THE WITCH AND HER SOUL

the witch & her soul

CHRISTINE MIDDLETON

For Mike
who makes everything possible

First published in 2012
by Palatine Books,
Carnegie House,
Chatsworth Road
Lancaster LA1 4SL
www.palatinebooks.com

British Library Cataloguing-in-Publication data
A catalogue record for this book is available from the British Library

ISBN 13: 978-1-874181-90-3

Designed and typeset by Carnegie Book Production

www.carnegiebookproduction.com
Printed and bound by CPI Group (UK) Ltd, Croydon, CR0 4YY

When women preach and cobblers pray
The fiends in Hell make holiday.

Lucifer's Lackey, 1647

Unto myself I do myself betray
Myself agrees not with myself a jot
I trust myself and I myself distrust
I cannot live, with nor without myself

Roger Brearley, 1677

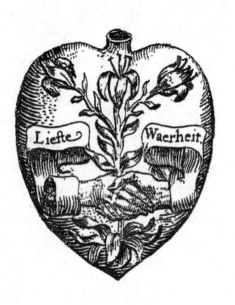

Liefte · Waerheit.

1612.

For a while, the only moving thing in the dim room is the flickering flame of a candle. The only sound is the occasional tumble of coals in the grate.

The man in the bed is still, now that the fret of fever has quieted.

The woman in the chair drawn close beside, leans on her elbow watching him.

Her hair is a long red plait. She sighs, touches his hand slightly, then stands, for a moment lost in thought.

She moves to sit at a small table near the fire, lights more candles, and picks up a quill.

She glances back towards the bed and then, begins to write.

Chapter 1

I, JANE SOUTHWORTH, Lady of Samlesbury Lower Hall, determined now to set down certain recollections . . .

I, Jane, that was born Jane Shireburn, natural daughter of Richard Shireburn, great knight of the realm and Master Forester of Bowland, resolving now to give some account . . .

I, Jane Southworth, in the year of Our Lord 1612, at the hour of midnight, seated in the light of three candles, by the bedside of the living corpse of my poor husband . . .

I do not know in any way how to begin this writing.

I, Jane, wife of John Southworth, grandson of Sir John Southworth, ancient knight of the shire, loyal servitor to Queen Mary, and Defender of the Faith . . .

It will not do, I cannot begin. I do not know how – which Jane I am, which child, which soul.

How truly vexed I am, that I cannot now begin after so long a wait. Does the prohibition weigh so heavy, of this dying man?

I have so longed to write; to shuffle words on a white page, words that could break into voices, remembered voices. For it is my own life that I crave to record, for all its unimportance. My own memories to be set in something as hard as the amber that imprisons flies. To net forever a butterfly moment of gaiety, cage in the shadows of fear, preserve some pearls of tears.

I will write now what I remember, for myself alone. Whatever words will come, I'll scrub none out. Seeking to please no man, nor woman, and I'll not fear equivocation neither, seeing as what pleases a papist would enrage a puritan, and what is given as a prayer may be spoken as a charm for a witch.

They say it is a lonesome thing to watch along the dying, and she certainly takes her time, the Lady Death, with my old husband, blueing his lips, pinching his nose, and fluttering his fingers. But still it drags on, and as I know her ways, I think I have some nights and days still to come, sitting here in this heavy room, waiting, waiting.

The world is quiet. Only the house stirs and creaks a little now and then, muttering in its old bones. And while I wait, Ellen comes to renew the candles and place another drink for me. At midnight, midsleep she comes in, greyer than her grey shawl now, a right grey mouse, she who was a little scurrying bright-eyed maid when first I took her on.

Her care is all for me, but still she pauses by the bed, to pull the covers, damp his forehead. Is her touch tenderer than mine that makes him stir?

"He spake my lady. Said a word, your name." I heard it too, just. Upon a breath I think he whispered "Jaynie." Two men only have used that softer form, and if my husband did some few times in early days, it was not by my leave.

Now Ellen is gone and the hollow hours stretch out before me, where I can use that license his feebleness has given me.

✳✳✳

It was my father who first prettified my name, from "plain Jane and no nonsense" to a word that had more of affection in it. And my brother when he was pleased with me. But more often to torment me he would sing a jingle:

Jane, Jane, plain as a drain
Sit in a corner and don't complain.

My brother: Red Rick, as he was known. Thoughts come tumbling now, jostling to be remembered, and though I scratch a pen as fast as any clerk, I have some work to keep pace. We were all redheaded; my huge red-bearded, red-maned father, and my restless, nervy foxy-red brother, and my own that was coppery and too much of it to keep tidy, as complained my mother. All, that is, all the baseborn children, even little Grace with her carrotnob. Not one of us inherited my mother's colour, nor her looks neither. Isabella with her crow-black hair and her name that made some servants whisper of Spanish blood. But she was no friend of Spain, no zealot, not she, 'La Concubina'. It was the mistress of the house who cleaved most ardently to the old religion. But how she walked, my mother, when he called her up from the low end of the table, to sit by him. How she loved to go gorgeous in coloured velvets that were the fury of Lady Maud. And where is the surprise in that, the old legal wife, with a chin like a spade and a long pious nose? Looking as if God had grudged her the superfluous flesh that was so lavishly bestowed upon the concubine. For Isabella was all in rounds; round cheeks, round breasts, and dimpled elbows. The pout of her small mouth was round, and perfectly so was the single black birthmark that sat below her collarbone, as to draw attention to all that lay below, and certainly succeeded to catch the ever-straying fingers of her lord. I thought then – or perhaps I was older when I thought – that same dark mole held all her power over him. But I never thought it to be a thing of fear.

So she was the favourite and unlawful, accustomed to quick translations, taking whatever chance and favour threw her. And I learnt that of my mother sure, for I too was often made a pet. I learnt – oh very early – the curious thing that I might be in two places, and all differently regarded, and still retain my single self. My dear Rick never learned it. Strove to make himself wholly in one world. But I took an odd pleasure in behaving in one way at the servants' table, sometimes waiting on them that were foremost, sometimes even taking a clout, or worse a fondling pinch, especially off that Simon Carter who took more liberties than ever his master knew. And then in the whisk of a rat's tail, I would be sat on my lord's lap and stroked and made much of, and given sweet things off his plate.

I did not flaunt though like Isabella. But I had my own ways of wheedling into his favour, which I very much desired to obtain. I suppose I was a pretty thing, but I know that I was clever, too clever for my boots, the servants said. My prattling, my inquisitive prattling, diverted him. And he would laugh with my forever asking why. He called me Jaynie Whyandwherefore. And said that I was as good as a wise fool to have in the house, with my asking why one was high and one was low, why brave virtue should be called base treason, why high and mighty Simon Carter could be so affrighted of an old beldame like Mother Goggins who was half out of her wits and all trembling with the palsy. He laughed a lot at me, my great father, but I do not recall that he ever answered my questions.

Of course not only I needed to learn dissimulation. The great hall of Stonyhurst had its own changes and secrets, sometime showing a jovial and convivial face to welcome all and sundry and keep the queen's favour, while its heart beat to a different tune: to quiet prayers behind doors, to hidden blessings and unspoken fervour, above all to the massing priests and their secret comings and goings.

And in the ebb and flow of that house, I had some work to find a solid place to put my feet.

It was when I was still too young to navigate those currents properly that I was first led to trip from one side to the other. It was a fine Sunday morning and I think I remember that we had well breakfasted. Also I had pleased Sir Richard with some fanciful saying. He spread his large hands, snowy cuffs and thick fingers, flat upon the table as to demand attention, and pronounced quite slowly: "I go to Mitton Church this day, to please our lady queen and do her bidding."

Such a silence fell. Most looked at their plates, avoiding to look at Lady Maud. Her long face grew longer, but her eyes stared most intently. I know because I, who have always been too bold for my own good, watched both of them. Sir Richard caught my curious observing, and laughed. "Come Jaynie, you look uncommonly decent today. You can accompany me to the new-fangled ceremonial."

My mother, Isabella, stirred. She might almost have risen, but did not. But Maud stood, in all her righteous dignity. "My lord, is it not enough, not shame enough, that you forsake our ancient faith? What need, what good reason is there that you offer to take the child along?"

And he, so used to ruling the roost but on this theme always placatory with her: "Aye Maud, would you have me pay more recusancy fines and bleed this great house white? You know full well that my whole intention is to preserve the family of Shireburn."

"But how will we protect our religion, my lord, preserve the faith of our fathers, if you are seen to assist, and a child of this household along with you, at the reformed service?"

"In just this way my dear. By heeding the queen's

command, we will play the game of state and keep the letter of the law. I will be bored for an hour is all."

"And if you do go there, in deference to the Crown" – Maud did not easily let go – "there is surely no need to take the child."

"She's not your child, Maud," he said more roughly, "and her mother makes no objection."

I can remember how Isabella dabbed her rosebud mouth with her napkin and looked into a distance.

He continued seriously.

"This girl may even be required to make a more politic alliance than we would wish. For God knows what discords still lie in wait, what protections we" – a heavy pause – "and your protégés may need" – then he muttered below his breath, but I heard – "as they come swarming now from Douai" – and loudly added – "No, no, I take some of my serving men also. I do not propose to attend Mitton as a yeoman farmer. And Jane will entertain me with questions on the sermon."

He had me by the hand, but paused by the porch door to seize a handful of fleece from one of the bales stacked there, "Or else we'll stuff our ears with this wool and not hear any of the heretical preachment, while you may spend this hour on your knees, Maud, praying for our immortal souls."

It was a fine thing to go with my lord to Mitton Church on a Sunday, but that night I had to make confession to a senior servant, as there was no priest just then in the house, and I was sent to bed supperless to pray forgiveness for my precocious apostasy. If Goody Goody Two Shoes Gracie threw a triumphant glance at my punishment, my brother Rick was not wholly inclined to displeasure neither, taking the opportunity of another nonsense rhyme:

6

Jane, Jane, silly and vain
Went to Mitton, favour to gain.
Pleased her lord, not Lady Maud
Got her a penance when home she came.

But there were other times Maud was never set aside, when she took on the mantle of real authority. When any of the wild travelling priests came to be harboured, the house ran to her particular direction. She personally supervised refreshment for the exhausted travellers, and personally set out the vestments and laid the altar. She and her maid alone decorated the chapel room hidden high in the eaves. Servants were dispatched to invite in the faithful and give warning of any untoward visitors. And a hushed, careful reverence everywhere. Pale Maud and her pale children proudly placid, serious and devout, Sir Richard much quieted and shriven, and of course the plump Isabella and her offspring hidden away among the servants.

I had always wanted to see them come, dark-cloaked on cloth-shod horses, with that strong sense of danger – mortal danger – that they carried with them. Sometimes Rick and I tried to linger about to see them come, but it is hard for redheaded children to be inconspicuous, and a few times we earned a slap and more for our curiosity.

Young as they often were, weather worn, dirty and very hungry, when they entered, the household would come humbly to greet them. Even Sir Richard himself would bow the knee and lower that bass voice to a husky "Bless me Father."

And when the folk trooped to make confession did my father confess all his sins? Did he confess to loving Isabella? Even to making a favourite of me? I wondered.

I do not now recall just how long after going to Mitton Church that I was first admitted to a secret mass. But in my mind there is a feeling of connection. It may have been because I had the good sense not to talk about these visits; a good sense not normally attributable to me. However it was, Maud had me called in to her.

"You are of an age to keep your counsel and to understand how vital it is to all and every life and soul in this house that our visiting missionaries and our celebrations of the Holy Mass remain close secret within these walls."

She paused and I did not speak.

"And it is my wish to save your soul, and return you to the grace of our Blessed Lord."

She looked down her long nose not unkindly at me. And indeed often times she was not unkind. I do think her hatred of the redhead on the throne far surpassed any dislike she held for her husband's bastard children.

Chapter 2

IT IS THE SECOND NIGHT of my lone watch. I am not sure that it serves a purpose to mark the intervals of this writing. John is sleeping placidly. My Lady Death holds him quite gently at this moment. Will I hereafter desire to measure his dying against my narrative?

I fear my own clumsiness. I do not know of any noble woman who has chosen to write in this fashion. I have no example to follow. But I am strangely coming to believe that this scrawling that I do, which diverts me from the close watching that I pretend, but helps to pass the long silent hours, that it is in some imperceptible way keeping him alive.

Or does She wait, knowing he is securely hers, to humour me?

For how long then? How long can my memories creep breath into his lungs?

Sleep on then John, as quietly as you may.

❋❋❋

Of course we knew very well about the visitations but to know a secret and be privy to it is a different thing. And my first permitted – and obliged – attendance at the mass was a wonder to me.

Rick came with me but Grace was too young. And Isabella, not sorry of an excuse to avoid appearing drably clothed among the servants.

After the midnight hour was well passed, about two

o'clock of the morning, when one hoped all informers and searchers to be well abed, we climbed the narrow stair to the long attic in the roof. And even as we mounted I could already hear the hush, if that is not a nonsense thing to say.

But then on entry, my soul stood still, enrapt with so much light from myriads of candles, with hanging linens and banks of flowers. And clouds of incense from a great swinging silver censer, that made my head fairly swim.

All was transformation. Those servants that were allowed were cleanly dressed and combed, all waiting with lowered heads. Even Simon Carter was bowed in humility. My dear father knelt, all gravity in his face, while his two elder sons in surplice and lace were severe young acolytes fit to serve a king. The truly wondrous transformation was of the scarecrow outlaw who had arrived in such a sweat of haste the previous morning. Now robed in silken alb and chasuble of Maud's embroidering, he appeared to be almost an angelic spirit.

The solemnity began. I have always found delight in words. If children pick up vocables like pigeons pecking peas, I was surely one of the greediest. Syllables were to taste, to weigh, to treasure, howsoever elusive their meaning. As the hush gave way to the recital of soft admonishing Latin, like and unlike the binding spells I had heard quoted in the kitchens, I joined with fervour in the mysterious repetitions. To the stern *Agnus Dei* I soulfully responded with the deeply woeful *miserere nobis*. And I beat my chest devotedly for *Mea culpa*. I bowed my head like all the rest for the elevation of the Host, flesh of God. But it was the human flesh that drew my fascination. Gazing at the hands that held high the host above his head, my earth-fast mind was remembering tales that Rick had told me of the torturing of priests. I wondered how unbelievable and terrible it would be to see the body beneath this glory stretched upon the rack, or hung in a noose, or disembowelled before his own living eyes. And I wondered at the ferocity of conviction that drove such a man to court those risks, to keep alive the flame of a forbidden faith, in the land of the Protestant queen. I did not then, nor do not now, fully comprehend it. But I was swept by the myth. And if Lady Maud had purposed to wean me from the humdrum services at Mitton, she entirely succeeded.

John, you neither speak nor stir. Neither will you ever read these words. But how my piety then would have pleased you now.

In my new-found devotion I found myself much reconciled with the severe lady of the house. I am sure that I did subdue my behaviour and I made some show of learning prayers. Truth to say I learned them better than any of the other children. I really believe that Lady Maud would have liked to like me, but her steadfast concern for the precedence of her own children prevented it. And she was forever insulted be my mother's presence. But life was peaceful for me in that house at that time.

Was it then weeks or months after we had started attending masses? Mayhap a year passed before the day when young Richard burst into the hall, crashing his whip upon the table with fury, and my Rick right behind him, with a fool grin he could not wipe off. Richard, his pale face grown quite flushed, shouting about this bastard boy, who had got himself, by who knows what parleying with the stablemen, too good a mount and led the chase.

Several of the local families had come for the hunt of a reputed fine large boar. It had been much talked of. I could easily see how Red Rick, shorter and broader than his stepbrother, but so much more eager to be foremost, how he would outride, outmanoeuvre Richard. But he maintained to me that it was more by luck than craft that he found himself close by when the beast sidetracked into a clearing. And without waiting for Richard, my brother had spurred after, straight in its path, and got to thrust his spear into the pig's fat throat. Minutes later the son and heir arrived to find the glory of the day taken from him. And guests were heard to enquire as to whether the Shireburns often gave their servants the right to the kill. Rick was too elated, oh by far. He crowed his success long and loud. What more fearful stupidity could any baseborn boy have committed?

His grinning stopped when he saw Sir Richard's face. My father's voice matched his cold face. "How come you to be so ignorant of a huntsman's service to his lord? It seems you require to be taught your place. And you have yourself to thank for the lesson."

It was Simon Carter who hauled him out then, with what pleasure I could see, to be whipped in the stable yard. And Red Rick was forbidden any form of hunting, except to tend the traps of vermin and small game in our domains, which would now be his occupation.

Lady Maud applauded his ire. "They are unruly my lord, all three of Isabella's children. They lack piety and humility."

He noddingly agreed.

"They need to be restrained in their freedom, put to more diligent occupation. It were good to exhort them to much greater prayer, prayer and abstinence—"

This last was not a word of great appeal to the Master Forester. He shrugged as to tell her to conclude, but she clung to her last word. "It is that they must be made to understand their place and adhere to it."

So who should next be found most lamentably out of place?

I found life more tedious with my companionable brother sent gamekeeping on the estates. And I lacked his protection from Simon Carter, who troubled me from time to time. For these reasons, and if I tell the truth sometimes to escape a dull chore, I did occasionally steal into the study, which was forbidden me.

My father was even then engaged with architects in designing the greatest, gracefullest mansion in all the Ribble valley. In his plans he was envisaging a monumental library, but the present book room was not so very large a place. It had great peacefulness though, with long windows that cast sunlight full of trembling motes onto the deep carpet. And books of course everywhere, smelling of sweet strong leather, and always some great tome open upon the lectern. And frequently there were architects' plans open about the room, which I regarded with less curiosity than the picture books. I remember books of the lives of saints and strange martyrdoms, illustrated herbals, and a compendium of mythological beasts to be found beyond the seven seas. I was even fascinated by the print itself, those rows of marching hieroglyphs which mocked my attempts to decipher.

At this time we had amongst our visitors one Nicholas Owen, a monk called by everyone 'Little John', because he was not much more than a dwarf. He was crooked of gait also, but of great gifts, they said. I took him for a learned man, as he was so often in converse with our master, and they spent much time together with books and papers. But when Sir Richard was not in conference the book room was usually unoccupied. Maud's elder children were never bookish and we lower ones were not allowed there.

On the day when I knew my father was to be taken up

with Shireburn Rental Day, and all the household mightily occupied, I crept in there. On this day there was a great quantity of paper lying about which I disregarded. I was intent on locating a picture book of saints which I had seen before. I could not have been in that room more than a dozen moments before I heard the swish of skirts and the jingle of keys which could belong only to the mistress of the household.

I looked up to see Lady Maud and she was angry beyond my expectations. She strode briskly towards me, catching me with a lump of my hair. Her voice was like a rasp. "What do you do here, miss? So far out of your place? Presuming on a freedom of the house you do not possess."

I was hauled out of the library and forced to face Sir Richard, who was just then preparing for Rental Day. He was in discussion with the bailiff and not best pleased to be disturbed. But when she told on me he looked most grave. I thought it must come to a beating. And then he said, "So Jane Shireburn, where did your curiosity take you in my library?"

I answered humbly at first, "I was looking for a story book." He waited. Maud glared. I could think of no excuse for my disobedience. My head hurt where she had pulled me, but I wanted not to cry. And I think, not unlike Rick, fear made me impudent.

"I do greatly desire to read, but since I have no teacher, I am obliged to remain with picture books."

"Insolence!" The word scarcely escaped through Maud's teeth.

But my father looked at me thoughtfully, and then turned away to speak with the dwarf monk, who was still breakfasting. It was an urgent conversation but I could not see that it had to do with me. He came back, gestured for his cloak, and while he pulled it on he nodded towards me.

"Well Jaynie Wherefore, if it is a clerk you would be then come into the Bailiff's court and give some help with the accounting."

I dared not look at Lady Maud again, but I followed him out as meekly as any of his hounds.

And there am I seated at the long accounting table, covering with blots and scribble the lump of paper before me, in feeble imitation of the clerk's tidy rows of figures and names.

I am half dazed by the turn of events, and deafened by the huge commotion of Rental Day. Part stifled too by the stench, for some had brought livestock with which to pay their dues. And so much laughter! My father, known to be a severe tax master when levying soldiery for the Crown, was a benevolent landlord to his own people. He knew, as did others, that there were tenants would gain more by their dinner than they paid in rent. He was loudest in the jocularity, as roars of mirth greeted the recited merits of produce brought up to the bailiff's table, as to the turgescence of cucumbers, the magnitude of duck eggs, or the plumpness of pumpkins. I understood the jests little better than I understood the tallies of the clerk, but I recognised that they were an important part of the general good humour.

Flummoxed as I was, I tried hard to concentrate on my task. I endeavoured to comprehend and take note, though I was clearly incapable of making record, of the great variety of tithes and tributes brought before my father and his bailiff. And I had a puzzled interest in the variety and even whimsicality of some. Beside the receipt of livestock and harvest dues, there was the annual tithe of a penny, a pair of spurs, a pound of pepper, a barbed arrow. I guessed at some indulgent remissions made by my father in his cups. William Gaunt, a respected old man, brought his single flower. My father took it seriously and carefully examined the velvet red rose. "It is as always a perfection, Master Gaunt," he said solemnly, "but I'll take it as a favour if in the future you will pay your dues to Mistress Jane Shireburn here."

There was applause for me then, as he laid the flower gracefully on the table before me. But he leaned over to me and beneath the noise his voice was quiet.

"You must and will be punished Jaynie. You understand that?"

Chapter 3

I DID NOT GET A BEATING AFTER ALL. I 'scaped the whip, John, which I have always feared right cravenly, as I once evaded yours. But I do not ever forget my marriage night, nor can ever make myself quite forgive. There is a little hard pebble of unforgiveness rests in my soul.

I was much more grown before I understood the true cause of Maud's fury. Nicholas Owen, our 'Little John', was in fact a man of legend. This was a dwarf who did not labour in the bowels of mountains nor in mines of gold. He excavated for a more serious treasure. He was the mastermind and hand who created subtle and secret hiding places, in the masonry, the very fabric, of houses, Catholic recusant houses. In chimneys and false flues, behind wainscoting and between walls, under cellars and in roof spaces, he made priest holes and tiny chapels. Those who knew him whispered of an ingenuity which baffled the pursuivants and defied the assiduity of Crown searchers for many years.

It is certain that at that time he was in consultation with Sir Richard and Lady Shireburn as to contriving similar hidey holes in the planned new Stonyhurst, since it is evidently easier to construct such labyrinthine passageways at the inception of a building. And fairly certain that the plans scattered about the library held incriminating secrets. Any disclosures as to the identity and purposes of 'Little John' would have brought ruin on many households and death to some.

He need not fear disclosure of mine now, Nicholas Owen, since he is dead and executed, and that most dreadfully. But in those days when I was young and he was a man of clandestine renown, the prowling among books of a disobedient child was easily enough to provoke alarm in Lady Maud.

And it was of course my lady who decreed my correction. Since my sin was not to know my place, so I should suffer a diminution of status that would point the lesson. I was henceforth ordered not so slight a translation as to wait upon the lower table, but sent to help cooks in the kitchen and work in the poultry yard. I was made equal with scullions and rough stable lads.

I spoke not a word in my defence – indeed I had no defence – and none spoke for me. I imagine Isabella shrugged her velvet shoulders. She had no interest in sharing my downfall. And she still had Grace, little Goody Twoshoes Gracie.

I did not fear the work so much, all the fetching and carrying, the sweeping and scrubbing, not so much as I hated the humiliation. But I already knew by then how unexpectedly Dame Fortune could spin her wheel. I had learnt how noblemen of substance, acquaintance of my father, could swiftly become exiles or prisoners of state. And ennoblements could fall upon those of no account. Queenly heads had been chopped on the common block. And I had seen ragged men changed into angels. Life was all change and translation, and I must needs take pains to preserve my single self. So I would be poultry maid, I thought, but not for long!

It was to be expected that there were coarse menials who took pleasure in jests at my expense, but I was always able to please Irene, the chief cook. She was unmarried, being greatly fat and moustached, but in her youth she had borne a female child out of wedlock, who had later died, and whom she still mourned. Was she red haired too, that lost little girl? Howsoever it may have been, Irene was kind to me, often sought to lighten my chores, and was well able to cuff the ear of a loutish joker.

One chore I did not so dislike was carrying out food to the begging poor. Ours was always a beneficent house. Lady Maud lamented the ancient charity of the monks, as much as she grieved for the ruin of their holy places. My father inveighed against the unrelieved poverty that followed in the wake of monastic destruction, and held loud arguments about the institution of a Poor Law. And the great Irene was no skinflint in the kitchen neither.

On the whole I carried out decent alms to those who waited, though had I been in favour still, I might have asked why the hounds in the hall had better meat and bones than ever the scurvy folk at the gate. But I did often manage to scrape extra bits of fat and fruit to add to their portion of daily bread.

At first the sight of them all hurt my eyes; their filth and warts and carbuncles. But I am sure their cringing gratitude was salve to the wounds of my pride. I never feared the old women neither, the witches that could so affright some of the servants, but I was wary of the men, vagabonds who could leer a menace out of even one good eye. That fear lay in the wrong quarter however; more danger lurked within the gate.

I was about collecting eggs in the long barn when I heard the man behind me. With one hand he seized my basket and swung it away, the other took my shoulder and shoved me to the ground. Simon Carter, that great dogface, had his member strut out before his breeches were well undone. As he fiddled with his laces I struggled to rise and I called out as well, so that with our contending we set all the fowl flustering and scritching. But he laid me down again quick, he with a grown man's strength, and

I lay helpless and wretched in the straw and hen muck, feeling more hate than fear at the sight of him, though I was also truly afeard. But the freedom blow I could not deliver came soon enough with the thwack of a wooden spoon to his head, and, better armed with the kitchen knife in one hand and the spoon in the other, Big Irene had him out of the barn in short time. But not before she had lambasted him some good thumps, dealt with all the authority of indignant virtue.

She took me back and set me ashivering and atrembling by the hot fire and continued her work with a good deal of muttering. There were sundry imprecations while she energetically kneaded bread, reflections on the villainy of fornicators, on the kindless greed of straddling men, on pricks too hot for the Devil Himself.

But for me there was only an endless series of comforting endearments, though in phrases that were strange to me: 'sweet child of grace', 'Christ's delight', 'pure soul', 'all inwardly lit', 'sinless and perfect'. If I was a little surprised by the generosity of these sentiments, being accustomed to the preoccupation of our priestly confessors with the black sinfulness of my soul, I did not then pay too much attention. I was too wrathful to dwell on anything but my abiding hatred of the senior servant.

She told me how she came to know that Simon Carter had gone after me.

"It was them two old women that often loiter. They came up to my kitchen door, old Mother Goggins and the Demdike, to tell me he was following you. Though what should make them so bold, or to so trouble themselves, I do not know." She sighed. "Except that all the peasants know him for a lecher and a forcer of young girls. And I wager he'd be pressing rents too if your father didn't have a good bailiff. He's a man well disliked hereabouts."

"I hate him," I said, "I hate him and I will tell my father on him."

"You'd best tell no one," said Irene calmly. "You would only smirch your own good name. Dirt sticks to the innocent as well as the guilty."

"But I'll tell my brother," I declared. "He will kill him for it."

She didn't answer that. We both knew that it was a fool thing to say.

She wiped her hands after and found me a clean cap and apron. "You can do some weighing for me and wash out those bowls. And tomorrow, first thing in the morning, you can take out one of the big barley cakes, and make a present to those two old women who saved your maidenhead."

It was a good cake that she made, Irene, thick and sweet with plenty of caraway. Old Goggins whistled a thanks through her few teeth. I did not thank them directly for the watch they had kept over me, but I did speak more kindly than was always my wont. The Demdike was the younger and less abject. She came up close to me and shoved a thing into my hand.

> *Here is a charm*
> *Will keep you from harm.*

she said in her sing-song voice. It was a very little thing wrapped in a dirty bit of rag, and I shoved it in my apron pocket.

It could have been only hours later, because it was before dinnertime, when one of the stable boys burst into the kitchen, all red from excitement and the importance of his news.

"He's gone now – for good and all! He's a goner, that Simon Carter. Fell off his horse and broke his neck. And some will say good riddance."

Whether his jubilation was at the substance of his news or whether it was the exhilaration of being storyteller to a kitchen of awestruck maids and squabs, I do not know. But I know that I was more amazed than any of them.

"How fell off his horse, and where?" asked Irene.

"Just riding a boundary fence with the bailiff. The pony tripped and he fell off awry and his neck got broke. They've just now brought him in."

"What was it made the horse stumble? Was it a hole or was it a poacher's trap?"

"Or just a loose stone. It was nothing special, they said."

"Unless it be the judgement of the Lord," one of the kitchen maids muttered. And I thought straightway that I was not the only girl he had pestered, and worse. The kitchen was full of a kind of pleasure; the pleasure of hearing any dreadful news, and the pleasure of relief too.

"A charm – to keep you from harm." The words echoed in my mind. I moved to the doorway, nearer the light, to examine Mother Demdike's gift. It was nought but a little bone, perhaps part of a chicken wishbone, all cleaned of flesh, and shiny white as with polishing.

But I had not much perused it before Irene was behind me. She shoved me out the kitchen door and then intently asked "Demdike?" I nodded and she pulled it out of my hand, and then she snatched the bit of rag as well. She went back into the kitchen and hurled both into the coals.

The girls were still plying him with questions, the stable lad, who was struggling to imagine details to embroider his narrative. Irene chased them back to work, but later when no one else was by, she spoke to me soberly. "That's two things then you best remember to forget." And then as if uncertain of my assent, she spoke very slowly: "There is light. And there is the darkness, Mistress Jane. You cannot live in both."

Chapter 4

GOSSIP IS LIKE THE BINDWEED, easy to break off at the surface, but sending many threads of roots in the dark soil, where you cannot reach. I do not know what whispers followed me after the death of Simon Carter, and if there were any, how far they might have spread. So far as Samlesbury Hall, John? Was your mind tainted even when you first lusted after me?

And Isabella, my mother? After all she did sometime gossip with the servants and she was one to know the appetites of men. What knowledge or half knowledge might she have had? Or was it Isabella who whispered sweet things in my lord's embrace and persuaded a termination to our punishment? Or did he simply grow impatient, Sir Richard, with the lowly status of his own born children?

❊❊❊

For all my trying I cannot remember just how long it was before Red Rick was recalled to congenial responsibility as head falconer, and both of us allowed to take our places with our mother. I was set such pleasant tasks as tidying embroidery silks and frames or ranging cutlery upon the table. And I had in particular the not onerous duty to check the refilling of the wine jugs when we had company.

Among that company were some who would not endure a harlot at the same board. Four men stand out in my memory among my father's frequent guests – two sour and two sweet.

Richard Hoghton of the Towers wore his importance very knowingly. He spoke as not to be contradicted and upon serious topics. He had a trick of quivering his nostrils when roused to affirmation. I myself did a tolerable good imitation of his twitching nose.

Roger Nowell, of Read Hall, I liked least of all. His nose was also large, nay larger, and his beard more profuse. In fact he had rich curlings of hair from every orifice, and my brother was given to wickedly speculate on the wondrous thickets of his nether regions. And if it were sinful to laugh, we could not forgo mockery of his sour puritany ways. I think he is not much changed now neither, but rather grown in state. Of course he would not tolerate the presence of a courtesan and Isabella did not come to table when he was a guest, but I waited on him with the wine.

From my father's intimates I liked best Thomas Walmsley, judge, and Richard Assheton, landowner. The judge, ever tending to corpulence and to extravagant dress, brought the wit and gossip of London into our northern hall. I have come to revere the man as much for the measurement of his opinion as for the excesses of his wardrobe. But as a small child I thought him a frivolous, if endearing, personage, because he made my father laugh so much.

Doughty Dick Assheton was as energetic as the judge was languid, as jovial as the judge was witty, and as hearty a country gentleman as the other was an exquisite courtier. And both easily and equably associated with Richard Shireburn's more irregular family.

It was Dick Assheton who occasioned my first acquaintance with Alice Nutter. I had heard of her amidst the generality of gossip, as a yeoman farmer – not just farmer's wife, for her late husband was without talent they said – known for her great skill of animal husbandry and the amassing of an ample stock of wealth. She was also known as a woman of notable charity towards the poor. Not such a figure as to arouse my particular interest at that time.

They arrived on an evening of violent summer storm, the sound of their horses clattering in the courtyard, beneath the strumming rain. Dick Assheton was thundering at the door before the servants had time to pull it open, and calling to Sir Richard before he was through the porch. Heaving his sodden cloak to the ground, he was shouting, "Such rain as never seen we have endured. And hail, lumps as big as bulls' ballocks we've been pelted with, all the way from Preston!"

Before my father could properly express his welcome, he gestured towards a tall, cloaked figure in the porch. "I have brought a fellow traveller with me, Richard. We have ridden from Preston together, and she's as well wetted as me. Mistress Alice Nutter – you'll know her surely? From Crow Trees Farm in Roughlee."

Of course there was no doubt that the broad sweep of my father's hospitality could encompass gentrified yeomanry, but it was still surprising that he should set this drenched farmwoman so near him in a place of honour.

She was a tall thin poker of a woman. Her face was as brown as any farmer's. I could not say – forgive me Alice but I could not – say I thought her comely. I was green in judgement then, and I saw eyes all wrinkled with much gazing after sheep on long fells, a nose of no interest whatsoever, and a thin, wide mouth that went from ear to ear when she laughed. But could shut like a trap when she was displeased.

There was no displeasure evident, however, when we took our places at the table, though Isabella murmured to me that she thanked Saint Catherine that she herself had not been gifted such a deep voice or flat chest. And it was not long before Lady Maud found a want of deference in a peasant woman taking such an easy way of discourse with the Master Forester of Bowland. But the great man himself was all courteous condescension.

"Dick tells me that you have quite transformed Crow Trees Farm, Mistress Nutter. How long is it since the death of your husband?"

She was not shy in her replies, but spoke consideringly, slow, in a deep-toned voice that seemed to give some weight to her opinions.

"He will be gone three years come Michaelmas."

"That must place a considerable burden upon you."

"I could not claim his death to have burdened me in the way of work. He was by a good deal my elder and sickly some long time. It is I have run the farm this many years."

"My family farmed that part over a hundred years ago. It is not the most hospitable ground – thin soil and short summers. You do well to make it prosper."

She nodded agreement.

"On what principles have you proceeded? Were you able to search out good markets?"

"I worked chiefly at improving the breed." She gave the thin grin that I have come to know. "Although I think the bluster on Pendle does in any case oblige our sheep to grow a specially thick fleece."

"What improvements did you seek? What additions have you made?" He was always avid for details of estate management.

"Well," she seemed to enjoy the inquisition, "I have bought two excellent rams, but of different extraction, and I believe the quality is already evident. We want to make better than rough yarn."

"Wool production is in fact your chiefest interest?"

"It is our staple. But we have taken on some Silverdale crag sheep for meat. They are of good flavour and tendency to fatten, as well as fine wool producers."

"Silverdale?"

"They are the big whitey-faced ones with horns."

She did not hesitate to use an instructive tone, and he took no offence but refilled her wine glass.

"And how did you know where to seek out these better strains?"

"One hears much of breeds at the markets of course. But I have read as much as I could on the subject. There are several works on practical husbandry that I have found of great value."

"You are a lettered woman Mistress Nutter?" This from Lady Maud, of condescension or disapproval, at first I could not tell.

"I were a poor woman else."

"Poor." Lady Maud considered the word. "You speak of the necessities of your commerce?"

"It is true that books have played a serious part in securing the prosperity of our farm, but I count them also as doorways to wisdom."

"Wisdom?" Maud dangled her word in the air, as it were, but Mistress Nutter did not hasten her reply.

"I do count it wisdom – to learn the thoughts, the great thoughts, and sometimes the foolish thoughts of other folk, from other places, from other times."

"To what end do you go scouring for these other people's thoughts?"

"Why for betterment I hope. To bite the silver of my own beliefs. To add whatever of grace I find," she paused, "and for the sheer pleasure of it."

"Pleasure." This repetition was all of ice. "So you would consider it – all this reading and writing – a fitting pastime for a virtuous woman?"

"As fitting as living and loving, as cooking and broidery, as . . . as playing upon the virginals—"

"Playing upon the virginals," Dick Assheton looked for a laugh, as he seized a cheerful entry into the conversation, "now there's a pretty thing. But I agree with you Maud. I don't hold with too much reading and writing. We need to sign a letter or a bond perhaps, set down the day of birth and marriage, and make our will. But so long as a father can recognise his own children, and a shepherd knows his own sheep, and maidens can see through the wiles of subtle bachelors and preserve their by-your-leaves, well," he waved a great gesture, "we can leave all this printing alone."

Alice Nutter grinned again. "I think it will take longer than the arrival of the printed word for maidens to discern the wiles of their seducers. But it will arrive I'm sure, even for us country folk."

"Mistress Nutter is in the right Dick," my father broke in. "Even the wild Lancashire gentry have need of print. And" – slightly bowing towards his wife – "the Catholics now are amenable to translating the Bible, so all the world may read the Sacred Word."

"There would be no need of translations of the Bible, were we allowed our priestly instructors," said Maud. "And there is in that freedom you speak of, great room for misinterpretation and heresy. It is a danger I perceive and would in all ways discourage."

She turned directly to Alice Nutter then and her hostility was plain to see.

"I bow to Mistress Nutter's trade requirements, and there are practical necessities we all understand, but there is in these books – pamphlets, writings, whatever – much obscenity and obscurity, so much of evil and error, from which we women do stand in earnest need of protection."

"Our best protection must ever be our God-given minds and our sweet consciences."

It was quietly spoken, even in the deep voice, but it was audacious to speak so to the lady of the hall. That same lady's reply came back like a whiplash: "It is just that mind and conscience that ought to keep us from vainglorious show of learning, or a fool indulgence in frivolity."

She stood then, about to leave, but Sir Richard placed a restraining hand upon her arm and gently compelled her to sit. With his other hand he meditatively circled the wine glass before him. And spoke with his eyes still upon the glass.

"We cannot banish learning from our lives and families. It were a nonsense to think so. We would lose all power in the land, and now when we have a most urgent need of information and influence. Also to be literate is accounted an ornament among many of the most noble rank – men, and some women."

He raised his eyebrows to signify more wine and continued evenly, "You have two sons Maud, presently at the university, and neither gives a jot for written wisdom. And there is in this house a girl straining at the leash for instruction. But we deny her. Let us send Jaynie to go to school with Mistress Nutter."

The maid had just passed me a big pewter jug and I put it down upon the table with such a clang that some of the wine spilled out, so consternated was I to be suddenly thrust into attention. My scarlet face must have also proclaimed my identity, for Alice Nutter immediately fixed her gaze upon me. She looked at me with such a long consideration as if she were assessing the purchase of livestock.

"For all I say," she answered slowly, "my own children were untroubled by a thirst for literature. Most times they crept like snails to their school books. It would be a very singular pleasure to instruct a child with an eagerness to learn." She looked at Lady Maud's stony face and then back to my father. "Lend me your earnest daughter Sir Richard, and I will undertake to teach her reading and writing, and something of pastoral skills also, if that should please you."

Lady Maud was subsided into a graven image, but my mother was at last stirred to deliver.

"I think Jane is required just now to perform her duties in the hall," she said. "And harvest time with extra work is not so long away."

Alice smiled directly to me then and gave a small shrug. "She will at any time be right welcome."

But my father was ready for an end to debate. "Let her go Isabella. She has pestered us long enough with her curiosity. And if the girl is clever we should not stifle her gifts."

He turned to the landowner. "Come Assheton, are we not overdue for a hunt at Downham? What have you in Pendle Forest to give us a good chase?"

It was a favourite topic. And it transpired that there was game ready and waiting in the Assheton domains, and this being the week after the summer Assizes, Sir Richard was at liberty to take advantage. Accordingly it was decided that if the storm had blown itself out by the morrow, I was to go back with Alice Nutter. The hunting party would set out a few days later to Downham Hall, where I was to be met, to be brought home.

Rick took advantage of the general cheer to secure himself inclusion in the party. It was well known to me that he had more than a passing fancy for Dick Assheton's daughter, and Dorothy not averse to my brother.

No one at all asked my view, and truth to tell I did not know my own, but I perceived that my life was once more to turn upon Dame Fortune's spinning wheel.

So I went to Crow Trees Farm in Roughlee. I had no

inclination to lodge in a farm house, nor ambition to learn country crafts, nor did I wish to diminish my rank in the world. But I was, albeit reluctantly, drawn to this plain personage, so bold in tenor, yet gentle in demeanour, so unafraid to speak her mind before her betters. I who had so often slithered on the slippery slopes of grace and favour at Stonyhurst, how could I not take note of a woman whose feet seemed planted on such solid ground? A woman who, I already suspected, would not budge for prince nor prelate.

Chapter 5

I DO NOT CATCH A VIEW OF PENDLE so often now that I am living close to the river. But the great hill, doglike recumbent, with broad head and long flanks of heather and bracken and sedge grass, it is a very constant bulk in the landscape, a something always there, that dominated my childhood vistas. It looms now in my mind as I try to remember this visit, where I was obliged again to slide down a rung or two in the ladder of consequence.

Alice's farm lies on the far, colder side of Pendle. It is tucked into the lee, stretching on the sun side into a thin-nish orchard of apple and damson. That was my first impression, that it was cold, and then that all was clean and orderly – and so quiet. After Stonyhurst Hall, with the clattering of many servants at the tables, with hounds underfoot and scampering children, some of seigneurial descent, some not, and my lord's loud orders and cheerful oaths, this was a very sober gathering that left me with a sense of being solitary.

And the good order that was continually pointed out! Chairs and chests in tidy rows, pots and pans upon correct hooks, plates and goblets neatly in place upon the table. Even the neat parcels of rushes and the cleanly-sanded floor where no one spat. I longed for the prodigality and overflowing life of my father's hall.

I was slow to appreciate the good will and devotion that lay behind this decency. Alice's daughters being married and away, it was left to her son, Miles, a gentle boy but dull, dull as a rain cloud, to show me the workings of the farm. I affected a polite admiration for the excellence of brewery, bakehouse and buttery. I endured the tedium of inspecting the outbuildings with what I thought to be a very good grace, taking note for better information of my father, of the 'cloth shop', where benches and tables were laid out with carding brushes, and rows of spinning wheels and some fancy looms were set up. Alice, not content with growing wool, was about the business of making cloth. I forebore to make foolish comment on the grotesque structure of paddles standing by the fierce little Pendle Water to pound the cloth, or the scarecrow frames to hang and dry it. And defying boredom, I opened my eyes wide at the sight of the huge empty vat in the great barn, and laughed with the merriest of notes to hear how for once Mistress Nutter had been obliged to forgo an experiment and acknowledge the superior resources of the Master Dyers of Manchester. I was imitating Isabella in my childish way, that I am none too proud of, but I fair flummoxed the lad.

But I run ahead.

When we arrived I noted that no stable boy but Alice's son came to take our horses, and Alice herself carried the heavy satchel into the house, flinging it onto the table as a tall, balding man approached.

"Food first Hugh Redferne, and then get out the ledgers." It was clear that she was not displeased with the trading she had done in Preston.

But if order was carefully observed in some ways in this house, it was mightily neglected in others. I was introduced to the farm folk with great simplicity.

"Jane Shireburn, this is the Family of Crow Trees." (I only knew later to use the capital letter.) And each servant was presented with as much gravity as a milord. Hugh Redferne, steward; Joan Gentle, cook; Martin Vere, shepherd; Tom Redferne, deputy to his father; Anne Whittle, laundry; these last two exchanging languishing cows' eyes. Even Mary Penny, scullery maid, and Tommy Fair, stable lad, were given the dignity of both names.

Precedence was most neglected, though Alice did take the tall, carved chair. But she did not lead the Grace, nor did her steward. A little murmur of invocation rose from every side. Each person there seemed to feel free to voice his own thought, to thank the Good Lord for spreading the table – simple as cold bacon and sheep cheese seemed to a child brought up at a table of garnished roasts and French wine. And all were of one mind in inviting God to bless the righteous here assembled, who were praised for sinlessness, such children of light as we were, such dwellers with the spirit, so pure hearted and sanctified. It was a litany of sweet congratulation, and a vocabulary that put me in mind of Big Irene. It seemed to me – how can I say – a peasanty, a silly sort of praying, used as I was to the Latin gravity of my own home. But I was not averse to being included in these flattering categories, having heard so many Jesuitical warnings as to my fallen nature, and my horrid propensity to sin. But from the outset I am sure, I was aware that the Family of Love was a more secret and a more devious congregation than my own outlawed Catholicism.

Later that evening I was introduced into Alice's 'counting house', which was no such thing, but an accounts room, an apothecary, a library and a parlour, all in one. Unlike anything at Stonyhurst, here were no gaunt embroidery frames, nor iron lecterns holding pattern books for Maud's holy needlework. No perfumed silks or satins neither, such as graced my mother's chamber. This was a long, warm, busy room, with cheap russet curtains, but a carpet unexpectedly rich. A quantity of potted herbs were ranged on windowsills, and these were neatly, carefully, labelled. But the same spirit of contradiction decreed that order appeared to be lost in the spill of books, books everywhere, upon shelves and tables and chairs – tomes of august binding aside penny pamphlets, little black doctrinal books and decorated volumes of poetry, illustrated herbals and much-thumbed books of husbandry.

Alice had spread out account books and was in conference with Hugh Redferne, and I was let loose to touch and finger and smell. I felt a growing excitement that I might soon be learning the key to this plethora of print. As I struggled to replace an enormous black-bound treatise, she looked up and laughed: "We should begin with fables, Jane. Sermons are for later."

Of course I learned to read most rapidly. Such a contrary combination as I had experienced, of prohibition and encouragement, was bound to light a spark in the dullest scholar. And Alice decided that I should learn to scribe as well as decipher. "Reading is for understanding. Writing is for making," she said, "and you are fit to make more than puddings and cushions."

Did my father intend me to learn the making of script? I do not know. I do know that I have made little use of it 'til now. 'Til now.

Of course fables are but small sermons made easy, and here I had a friend who was prepared, most pleased in fact, to answer questions. Alice you are the only one with whom I could ever hold amicable or profitable argument. And that began in my first lessons.

I remember objecting to Aesop's moralizing, finding the ant was surely mean-souled to refuse all winter shelter to the dancing grasshopper.

"And think you," said Alice, "that all that are warm should take in all who go abegging?"

"The grasshopper sang. And my father would not refuse. Our door is always open for poets and minstrels and dancers."

"Well for poets and minstrels," she nodded. "And the ragged and the ugly and the botched and scabbed. Would they be let warm themselves at the great firestone of Stonyhurst?"

"Why no one can succour all the wretched. Even if the monks were still here—"

"The monks did not relieve all there was of poverty. And they did mightily enrich themselves."

"So there is no remedy?"

"Oh there could be a remedy." She has a trick, Alice, of linking her fingers into a steeple shape. I have observed it often.

"It needs a world set altogether on a different cart. It is possible for none to starve. This is a plenteous earth and there would be enough for everyone, were its fruits to be fairly shared among. Enough for all, but not enough for some to be foremost, for some to take the fat share."

"Some are cleverer," said I.

"Let us see what Aesop has to say about that," she said with her wide grin.

Peaceable though the little farm seemed to me, it was not always so harmonious. The day the 'cloth shop' was set in motion, other folk came for temporary work, among them Anne Whittle, Annie's mother. She shared little of her daughter's sweet nature or swift grace. But she was reputed well-skilled at carding wool, despite that she shook most extremely with the palsy. She it was who introduced a note of disharmony into the mealtime assembly. "They all spoke in Burnley yesterday how Lizzie Southern was taken for adultery. There's none to tell who the father might be, but some said there's a babe come with a face near as crookedy as her own."

Young Annie spoke without her mother's zest: "If she's been taken by the constables, she'll be stocked for sure."

The old one hastened to agree. "And very like some strokes, for she's an ugly sinner, as well as a whoring thief."

I looked to Alice to see her speak sharply to this woman, but it was the steward delivered the rebuke. "For shame Anne Whittle, such pitiless words become you very ill."

She was not stopped so soon. "They are a bad family, the Southerns, foul-faced and foul-mouthed. And Lizzie the ugliest of them all."

Hugh Redferne spoke with a solemnity that would have quieted me: "They are a troublesome family, heaven knows, but their poverty is extreme and they scrat around to find a living. You with a roof above your head and two fine daughters might find it in your heart to wish a little Christian charity on a poor destitute and deformed."

Anne sniffed and mumbled into her bread. Joan Gentle, ladling out the soup, paused to murmur, "You cannot wish harm on her, Anne, when you yourself had the bringing of her into this world."

"And bitter thanks I got for it." Anne Whittle's head bobbed agitatedly in recollection. "Three days and nights sweating like a sow and screeching like one. 'Til I would have been glad to leave her to her pain. But I did not. I brought that strangulated babe out into the living world."

"And it was well done—"

"And when she saw its squashed up face and the one eye sitting above the other, she commenced to curse, and has cursed me ever since, old Demdike."

"Elizabeth Southern," corrected the steward.

"Nay she is known as Mother Demdike in these parts. I can tell you she is known and feared even as a most potent witch."

Joan persisted, "She is old and very poor and going blind. And that is enough to be called after."

"And free with curses for the midwife who struggled with her."

Finally Alice intervened: "The midwife is often blamed for the bad coming of a babe. But you also had thanks of very many folk. How many babes came out well and safely through your hands?"

"Until the shaking sickness came," the old woman said bitterly.

"Aye, until then. But I do not think that poor squinting Lizzie had any midwife by to help her." She made the steeple with her fingers and the deep voice softened as her face grew pensive. She looked far away as she might have been counting sheep. "Those of us who bring forth children between clean sheets, what do we know of the ditch delivery of a drab? What fear and loneliness goes with the pain? Many a young girl, a young child, is taken by force, by force or ignorance. Or then again it may be the babe was conceived with as much tenderness as in the great four-poster. Perhaps they even loved a little when they made it." Her fingers twisted. "But for all that, she will be whipped 'til the blood runs, in front of Hell's laughter in the market square. Lord save us from such judgementals."

Everyone stayed quiet after, I remember, 'til Joan Gentle fetched out a jug of elderberry wine, and they began to talk over the day's work.

Later that night when we had retreated to her office and I was endeavouring to copy spidery streaks of letters, I could not forbear to question her. "You were very mild with Anne Whittle, Mistress Nutter. I would have expected you to check her at the outset."

"Hugh Redferne did correctly reprimand her."

"And Joan Gentle. Should not you, in your own house, have the first authority?"

"Ah, we have no place here for the great idol, Authority, whether it comes cassocked or crowned. It is not for a single one to preach. In this place anyone may speak who is moved by the spirit, and if not, may stay silent. Indeed that is the rule – nay you cannot call it a rule. We are exhorted to learn to hold our peace, to hold our souls in quietude, for there is a very great virtue in silence."

She prevented my comment with a smile. "I know, I know, Jane. I am very disposed to pronouncing my opinions. Of all my many sins it is the most besetting. I am not a hoarder of words, but on occasion I do attempt to set a bridle on my tongue."

"Many sins, Alice?" I grew impudent. "Are you not then perfected? As of the Family?"

She ceased guiding my hand and asked sharply, "What do you know of Perfects?"

"What I see, what I hear. And what I guess."

"What you learn of Anne Redferne when you gossip in the laundry. She is a sweet girl, but a silly goose and she chatters more than is safe, and you Mistress Shireburn are too quick. I should have known that you would find us out." She looked at me seriously, severely. "I most sincerely did not bring you here to convert. I had no intention to attract your belief into the Family of Love. It is a group with many enemies and some say detested by the lady on the throne. I must pray you for your secrecy. An idle word could much endanger us."

I had grown a great liking for Alice Nutter, but I cared not a jot for her Family of Love, and I had no patience to enquire which of all the beliefs in the world was the shorter road to Paradise. But I was very tired of secrets and resentful to be burdened with yet another injunction for secrecy. I threw down my pen and pushed aside the copying paper. "I am aweary of tell nots; tell not of massing priests, tell not of dissenting conventicles, tell not of your father's wenching, tell not of violators and old women with charms, of power to do harm—"

"They have no real power to do harm," she said gently. "It is only ignorance and fear that lend them reputation."

"But I – I have a power," I think I whispered. And even now I shrink from writing what I believe I said. But Alice took my hand.

"No Jane. No. Do not make that mistake, ever. Simon Carter got what he deserved, richly deserved, when his pony pitched him off. But it was no evil spirit that procured his death. Nor good one neither. It was the accident of a stone and a hoof, such as happens a thousand times."

My turn to ask, "What do you know? How do you know I spoke of Simon Carter?"

"Whispers drift like scraps of morning mist in these damp valleys. They collect, change form and dissipate. They are malevolent but insubstantial. They are to be forgot."

"And not spoken of."

"Exact. Jane, life is so full of don't tells, why does it weigh so heavily upon you?"

"Because I am afraid of the dark."

"Why the dark is always prowling round us. But it cannot touch the light that is within, the light of our Blessed Lord in your soul."

"If you are a Perfect."

If there was a sourness behind my words she laughed it off. "I am never like to be perfected in this life, old money bags that I am. But I do strive after virtue, and I do revere the teachings of the Family."

She handed me back the pen. "And now it is for me to try to be not verbose, and for you to put your mind on the printing, if I am to send you home a lettered woman to your father."

With which she set me back to copying.

Chapter 6

TO EVEN SPEAK OF FEARS is to give them shape, space in the mind. Despite the gentle manners of the farm household and the neat tiny chamber Alice had assigned me, I did not sleep easy at Crow Trees Farm. On the last night I thought I heard a rapping at the door, which had come ajar. I leapt from my bed to cross the very little space, but my feet were leaden-heavy. A gust of wind blew through and before I slammed it shut, I had a faint sense of a something, a breathing something, that was invisible, a sound that was inaudible. I lay awake some while, listening for whatever presence hung about behind my door, and at last fell into a heavy but unquiet slumber. I woke to the clatter of early morning in the farm kitchen and my own heart still thudding in my breast.

I hope that no such dreams come to pester you John. As little as I love you, I would have you lie untroubled in My Lady's fast embrace. And if I do not trust My Lady to deal with you mercifully, I do trust Ellen's concoctions to smooth the creases from your forehead, to settle the motion of your chest.

But I was glad, I confess, to ride away to Downham Hall, to see the sideboard spread with plenty and mine host with oaths and jokes, and I with nothing to consider but how to please my father. Who was jovial after good hunting and purposed that we should travel via Clitheroe market, as it was the monthly gathering there. And Alice of course had business and was bid come with us, and since Dick Assheton had reserved in the inn, she also was invited to dine with the rest.

It was merry on the way into Clitheroe, making our grand passage through the crowds of folk and beasts who pushed back to make way for us. The noise grew steadily as we entered the town, threading our way through the maze of stalls, stalls piled with eggs and cheese, mounded with vegetables, clumped up with caged poultry or laden with beer kegs and jars of liquorice. At a little stall offering fresh flowers, I made sure Rick would purchase a nosegay for Dorothy, but my idiot brother must needs press forward towards the sounds of tumult, the waves of hurrahs coming from the centre of the marketplace. But it was no bearbait that we encountered there, to his disappointment, nor no cockfight neither, not even a match of mastiffs. It was different thing altogether. They had Lizzie Southern there, strung between two posts. She had no garment to cover her sagging, milk-heavy breasts, and the bit of a skirt left her was for neither here nor there. And if it was not blood that had wetted it, the girl must have been prodigiously pissing herself. As we halted there I heard the sharp whistle of a whip, and she lifted her shaggy head, misshapen face the more deformed by the grimace of a silent scream. A scream drowned out by the cheers and jeers of the market populace. And then it fell, that heavy head, like a rag puppet, while the two constables flexed for the next stroke, turn and turn about.

But the worst of all to me was that I had already seen, or almost seen, that dreadful face in the crack of a door, had seen that silent scream in my haunted dream. My mouth was all ash, but my pony held her place for all the press of people. Until my father was behind us, and ordering us roughly, "Away now – Rick, Jane. Come out of this. You

42

are waited for at the inn." And he seized my horse's bridle and fairly dragged me away.

But even as we left the spectacle, this fool jingle rang through my head:

> Jane, Jane, who is to blame?
> Who dreamt the dream? Whose is the shame?

I was right glad to be taken in charge to the inn. That was a different noise – cheerful greetings, the clatter of crocks, the 'pass, pass,' as steaming bowls of mutton broth were carried through, and much attendance of course paid to our party, to find good seating and debate the dishes offered. And as it happens in noisy crowded places there was a momentary lull, and then it was I heard Alice's deep voice: "Who gave the order for that whipping?"

A silence fell, and it was the justice of the peace from Read who answered her. Roger Nowell at a table nearby paused in his slicing of a lump of beef. I remember how I could not avoid observing the black hair that frilled his knuckles as he sat down his knife and fork. "I ordered that whipping. Do you have complaint to make?"

"Is it not very harsh – to whip so poor a creature for so human a sin?"

"But sin it is and requires castigation. Or are you advising that we suspend judgement mistress—?"

"Nutter. Alice Nutter. Only I find the correction too severe – to flog a beggar girl in front of the laughing scabs of the market place. Were it not a better thing to temper justice with mercy?"

"And fill the parish registers with bastard children, who already struggle to maintain the rogues and vagabonds hereabouts. What foolishness do you presume to offer a justice of the peace?"

She did presume, presumed to continue. "How many stripes did you order?"

"You question, mistress, you toss questions at us, who administer the queen's law in this most unruly patch of her realm?"

"Nay Master Nowell. You are the authority here and not to be gainsaid. It is just that I never cease to ponder the words of Our Lord as who should send the first stone. And I wonder who could be so far without sin."

"Presumably you do not question that our clergy should guide their flocks, that justices enforce the law?"

If his voice was heavy with sarcasm, hers was clear as a bell. "Indeed no. And yet it still vexes me. Who could it be Master Nowell so far without sin?" She shook her head in mock confusion. "I think only our Blessed Lord Himself, who is without stain." She let the silence run a little minute before she said, "Can you imagine Christ Jesus flogging a cripple in the stocks?"

Nowell made to rise. I am sure he wanted to hit her. But my father, who had been impatiently drumming his fingers upon the table, intervened. "We have heard enough of your preachments Mistress Nutter. This is not the place for a pulpit. Nor rightly considered, is it a woman's part to give us lessons in religion."

Alice gave but the shadow of a half-smile. "I never learned that gender was an attribute of the soul."

But no one paid that any attention, nor paid any more attention to her. She did not speak again, but long before the meal was finished she picked up her cloak and took her leave. I am sure we were all very glad to see her go.

"She has a face to curdle milk, old Nutter's wife," Assheton amiably remarked to the world in general.

"Widow," corrected my brother, "and because she has the running of a farm she presumes to sit with her betters and make contradiction to a justice of the peace."

Nowell, also preparing to leave, drew on his gloves and nodded across to Rick.

"The fault is in our laws," said the justice. "Because a widow has full legal charge of her estate, she therefore takes upon herself the prerogative and pre-eminence of a man. It is a thing requires correction."

Thus encouraged, Rick grew heated. "But she does pass all limits, the Widow Nutter. To speak so insolently, so audaciously to take upon herself to make pronouncements – and then to leave so gracelessly precipitate."

My father spoke very calmly: "She has gone to solace the beggar girl. They must have cut her down by now."

That surely had been Alice's intention, but the scourging over, Lizzie had already crept away – no one knew where – and was not seen for weeks. Perhaps she beat her own pain out onto the baby boy who was the cause of all her trouble, for it was soon apparent that he was an imbecile. He does no hurt in the parish though. Silly Jimmy thieves a little but leaves the lasses alone. He sings to himself, tells crazy little stories, and tries to adopt every stray puppy dog he finds. And I doubt not that such philanthropy earns him many a beating from his half-starving mother.

Chapter 7

IT IS STRANGE HOW a very little absence can alter the lineaments of familiarity. Something in my home had changed, or something in my way of viewing it. What most jolted me with surprise was the deterioration in Lady Maud. If she had been growing frailer before I went to Crow Trees, I had not observed it. What I suddenly saw was the stoop of her shoulder, the dragging lines about her mouth.

My father, kindly in a general way, paid her very little attention, and the events of the great world did little to bring them close. Margaret and Mary were attentive in a dutiful way, but I think they were always in awe of their mother. My sister, Grace, watched the weakening of her stepmother with little pity, with something like grim satisfaction. Grace had never borne the brunt of punishment from Lady Maud, had rarely even taken correction from her, but she held an unremitting resentment for the lady of the hall which was more real and more unforgiving than any sense of injury that Isabella ever expressed. For myself I could never avoid the belief that the Lady Maud would have liked to love me. My very little gift to her was that I did not avail myself of a permission to pursue my new skills in the library, but kept to household ways.

I think that it never left off raining that autumn. Leaves without colour fell into sodden piles. Acorns scattered down and were squelched into mud before children could gather them. And I began to lose my brother.

I find it of some interest that I generally remember so

little of the weather and attendant circumstances when I delve into my early memory. Always it is the voices that come back to me, loved voices and less loved voices. And the words that leap into my mind, that come crystal clear and sharply formed, demanding record, until my pen can scarce keep up and my wrist is aching.

But this autumn damp I do remember, linked as it is with ailing Maud, and with the sense of loss, as my brother changed. Or I changed towards my brother. I always knew Rick had his way to carve in the world, and that he detested subordination, but I had never known him depart the ranks of chivalry before his outburst in Clitheroe. And this theme of insolent widow he never left alone. As if he borrowed legitimacy from Alice's solecism, from her stepping so far out of her station. And if he felt a faltering of loyalty in the little sister who so devotedly had followed him throughout childhood, well then it did but spur him on.

I remember the subject recurring again some days after we had heard of the death of Margaret Clitheroe. Judge Walmsley was in the house, as we had held a jousting party for the elder legitimate sons, before their return to university. He was of all our guests the most gentle towards Maud, and without ever abandoning his London drawl, or his air of languid insouciance, he treated her to a multitude of tiny gestures, of bows and nods and half smiles, that served to reiterate her importance in the house.

Rick had watched the archery display of those who were nobler born, with the frustration I always recognised in him when he longed to compete, to outshine. It was perhaps this pent-up emotion which vented itself in a furious recounting of Alice's temerity against the Justice of Read.

Walmsley smiled faintly, "Ah compassion. It is such an outmoded virtue. Especially among our Christian gentry.

And it is not the least of Alice's peculiarities."

"Do you know Alice Nutter?" I asked.

"Not perhaps as well as you, Jane. But she is known in many unexpected parts of the kingdom, with her canny trading. An old spider with surprising webs."

"A spider?" I very slightly would have objected.

He laughed, "But very learned I grant you. And known for charity."

Maud frowned, "I do account myself a stranger to newsmongering. But I am given to understand that Alice Nutter attends church service with as little fervour as any good recusant. And yet it seems clear that she has no fidelity or attachment to our ancient faith."

This remark elicited no response. The judge busied himself with the pretty little tobacco box which was just then his favourite plaything. But Maud continued, "But there is talk of a sect, of atheistical or heretical subversives, who seek to undermine the foundations of the state."

When the judge still did not reply, although he attended to her, she said, "They say there are Familists even here in Lancashire."

"Familists." Walmsley slowly lit his pipe. "If any such there be they are well hid. They are secret and cooperative, and apparently conforming. And very peaceable."

"But not impossible to discover?" Rick spoke with eagerness. "One could learn where to search them out?"

Walmsley ignored him. "A very mixed bag. Farmers, merchants, yeomen and some in the highest places."

"At court?" my father questioned.

"There was a push some years back, and a Bill was drafted to clip them with a sentence of death. It was thought with support from the Privy Council. But it was quashed. Someone had said a good word. Someone close to a royal ear."

"Who does not recognise the danger?"

Walmsley's look to Rick was tinged with disdain. "Danger that they represent or that they court?" He puffed thoughtfully. "The first is imaginary. The second, so long as they keep mum – they should keep mum."

He leaned back in his chair to indicate an intention to follow his own advice. But he looked at me carefully through the smoke, and that not with disdain.

Maud gave a long sigh. "No such leniency or sweet safety for our brethren." She spoke bitterly, "Margaret Clitheroe has drawn a vicious fate as reward for her service and faithfulness."

That quieted us all. That not so many days before, a distant kinswoman in York had been crushed to death beneath a wooden slab as legal punishment for the harbouring of priests, this frighted me more by far then Rick's gory tales of priestly executions. Her crime was after all no different than that committed in our own household these many, many times.

Walmsley nodded. "She refused trial by jury. She was strongly advised to trust to the mercy of a jury."

"Because she would not have her child called as witness. Such a saint and holy martyr is that woman. And when the jailers would have hurried her death with piling on more weights, she even bade them desist."

"Indeed." Walmsley lay a calming hand, a much-ringed hand, on Maud's.

She was breathing heavily and it cost her to speak, but she did not desist. "She did so in intention to prolong her own agony, for the glory of God and the radiance of her own immortal soul."

"So they say, my lady. So they say," said Walmsley, and if she heard the cynicism in his voice she ignored it. As I believe she was ignoring the gradual defection of her husband. My father had never been a model of abstinence, but despite that his concubine was allowed her presence, Maud's pre-eminence in the house was never in dispute. Now though he was becoming less indulgent of her religious fervour, and in any case was oftentimes from the hall with journeying to London, with meetings of loyal gentlemen, with pledges of loyalty to the Protestant monarchy. From one of such journeys he brought news of the capture of 'Little John'.

Maud ever paler, ever thinner, with her chin like a shovel and eyes deep sunken, was but the fiercer in spirit. She gave orders, whispered orders but compelling, that all the household should gather in the chapel. Even my father on this occasion heeded her. She kept us all, long time, on our knees, intoning interminable rosaries.

"We will pray," she insisted, "we will pray for his release. We will pray down a miracle from Heaven itself."

I thought of the little dwarf with magic hands, the builder of such skill and ingenuity, who had very like saved me from a whipping. I would have been glad to pray him from captivity, but my own faith was not so robust. Rather I watched and wondered at the unflinching will of my stepmother. Could she make miracles happen? Would she procure his release? What kind of mental resolve did any woman need to control the laws of chance? What secret power might interfere with destiny? I long debated this with myself. I was yet something dismayed, and I know not why, when we heard the glad news that Nicholas Owen had escaped from the Tower.

By the time that Mary Stuart lost her head on the chopping block, Maud was too weak to rise from her bed. Only tears coursed her cheeks and dripped off that poor jut of a chin.

Chapter 8

IT WAS A SINGULARLY UNFORTUNATE MOMENT for Lady Maud to die: the year of Armada.

The threat from Catholic Spain had even ousted fears of plague. It was no time for demonstrations of allegiance to the Pope of Rome. The Lady Maud who had spent such care in long and elaborate contrivances for masses of secret splendour and brilliance, for her the obsequies were hasty and scant. I could not but be saddened by the pitiful lack of ceremonial for her. I look back even now with slight surprise at the ardour of my father to join the League of Lancashire Gentlemen.

My brother Rick was not surprised. I still retained the habit of visiting my brother in the falconry, and as he worked he would discourse to me on the changing nature of allegiances. To demonstrate his new understanding of the Protestant view point he even went so far as to mention the bonfires of Smithfield, when the King of Spain fingered these islands through Queen Bloody Mary. I was amazed to hear him speak of her in this way, here at Stonyhurst, but he went on to explain that these divisions were now of no matter. "It is no longer papists against Protestants. Nor white rose against red. It is simply staunch Englishmen united against a common foe. Bound in our duty to prevent that black-souled Spaniard in his attempts to breach the ramparts of our silver seas."

With such sentiments went a wholehearted engagement in my father's efforts to recruit a body of men for defence, and for the building of a huge beacon to stand atop of Pendle Hill, one link in the chain of watch fires that threaded across the country. There was a fever of activity in and about the hall – felling and chopping and carting. There were smithy fires roaring and armoury work clanging all hours of the day and night. There were hoards of men in the hall and in the vicinity, reluctant farmsteads pressed to take them in. All was robustious in our house.

But my Ladye Tyme, as indifferent to all of this, took charge of her thin fierce daughter, and she was soon forgot.

However, in some sign of respect the concubine's family were made to vacate the hall. Isabella was sent into Derbyshire, from where she hoped and planned to return a blushing bride. Rick and Gracie both, not without pleasure, were sent to sojourn in Downham. And I – why I was chosen I could not guess, but that the Gods had briefly taken favour from me – I was sent to Samlesbury Hall. To the house of a penniless, ferocious, recusant lord.

I helped my mother pack her possessions and to change into mourning clothes. I could not prevent a smile to see her attach a high ruff, which quite obliterated her beauty spot. She caught my smile and tossed her head with that gesture she had.

"You need not smile, Jane. You have the self-same spot growing between where your breasts will come. And you should value it. It may be a better help to you than any love potion."

I did not answer back, but I reflected that a love charm was a puny gift compared with the ability to flit a man out of the Tower of London.

When I came to your house John, I was neither child nor woman. No – I strive for exactitude – I was a child still but with a woman's knowing of some things, which must be the same for any harlot's daughter. And not unaccustomed to small slights.

So I was not unduly discountenanced by the lukewarm welcome. Your grandfather's influence was immediately apparent, not only in the many forbidden images and crucifixes, but in the poverty of the appointments. It was Sir John Southworth's, not your father's house – the old knight famed for valour in the field of battle, and for a stubborn clinging to his faith, in despite of prison term and the recusancy fines that had bled his estate white dry.

He was one of the few who had resolutely gone to Lady Maud's funeral. I marvelled that an absence could so fill a house with presence. So that to me it seemed all other members of the family were drained of interest. Your father, Thomas, too hesitant to have charge of the hall. Sweet Rosamund your mother, with her plump worried face, fluttering anxiously about the house, a house bereft of books, since all had been confiscated for sedition. Though she was kindly to me, teaching me how to Irish stitch a cushion, and other small skills to pass the time.

And you, dear John, oh you were of no interest to me. A brawny, bonny, brutal lad with no more conversation than a turnip. And if I paid you no heed it cannot be said that you vouchsafed me much attention neither. Not then. Not then you did not.

We all seemed to exist in a state of half waiting, until the master returned. My father's homecomings were always noisy, almost festive, with the clattering of hooves, and oaths and shouted commands and barking of dogs, and his own huge voice over all. Sir John Southworth came back to Samlesbury alone with his dour serving man. The clangour of his arrival was like a note of iron. He entered without fuss, but I thought that the house seemed to tremble to receive him. I could not fail to remark the deference of his son, the excessive timidity of his daughter-in-law. Safe to say, that I kept as low as possible, sitting humbly at table, adventuring speech to no one. But even so I did not escape notice.

He spoke the Grace before the meal, asking the Lord for blessing on the assembled company, for all the gifts that lay before us on the table, and beseeching forgiveness of our sins. "And for the sins of those that have reneged," he suddenly added, "for those who have forsook the paths of righteousness, and suffered that faithful servant Maud Bold to depart this life with such scant ceremony and so little respect."

He sat after that and took a swill of wine but he did not let loose his theme. "She who in life was made to endure the presence of a concubine at her own table, even in death was not allowed her due, deprived of full requiem, deprived of that recognition and attendance, which should in justice accompany the passing of a faithful daughter of the Church."

The waiting man, John Singleton, he alone seemed not in awe of the old man, but to enjoy the rant. He muttered 'ayes' and grunts in accord with his master, and kept his goblet refilled.

We all commenced to munch in silence, but the knight suddenly banged his fist upon the table with force to make the platters bounce. "And who fetches a redheaded devil imp to my table? Did I leave Lady Maud's feeble funeral to find the harlot's child lodged in my home?"

I spake not, swallowing my crust with difficulty. No one looked at me. Thomas hemmed in his throat.

"And not alone is this girl the fruit of mortal sin. It is the child all know to have accompanied Richard Shireburn to Anglican services. So early to throw mock at that religion which Maud was upholding in their home."

He reached for bread and my cast-down eyes observed the old, knobbled, veined hands beginning to tremble. He dragged a plate of fish toward him, mumbling somewhat, something like: "And if it takes a grown man but few years to lose his faith through conforming, who knows how quick apostasy breeds among children."

John Singleton, then I clearly saw, took it upon himself to touch the knight upon the shoulder, and what he whispered did nothing to abate the old man's fury. He turned his angry gaze on Thomas. "And at this time, this very time, should we endanger our own kin with such besotted hospitality?"

Thomas opened helpless hands to indicate – what? A favour requested not refusable, the claims of friendship and influence, the smallness of the hazard presented by a young child? Whatever he might have said, the gesture infuriated his father.

"Are we expected to endure ill-begotten bastards on every side? The daughter of a goggle-eyed whore on the throne, and the daughter of a Jezebel at my board!" He thumped the table again – I was already rising. "Get her out, get rid of her! Clear her from my sight before she brings the very Devil to sup with us."

I had already cleared myself, was stumbling wretchedly clumsy from the room, for tears were blotching my eyes, and sobs tore ragged in my chest, struggling into my throat. I rushed past paralysed servants standing foolish with dishes in their hands, rushed to some place I knew not, but to somewhere, anywhere, out of his way. And in my half-blind progress, I pushed against a hanging tapestry that swung away to show an aperture that seemed a hiding place, but was in fact the well of a tiny narrow staircase. I followed it up and round to a little low door, not easy to see at greater than my height, but promising a longed-for hiding. Still part-blinded by salt water I entered a room that was darkish and square with an immensely large crucifix depending on the opposite wall. I shut the door and leaned my back against it, struggling for breath and to stop the sobbing hurting in my breast.

When I properly opened my eyes he was standing staring straight at me – a tall, gaunt boy in a soutane. Who was the more surprised I could not say. And he did not speak until my chest had stopped wildly heaving, though my eyes still streamed. His voice was deep and gentle.

"What is the cause of all this woe?" I know not what words came out – even with my prodigious memory for speech – I cannot think which words emerged through spluttering sobs and gulping tears and snot, but he contrived to pull the meaning out.

That room was barely furnished, an iron cot with a dark blanket, a large oak chest, a shelf with a missal and some altar vessels, and a table carrying a jug and ewer, from where the young priest picked up a towel and came across to me to mop my storm-washed, mossy face.

His kindness did little to stem my tears. They only flowed the faster until he picked me up in his arms and sat me on his knee, so I could weep freely against his shoulder. It was a bony shoulder and a bony knee, but it was the balm of comfort after my shaming in the dining hall.

When I had somewhat subsided into a few hiccups, he asked, "Who is this girl upon my knee?"

I sat up straight to say that I was Richard Shireburn's daughter and if I was a bastard child, I was still much loved by that great man. And honourably raised. And neither ignorant nor faithless. He interrupted my prideful assertions. "You are evidently a noble young lady and welcome to my narrow abode, but you must know that you have stumbled on a dangerous secret. I do need to ask you to be very close as to my presence here."

Tell nots again! My bruised pride fuelled indignation. "Think you we know not of hidden priests at Stonyhurst? And that I know not how to faithfully protect and honour a fugitive holy man? It is not necessary to ask me." And with a child's boastfulness I said, "I have already guessed, sir, who you are – Sir John Southworth's son, Christopher, that went away to the Jesuits at Douai to be ordained."

He nodded, "Well guessed, and I am most unlawfully given this small reprieve to visit my father's house, as I am being officially conducted to Wisbech Castle."

"You are come for Lady Maud's funeral?"

"Alas, much as I would have wished to help officiate in her requiem, I fear the trail I leave may bring too many spies after me. I could have been the cause of a very grave disorder."

'Grave disorder.' These seemed to me light words, for what I knew might be the consequence of spies finding a gathering of Catholic clergy at our house. I was very sorry for myself but not so sorry that I did not also feel my oft-times puzzled pity and reverence for the outlawed priest. "But you must still go – to the castle?"

"I have made a promise."

"And is it not fearsome there? Wisbech Castle is a house of dread, so they tell."

"No more than any prison. There are other priests there incarcerated. And other trials for the soul, perhaps more dire than the confessionals of simple felons."

I did not know the trials that he spoke of, only that I could see he was a very troubled soul, and that his troubles were more weighty than my own. "I do understand Sir John's vexation with my presence. And his fears for you," I said, "but I would never betray you, Father."

He stroked my hair absently, and then replaced my cap straight. He was about to set me down when there came a quick treble knock at the door. John Singleton entered with a supper tray, which he very nearly dropped to see me sitting there upon Christopher Southworth's knee.

"The child was distraught," the young man said. "I think my father was very fierce with her." And as the serving man made to protest, he gestured him to silence. "She is faithful, and of a faithful family. No need for alarm. I will send her down shortly, and you must arrange a servant to take her home."

The older man placed his tray and bowed out, though his look for me was not a friendly one. I stood uncertain, ready to follow, but the young priest gestured me to a little rush chair. "Well Mistress Jane Shireburn, will you do me the honour of sharing this simple repast?"

Chapter 9

IT IS TWO NIGHTS NOW that I have not written a word. I am more than imperfect in my attention to you, husband, but I could not leave you to suffer unattended. I could not so withdraw from your present moment, into my own so much more tempting reveries. I do the little things ill that Ellen does for you so well. Nor can I rejoice at that stronger breathing and motion, which seems to bring you only pain and disquiet of soul. But I wish you ease with all my heart. And I also wish – and hope it is no sin – that My Ladye will come tenderly to you and not delay too sufferingly long. As she was painful slow in gathering to her bosom poor Lady Maud. But not too late for that other dame who governs my life, to swing her wheel full circle, as the courtesan's family were reinstated into full favour and position.

❊ ❊ ❊

My mother, properly wed and sumptuously, I could say, clothed, was only poorly gratified. She had spent nigh on a year in Derbyshire, and I think it was a year of indolence, not foreign to her nature. However she took my father's ring, she did not noticeably increase his ardour. Was it legitimacy or amplitude? I was well aware that it took younger naughtier girls to light the flame in his ageing but indomitable loins.

Of course my brother fairly shone, although he must needs always give place to those sons were purchased in sanctified sheets. For me what can I say? Life opened with the slow surprise of a flower. Congratulations, compliments and invitations edged us into the world of great ones.

We went – and Gracie of course – on county visits. We were well received at Hoghton Towers and how little did I care whether Sir Richard Hoghton twitched his noble nostrils with disdain or appreciation. Even at Lathom, the Earl of Derby greeted us with warmth and we were invited to participate in the dancing and masques and music, and all the subtle entertainment we had – I had – so long desired.

Sir Thomas Walmsley became a member of parliament for the county, as well as queen's judge, and was most pleased to receive us at Dunkenhalgh. I loved him for his urbanity, his finery and his good heart, and most of all for his affection towards me. In a newly-widened world, I was able to be often in his company.

I received inevitably the freedom of the library, to read and write as I pleased. In fact it pleased my father greatly for he was grown obsessional with the new building, and I was well able to decipher masons' plans, and abominably written architects' notes. I took pleasure in adding my pennyworth to the arguments – for if you employ one architect from France and one from Italy, you may anticipate discord. One small curly-headed Italian buzzed like a fly about me, and it was perhaps then I learnt, before I told on him to my father, that I would most enthral men with my copper hair, rather than with any other thing.

There was also John Spencer, nephew of old Sir Thomas Gerard, was caught up with me about this time. He was a courtier of sorts but dwarfish and not well favoured. How is it I have so much to do with dwarfs? He let it be known that he was a gifted poet and friend of poets. He boasted of his friendship with William Shakeshaft, who, Walmsley let us know, was becoming great in London. As well as penning verses and composing compliments, John Spencer was making an elaborate study of sculptured monuments, which gained him entry to my father's conference, and the possibility to persecute me with his attentions.

What gave me great satisfaction too was my position at the high table. I wielded no more wine jugs, nor was not so required to keep my eyes lowered, but I might listen and observe fully those conversations which I now still easily remember.

I kept mute when Sir John Southworth was invited, and it was with malicious pleasure I saw how reciprocally he was detested by Roger Nowell. We knew – all the world knew – that it was Nowell's kinsman, the Dean of St Paul's no less, who had conducted the prison examination of the Samlesbury knight. Of course the blustery old man could not counter nor endure their condescending attempts to wean him from the breasts of error. Error, if so it was, to which he so devotedly clung. And if his fidelity to ancestral beliefs had more of passion than subtlety, it was still in my father's view an ill judgement to pronounce the old man 'an illiterate bigot'. And Nowell repeated that in too many houses.

It would be difficult to say whom Roger Nowell did like, including the long-suffering, bulging wife, whose womb he did so continually populate.

My father's hospitality was always large and would certainly not be stinted towards a powerful neighbour with augmenting fortune. But I knew when pleasantness was pasted on his face and when his voice was modulated with care.

He could, however, always surprise me; as by admitting Alice Nutter to his board. After her unseemly outspoken utterance in the Clitheroe inn, I had thought that she would never again be made welcome at Stonyhurst. But I believe that Richard Shireburn was large-souled enough to perceive how little difference lay between his own seigneurial whoring and the petty lechery of beggars. And even to carry Alice's reprimand on his conscience. I think on this account he would never refuse entry – nay invitation – to a widow woman, as comfortable to entertain in some companies as a bed of nettles.

Or did he simply wish to pick her brains for the breeding of cattle and sheep? For he often asked her to perform commissions for him. And if that favouring surprised me, what caused me to ponder – and I ponder still – was an obscure current of sympathy, which I sensed between an elegant royal judge, and the plain as a pikestaff herdswoman. It was never stated or owned to, but I have felt it a score of times. How they understood each other. Was it just to do with wit and learning?

It was a short night that you granted me last night John, and I fear a restless one again. I perceive that I must hasten this narrative if I am to reach the present. But I will not skimp the telling, not now, just as I am at my high years.

One time my father was recounting anecdotes of family history. It concerned an attack made by Lancashire men on Yorkshire Talbots, and the revenge that Yorkshiremen took some eight years later. Their vengeance had been wreaked on one woman: Adelaide Simpson.

My father gave the relation very ironically: "That was a brave foray. John Talbot, gentleman, struck her with an arrow on the head, unto the brain, a mortal blow. But that was not enough. Waddington, yeoman, struck with a thick stick on her belly, enough to kill her again. And then other

Talbots and such gentlemen – a list long enough to fill two pages of the rolls – set about her, lambasting the corpse with true Yorkist gallantry. And all of them, for sake of flaunting the white rose, obtained the king's full pardon."

Nowell nodded and commented ponderously, "An exaggerated method to reassert Yorkist supremacy certainly, but one feels that Adelaide Simpson must have been a particularly unpleasant virago to provoke such a wealth of blows."

Alice could not prevent that wide grin. The judge caught it and half returned it. He leaned back in his chair and said sorrowfully, "I did myself hold off marrying a wife long time, for fear I might be compelled to muster a regiment of soldiery, if she should give me aggravation."

Alice gave a splutter into her wine. The judge danced a kerchief before his face. For some moments they were both misbehaved. My father was not overly pleased. The justice's face reddened. How little he did like Alice. And sometimes could not prevent himself expressing it.

One time her name was in the conversation. The men were back from the Assizes and the subject was defaults of payment, which in some way concerned her. Nowell spoke with sudden heat.

"Among the numerous threats to the solidity of the state, and the safety and serenity of our good queen, I rank not least such a scolding woman. It is her fashion to ignore degree and disrupt hierarchy. This is a way to open the gates of chaos, of disorder and confusion."

My father said thoughtfully, "Nay I know of no disorderly actions or tumults in Alice Nutter's house, but I do hear frequently of the Christian charity of her kitchen."

"Charity she may perform, seeing as she has so indecently grown her holdings and wealth."

"Simply to prosper – do we Puritans hold this a vice?"

I have many times observed how Judge Walmsley fiddles with his tobacco to hide his irritation.

My father warmed to her defence. "She should prosper. She knows her sheep. She breeds and doctors with skill, and she trades her fleeces up and down the land. It is an energetic commerce that she drives."

"Commerce with the Devil more like." Nowell was never pleased with contradiction. "There is more than wool to be carried on a packhorse."

He waited to be questioned, which no one did.

"Books," he announced, "books, pamphlets, polemics, translations!"

"Translations?" Judge Walmsley lifted interrogative eyebrows.

"Just so," replied Nowell emphatically. "Of all manner of foreign opinions unwanted in this county: German rant, Italian idolatry, Dutch mysticism, French sophistry—"

His list might have continued but the judge sighed mournfully: "Ah Dante beloved, clever Machiavel, Erasmus, sweet Montaigne, dear bawdy Rabelais. Are you all to be lost to us?"

Nowell breathed heavily and drove on. "Make no mistake, this is a contraband of evil. It may be disguised by harmless parcels of poetry and plays, but I know, I have information that there is carried up and down material that would warrant more than a prison sentence."

"Come, man," my father amiably remonstrated.

"No sir." The Puritan was eager to prove his point. "There is to be found in these satchels, in these bales, works of blasphemy and rebellion – subversive teachings, Arminianism, Nicodemism, antinomial trash – all stuff to stop up the nose with the stink of foul and filthy error."

I thought he had reached the peak of his oratory, but he lowered his voice – and his thick eyebrows also – to say,

"These drovers' roads are veritable channels of heresy and sedition."

Walmsley smiled slightly and leaned back to exhale. "Conduits of thought," he said, "to connect the dark little vale of Roughlee with the wide world of learning. We should congratulate this woman."

The judge's mockery was an irritant too much for Nowell. "This is a business for castigation, not congratulation! You are all frivolous, you great nobles, lax in morals, lax in manners."

My father placed an admonitory hand upon the other's darker one, but the justice, too inflamed, turned to his host: "Even you Shireburn. You may not subscribe so far as the Earl of Derby to the religion of Good Luck, but you were ever ready to trim your sails to a strong wind."

I was astounded by his effrontery, but my father answered quietly enough.

"I hear this criticism from every side." He used his swirling wineglass, I thought, as the judge used his tobacco box. "There are those who would have me beggar myself in paying recusancy fines, to keep up the old religion. And others who send high and mighty messengers to upbraid me that I do not sell my neighbours to the queen's law and lay information on those that harbour massing priests."

Nowell's tone quite swiftly altered to one of eager conciliation. "If you had such knowledge, Sir Richard, and laid it before the state – as is your bounden duty – it would be a true service to our sovereign, and such duties do not go unrewarded."

"I am not such a fool as not to know I am reported on," my father continued evenly. "And of course I know in which houses secret masses are still celebrated, and which noblemen cleave to the old faith. But I am not about to shop my neighbours for a nod from London."

He tossed back what was left of wine in his glass, and his anger was suddenly evident.

"I hold to the law, God's and the Queen's. I keep an orderly household and succour the needy of the parish. I press soldiers for the Crown and I build a great house to grace this county. But I will ransack no man for his conscience."

He paused as if there was need to secure more attention. Which there was not.

"And I will tolerate no man to meddle with mine."

He gestured for refilling, without a word, and the men drank in silence. Judge Walmsley raised his eyebrows to watch ascending spirals of smoke. Then the Justice of Read, seeking to draw together the tatters of his robe of authority, embarked on a new topic.

"But there is a real scourge in our midst. If ever James of Scotland sits on the English throne, I think we would be well advised to take heed of his learned opinions, and root out the witch covens that infest our country."

My father did not pick up his olive branch. Judge Walmsley sighed lengthily and blew careful smoke rings into the air. Nowell was left to meditate on his excellent theme.

Much later I repeated this conversation to Alice. "You can say one thing for Puritans," she remarked, "they are never short of a word or two."

Chapter 10

THERE ARE THE HILLS AND VALLEYS OF FEVER. And now we are come to a level place, for which I can only be thankful. So you may rest and I have liberty to delve my past. I cannot delve yours, John. I wished never to set foot in Samlesbury Hall again, and yours was not a family that came very much into society. So your growing from taciturn child into tongue-tied youth, I do not know how it went. Did you sport and hunt, chase deer and boar, as a country gentleman would? Did you fast and pray and genuflect as a hidden Catholic ought? Did you learn to despise your well-meaning father, because of a boyish devotion to a fierce old warrior?

✳✳✳

While I was become a summer grasshopper, I danced, I played, I sang. I read many books and I wrote many poems, earning extravagant praise from John Spencer, for the sake of which I endured his more tedious compliments.

But it was my father ever the first in my affections. And yet I was not sufficiently observant to understand how he was labouring for the legacy he wished to leave. His passion for building the great house of course had never diminished, and he had commenced the construction of the gatehouse. But he was also taking time and care to secure alliances for his children. I was the last to be so served, and I believe that he liked to keep me about him.

"Wives may come and wives may go," Judge Walmsley

once observed to me, "though not always with the alacrity of Harry Tudor's consorts. But a favourite daughter may hold fast to her father's heart forever."

And I was very content to be such a favourite. Able also to be glad for Rick, that marriage was arranged with sweet Dorothy Assheton, along with gift of the manor house at Dunnow. As the time for his leaving grew near, our lately coldness melted, and we returned to something like our childhood's camaraderie. I hung about him, advising on many things; his wedding clothes, the attentions he should be lavishing on Dorothy, or moderation he might observe in sporting and drinking with his father-in-law to be. And when he had endured enough he would retaliate with endless jingles at my expense:

> *Jane, Jane, silly and plain*
> *Needs some help to find her a swain.*

But he did on occasion return my advice with some seriousness. I had received a little note from Alice Nutter, advising me that Anne Whittle was shortly to wed with young Tom Redferne, and expressing what pleasure I could give them, were I able to attend. As chance fell out, this ceremony was to happen in the same week that Rick's wedding would be celebrated at Downham Hall. I received my father's permission to prolong my stay from Stonyhurst. My father's permission but not my brother's pleasure.

"You should avoid Widow Nutter's company, Jane. There are whispers of this Family of Love. It is to be shunned as" – he stopped before the word plague – "as a noxious evil."

"Alice is no evil woman," I began, very much in my father's vein.

"You have no idea what it is about. They derive their

dogma, or their lack of dogma, from a Dutch mystical fellow, which is bad enough for any Christian man."

"So?" I am sure I gave but a careless shrug.

"Jane, grow into your senses. The license this group demand is out of all reason. On account of carrying Christ within, or some such dreamy blasphemy, they make claim that women should stand equally with men in all things, that folk should love freely where they will, and whomsoever they would, that people who sit in high places should be toppled, and every common churl the right to his opinions."

It was in the falconry as usual that Rick had chosen to deliver this brotherly counsel. I remember stroking his face with a long feather I had picked up, in an effort to distract him from his sermon. "Where have you been learning these informations? You who should be wholly taken up learning the duties of a groom. Do you know Dorothy's chosen flower? Her special colour? Her favourite jewel? What interest have you shown in the arrangements at Dunnow Manor? What erotica have you studied to grace your service on the wedding night?"

Rick frowned impatiently. "Leave off this frivolity Jane. This is a business that could touch you. They would have no distinction at all be made in religion, claim that every knave should have entitlement to preach, every sect freedom of operation. In short they do exercise and demand a monstrous toleration that would disrupt every organ of state and would wreak destruction on us all."

"That would set the world on a different cart," I think I said.

He frowned mightily, not grasping what I intended to say. I suddenly wanted not to lose the fragile peace between us.

"Rick, my dearest brother, for Anne Redferne's wedding

I am already promised. But I do hear your words, and I do take heed of your warnings. And I will bear them in mind. But do you also graciously heed the admonitory words of a little sister." I took hold of his hand and held it warmly. "You will be loving and gentle to Dorothy I know, but because you are to become a landowner and a personage, do not come to play the cock in the barnyard."

"Like our father," he said, "taking my choice of the fowl?"

"Nay I was speaking not of libertinage. I had better have said 'cock on the midden,' crowing out opinions loud and long. Too many opinions, Rick," I said, "and not all your own."

He was stung and affronted, but still kept some humour in his voice. It was not only I who wished to preserve our friendship. "You should not speak so to an older brother, and to one so soon to be a married man."

And I had enough sense to ask forgiveness, and beg it with a loving kiss. And he still fond enough to take me by the waist and whirl me round, as he sang that time:

> *For Jane, Jane, pretty and vain*
> *Nothing less than a prince of Spain.*

The last jingle my brother sang to me was in the early dawn of his wedding day, when I was loitering in his chamber eager to give my view as to the final choice of jewel and feather upon his imposing bonnet. He was excited and full of laughter, and to hush my insistent opinions he chanted:

> *Jane, Jane, a favour I claim*
> *Bring out the sun, banish the rain.*

And I did. The damp morning mist was burned away by a spring sun that flooded the landscape with benediction.

A benediction I had wrought. I am sure that Rick quickly forgot the favour he had asked of me, and would not have believed in any case that I could cast a spell upon the weather. My family were all disposed to attribute the fair day to the generosity of heavenly powers. Nor did I truly think I had rain clouds at my bidding. But I could not rid myself of the conviction that I had contributed no little part to the glory of that sun-drenched day.

Or is it memory that gilds that day and those few following? Was the village so extravagantly prettily decorated with birch and willow? And the hump of the great hill so protective? Was the feast that Dick Assheton had set out so prodigious, the roast swan so huge? Were we ourselves so elegant as I like to think in our wedding finery? The old folks so contented sitting with full bellies at their cottage doors, and the music so merry?

But since sunlight is better defined by shadow, there was a darker moment in this day, when a commotion happened at the bridge. Two female figures in rags and tatters had arrived there. Nor poverty nor age had been kind to Demdike. She had grown sunken and stooped, and besides the stick she leaned on, she used also the shoulder of her young granddaughter, a twig of a girl. Nay hardly a twig, Alizon was as fluttery and nervous as a leaf, and clearly very much at the bidding of the old woman. She was not an uncomely wench, and had that in her features to suggest that her mother also might have been a very proper woman to look upon, if nature had set the two eyes square in her face.

But the two of them on the bridge in their scarecrow clothes and their destitution were like spectres at the feast. And it was not pity stirring the crowd but like a chill of fear that passed over.

There were many tales of the Southerns circulating in

Pendle. Folk had even words to say about the Whittles, seeing as old Anne mumbled uncontrollably in her palsy, and got named Mother Chattox for her affliction. Rumours floated of lamed horses, spoiled crops, sour milk and sometimes of human sickness. Yet these bits of witchery seemed to me trivial compared to the lurking dread of plague, which, threatening cottage and manor alike, we tried to banish from our thoughts. Howsoever I may have thought, Demdike could scare more than crows, and the folk were consternated at her presence there.

Seeing the fuss and scuffle round the bridge, my father strode quickly down the hill, and I followed him. He reached out of his pocket a good jingle of silver coins and poured them into Alizon's ready outstretched hand.

"My son is married on this day and we make festivity. Take this and go, go to drink the health of the young people."

The old woman fingered what lay in her grandaughter's palm. I saw how many coins. It was munificence.

"Thank ye," she said, screwing up her face to see him. "I thank ye. We'll go and pray for their good fortune."

My father was already away. I lingered a moment, perhaps curious to observe their pleasure at sudden riches, or just curious.

The old woman turned towards me, her eyes straining. "Shireburn's girl," she asked, "the lowborn one?"

"It is," whispered Alizon.

Demdike nodded. "I give ye a charm once Mistress Jane. To keep ye from harm."

I gave her no answer but she hesitated as if searching around for some token. "Will you take a word now?" she asked.

I still gave no answer but she asked, "Three Johns in

your road?" I shook my head, which mayhap she could not see, for she went on in her sing-song voice:

> *One you do not want*
> *One you cannot have*
> *One will be your fate*
> *That you cannot scape.*

I made to leave then. I suddenly had no desire for her riddling conference, but she held my arm a moment, her hand a withered hook on my bright taffeta. Her eyes were still screwed up. "I'll tell ye," she said, and she lifted her head to take her blind inspiration from the sky, and intoned slowly, as if reading from that inscrutable canopy:

> *One with a silver poet's tongue*
> *One to sing a lover's song*
> *One who is hale and strong*
> *Which one to do you wrong?*
> *He the one who will die young.*

I released myself. "Thank you Elizabeth Southern. I do not wish to know more of my future. Go in peace and enjoy my father's bounty."

How wry was that twisty smile? "*Sancti sanctorum in coelorum,*" she bestowed on me, which garbled Latin I chose to believe was meant as a blessing.

Chapter 11

WHAT DID SHE REALLY KNOW OR GUESS, the old
Demdike? What veil of the future could those half-blind
eyes pierce?

Certainly you were my fate, John, my unwanted fate.
But what wrong you did me would weigh feather-light in
most scales, though I keep my accounting strict. As I look
upon your face, hollowed by pain, yellowed from fever, I
cannot call you a young man. But you are not old neither,
and far from living out your three score years.

So you could squeeze her words into a half truth, half
guess. I did observe how young Alizon listened to her
grandam's words as to an oracle. But on that sunlit day,
I paid but little heed to her puzzling predictions. I have
heard mountebanks do as much to gull the crowds at
country fairs. And I did not care to have an ancient beggar
meddle with my fortune.

"Chatter on old woman," I said to myself, "you cannot
cause the sun to shine."

Richard Shireburn's gesture had earned general approval.
Thomas Walmsley had his arm flung across my father's
broad back in affectionate approbation. Richard Hoghton,
I remember, his aristocratic nose quite reposeful, uttered
words of dignified commendation. I myself was made
beneficiary of some of these compliments. My poet was

on hand of course with sundry praises. And his patron kinsman, stiff but kindly Sir Thomas Gerard, spoke warmly to me of the alacrity and generosity of my dear father. I was aware that he regarded me with appraising eyes, not to my detriment I think.

And you dear John, quite hesitant and awkward but determined, you came up to me to let me know "That was well done – very well done – of your father, Mistress Shireburn, to clear the old woman off, before—"

"Before she cast a blight on this bright day?" I offered helpfully.

Oh the intense eyes of a Southworth! How they burned while you faltered in conversation. Easy to see that you were smitten. And I, in my apricot and gold brocade gown and my gold thread cowl, I felt able to captivate the attention of whomsoever I pleased, on that day, at that time.

I did appraise you for the dancing, for if your speech was lacking in vigour, you stood four-square and manly built. But you confessed to being a poor dancer, and as I laboured to find subjects of easy communication, you were also discovered to be a poor reader, that you did in any case, regard most books as receptacles of error at best, and heresy at worst. And merci to the grandfather, thought I.

And I wondered also how I would choose between the poetry and praise of ugly John Spencer and the stalwart frame and poor speech of Southworth's grandson. I was obliged to conclude that neither would hold me in thrall very many hours.

So I was not too sorry to be led away from the dance. And the more pleased to converse with my new brothers-in-law. It seems the Asshetons must ever bring forth stout vigorous branches, and delicate fragile twigs, and nought between. Young Nicholas was as ruddy and noisy as his father, and the eldest, Richie, as gentle and sweet natured as Dorothy. But frail and sickly also, so that I always felt a great desire to place protection round him. He was of course extremely glad that my father had removed an anxious moment from the day.

My own brother, well steeped in his father-in-law's hospitality, was inclined to a more critical view of our father's complaisance. He was drunkenly affectionate towards Dick, whom he was counselling to avoid such leniency, and rather to take precautions against the pestilential stench and thieving propensity of old crones, promising that he himself would keep all such well clear of Dunnow, and the fair Dorothy.

But the master of the feast was too well soaked in his own good wine to be lured into ill humour or even senseful reflection.

"You know what they tell about old Demdike in the village, Rick? How she caught silly Jimmie straddling the nanny goat – having no solace else – there's not a maid would let him near. She screeched at him so loud that his John Willy fell off, and he a lad coming into his prime. So he begged and begged his grandma give it back. And in the end she relented and bid him climb up a tree and see could he find it in the big crow's nest. So up he goes and down he comes with a handsome great prick, near a yard long."

"Can I have it Granny?" he says.

"Put it back yer silly feller," screams the old woman, "that's the parson's!"

And he laughed so hard, Dick, that he fell off the bench and lay spread-eagled in the grass, in the very bliss of drunkenness.

But if I unstitch my memory a little further, I can detect another faint shade lurking behind the gaiety.

Subterfuge, that ungainly fellow, had long served in our

household, but now that Maud was gone, the hidden chapel empty, and Margaret and Mary content to tell their beads in pious quiet, we all breathed easier. But never completely free of alarms. Shifting factions in London could mightily affect our lives. So savage a proposal as to remove recusant children out of their own families was never implemented, but about the time of Rick's marriage, a bill was passed forbidding recusant gentry to travel more than five miles beyond their estates. Of course such measures were more largely flouted than observed, and even Roger Nowell would not attempt to enforce a fool edict. But many guests at the Downham wedding must have been aware of the uncertainty of their freedom. It was an Act that greatly incensed my father, and roused his spirit of contrariety. Which I am sure was responsible for the largesse of leave he insisted on giving to me: "Ride where you will Jaynie, and as far as you want. Go visit with the Widow Nutter if it pleases you."

So with one servant I rode the little way to Grindleton, but I might have been leaving one world for quite another. The parish had been chosen by Hugh Redferne for its congregation of like-minded souls. I found all on such a modest scale as to be practically invisible. Indeed the trestle tables set out in the field by the church were forbiddingly bare when I arrived.

Good cheer grew, however, as the Family gradually assembled, each member carrying a dish for the table, as well as a small gift. Such small gifts though. A variety of gifts to be sure, and nothing grandiose – a tankard, a spoon, a kerchief, a spade, a bag of lavender, and all of such pronounced utility as made my broidered cushions seem quite a frivolous offering.

Dear Anne, in a simple linen gown, needed no farthingales nor stiffeners to proclaim her queen of the feast. And a very pastoral queen she made. My apricot taffeta did quite sink into ordinariness compared with Anne's spring floral finery. She had sweet violets tucked in her bodice, and in her hair, which she wore loose-flowing in the old style, she had a type of bridal wreath, woven of primroses to outdo her own yellow, and white wind flowers and more violets. Though what pain and bother it would have cost old Anne to weave her daughter's coronet of such delicate fabrics I could only imagine, seeing the spasmic tremors of the woman's hands, and the frightful wobbling of her head.

Hedgerows and woodlands had not only dressed our queen, they had provided the large part of the refreshment. Every sort of berried juice was brought to the tables, in colours to rival Dick Assheton's wine. And food in the end was plenteous, with more of pasties, I noted, than meats. And a large sugared caraway cake that might have come from Big Irene's kitchen.

But before we ate, such a simple ceremonial took place as I have not seen elsewhere. Neither prelate nor curate held sway at Anne Redferne's wedding. Tom simply took her hand and declared before us all: "Before God, I love thee Anne and I will love thee all the days of my life, and whatsoever may come to me of good or bad fortune, I will share with thee."

And Anne, so softly I only heard from being in the front pew, made her vow. "I love thee Tom, and will do so always. I will care for thee now, and in old age. And if God would send us children I will be a good mother to them."

Then Thomas Redferne stood and presented to the couple a green nettle. He was very solemn as he intoned, "This is the stern dispensation of the law."

William Gaunt, whom I had not known to be of that persuasion, had fetched an early rose, and he tendered it carefully as he said, "A blood red flower which is a sign of the passion and forgiveness of the Son."

And Alice, from some corner of the world, had procured a tall-stemmed lily, and her deep voice was strongest in that little church: "May lilies come to bloom in our cold northern county, for this is a symbol of the love and peace of God come to dwell amongst us. That through purity of spirit we may make a heaven in this life and a paradise on our green earth."

After which singular heresy, everyone approached and kissed the wedded couple. And all was a pitter-patter of gentle endearments and that humble self-congratulation which made me want to smile, as the children in God without sin, the souls lit by the light divine, the clean of heart and the blest of spirit, the very walkers with God, shared their joy and their community in that secret Pendle village.

We rambled rather than rode back to Roughlee through the beneficent afternoon. Hugh Redferne was mostly lost in thought, or memory I surmised. Part time Alice and I kept our silences, content to enjoy the scatter of sunlight through nets of young leaves. But we would have little rushes of talk, like the sudden noisy brooks that crossed our path.

I remember asking, "It cannot be true that the peaceable folk of the Family of Love want to topsy turvy the world?"

That earned a smile. "Think you not the world is topsy turvy as it is? Great villains sit in seats of power, and small villains sit in the pillory. The church of mercy sucks tithes from the poor. And our consciences are not allowed to be in our own keeping."

"And they are going to set all to rights, your Family?"

"Oh I think not. They endeavour always to avoid discovery and commotion. But there are many others – malcontents and visionaries – who seek a better world. There is a buzzing of angry hives up and down the land,

and if they should swarm, there will be a right stinging."

I turned in the saddle to observe her face: "And are you a busy bee Alice?"

She plucked at her horse's mane and laughed, but ruefully. "I am neither flesh nor fowl nor good red herring. I know not what I am, but that I seek always – I am a seeker, an everlasting seeker after truth and righteousness."

She added in a more sombre voice, "Though they that call themselves Seekers, they do but erect a new dogma it seems to me. And where there is dogma there will surely follow persecution of one ilk or another."

She still played with the horse's mane. "I love the quietude of the Family, but they will not change the world." Then changing her tone again she quickly smiled: "But still let us say I am a seeker, it is as good a word as any. And you Jane, where are you growing to?"

"I am like you Alice. I do not truly know who I am."

"Perhaps you will be like me, and wait upon the gentle Ladye."

And she waved off my next question, saying, "I will show you a thing when we are back in Crow Trees Farm."

Later, it was Alice who remarked, even as shadows were beginning to creep over the land, "I am glad Elizabeth Southern stayed away today."

"I had thought the same. Seeing as the old one and young Alizon were at Downham, and there was a fear they might trouble the feast."

"That is why I went to persuade them."

"You went – to Malkin Tower?"

"Where else? One cannot reconcile these families but they promised no disturbance."

"I would not care to go to that place. What is it . . . what did you—?"

"What did I find at Malkin Tower?"

Flying brooms and a black cat's glower
Cauldron's stew and the milk gone sour
Toads and crones in the Devil's power.

Her laugh was all mockery of me. "I saw a nearly blind woman and a deformed one, an idiot boy and a beggar girl. I saw them spending an unaccustomed hour of happiness, because someone had filled her hand with silver."

"It was my father."

"I know it. All the world knows it was your father." After a pause she said, "You will find it hard to replace him in your affections."

"He will never be replaced in my affections." I spoke with passion, and she replied, "That is possibly true."

But since she had mocked me over the Southerns, I resolved not to tell her about Demdike's predictions.

Chapter 12

WE ARRIVED LATE and too fatigued to eat supper, but Alice made me a bowl of metheglin – sweet honeymead ("from a receipt I brought out of Wales when I fetched the big ram") – and I slept long and deep in the tiny chamber. No rasping breathing spirits came to the door, and I reflected how easily one grows out of childhood terrors. So long and deep I slept that breakfasting was over when I descended, but I heard many voices in the kitchen.

The room was full of folk and talk, but I was stopped in the doorway at the sight of two great men seated at the table. One I knew well: John Law, the gross fat pedlar, who keeps all the lasses of Pendle supplied with ribands and such, was as usual filling his face at the board. The other was not fat in any way, but of a great height when he unfurled himself to bid me the good morning. Here was a London man, wearing his hair long and curly as gallants do, his soft-falling collar of some gauzy stuff, and an emerald drop in his ear. His face was bespattered with freckles, Scottish freckles, naught to do with the pox. His eyes were the grey blue of an uncertain March sky. But his smile, when he smiled, was all of midsummer. I did not fall, I flew into love!

"Mistress Jane Shireburn, of Stonyhurst," Alice presented. "John Law you know of course, but I think you are not acquainted with John Armstrong, though he is a friend of your sometime guest at Stonyhurst, John Spencer."

"Your admirer I think, Mistress Shireburn," smiled the giant.

For a long moment I could think of no word to say, and Alice helpfully continued: "John Armstrong is sometime of the company of the Rose Theatre, but this season all the actors are fled into the provinces. For fear of plague?" She glanced in query toward John Armstrong, who nodded an affirmation.

Assembling my dignity, I contrived a decent curtsey and I spoke, I think, without a tremor and even sternly.

"I am glad to hear your profession, sir. The names of John and Armstrong have a hollow echo in our country, and may still excite emotion, even so far south of the border."

He did not cease smiling. "That was all a long time ago, Mistress Shireburn. I am sure that Lancashire cattle sleep peacefully in their byres these days. And our clan being now dispersed, I think the fiercer elements in our blood are much diluted. No reiver or raider I fear, but a humble minstrel, at your service."

Alice interrupted briskly. "John Armstrong is normally living and working in London, but he is here just now on a kind errand, to repay me an old debt from an old friend. And I have prevailed on him to spend some little time with us at Crow Trees, before seeking temporary employment in some of our great houses."

"You are looking for work as a player?" I asked.

"As a player of instruments, madam. I am a music-maker. I am not one to tear a passion to tatters, nor to cavort and juggle as a fool, upon the stage."

I was not sure whether I was reprimanded, but I ventured on: "Which instruments do you play?"

"I am obliged to demonstrate a facility with every instrument required at the playhouse. I also sing a little if petitioned."

I thought I should perhaps tread carefully around his

self conceit. But it did not prove so difficult. For one thing my exalted status was soon put into doubt.

Alice said, "We won't ask you to sing for your supper, John, but I daresay you will be pleased to entertain Mistress Shireburn during your stay."

For which I was rewarded by a somewhat extravagant courtly bow, and a mock humble request to enquire as to the length of the young lady's sojourn at Crow Trees Farm.

She has such a wide thin-lipped smile, Alice, when she is really amused, or when she is full of warm feeling. "As to that, Jane Shireburn is as welcome in this house as the flowers of the May, and she shall stay as long as her inclination persists. But she may well be required to work for her keep."

It was an old jest between us, but I noticed that it confused the young gallant, particularly when she slapped a dish of curds and whey on the table before me and then a garment of much the same colour, a rough linen apron, on the chair beside.

"You would be well advised to use this Jane, if you propose to stay about the farm."

Which I was not sorry to do, although I had left off the taffeta for an everyday gown. And it was such a voluminous cover she had given me as would have served for the giant himself, which she suggested with raised eyebrows only, and he declined with a dismissive wave.

"What would you have me do then?" I asked half laughing and she laughing but deliberate. "Dear Jane, if you are truly of a mind to help me, I need someone to be abroad to carry some few victuals up, to check the flock and speak with the shepherd. And fetch down any orphans. I am bound to stay in the house today to reassign my household, having lost two servants much valued—" she glanced towards Hugh Redferne "—and beloved."

I said with the faintest or most feigned reluctance, "It is late in the season surely, Alice, to find newborns?"

"We put different ewes to tup at different times for a reason: to prolong the lambing. Are you growing an interest in sheep rearing, Jane? You will be worthy of your father."

The new guest broke in: "Mistress Nutter, I beg you let me be of assistance too. Let me aid this fair maid in her scouring for sheep. Permit me to accompany her on a mission of allegorical as well as practical import."

For someone who scorns the playacting, I thought, he had learnt many tricks from the stage. But it did not make him less delightful in my eyes. Alice was too sage to take notice of his humour, but she clearly liked the man and saw that I was not averse.

That was how it fell out: that a lowly (how can I say it of such a high man?), work-wanting minstrel could raise his eyes to pay court to the favoured daughter of a noble house.

But that daughter was already well versed in fortune's tumbles. I had learned to dance a jig to the Dame's turning wheel. Why could I not play Phillis to his Coridon? Why not be a coy shepherdess to gain a beauteous love-sick swain? Who furthermore would be most able to play upon any pipe I chose, beneath the greenwood's crowded boughs?

I admit to all these foolish thoughts, while I had not yet spoke above twenty words to him. For it was a game of looks we played at first.

When we rode out onto the slopes of Pendle, if I could still cause the sun to shine I could not force the blow to cease. The wind blew our words back into our faces, so we did not talk but looked. I laughed when the wind blew his elegant half shoulder cape smack into his face, and he laughed when my cap let go, and my hair flew wild into the air. To make me look like a banshee is what he said after.

But I still attended to my task. Speaking with the shepherd was the most difficult part. Martin Vere was a deceiving man. His considerable height was disguised by an ungainly stoop, and his amiable nature by an extreme parsimony with words. I endeavoured to discourse learnedly on loose wool and wormy feet, as well as checking which lambs had good suck, and what the need for rescue. With little more than nods, he indicated two trembly little creatures, ill-balanced on thin legs, whose mother had not survived parturition. We brought them down, one a piece in our saddle bows. And he continued to accompany me, this tall fellow, as I made myself useful to Alice.

Feeding the orphans was a task that I always liked at Crow Trees. He watched me showing the lambs how to take the teat from my milky fingers, and the heat came into his face. And I knew – for I am Isabella's – that I had him. And I could imagine my brother singing:

> *Jane, Jane, your man is slain*
> *Cupid hath pierced his heart and brain.*

That evening, when we were retreated into Alice's study, John Armstrong entered with two gifts. For me there was a tiny silver pomander upon a scarlet ribbon, which had been purchased out of John Law's pack, when I was not aware. He begged me not consider the offering an impertinence, but he had taken advantage of the happy coincidence of the pedlar's presence there that day et-cetera, et-cetera. I have it still, wrapped in silk, in the bowels of the big chest upstairs.

For Alice, the debt payment already made, there was a gift he had been charged to bring from Master

Shakespeare. That name was already become well known, even in our benighted north, and of course I asked which Master Shakespeare, and how Alice came to be acquainted.

"It is the playwright's father," explained Alice, "who dealt in wool like me, and once having strained too far his commerce, he ran into a difficulty which nor he nor his family could easily resolve."

"You lent him money?" I prompted.

"And never looked to see it again," Alice nodded. "We had a good trading relation, old John and I. I begrudged not a penny of it."

"But now it is returned," John said with more simplicity than I had observed in him that day, "and he would have me also offer you this very small gift, for your personal comfort, and with affection and gratitude."

When she unwrapped the waxed paper, Alice had in her hand a tiny white clay pipe, and another smaller packet of tobacco.

Her grin went from ear to ear. "That man knows my secret sin!" And then seeing my face, which expressed at least surprise, and at most reprobation, she laughed: "'Tis but to keep the summer flies off my maggoty old ewes, Jane." Then glancing at John, "But I daresay I may draw some cheer from it of a winter's night. And it will surely act as a singular aid to reflection." At which she proceeded to load and puff the thing, with what was evidently an accustomed ease.

Was it the same night or the next that we joined the servants in the kitchen? Hugh Redferne had been melancholy ever since we left Grindleton. It cost him dear to lose his beloved Tom, even though it was no very great distance to the rented cottage at Greenhead. He had perhaps been praying for some time alone, but when we heard that solitary bass intoning psalms, the household gathered to share his worship.

It was a melodious choir that we assembled. Joan Gentle was tuneful and Mary Penny's treble was a dulcet note, while Alice did her best to soften the dark resonances of her voice. Neither Miles nor I were of great advantage, but when John Armstrong lent his voice he sang so strong, so true, and so swelled our little harmony that we thought we were become a celestial choir. His London loftiness quite fled before this rustic music-making, that could never have been part of any theatre repertory. He sang without irony or affectation the rough plain chants of the Familists:

> *Our heart is to the mind of God most High,*
> *Our being amiable, as the sweet Lily,*
> *Our faithfulness, love, and truth upright,*
> *In God's light life, and clearness bright.*

And I thought I had been much in error to so lightly value the service of the Church of England, when John gave us to sing:

> *If ye love Me, keep My commandments,*
> *And I will pray the Father,*
> *And He shall give you another comforter,*
> *That He may abide with you for ever,*
> *Ev'n the spirit of truth.*

It was on the last evening of that memorable residence that Alice remembered the 'thing' she had promised to show me. It was after all just a book, one of the small black volumes that held pride of place in her study. It was a Familist tract entitled 'Temporis Filia Veritas'. I did not, could not, put my mind on it, though I skimmed through enough pages to sense a very eloquent argument for compassion towards all forms of sincere belief, a plea for the monster Toleration.

Johnny was humming softly as I read, and Alice puffing on her infernal pipe.

She said, "It was just to explain to you how I wait upon her, through trouble and travail if need. I wait for the gentle Ladye Tyme to bring forth her most beautiful daughter, Truth."

"You will need have patience, Alice." I spoke with levity.

"She is my mistress, the gentle Ladye," was all she said in reply.

Chapter 13

PERHAPS I ALSO was waiting upon Alice's gentle Ladye, but I felt as if she was waiting upon me, or had at least suspended her motion. I tell these hours off now, like golden beads, but the rosary then seemed endless. I could not believe that the summer would ever end, and happiness seemed as easy to capture as a butterfly on a lavender bush.

John did not find employment immediately and his musicianship was not in great demand until the winter festivities. We had hours to spend together, could we find pretexts for meeting. The most of our contrivances was poor John Spencer, who found himself frequently tagged by his tall musician friend. They were both made welcome by my father, who, already in the grip of building fever, was now consumed by the need to create memorials. Great men have a terrible fear of obscurity after Nature's full stop, and a need to commit their fame to stone and mortar. For now he determined that, in addition to the Stonyhurst build, he would erect a new side chapel to Mitton Church, designed to house statues of himself, of Lady Maud, and subsequent Shireburns. What Lady Maud would have thought of this defection cannot be known. However, if a family chapel of any consequence is to be graced by impressive statuary, then who better to consult than a scholar who makes a particular study of funerary monuments? John Spencer, already much in my father's conference, became his favourite counsellor, summoned near every day and accompanied often – very often – by his tall friend. I think it may not have been the easiest patronage for Spencer. Endless discussions were engaged in, endless designs pored over. Tables littered with architectural plans were now overlaid with sketches of armorial devices, and ornate embellishments of our family motto, *Quant je puis.*

John Spencer himself brought portfolios of drawings – of heraldic unicorns and allegorical draped nymphs, and classical heroes, undraped. Wreaths of winged cherubim danced across the pages, and motifs of the chase, hawk, stag and hound were used to give vigour to his sketches. And all designed to support and flatter the recumbent effigies of a knight and his lady.

All such as would have been a fascination to me, were I not bound on securing the release of my minstrel from this conversation. And if John Spencer threw a wistful glance as we made our escape I did not admit a care in my heart. The great knight himself was so taken up as not to take sufficient heed of a departing daughter.

It was the high summer of my life, although it was the springtime of my years. And I had not so long left off being a child that it were much labour to return. For we were like enchanted children, in our escaped moments, wandering in make believe, dreaming dreams of a future as insubstantial as a palace of cobweb and cuckoo spit. We hid and sought in thorny woods, watched hay mow bleach green fields, and made a pretence of fishing on the wide river. My troubadour needed no petitioning to fill my ear with his sweet voice. He sang to me every sort of song: fools' fancies and lovers' petitions; plaintive ballads and scurvy street songs; mournful dirges and bawdy bits; devout hymns and fierce little ditties from the gutter. And so many woeful tales of unrequited love that I made him desist: "Let me hear of no more woebegone maidens or languishing lovers. I am tired of rose-petal cheeks and dewy eyes. Sing to me of a brave youth; sing to me of a girl made of sterner mettle." Upon which, leaning on the oars, he composed an impudent lyric: "Here is a song for a girl of fiercer metal."

> *My love is no milksop girl*
> *For her hair is all of copper.*
>
> *My love has a will of steel*
> *And her hair is all of copper.*
>
> *My love has an iron hand*
> *And her hair is all of copper.*
>
> *My love has a heart of flint*
> *And her hair is all of copper.*
>
> *My love has a voice of brass*
> *And her hair is all of copper.*

I splashed him with a handful of river water in punishment, and he revenged himself.

> *My love is alchemists' delight*
> *Tho' her hair is all of copper,*
>
> *For her cunt is all of purest gold*
> *Whilst her hair is all of copper.*

Then I leapt as to throw him out of the boat, which rocked and lurched alarmingly, so that I fell. I fell into his arms, and then I punished him severely enough.

My father knew of course, must have known, but so long as reputation was preserved, he left matters of prudence to our mother. And Isabella, apart from advice as to the use of a sponge well-soaked in vinegar, was indifferent to the problematics of virtue. Richard Shireburn, after all, had sown his own oats, both far and wide. And in that golden summer, I believe he knew how little time was left, for him to live, for me to play.

I did not share this wisdom. I was too young to believe in endings. Not the yellowing leaves, nor the shortening of daylight, nor the fleeing of swallows could warn me of love's mortality. Nor the croaking of old women neither. But into the flimsy tissue of our dreams I attempted to weave a stronger thread, a narrative, which seemed to me compelling: of Johnny Armstrong, in pursuit of fame and fortune; of providential patronage and successful performance; the buying of shares in London theatres; and the friendship of famous great men. And this to culminate, of course, in wedded bliss for me and everlasting love.

Our flame burned brightly even through the winter and its rigid boundaries. In stolen moments in great houses, in conversation between performance, we touched fingers, whispered entreaties, made vows, endless vows.

Where John was employed we were frequently invited. He joined a small group of violists to sweeten the interlude of Richard Hoghton's grand banquet, became a celestial lutanist for the faerie masquing commissioned by the Earl of Derby. He played upon bagpipes for the ball Judge Walmsley gave. He was hired to do, in truth, very little for Christmas at Stonyhurst, for our tenants were so eager for the mumming and the carol singing that they left little room for courtly musicians.

That is what I remember most: the Christmas feast at Stonyhurst. My father had stripped half of Bowland Forest for the berried branches that covered all the walls, with skeins of trailing ivy from every hook and nail. The servants wore new liveries, and extra men were taken on to hold heavy flaming torches in the hall, which, together with the many candles of the great rood beam, illuminated the revelry and the feasting. It was a rude entertainment compared with Lathom and Hoghton Towers, but to my mind it was the merriest.

Isabella was the only sufferer. Being incapacitated by a fit of the gout, she was confined to a great chair and padded with a multitude of cushions. Judge Walmsley, in his everlasting gallantry, sat by her much of the time earnestly discoursing on the relative merits of various plasters and philtres suggested by his physician. It was after all a subject beginning to be of serious interest to himself.

For the rest, all were resplendent in Yuletide finery. Decorous Margaret and Mary looked well in rich dark velvet gowns. Gracie had enough hoops to her farthingale as would have satisfied Queen Elizabeth. For myself I thought to catch attention by a choice of fabric rather than by width of skirt, and I was pleased with the effect of seawater-green satin overlaid with blue sequins and silver lace in a design of peacock tail. I hoped to glitter in the torch light.

I pleased my father I am glad to say, and I also pleased my lover. And he pleased everyone, with his solo part, and with the accompaniment he so graciously provided the rustics. We knew already, both of us, that he must soon leave, for the London theatres were said to be reopening. I could not look to see him return while winter mired up the roads, and iced the bridleways. As his departure drew near, his presence was more vivid to my senses. I could feel his look, almost his touch, across a long room, and all about him else seemed to shrink and fade into dull colour. When he came to sit by me I was as dazed by his nearness as he was, he said, dazzled by my shimmer.

And he was very urgent then, urgent with promises of unshakeable fidelity, of certain return, urgent for me to know the ardour of his love, for me to find him access to my bedchamber. I was no unwilling lady, and did I wish to sequester a tall gallant until the household were abed, I had a friend with more access to closets and pantries then any servant in the hall.

As the evening was drawing to a close Judge Walmsley wanted more music. "Come Johnny," he called, "you have played a little and pleased us mightily. Give us a taste of your singing." And when Johnny affected to decline, protesting that all his skill was in his fingers, Walmsley laughed. "If not for me young man, you will surely not refuse that peacock lady sitting next you, if she should make request."

I chose a Dowland that I knew to be a favourite of the judge's, full of plaintive amorous dalliance. I write it down now to bring alive the memory, so that I hear that voice again.

> *Awake, sweet love, thou art return'd*
> *My heart which long in absence mourn'd*
> *Lives now in perfect joy.*
>
> *Only herself hath seemed fair*
> *She only I could love*
> *She only drove me to despair*
> *When unkind she did prove.*
>
> *And if that now thou welcome be*
> *When thou with her dost meet*
> *She all the while but play'd with thee*
> *To make thy joys more sweet.*

He sang with such pitiful reproach and alluring malice that I thought every dame in the hall should have swooned, and indeed he received very warm applause, and a cup of the best wine was presented to him. He stayed on his feet, a tall graceful figure he made, and bowed and said: "I would offer another of my own choice for Mistress Shireburn. The words are those of a poet who has sometime honoured me with his acquaintance."

> *Ah, dear heart, why do you rise!*
> *The light that shines comes from thine eyes.*
> *The day breaks not, it is my heart,*
> *Because that you and I must part.*
> *Stay, or else my joys will die,*
> *And perish in their infancy.*

Even as I write the words I feel again the stab of parting, recognise now the message in the song. For John, that subtle courtier, knew more of the world than I, while I, I saw no reason why our young joy should suffer a cruel termination, since I would stay for him, would always stay. As I stayed that night, pacing the cold chamber, until a young gallant could find his way by Irene's candle.

And there I would have stayed forever, in the explorations and delights of my small bed. But though I tried – and by Hecate I tried – I could not summon up a spell to hold back the morning, or to keep fast the curtains of the sweet confederate night.

Chapter 11

SO THERE IT IS – the story of my love – told in one night's scribble.

And I do not know if I have the heart to go on. What is there left to tell myself? All is so dull beside. Do I sit the long nights out looking upon a man that used to be? John labours but he does not die. He has lingered so much longer than I expected. His breathing is heavy but regular. The quill in my hand is heavy, and reluctant.

Still there is more to say. Last night what I wrote by your bedside, husband, was the veriest infidelity, I know. What the Bible says of adultery committed in the heart – it must apply to memory. I have, I think, lied to you John, all this while, lied to myself moreover. I am discovering that I do not write solely to rekindle ancient memories, to relive my youth. But I have all the while been preparing a balance sheet, between us two. And I cannot finish that, not put the last farthing in the right column, while there is breath yet left in your poor body.

❊❊❊

So back to dullness. For it was a dull house when John Armstrong was gone. And Rick was gone. And Isabella was in a constant low rage with the gout, and demanding so many trivial attendances that even the maids were in a fret with her.

And how slowly, greyly, drearily slowly, that old winter crawled back towards his lair. The fierce brave snowdrops were ignored in his surly refusal to depart. It took the oncoming clarion of daffodil and the everywhere mustering of incipient leaf bud to shove the old one back, and free us all from his cold clutch. To persuade the birds at last to start their jubilee. And though she would come at last, cautiously dripping, the spring, that green girl was still some way off when my father returned from a lengthy visit to the capital. But there was a certain damp hopefulness in the air, which matched the tentative hope with which I hovered round his return. It was not until the evening that he sent for me, to speak with him in the library.

He was seated with magisterial air at his desk piled with documents and ledgers, and he waved me to a seat, with but a nodding smile.

"Jaynie it is time, it is more than time that we give thought to your future," he began, and I, too quickly, too precipitately, answered him.

"My lord, dear father, I thank you for your care of me. Will you give me permission to open my heart to you?"

"Your heart is not my concern. I am speaking of family settlements, of wedding arrangements, of financial agreements."

I opened my mouth to speak, but he went steadily on. "I have arranged an alliance for you, a good match—"

And I could not forbear to interrupt before he uttered words that might not be taken back.

"My lord, I have given my love, and would plead that I might give my hand in wedlock to John Armstrong, who is an honest courtly gentleman—"

He was truly impatient now.

"I really did believe you had more understanding of your position. Can you imagine that I would donate a daughter of this house to a penniless itinerant, descended of the worst tribe of cattle thieves and marauders on the Scottish border?"

I drew my breath to speak, but he would not hear me. "It is decided. I have made you a most honourable match, and one that moreover Lady Maud did approve for you, whilst she was still alive. It will cost a fair dowry, but you are to be wedded with John Southworth. Their coffers are empty, the Southworths, but their name is clear. You are a fortunate girl."

So I could not but break out, "I will not marry that great lummock. He bores me extremely. He is without learning or refinement. I would rather marry my grave. And his grandfather has a particular hatred towards me."

"You are not marrying his grandfather. John Southworth is a seemly honest and young man. Great Christ, Jane, I am not marrying you to an old syphilitic. I am giving you a name that is respected in this county. You will be Lady of the dower house. You will be secure – and safe. Do you not understand?"

If I understood or no, I could not reply. My throat was stopped up and he said more gently, "What is required is simply your duty. Johnny Armstrong is a charmer and you have had your dalliance. And now you are bound to uphold the name of this family, as we are all bound to do, all of us."

I made a motion that I still do not know whether I intended to kneel in supplication or curtsey in submission. I do know that in that confusion of emotion there was born the first truly rebellious thought I had ever had against my father. For I thought how he might well do his bounden duty to his family, but he took a wide field of freedom to himself as well.

But he came round to me with an affectionate gesture, and kissed my forehead. "You know I look to you Jaynie, ever to protect my honour."

And then himself reseated, "And now depart for I have weightier matters than your affiancing to settle."

I had hardly closed the door before my sobs leapt out. I broke into a storm of weeping that I could scarce get back to my chamber. And I fell upon the bed where I had once known the sweets of love, to abandon myself to sorrow.

I went on weeping for days. I seemed to have an inexhaustible flow of tears. I wept enough to fill buckets and pools. I would have overflowed the Ribble river; I might have filled up the Red Sea over again, and prevented Moses ever reaching the promised land.

That is how I jested later to Alice, but in that little bed I wanted to die – and resolved to do so. Surely a girl who had brought about the demise of a lusty violator could encompass that same end for herself? And now casting back, I cannot reckon how many days I spent in the grip of that bitter disappointment, refusing food, my face towards the wall, but I think I did in the end cause some alarm.

It was always Margaret who came knocking at the door. Gracie had nothing to do with me, docile Gracie, who could hardly understand the notion of disobedience. But pious Margaret brought little bits of food and gentle urging of submission to God's will, if not father's.

It was Margaret who brought a message from him, from my father, that I must learn some temperance and wisdom, some understanding of necessity and that perhaps I would learn it best with my old tutor.

It seemed that Miles Nutter was below with delivery of a ram that Alice had procured for my father, and he was to go back with monies. The suggestion – the order – was that I was to be prised from my bed, return with Miles Nutter, taking charge of the monies, and stay at Crow Trees Farm some few days, after which a servant would be sent for me. So I might have a change of air, a change of disposition and come by a little sense, assisted by the 'wise old bird'.

I had a night to compose myself for the journey and in the morning early, Margaret dressed me and fed me sweetened bread and milk, and bade me be of good cheer for all would come well. I found myself very weak and staggery, but I have always enjoyed being in the saddle, and Miles's heavy cob set no helter-skelter pace.

I noticed as always the chilling of the air as we rode east and high, and as the forest thinned. The wind that thrashed the fells and scudded clouds across the grey sky also stung my cheeks and chafed my lips and brought to my eyes tears, that were not dredged up from a thwarted will, and had nought to do with collapsed dreams. And that awareness of something more immediately present and more momentarily hurtful than the dull bag of grief I had been carrying, brought me back into the world of real sensation and proportion. It was a wind, Alice's wind, that blew cloud castles out of my skull, and mayhap blew some sense into.

When we reached Crow Trees, I near fainted off my horse. Miles bore me into the kitchen, and Joan Gentle set me by the fire, wringing her hands in distress at the sight of me, complaining that I was become thin as a needle. Finally she set a jug of metheglin to warm for me.

Alice came down from the hill at early nightfall. She entered the kitchen, did you not Alice? You ran to me and, between commanding Joan Gentle, and seeking out shawls and preparing concoctions, you knew not which way to pamper me first. I think I must have been a poor thing to look upon. But the kitchen warmth, the honeymead, the affection all grew comfort in me. Out spilled my little story: the love, the songs, the prohibition, the new instruction. Alice listened smiling, not her face-splitting grin but a small sad smile. "Hey nonny nonny," she said, "the world is so bonny." She took out her little pipe and was a long time packing it. "One day folk will marry for love, when Property is unseated and Degree is scrambled. Not in your day though Jane. We must wait on my Ladye Tyme."

Chapter 15

IT WAS NOT SO MUCH that it was early, the lambing, as that it was so prodigal that year. On the morning there was much bustle and commotion in the house, with extra workers taken on, among them Bess Whittle, brought in to replace her sister at this busy time.

She was like and unlike Anne, pretty certainly, but in a more countrified fashion. She was cheerful, loud and energetic with an inclination to superfluous ribandry. She had pinned so many little bows to her cap as to be slightly ridiculous in that sober industrious farmhouse.

Breakfast was briskly served and briskly cleared. But Alice refused me leave to so much as step outside the house.

"You should stay," she said, kindly but firm. "You can help keep an eye on young Bess here, and make sure she does Joan Gentle's bidding. You may have doses of hyssop tea and dollops of reading off my shelves, if that pleases you."

Then she added, "But mayhap you should leave aside the Familist tracts. I would not lead you into schism as you are about to make alliance with a pious papist house."

"You think they are so very seducing, your tracts? And me so easily converted?" I spoke half in jest, half not willing to be ordered. "I think I can make up my own mind."

"But your mind is not yours for the making up," she said, buttoning up her great cloak. "Your mind is now for the buckling down." She smiled round the door, "Like you yourself dear Jane."

I was not sorry to be left behind. I still felt weak and

with a swelling in my throat that pained me somewhat, I did not want to come down with a quinsy. Yet I did not thoroughly avail myself of Alice's invitation to peruse her volumes. I was content to talk to Joan Gentle as to the ordering of brewhouse and buttery, since I was soon to have the running of a house myself. And Bess was most prone to chattering. Although I could not fault her for an indolent worker, I thought that her free and easy manner would have earned her a scolding in Big Irene's kitchen. And to my shame I was more taken by her tattle than Alice's tomes. Over the paring of swedes she began her recital of gossip.

"Demdike's girl has got herself a man now. She bought him out of the stocks, and set him to a cobbler in Colne."

Joan Gentle joined in. "She put your father's silver to good use, Mistress Shireburn. John Device was to be whipped as a sturdy vagabond – there's many a decent man caught in that trap. Lizzie paid his fine and an indenture to the cobbler. And they are wed."

"And John Device is a decent man?" I asked.

"I do hope and believe he may be. For a man with a trade to follow could lift that family out of misery."

"Oh if there's better than bean bread on the table at Malkin Tower, and more than rags to their backs, it's not for the wages of a cobbler's prentice," said Bess. She attacked her vegetables vigorously. "There's a more ungodly trade brings in a better revenue. Old Mother Demdike, and her Lizzie too, both are afeard the length and breadth of Pendle for threating begging."

"People are afeard of their powers, above natural." Even little Mary Penny had a word to throw in.

I saw gentle Joan Gentle frown and I interrupted very loftily: "Elizabeth Southern is a licensed beggar. She has no quarrel with the law."

Bess paused in her scraping to observe me. "Aye

Mistress Shireburn, you are surely right. But I daresay a spoiled pan of milk or a lamed horse is of no great consequence to you, begging your pardon."

"Horses go lame and milk gets spoiled without any help from old women begging for their living," said Joan.

"There's beggin' and beggin'," replied her assistant. "There's beggin' and there's terrifyin'. Lizzie, she can curse fiercer than seven sailors, but it's the old one with her milky eyes and her waily waily voice that freezes the blood in your veins. And woe betide if you're not quick and open handed with your alms."

I laughed. "How should a brawny girl like you be so afeard of a withered old woman?"

"Them as the Devil favours should frighten any Christian man." Bess was in full flow. "She frights even her own granddaughter. Alizon quivers like a river reed when Demdike starts on charms and witchings."

"Poor Alizon," said Joan, and then summoning her authority, "And now I want to hear no more of Whittle words against Southerns. If you've finished them swedes Bessie, there's milk waiting for churning in the buttery."

In such a leisurely way my day was passed. That evening Alice pronounced herself pleased with my look, and all agreed on the sovereign efficacy of hyssop and rue. I was well enough to accompany her on the following day, despite that there had been a thickish snowfall in the night. I remember that ride well. And that day. And its following. The time when I, not without struggle, began to cast off being a child.

The perishing frost had crisped the tussocky grass and some of the boggy parts. We could ride more easily, but still circumspectly, for snow had filled in the declivities of peat hags. It had also blanketed out the wind. We rode slowly, able for once to hear each other speak.

"I had bought in a young ram – same as the one your father commissioned me to purchase for him. I let him in to graze with the ewes, thinking him too unripe to do any harm – or good. But behold what a noble tup was there! Here are my ewes dropping scores of lambs, and the weather still very bitter."

"You are pleased Alice, or vexed? There are too many?"

"Nay they will not rot if they can find suck, but there are so many threesomes and my poor girls have but two teats apiece. We will have to cart a number back to the farm and make shift to feed them there. But it is a poor farmer would complain of a good harvest."

She carefully inspected the wattle enclosures, the shelter for the extra fodder we had helped to carry up, and the farm cart already part loaded with a few exhausted ewes and orphan lambs. She exchanged judicious few words, and many nods and silent signals with Martin Vere, that most reticent shepherd, as to hopeful adoptions. We rode slowly in ever widening circles to pick up any overlooked or helpless ones. The tiny things were shivering with fright and cold.

"In Stonyhurst it is almost spring now," I told her, shivering along with the lambs.

She nodded. "That is for you Lady Jane – the valley and its pleasantness, the river with its changes, its ebb and flow, like human passion. Up here is emptiness. I love the cold hill."

"Hugh Redferne told me you were hefted to the hill, as fast as the wildest sheep."

"That is a saying of Martin Vere's, I think, in one of his rare moments of loquacity. And it is true of that man. But for me, dear Jane, it is a place where it is easy to pray and to ponder. And to wonder. On Pendle I feel I nearly touch the skirts of God."

I was pert that day. "I thought that God was already with you, indwelling even, the light within. Is that not the Familist belief?"

She answered me seriously. "That is what I strive for. But I think that light is not uncovered without effort. And I do not flatter myself to be a Perfect in this life."

I found her tone reproving and I was suddenly beset by annoyance. "That is an interesting distinction you make, Alice, between your own prayerfulness and my . . . changeableness. You make me out a weathercock?"

"My dearest Jane, much as I love you, which I most dearly do, and like as I am to lose you soon, still I cannot tell who or what you are, since you likely do not know yourself."

"What makes you say that? Papist, Protestant, Puritan, these are hardly choices to addle the brain."

"As to those adherences, you will decide in the course of life. But you play many parts Jane, and you play them well. You are as easy in my farm kitchen as I daresay you are in the Earl of Derby's hall. I know that the soul of every other must lie somewhat in obscurity, but you are the greatest puzzle of all to me. Who is Jane Shireburn?"

"How should I know," I answered angrily, "I know not what name to call myself: greasy poultry maid, or muse of poets, bastard daughter, or jewel of my father's eye – a jewel to be sold off cheap moreover—"

"Nay—" Alice attempted.

"A London man's plaything – a wanton do you think, or have you harsher words yet?"

"Jane—" I know she endeavoured to halt me, but I would not be hushed. I was hurried on with passion that she should confront me with such a question, and stinging with the pain of my own uncertainty. "Oh there are worser words in plenty now I am of a mind:

loose jade, unbeliever, nullifidian, or let us go to it – a murthering witch."

Alice rode near to me then, took hold of the reins of my horse. "My dearest Jane, dear child of grace, cease this . . . clamour, and this . . . unreason, which I never intended to provoke. I only wondered, and mayhap it is an idle wonder, where your spirit flies, your so free spirit."

My anger faded as quick as it had flared. "Alas I am neither spiritual nor free. But you are somewhat in the right Alice. I do not know who stands at my centre." There was still snow in the air. For a moment it blotted the space between us. I spoke almost to myself. "Are we not all many ones, bundles of beings? Is there only one selfhood?"

As the flurry cleared, she said firmly, "Surely there is only a single soul. Else how should we make a dwelling for our dear Lord?"

I felt so much confusion on that day, but I think it was her sermonising I minded most.

"But I could turn the tables, Mistress Nutter, to ask what designation your seeking would lead you to adopt, who are not a Perfect nor a thorough going Familist. Who are *you* then, Alice Nutter?

And since she did not immediately reply, I sang a childish jingle:

> Teacher, preacher, counsellor, clerk,
> Which of these is nearest the mark?

Then she laughed. "I am as I am. Today I am one singular fortunate market woman with a fine ramrod of a tuppity male, and too many little lambs to feed. Here's one for you."

She gave me a parti-coloured shivering bundle, and for herself a tiny black, black-nosed, black-tailed and already mewing lamb. She lifted it to bury her face in its wet wool, and then gave me that grin that cut her face in two. It was all in that look, the maternal pleasure of having so many young things to care for, the calculating satisfaction of a successful trader, and sheer delight in the virility of a young ram.

I have pondered on my behaviour to Alice on that day. I seemed moved to impertinence at one moment, and to affection at the next. I was not pleased to be the object of advice or correction. But I think my impulses were like those of children, who hurl waves of malcontent against the rock they know to be immoveable. I am sure I dared not further indulge my anger against my father, but I incline to believe that Alice was the most like a loving mother to me, more than Isabella, more than Lady Maud.

I keep that image of you still, Alice, though it is long time since we have met. I see a tall woman on a hill, the rising wind whipping flocks of snow into your untidy brown hair, a black lamb close to your cheek, and a smile for me.

As we slowly came down from the hill for midday, each with a throbbing little thing wrapped in our cloaks, I said, "But you are wrong about the river. I have no inclination to live by Samlesbury ford, and I quail at the thought of—"

"Of bedding John Southworth, who is after all no bad fate for you. It is time to accept, Jane. He brings you a good name and a secure place. He may well even make a sturdy lover, if you let him."

"I thought that you in your Family of Love believe that one should love and choose freely, men and women."

"And I believe in a silver city of holiness, that will one day be set upon the earth, but in the meantime—"

"In the meantime?"

"In the meantime we are all subject to necessity and must needs accept our lot, with as much grace as possible."

What my head was learning my heart was resisting. I disliked her stoic words, and my displeasure must have been evident.

She sighed lengthily. "It is so for us all Jane. I was married off by my father to an old man who begat children off me but gave me little merriment in the making. While my young heart was turned a different way altogether."

Even then I could not resist a small jibe: "And who captured your young heart, Alice? Some poet or philosopher sure."

She said, "It was a travelling joiner I loved, one alight with the word of God. Who believed moreover in the right of a woman to speak the word also."

'Teacher, preacher' jingled in my brain, as she shook her head, saying "But all so long ago," and lapsed into silence.

But the peevish child in me did not yet let go. "Anne Redferne married after her heart," I said.

Chapter 16

ANNE REDFERNE: I had hardly spoke her name before she was thrust into our attention.

Her husband, red and sweating from the gallop, accosted us at the very farmhouse gate, begging that Alice come back with him to Greenhead, for Anne was bad, very bad, and the old one no help, but near in a fit herself.

The story came out mixed and garbled with the man's panting and anxiety. Alice did not wait for details. She passed our lambs to the stable boy with brief instructions and we turned our horses and made haste to Greenhead. On the way she wasted little time in catechism, but Tom said enough to let us know that one of the Nutters, who had been after Anne, had made entry into their cottage and forced himself upon her.

Since my own escape as a child, I had not been that close to a violation. People talked – they talk all the time of such things, even of my own father. It is a subject comes with much clucking of tongues, or deep sighing, or jests and jibes, depending on the speaker.

There was no jesting in that little cottage at Greenhead. Anne lay upon the bed, straight as a stick, but from moment to moment a shiver coursed through her. Old Anne, seated close beside, quivered and shook as if in convulsive imitation of her daughter's trembles. But the girl on the bed was silent as if struck dumb, while her mother mumbled and chattered like one out of her mind.

Tom came to stand by the bed, taking his wife's hand. "It was the kinsman of your husband, Mistress Nutter.

Robert Nutter has been coming after Anne, he's been bothering her some time."

"They are known for it," sighed Alice, "he and his brother. Sorry kinsmen."

"They are known," old Anne's grumblings cleared into speech after Alice spoke, "known as louts and lechers, and it's ill chance that she's been brought to this cottage that stands on Nutter's land."

Alice nodded. She had a little bag that always hung from her saddle, containing decoctions and unguents and I know not what. I had thought it was meant for treating sheep. But she took out several pouches and flasks – such a strong scent of musty bracken and pressed leaves and desiccated petals near made me dizzy. She bade Tom heat water to boil the comfrey root and had old Anne fetch some cloths.

Swiftly she drew back the coverlet to overlook the young woman. Her shift was ripped all down, and there were bruises evident upon her breast and body. There was some blood too, not much. Her face had been wiped already, but a wound to her mouth kept dribbling.

The old one came back with the cloths and stood cursing at the sight of her daughter. "Bob Nutter – he is the very Devil out of Hell! I pray that he rots, rots his gangrene soul. Let him burn in filthy pitch 'til he screams at the pain of his own melting bones."

"Hush, hush Anne," said Alice curtly as she commenced to bathe the girl, speaking to her in a lullaby way. "There my dearest bright girl. All that is over and done. No need to fear now. See, Tom is by and caring for you. No need to fear, child of grace. God is loving you. Feel those great wings holding you."

And on she worked, interspersing little Familist endearments with a catalogue of her own ministrations. "Here's lavender flower water to bathe your temples, to revive you from fainting and swooning. And these tender places will heal the quicker where I put the comfrey Tom has boiled for you. And we have marigold juice with vinegar and honey, to calm the swellings, and some for your mother to sip, for marigold is a great comforter."

Little by little the girl's tremors ceased and her rigidity unbent, and Alice lifted her a little in the bed.

Tom came to stand by me as I made the chamomile infusion of Alice's prescription – I was become the veriest serving girl. He kept repeating over and over, "I did get here just in time."

Alice turned to him then. "All's well now Tom. Sit and take the drink that Mistress Jane has made." She herself took a cup to spoon feed Anne.

The old one came over to sit by the fire, her breathing steadier, and though her head wobbled agitatedly and her lips quivered, she delivered her story clear enough.

"He was at her already when I came by the cottage. He had cast his breeches and thrown her to the bed. He was standing up when I came, his warty face all grinning, his belly bare, his stinkhorn up, bursting to come at her, and every time she tried to escape, he knocked her back with big blows, seeming—" she gulped a deep breath "—seeming to enjoy the hurting as much as what he was going to give her. When I came in I flew at him but he knocked me down easily into the corner. 'Stay for the fun,' says he, 'and watch how I'll ravish your daughter.' And he pushed her back on the bed, tore at her clothes, and lapped her skirt over her face . . ." She trailed off into sobs.

"I got here just in time," said Tom determinedly, "I did get here just in time. She was near stifled under that skirt. I plucked him off her and I threw him out and his breeches after him."

"You threw him out," said the mother, "but that's all you did. You should have beat him, you should have whipped him. If I were a man—"

"If you were a man you'd be a fool," said Alice. "What good in the great world can Tom do in thrashing the landlord's son? And do the Children of Love show peace only to their own kind? It is the test of his light, woman. Do not make it harder."

She sat herself opposite Tom. "Was he chastened when you evicted him?"

"Nay, he was in a fury, yelling he'd have his father turn us off the land."

"He'll not do it Tom. The Nutters of Greenhead are distant in my husband's family, but what I know of them the father is a decent man. He'll not be ruled by a libertine son."

"He's always been a good landlord." How like Tom was to his father, so carefully weighing the fairness of his judgements.

"He'll never send you off," said Alice firmly, "and before he dies, and the other inherits, there's many a year to change the story."

"Aye," said old Anne. She had chuntered herself, perhaps aided by marigold syrup, into a peaceable state. "And there's a great likelihood that he'll be dead of the pox before that happens."

As the old woman settled, Anne came slowly back to us. I made shift to lay out some food, and a little peace had returned to the cottage before we left.

It was a sombre gathering sat at supper that night. Alice told the story sparely, just briefly mentioning that old Anne had been incensed against Tom. Bess broke in, "She is in the right, my mother, Tom should have beat him." But a dark look from Hugh Redferne silenced her.

In the uncomfortable moment that followed, I hazarded, "Strange thing Alice – in your family, lechers like the Greenhead men, but also holy priests and martyrs. Like that John Nutter, hung and quartered at Tyburn."

"Libertines and martyrs," she said sadly, "all sin against the sacredness of life."

"But still it is a noble thing to die for one's beliefs," murmured Joan Gentle.

"It is the very stupidest of games to call yourself a merchant with a luggage bag of five hundred catechisms, and fifteen Rheims testaments," said Alice angrily. "What are these religions that are so avid for the blood of martyrs?"

"Martyrs and libertines," repeated Hugh Redferne, slowly pondering, "are not the same. Where a martyr dies, pinning a sin on the soul of his tormentor, the libertine does often procreate life."

The shepherd had silently supped with us. He picked up his scrip, took down his cloak from the nail. "It is the same with the sheep," he said, "pillicock sits on pillicock hill.

> *Young men will go blissom,*
> *When maids are in blossom."*

"You are in the right as always Martin Vere." Alice glanced towards the tall, hunched figure in the doorway. "It is deep writ in the pattern book of Nature. And we, we rejoice in the energy of rams at the tup, the bellow of a rutting stag, the impatience of a stallion at stud." She let her deep voice slip into dreaminess, near fading away. "The pressed apple, the pounded spice, threshed grain—"

It seemed Hugh understood her best. He nodded, "Generation or germination, life will not come without bruising."

"But we must dispute with great Nature," Alice recovered her voice, "and rightly condemn the injurious lecher, the cruelty of a forcing man."

I spoke, even before I thought: "Was God therefore compelled to make a hurting thrust in order to create the world?"

She gazed at me. "Oh my dear Jane, I love you for your questions."

But abruptly, shaking off her dreaminess, she turned with some tenderness to her steward.

"For the sake of the divine, Hugh Redferne, give us an anthem to set our hearts and souls to rights."

Which he most sweetly did.

✳✳✳

I spent the next day with Anne Redferne, leaving Alice to concentrate her mind on the lambing. Bess was released to spend the morning with her sister, and Hugh Redferne was to come for me after dinner.

As I rode with Bess to Greenhead, she gave herself more freedom to bewail that ever her sister was took to that place. "The man's malice is well known. He has tried to break Anne to his will more than one time. And once my mother sent him off with a flea in his ear, and he went away cussing that he would so baulk us of roof and bread that we'd be glad to chew our own lice."

"She ought to be protected from such a lout," I opined.

"That's just the rub. Tom Redferne is no sure protector. His valour's no longer than his prick and his prick's no better than a pudden."

I could see that she was rousing to greater invective, and I stayed her there.

"You would do better, Bess, to mind your speech.

Your mother is already in turmoil and speaks without bridle. She pains Anne and she pains Tom, and those are wounds you are perhaps the best one to heal."

Bess was a lively girl, but not obstinate. She agreed. "Aye Mistress Shireburn, you are in the right of it again. I'll take heed of what you say."

She was as good as her word. She greeted her sister softly enough, and when her mother left off muttering to begin swearing, Bess said sharply, "Shut your gob mother, or you'll be cried out for a witch, same as Demdike!"

While Bess and old Anne busied about the cottage and the yard, I sat quietly with Anne. She was much recovered and insistent that I talked of my affairs. She took a grave interest, expressing some sympathy, but delivering the same implacable message. "At least you will be safe Mistress Jane. No one will be able to turn you off your own land. No one will push you into beggary."

"You will be safe too Anne. Alice is confident that Robert Nutter cannot rule his father."

"You heard what my mother says. She is right about his warty face. I am sure he carries disease, and that may carry him off."

I did not say "Let us hope so," but Anne said calmly: "We had a good life here before he got set on me. I do wish him dead."

Hugh Redferne came early for me. He would have liked to pass some moments in the cottage I know, but a Stonyhurst servant was at Crow Trees, waiting to take me home.

Alice was loth to let me go. She pleaded with the man to rest for one night, having regard to my still-feeble condition. But my father's orders were clear. He would have me return that day, that evening as it would be.

The snow turned to sleet, and the sleet drizzled into rain, as we rode westwards. It was late when we came to home, and I was sopping wet. The only light in the great hall was a tall standing candle by the hearth place, and next the candle in his high carved oak chair, my father sat watching the flames.

I threw off my wetted cloak and went to him. He indicated that I should sit on the footstool, and bade a servant warm some wine for me.

"Come and sit by me Jaynie Whyandwherefore, and tell me how you are disposed to respect your father's will and honour his name."

I sat and kissed his large hand. All my obedience was in the gesture, which he understood. But he still wished to converse and encouraged me to tell him of events in Roughlee. He nodded smilingly when I described Alice's excessive flock, and was thoughtful to hear of Anne Redferne's hurt.

"Do not grieve yourself, Jaynie," he advised, "Anne Redferne is a country girl. She must know such things are not uncommon."

"But a rape is a sin father, and also a crime before the law."

"And turning peasants out their hovel is neither."

When I did not answer he stroked my hair, picking up loose strands to examine the colour in the fire light. "It is life, Jaynie, that is all."

"You speak like the shepherd," I told him.

> Young men will blissom,
> When maids are in blossom.

He laughed, but it was more like a short dry cough than a laugh. "I have blissomed more than my share," he said, "in my time."

We both gazed into the crumbling fire. He repeated, "In my long lifetime."

It was the moment when I knew that he was dying.

Chapter 17

HE WAS A LONG TIME DYING, the Master Forester of Bowland. Though not so long as you my poor husband, who has wandered the banks of Lethe these so many days, keeping the ferryman and his boat waiting upon the shore. Wandered in some fields of unknowing, untouchable, unreachable.

***

The great knight gave almost as munificent hospitality in his dying as in his life. They came from all corners to say their farewells, high and mighty visitors, and humble folk also. The rain I had brought back with me continued, as though the heavens themselves could not contain their weeping. Sodden garments were hung before the great hearth and in the kitchens, where Irene was kept near as busy as at the funeral itself. And she herself wept with an abandon that forced the skivvies into silence. No one in the kitchen dared laugh to see the great fat cook constantly wiping her wet moustaches on the edges of her apron. I think only I knew that she wept also for a lost red-haired child.

For me the tears were locked away. The sorrow was something I had never tasted before. No more lovesick tantrums, no more beatings on the doors of wishfulness. My lord's passing was beyond question, and I already fore-tasted the emptiness beyond, with a cool dry grief, that crowded out all impulse to thought. We all worked hard, Gracie and I, Margaret and Mary, waiting on the endless stream of visitors, receiving broken-hearted words, or studied pompous phrases.

Judge Walmsley gave neither. He seized me in a rough and perfumed hug and went into my lord dry-eyed. He stayed long – my sisters thought too long – audaciously smoking and joking, and even made the huge hollow man laugh. And I believe it eased the pain. As I believe did the little phial of poppy juice that Alice sent, that I myself diluted and administered.

If as we went about our chores I noted a gradual diminution of status, I cared not. The Dame could swing her wheel as she liked, my heart was but a heavy lump, as hard as any stone.

His death at last was the clanging to of a door, that had oft times shifted with the wind, but would never now be opened to me again. And this side of it I was left in a desolate place, where I performed like a puppet doll. Custom and courtesy pulled my strings, gave me words to say, but I myself was empty as an eggshell.

My mother, oh my mother, how she clung to the threads of her magnificence. She ordered sumptuous mourning for us – garments of dark hue, but excellent stuff. She solved the problem of a too-modest ruff with a transparent partlet cut low over the breast. I had no patience with her trumpery; I found an old sober gown of Maud's with a square neck and a sliver of lace ribbon. And I endeavoured to distance myself from the growing stir in the hall, which marked the preparations for the requiem that Margaret and Mary were determined to celebrate.

I mind well how John Armstrong came and went. We had only the briefest opportunity to converse. He wept freely for my father, for our parting, for my enforced future. "Between a rough boy and a crazed old man, how will you survive?" he asked me piteously. I said with my voice in a careful monotone, "I shall have a great many children."

In his farewell embrace I had no more juice than a strip of old lemon peel.

But the body has tricks the soul knows not. On the day before the Requiem Mass, Margaret met me with a tray of meat and wine. "Pray take this to the priests' room, Jane," she said, "there is a weary pilgrim there and I have the Heskeths to attend to."

It was a heavy tray, I remember that, and I had ado knocking at the door with my foot. And then he was there, so tall, hooknosed, lines of suffering too deep-etched for a young face, gazing at me with dark Southworth eyes. He took the tray. This time the surprise was all mine.

"Father Christopher, I thought you were incarcerated in Wisbech Castle."

"Great friends," he nodded, "I am secretly 'loaned' to help my brethren tell the requiem for one of our greatest knights. I am most honoured to be here."

"And we," I began, "are honoured—"

But he interrupted: "I have thought of you often and often. A child with dark-gold hair invading my hiding place. It was an image to cherish, in the darkness of Wisbech."

I could say nothing. None of the words of custom so often lately mindlessly repeated came to me.

He said, his voice so quiet, "But I did not know you would grow into a maid so fair."

And then against my silence and perhaps repenting of a courtly compliment, he said, "Are we to meet always at times of funeral, I wonder? I am very sorry for the loss of your great father. And for the grief I see you feel. Can it be that you are in need of consolation at this time also?"

They came at last, the unwanted tears. Why then? Was it the gentle tone, the furrowed face, the memory? They came, hot enough to burn dry eye pits, not in a flood, but a trickle that tasted salt at the corner of my mouth, that wetted my chin.

His voice was husky when he said, "Alas I have no towel now."

But he did wipe my face with the tips of his long fingers, wiped my cheeks and off my chin to touch my throat, to stray to my shoulder, to push at that ungiving ribbon. I staggered a little. He steadied me with a strong grip to my shoulder, his other hand exploring the little rectangle of my dress, probing the resistance of the lace, finding how he could shove it over my shoulder, discover the hollow of my armpit, make me gasp for breath, until he caught hold of my breast, throbbing, as I could feel it, like a captured bird. When he closed that bony hand so urgently upon me I felt a rod of flame coursing down my body to scorch the secret parts.

I had never known it before, the fierce dark flower of desire that so swiftly unfurled tendrils of pleasure within my breast, driving hot roots of longing into the very closet of my virtue. And like a flower I swayed irresistibly towards the source of heat and light. The thick cloth of the soutane was between us, but I searched for his mouth, greedy as a fledgling bird. And there I stood, or swayed, avid for his taste, even as sounds were indicating steps upon the stairs. And could not let go of him, 'til he wretchedly pushed me from him, and only just within the nick of time. The door opened and Gracie entered with another tray and two elderly priests beside.

I could only make a feeble curtsey. Christopher said some nothings to them. I suppose they thought me a servant girl for I could not speak. Gracie did not speak to me either, but as I descended the staircase through my head danced a stupid jingle:

> Jane, Jane a strumpet's fame
> Is this the fate that you would claim?

If I had been a puppet before, I now became a ghost. I wanted to lose myself in some fog, dissolve into mist or shadow, even as the house was swelling with expectation. I had even forgot to be afraid, although it seemed that all the fugitive clergy of the county were gathering to serve the obsequies of Sir Richard Shireburn. There were ever footsteps in the upper room where priests were gathering and confessing. And a constant assembling of Catholic friends below, with still need for attentive welcome.

Young Richard, now master, although entering into his inheritance, still politely vouchsafed a respectful place to his unloved stepmother. The throng was so great that I was obliged to share a lectern with Grace. But nothing seemed real to me. Margaret and Mary had thrown all their disappointment at Lady Maud's scanty rites into a magnificence of decoration for their father. They had taken down a whole tree of wild damson to fill the chapel with white flower. The candlelight and the incense, the blossom and the murmured Latin all intensified my sense of being absent, in a dream.

A long row of priests officiated, the chief celebrant in chasuble of gold and white satin, while serving priests, for lack of enough vestments, waited on in black. On one black figure I concentrated my gaze, much fearing that I might be obliged to take communion from him, and commit some fearful sacrilege. If I was spared this sin, taking my turn with another, I did not abnegate the fearful pleasure of observing him. I watched those long fingers extracting wafers from a silver chalice, tendering the consecrated bread to the devout, fingers which but a few short hours away had plied beneath my bodice to my inexplicable delight.

But if I kept my eyes open, I tried to clamp my mind shut to keep away those foolish rhyming couplets.

Chapter 18

SO, DEAR JOHN, I have told of my sensualities, my trespasses. And you have made no moan, no signal of reproach. Not so much as a tossing of your head upon the pillow, a flicker of eyelid, as I relive my life.

I am not yet even come to our wedding. Grant me one more week, John, for the telling of my tale. One more week of seven nights; seven nights of peace with no soul to interrupt or question or distract me. As Richard was persuaded to give me one year of respite before the expiry of my youth.

***

He was, like his mother, narrow and pious, but also just and fair. When I pleaded for a decency of time to mourn my father before whatever festivity might be made of a wedding, he acceded to my request. I should be lower in the hall, of course. I understood that. As I always understood the seniority of Margaret and Mary. They were ever gentle sisters. And no visiting with the gentry, though I was not excluded from the hospitality of Stonyhurst. It was not to be thought of that I should visit Roughlee. That I did not question.

He was so formal, so painstakingly, so dutifully formal in his interview with me, the new master of Stonyhurst. He explained our bequests, that my father had so particularly made – my mother already gifted with the little manor house at Wigglesworth, my brother, with moneys he would know well how to use, and Grace and myself, of course, our generous dowries.

I played the new part tolerably well. I understood the wider terms of my stay of execution, though they were vague and not expressed in words. I dressed soberly, even meanly. I buttoned my lip. It cost me little to be subservient to Margaret and Mary. I minded more relinquishing my right to the library. But this subdued role suited my melancholy. I lived in a grey garden.

But even a winter garden is sometimes visited by the sun, and my determined gloom was not proof against occasional flashes of sunlight. One came with the perfect rose that William Gaunt brought for me on Rental Day. It pierced me with a memory bitter sweet of my father saying, oh so long ago, "You must be punished Jaynie. You understand that?"

Or my life was illumined by the visits of Judge Walmsley, who seemed to have no inkling of my reduced status – or took no heed – but spoke to me with his always jesting affection. He oft times brought little things to amuse me, inconsiderable trifles mostly – a ballad sheet, a verse riddle, a pretty leaf, once a scrap of jewelled lace. "Your Catholic brethren may choose to search for souvenirs in the debris of the gallows, but I bring you the leavings of the most exalted bed chambers."

But there was one gift he brought that counted most for me and I knew cost him most.

"I have ordered table plate to present upon your wedding, and I think it will please young Southworth. But this, Jane, this is for you." And he tumbled into my hand a silver chain and locket. The locket on the outside was chased with a pattern of forget-me-not, and inside held a miniature, a tiny engraving of a man with fiery hair and beard. I did not need that indication to recognise the subject, for the execution was both delicate and masterful. Near small enough to be set upon a thimble, the portrait drew the man to the life.

"My father," were all the words I could utter. It was too rare a gift for easy thanks, and I was overtaken by a mist of longing.

He smiled at my emotion and at his own amused recollection. "We once had a flaming dispute about his fishing rights on my side of the river. I impounded his boat. He was as furious as seven devils, and went to law and had the right of it. He won by legal device, fair and square, loth as I am to say. And afterwards we had a great drunken reconciliation. And since he had gotten his fishing rights, I demanded a fee of him, a portrait of the only man who was ever going to best me in law. And he gave it, the tiniest thumbnail portrait he could have had made. But it is like I think. It is like."

"It is . . . it is very like," I feebly repeated, and he took me in his arms as I went to kiss my thanks. I pricked my cheek on the points of his ruff, and I likely did some lasting damage to that pearly collar piece. It was of no consequence. We shared the warmth of our grieving. I learnt in that moment how sorrows shared may even be sorrows lightened.

I said then, "I know that you loved him, my lord."

And the judge with unwonted gravity agreed, "Yes. I loved him."

❋❋❋

Then one day I saw Alice again. She came to settle estate business with Richard, business that my father had not concluded. Richard had very courteously invited her to dine, surely against his whim, but he strove always to fulfil the supposed and the expressed wishes of his father. He had taken upon himself all the charge and drive of the build and supervised the funeral monuments. It was a very small nod to his father to condescend briefly to the Widow Nutter. That was a day of coincidence, for she came on a day when Walmsley was visiting, and later – for Richard had other affairs of his father to discharge – we were honoured by Roger Nowell.

As the gathering round the table grew warm in discussion, I wondered if I would ever hear such voices, such talk, in the dower house at Samlesbury. Or would my days be full of cows and prayer books?

Inevitably Nowell discovered a topic on which to vent his disapprobation.

"This is a terrible business with the Earl of Derby's son, so great a personage to die victim of witchcraft."

"I heard Fernando died with a profusion of vomiting." Walmsley was ever ready to pinprick Nowell's swell.

"It is believed witchcraft." Nowell was not deflected. "There have been witches found in Essex and now in Huntingdon. I believe the witch fever is blowing through the country."

"You mean witch-hunting fever? There is much crying out and much foolery on the subject. Show me a witch and I'll straightway find you a village feud."

"Do you deny, sir, that these women were witches, when they themselves confessed their guilt?"

"I do know that Justice Darcy was very liberal with promises of mercy upon confession, and that those promises were not honoured."

"But still," Nowell persisted, "the fact of witchcraft exists. And it is said by Bodin and King James that those who deny the existence of witchcraft are almost always themselves witches."

"Nay then you must win all your argument." Walmsley shrugged carelessly. "If the declaration is the proof, who can stand against you? I prefer to keep an open mind."

"An open mind is the gateway to error," said Nowell ponderously. "It will produce books like this damnable *Discoverie of Witchcraft*. James has promised a public burning of the volume when he ascends the throne. It will be his first edict I do verily believe."

"Have you read this *Discoverie*, sir?"

If Richard's polite intervention was intended to dampen the ardour of the debate, it was quickly set aside.

"Of course not. I know enough to know that he seeks to disprove the very notion of witches, and undermine the principles of our proceeding against them. It is a devilish work in my view."

Richard strove for mastery at his own table. "Have you read the book, Judge Walmsley?"

"I have. I believe it a very honest work, full of common sense, and what is more, common humanity."

"It hath enraged the King of Scotland." Nowell was of no mind to abandon the royal camp.

"All Reginald Scot's intention was ask the judges of the land to be exceeding cautious in their treatment of such cases, on the grounds of Christian compassion towards the weak and the helpless, it being the ignorant poor and aged who do mostly stand accused."

Then must Alice butt in a word. "It is ever so. The accused are almost always most defenceless. Why are depositions never laid against those who are able to speak for themselves?"

"It is a fault, Mistress Nutter." The magistrate turned a baleful eye upon her. "You speak truly. We have not cast our eye into high places. It is a fault we should remedy." He turned back to the judge. "But it is a lie we are not cautious in our proceedings, and careful to establish proof. The king himself personally supervised the trial of the North Berwick witches and confessed himself well satisfied with their guilt."

"Scot's other argument," continued Walmsley unruffled, "aside from the exceedingly incredible and stupid nature of the evidence brought in such cases, is the notion that the power of God may be so easily abrogated. In the case of the North Berwick women, are we to believe that the Lord God Almighty would have the power of storm and tempest wrenched from him by Satan, so that a bunch of silly women could shipwreck the King of Scotland?"

"But it was proven, it was proven." Nowell leaned forward. "The women confessed. Each and every one confessed their guilt. And James himself in constant attendance at their examination, and well pleased with the proceedings."

"I have a friend in Scotland," Alice's deep voice was almost dreamy and I remember how she twisted her fingers into a steeple shape, "knew Agnes Sampson well. He carried wool for me up there. They make a special weave in Berwick and never could get enough from me. Agnes Sampson, she of that group you speak of, was a gentlewoman, a gentle and a modest lady, and my friend was great friends with her husband. He attended the trial. She protested a long while her innocence, her full innocence of all knowledge of witchcraft. And so to prove her guilt, they had to search for the Devil's marks upon her body. They stripped her bare in front of all that great assembly, and she a shy woman of the kirk. They stripped her of clothes and hair and searched her to find the place the Devil made his mark and made immune from pain. You know how this is done, with a needle very pointy but quite big. It was stabbed into her legs and arms but since she cried with pain, it was clear no Devil had been there. They tried more places and since the Devil is very crafty and concupiscent they stuck the pin into her female parts, her breasts and then her nipples and then last into her privities, by when she was screaming, anything they wanted, any confession of guilt whatsoever, screaming out nonsense beyond all measure." She paused. "I am impressed that His Majesty was so contented."

There followed a moment in which I had sense to get to my feet. The justice was breathing heavily, preparatory, I supposed, to a furious riposte. I begged Richard's permission to leave his table and accompany Mistress Nutter to the stabling where she might verify the commerce she had made before starting the journey to Roughlee.

Nowell was beginning: "If the only way to catch a witch—" but as we left the hall I heard Walmsley interrupt him. "If the accusation is itself the verdict, then God help us all."

She came out with me in silence. I knew she had some beasts to look over before returning to Roughlee, and a dovecote that she had bargained hard with Richard for. "It is a pretty thing," she said, as we watched the men strap it on her packhorse. We were leaning upon a field gate, and when I did not answer she said, "So you see Jane, I have not yet learned to hold my tongue." And she sighed mightily, "So old and so unwise."

"You are as you are, Alice," I said. "I would not have you changed."

We held our silence 'til the men had finished. She made to leave, and then turned back to me. "Jane, I think we will not meet again, not in a long while, but I have cudgelled my brains how to help you to ease the fate that seems to weigh so heavy with you. I think you do not so much dread the raw young squire, who is lovesick any roads. But you are perhaps in the right to fear a harsh welcome from his family, and perhaps a time of loneliness."

"Aye, I do fear it."

"And I think that a good serving woman, a woman of sense and quality, can be more than a friend to the mistress of the house. So has Joan Gentle been to me."

"And where would I find such a good and trusty waiting woman? I fear I must take what servants are allotted to me in Samlesbury."

"I think you might well ask for the choosing of your personal maid. And what I thought to tell you is how I met a most amiable family in Rochdale. Abel Brierley is a substantial woollen draper in that town. He is quite a lettered man and acts as parish clerk."

"Of the Family?" I guessed.

"I chatted with his aunt and cousin, kindly gentle women who live in Samlesbury, a little place called Turner Green. I think that is not far from the dower house. Janet, with Henry her son, and his wife Ellen, they keep a little alehouse there. I am sure it is a proper and well-regulated establishment, but properness is not always the road to make a fortune in an alehouse, and I have good cause to believe that Ellen would be grateful for a steady place. There is a hare-brained sister too, but I do not know her."

"And you like this Ellen?"

"Yes, very much. She is kindly and with all her wits at home. She can read a little. I have no doubts as to her honesty. I feel confident that she would please you."

"I might be very glad of such a serving woman."

"Shall I send her a word for you?"

Of course I agreed. It was a small break in the looming cloud of my future.

And that is how I first had mention of her, John. As a possible friend and support for myself. But you see how life rings the changes. It is Ellen who has nursed you through this dragging sickness, who has soothed and comforted your days, while I watched with you, and escaped from you, in the nights.

Chapter 19

LORD, IT WAS LONG that year; that year that I held off marrying, held off even meeting with you, poor dear John.

And in this I was much aided by the new master of Stonyhurst. I am sure that Richard approved my desire for a prolonged and marked period of mourning for our departed lord. He may even have found some solace for his mother's endured insult in my downcast condition.

Very little time elapsed before he sent for me again, this time to inform me of large recusancy fines newly imposed on Samlesbury Hall, and that Thomas had tried to mend their fortunes with offers of conformity, Sir John therefore threatening to disinherit him. Which action was only prevented by the personal intervention of the Earl of Derby.

"The two men are locked in conflict still, and you are something of a rag in the middle. The old man would throw you off and cancel the marriage, but Thomas clings to his word, and doubtless his expectation of your dowry."

I found nothing to say, but my face surely spoke for me.

"I am sorry I cannot undo this for you. And it does little honour to our house. But it was my father's making. Though Thomas and John, of course, will carry through with the wedding, Sir John is still head of the house and he dictates the scale of celebration. It will be very small, Jane."

I answered that quick enough: "I do not care a whistle for the scale of the celebration."

"But if you are not sufficiently honoured I cannot

attend, nor other family friends, who have warm feelings for you."

What could I do but nod in glooming acquiescence.

"Richard of Dunnow will take you to Samlesbury and give you away. And I imagine your mother and sister will go with you." We both knew that my mother would not care to play a reduced part in any event, let alone a marriage of such dubious jubilation. "And I have disallowed John Southworth to break into your mourning reclusion, save for a brief betrothal ceremony."

Brief it was, I thanked my saint. How uncomfortably we sat in the great hall, John. You must remember how dumbly you sat, hands all ungainly and discomposed. While I stayed in my place, seeming all maidenly modesty, eyes cast down, staring at floorboards, but silently, vehemently, unwilling. And your anxious father and my rectitudinal stepbrother conversed in stilted phrases, agreeing the time and place of our conjunction – which, we were assured, would not be grand.

When Christmas came Richard kindly suggested that I might visit with my kinfolk, and I was not sorry to escape whatever his severe regime would make of festival.

I went first to my brother at Dunnow, and though I was made very welcome I was aware of the shifting surfaces of things. I was dismayed, though not altogether surprised, that Rick was growing after the pattern of his father-in-law. He was louder and coarser and even redder in the face than I had known him, while Dorothy had even more of the wan, slightly plaintive look of her brother.

I was not so very much cheered at my mother's house neither. She was not celebrating her widowhood with any great restraint or dignity, it seemed to me. Indeed when I arrived it was to find John Law, that huge fat pedlar man, well ensconced in the kitchen taking full advantage of Wigglesworth's plentiful pantries. The contents of his pack were strewn about in the parlour, under examination of Isabella and Gracie.

It was good Christmas trade for the pedlar. My mother had I know not how many pairs of gloves from him, and my sister, newly affianced to William Hoghton, was pleased to make a considerable order for satins from his sample book. Even the kitchen maids relieved him of some trinkets and gauzes.

Of course I was urged to make a selection, at least to choose a Christmas gift. But old sobersides as I had become, I would take only sewing silks. He had some silvery blue thread, gotten I think from France, that pleased me, and I purposed to embroider monograms upon the bed sheets that were my mother's wedding gift. And under her approving eye I did indeed set to work, creating a figure of J for John and J for Jane, and an S for Shireburn and an S for Southworth.

"I am glad that you have accepted your father's purposes and appreciate the decent match he had procured for you, as for Gracie."

"Do you love this William Hoghton, Gracie?" I could not forbear to ask, for I had heard that he was neither very young, nor very personable.

She answered with a shrug she must have learned from Isabella, "All cats are grey in the dark, I do believe."

So take heart, thought I, as I stitched diligently. I had rather be a wife than a concubine after all. And my other little brain rattled:

> Jane, Jane, where is the pain?
> Husband and lover all come to the same.

And as if she had heard my silly silent jingle, my mother leaned back into her cushions and echoed:

> "It's a game, it's a game"
> Said the Queen of Spain
> "One night's pleasure
> And nine months' pain."

And Gracie, docile little pupil, added:

> "Wean the babe,
> Then to it again."

And more wisdom than that I did not glean from Wigglesworth.

I had purchased of John Law, for a Christmas remembrance for Big Irene, a little broidered kerchief, in token of all the tears she had shed, and the yards of apron she had wetted. But I was forestalled and greatly amused to find the pedlar already at Stonyhurst when I returned, well seated at her scrubbed board before a platter piled with mutton and pease.

"John Law," said I, "it is a very short while since I saw you consuming mountains of food at Wigglesworth, and behold the next time I clap eyes on you, you are filling your face again!"

Irene laughed. "I tell him that he carries more in his belly before him than he does in the pack on his back."

"You should beware a double burden," I said with mock sympathy.

"I need sustenance," the pedlar cheerfully insisted. "I have a great way to walk if I am to supply all those who wait for me in Lancashire. It is the belly carries the legs and not t'other way."

"With such a quantity of ale to steady the legs for the walking?" suggested Irene.

"I am a steady man," he agreed, nodding at the maid who filled his mug. "And I carry more than geegaws in my pack." He took a great swill, and said portentously, "I carry philosophy and poesy and all manner of such inflammations."

I laughed unbelieving, and he pushed his plate aside to extract a small slim package from some inner pocket of his pack.

"This is for Mistress Jane Shireburn. To be given into her hands only. It is a bookish thing I would wager."

It was indeed a bookish thing – a slight volume of poetry entitled *Venus and Adonis*, with a letter tucked under the cover.

> *Dearest Jane,*
>
> *I am glad to tell you that all's well and arranged with Ellen Brierley, who will be pleased if she may serve you.*
>
> *John Armstrong gave me this volume. He wishes me to tell you that he has secured great patronage, and his fortunes are on the mend. Also that I assure you of his unending love and that you will ever be the soul of his music. But he wishes you well in this marriage and hopes that you may find satisfaction and comfort therein. The poem by Mr Shakespeare is his small gift to you, if I deem it suitable to offer it. I know not whether such amorous versifying suits well with your present seclusion. But if the passion of this poem should inflame your heart to warm your marriage bed, it may be no poor thing.*
>
> *Dear Jane – look for joy as well as consolation.*
>
> *Your ever friend,*
>
> *Alice*

I slipped the book into my pocket. I confess that I was not clear myself, whether such a gift violated the terms of my abstention from frivolity.

There were other things in the pedlar's pack for me. Margaret and Mary had charged him to bring a package, a small velvet box crammed with tiny seed pearls. They were eager to help me decorate my bridal gown, the more eager, I suspect, to beg pardon for their enforced absence at my ceremony. The pedlar was congratulated on his commission: "Enough here," said Margaret, "to embellish gown and cap and more beside."

All in all, John Law had made good profit from my family, though I guessed that there would be little call for his services at the Lower Hall.

But it comes at me from all sides, I thought, the pressure to bend my inclinations and my affections even, into the path of duty. And I also thought that it needed neither poet nor farmer to teach Isabella's daughter how to warm her husband's bed.

So heigh-ho, I came in a more proper frame of mind when Richard next called me.

"We have dawdled long enough Jane. You have not seen your house, nor acquainted yourself with your household. We should rectify this now. I have given permission for John Southworth to take you on a visit."

"I should be very glad to do that," I said not untruthfully.

"Then John rides over for you one week hence."

Chapter 20

So you came riding for me, John, and my tables were topsy turvied once again.

You chose a white morning. Despite the day's bright sun, powdery snow was frosted fast to the trees, and every branch and twig was woven into the crystal lace of winter woodland. The world was lit for your entrance, and you came bravely enough, on that heavy cob you favoured, great-cloaked and full of cheer and vigour as a boy – which you very well were. And I, I was determinedly content, and did not find it difficult.

I do not forget that ride, John, how the horses near danced in the keen air, clattering across frozen little brooks, trampling the crust of silvered leaves, as we wove in and out of woods along the river.

Nor do I forget your willing gallantry as you held back branches from before my face, nor your smile when the rime was scattered down upon my head. It was a merry ride.

But it was not until I beheld the little dower house that my heart was thoroughly won. When I felt what it might be to be mistress of my own place.

We approached the house from the north, crossing the river by way of the ford. It stands long and low in the east–west loop of a cleared valley. Where in summer I watch long-horned Lancashire cattle browse on sweet grass, on that day I saw a virgin snow sheet to the border of the river.

Of course you were proud of the home you were offering me, and eager to see that I was pleased.

"We are lower than Stonyhurst and nearer the sea," you pointed out. "That belt of limes is the path to the ferry and the church – apostate now, to our shame. The avenue does catch the wind, but our house stands out of the draught."

***

Lower Hall was angled towards the sun, and snow was beginning to drip from the roof edges. It pleased me entirely, this old red sandstone building, with its generous provision of window and its balanced proportion.

There were few servants in attendance, the house being presently unoccupied, but I remember how willingly the herdsman, Bernard Billington, came to take our horses and to be introduced. The door was opened by Mary Sowerbutts. She was, as often, in a state of pregnancy – favoured but disorderly in appearance. I learned that she was cousin to Ellen Brierley and wondered as to the wisdom of my choice. For the house gave little show of good housewifery. The fires were lit and furniture was in place, but there was no smell of cleanliness, no shine or glow at all, and many corners that might not bear inspection. I had a great desire to take this neglected house in hand.

We stood in the long room above the stairs, looking down at the river flowing so darkly between its frozen edges.

"In summer—" John began, and I stayed him with a smile, and a sudden desire to plant a kiss upon his pudgy face. Which perhaps he guessed – did you? – for he said, "I thought Jane that you might have this room as your personal chamber or parlour, for sewing or embroidery or prayers or such. It is light and private, but with quick descent to the kitchen."

"I should be very happy with such a provision. I have a little writing desk left to me by my father would stand very gracefully in this embrasure. And on that long wall we could mount some bookshelves."

That drew a frown. "We do not hold with book learning in this family. It is the reading of the English Bible has loosened the ancient true faith in this land, my grandfather believes. And I myself hold it unseemly and frivolous in a woman."

"Oh John I do not wish to contradict you. But it was my father who ordered my instruction, and I am certain that he would have wished me to retain this freedom. I would expect Richard to be of the same mind. Ought I to consult him as to terms?"

He answered quickly. "No, no. We shall not disagree on this. You may do as you wish."

Neither of us wished to sour the pleasant day, so I said feelingly, "It will never cause me to neglect my duties, John, you may be assured."

He took my hand – it was a gentle gesture for such an awkward knight – to take me down the stairs, and the more to prove my more good will, I added: "You will see how assiduous I am in my duties to you – and any children God may send us."

And perhaps that served me better than a kiss.

Did it so? How is it, John, that I seem to write to you, and for you, words you will never read?

I do not remember what my expectation was of Ellen Brierley. I do know that I was surprised by her very slight stature. But then all was dwarfish in the little alehouse on Turner Green. The door was opened by a low fellow – a hunchback with a gentle smile who put his hand on John's shoulder to caution him from butting his head on the low beam. It seemed to me a house in miniature, like a child's picture book. The rooms were low, the stools were low, the mugs and jugs were small, even to the fire irons, and the neat little flame that burned in the grate. All in great good order though.

The picture was completed when Ellen and her mother came to greet us. Capless, shiny hair brushed smooth, a pointy nose and bright brown eyes, Ellen minded me of nothing so much as the field mice which dartingly run among the corn stooks at harvest time. If Ellen was a brown mouse, her mother was the grey, chiding her children to make haste to provide for the guests. For if the Brierleys' stature was not great, their hospitality was all largesse. We were pressed to partake of warmed ale and spiced wine, of sweet tarts with curd cream, and ginger biscuits, and simnel cake, and I know not what we could not prevent being laid out for us.

But while her mother scurried, Ellen stayed to discuss the conditions of her service. She would not sit but stayed standing. And she standing so, and myself seated, we were a near equivalence in height. I described how she should wait upon me personally and supervise the running of the house and kitchen. Mary Sowerbutts would be occupied in brewhouse and buttery, with other maids to be found. Ellen nodded, expressing all willingness to fulfil what tasks I chose to give her, and well and carefully.

"But—" I was stayed by the caviat, and John set down his mug, frowning at the forward girl. She clasped her hands before her apron front and bravely continued to say that she must in all truthfulness appraise Mistress Shireburn that, "My cousin Mary and I, we are very different" – she glanced at her mother for support and went on – "we are quite different and we do not, always, agree well together."

She seemed to take a deep breath, and then in a rush she vowed how she was grateful, most grateful, for this chance of work and that she would most faithfully serve her mistress, and so she was sure would her cousin Mary, but there could be difficulties between them, and since Mistress Nutter, who had spoken for her, for the place, did not know of the problem, it behoved her, Ellen, to speak honestly about it. "So that if it falls out in time that you have need to part with one of us, and as I am the newcomer, I mean to say that I should understand. And I did want to appraise you of this, Madam, because I come recommended, and could not deceive you."

I did not think, as John did, that this was effrontery in a serving woman not yet took on, yet I was surprised by her boldness in advising me as to hiring and firing. So small, I thought, and so audacious. But quickly I recognised that this was a woman who clung to her honour, who could not abide to deceive and who had not a little pride. I said with a dignity new found for my role of mistress of the house, "There is plenty of work for us all I am sure Ellen. We will divide it fairly and strive to make a courteous Christian household. And a worthy home for my lord. Let us begin with good heart."

I did not need to ask if they were Family of Love, the Brierleys; indeed I have not asked direct to this very day. Nor did I feel the need to enlighten John when he suggested as we rode home, "They are somewhat puritany, the Brierleys, do you not find?"

I answered with a question: "And Mary Sowerbutts? She is of the same family?"

"Not puritan at all." John's laugh was knowing and perhaps even lewd. "She is known to be lightest and wildest at maypole dancing, and in other sorts—"

"—in no way like her cousin?"

"Mary is comely and has a fertile womb. Ellen has a barren marriage and a crooked husband."

"And Mary Sowerbutts's husband?"

"Thomas is also a wild one, son of an Irish tinker. He is a matchless player on the fiddle. And he can drink over any man in the parish."

"And he does his drinking at the alehouse?"

"He was not allowed for some while. Henry Brierley forebade him entry."

"For what cause?"

"Oh for some disorderliness I should suppose and a too licensed tongue. He can be free with his fists and he has no qualms in mocking his hunchback brother-in-law."

"This sounds like a tinder box John. Is Sowerbutts your father's tenant?"

John nodded. "He farms close to the hall. He is a good tenant mark you, pays his manorial dues and not stinting with labour."

"And favoured by your grandfather?"

"Of course – a loyal servant and a true staunch Catholic."

And that quits all faults, thought I.

Quittance was the name of all my days from then. Time scrambled through my fingers, however hard I tried to clutch the last moments spent in my father's – once my father's – house. I could have counted moments in rosaries of pearls, as the sisters diligently sewed the decoration to my wedding garments.

My farewell to Richard was as stiff as I could have expected, save for my feeling that the scales of approval and correction had slightly tilted.

He presented me with a box of various bonds and deeds:

"My father, in his testament, did so particularly command generosity to his baseborn children. I hope I have been just to you, Jane?"

"You were always just, Richard," I answered, suddenly knowing that it was mine to give or withhold commendation. "And generous," I said slowly, even doubtfully.

"But something less than kind?" he suggested.

I shook my head. "I have never made complaint or had cause. I have been grateful for your care of me, Richard, and I am sorry to leave it."

That he allowed me to speak so loftily, and did attend to my pronouncement, marked something changed. I was becoming a married woman, not a bastard girl of little consequence. And I might claim a voice. Speak and be attended to.

Chapter 21

AND SO TO WED.

No charms this day to conjure up the sun. The rain fell fitfully, not in copious lament but uncertain how to baptise my leaving. And I too was uncertain, never having expected to leave my childhood home with so little, so very little, ceremony.

In the end there was only Big Irene. As we prepared to leave she took me in a huge smother of embrace. Then she pressed into my hand a silver coin.

"It was given to me of your father, to comfort me for losing of the child. I never spent it."

I had barely time to thank her, no time to ponder on my father's act. Rick was impatient to leave. I knew that it was the best gift that she had to give, that and a solemn admonition that I walk always in the light. The tears I shed on parting from Irene were my last childishness.

At Samlesbury I was greeted by Thomas and Rosamund with careful politeness. I was well wetted by the time of my arrival. The perfidious drizzle had provoked my hair to some disarray, which did little I am sure to bring me into the favour of the old man, who lingered behind, leaning on his stick.

Rick was uncertain too, and severe with me as we approached the chapel door. "Just be good Jane," he said frowningly. "Do as you are told, be biddable and quiet, and all will be well."

I spoke my vow not trembling but clear, to mark my resolute good will. But it was a long mass with nothing left out. I cannot have been the only one glad of the conclusion. I was thankful to reach the table after all the obligatory greetings. But not only the children found the meal ample and interminable.

Rick and John had comfortable talk, to do with hunting mainly. Thomas and Rosamund paid solicitous attendance on old Sir John, whilst his serving man, John Singleton, did not neglect his master's cup.

I crumbled crumbs upon my platter and was glad to relieve the tedious time by exchanging wry faces with a round-cheeked boy, who then brought his sister up to inspect the bride. To divert them and myself I played at poking currants into the flat flaky pastry cakes that were a speciality of the hall. I made a grinning face, and then inspired I started on our monogram, with a J and a J, and was about to lace them together with an arrow when the old man suddenly thundered, "Are you about teaching letters to these children?"

I was too startled to reply. He threw down his napkin and growled, "We'll have no lettering or writing or reading in this house mistress. Nor in the Lower Hall neither."

I said quietly, wrapping my dignity around me, "I have permission of my husband, sir, to pursue my studious pastimes."

John looked in some alarm, muttering that it was not permission to teach children he had given.

"Why John that is not just. You surely meant that promise—"

I had but begun, but the old soldier silenced me: "She calls the tune already in your home? You have need call her to heel, your saucy wench!"

I was dismayed beyond description. For all my silk and pearls I felt unclothed at my own bridal board. And much the more dismayed that my husband did not speak for me. But if I was shamed before the assembly, before even Southworth servants and minions, I would not give way to the blustery knight. I did not cast down my eyes but sat in icy stillness watching him, watching the manservant puff fresh wind into the old man's sails, who nodded vigorously: "You have done well to remind me." And to me: "They say Ellen Brierley is to be taken on at the Lower Hall?"

I merely nodded.

"Mary Sowerbutts has kept house for us there. She is just now delivered of a stillborn babe." He crossed himself with demonstrative piety.

I said, "I am sorry for it."

"She has been employed down there since a young girl. She has not displeased us. She wishes to be retained in her old position and has asked me to speak with you."

"Of course we have work for her in the house."

"Not just any work. It is to be first woman that she makes petition. Whoever is your personal maid is chief maid in the house. Mary Sowerbutts has always had charge at Lower Hall. She is a good girl and attender at every Catholic mass. Which cannot be said of her cousin."

He was loud and I was quiet. "I am afraid that I have given my word."

"That is no matter. John will take the business in hand. He can explain to Ellen Brierley that you misunderstood the position."

"I thought a lady might have the choosing of her personal servant."

"A lady mayhap," he offensively began, but before he extended the insult Thomas was plying him with a plate of sugared fruit, and some anodyne remark.

Rosamund, with habitual kindness and prattle, took my attention. "Why Jane what a dainty locket you carry there, near lost in the beads of your bodice. The pattern, is it not forget-me-not?"

"It is a present from Judge Walmsley. It contains a miniature of my father which is most precious to me."

The knight chewed on his plums, which did not prevent him from suggesting, "You had better carry a saint's image if you will not wear a crucifix. Rosamund, can you not find her a picture of the Blessed Virgin?"

"Thank you, but I will rather keep the picture of my father. It is my greatest treasure."

"Your greatest treasure is your immortal soul," he grew wrathful again, "and you endanger that with every disobedient word you utter! You will do in this, as in all matters, exactly what your husband tells you."

So he attacks my pursuits, my household and now my private ornament. He made me weep as a child, and frighted me from the table, but he would not best me now, not if he threw my bastardy in my face. I rose from my chair.

"I will obey my husband in every aspect of the marriage bond, as I expect him to keep promises made to me. But my father is my first lord, and the love I bear him, the honour I owe his memory, is imperishable."

Ah, then his temper flared in his face.

"You will do as you are told mistress and exactly as you are told, or my grandson will thrash the rebel spirit out of you, and if he does not, I will take the whip to you myself!"

He rose also and I clasped my hands. Erect I stood, and dared a small contemptuous smile.

And then he simply frenzied. His face was scarlet as he stab, stabbed his finger towards me. I think no one at the table knew whether he said 'redheaded bitch' or 'redheaded witch' because his speech boiled into incoherence, before he clutched wildly at his chest, and then fell heavily forward, with plates and goblets crashing round him.

The next is hard to remember. Rick dragged me away from the table. Someone – a servant – put a clout about my shoulders, as another opened a side door, to where the rain had made up its mind and was pouring down in rods.

We rode through this heavy falling rain as fast as we were able. I dismounted, the clout and all well sodden. I stood at Rick's stirrup, my few tears well drownded by the water that streamed over all. A piteous figure I must have made. I would have asked him to enter, wished him to enter, but he shouted through the driving rain, "You are not the darling of Stonyhurst any more, don't you understand?" He leaned down from his horse: "You are a married woman Jane. You will perform your duty and obey your husband, or you will get the stripes you deserve."

He wheeled away as the herdsman approached. Bernard Billington for very pity took me by the elbow and led me to my own house door.

Then Ellen took me in charge. The bed chamber fire already lit, wet garments cast, a wet rag of a pearl-studded gown changed for a shift that still gave evidence of Margaret and Mary's handiwork. And one of Alice's good dyed blankets wrapped around me. Two young girls, brawny and amiable, were coming and going to tiny Ellen's orders, fetching hot milk and brandy wine. My hair rubbed dry and then brushed out. And all the while Ellen, asking no questions but murmuring endearments and comforts, in a lexicon I had come to know.

"Now little bird, now you will soon be warm. Warm and dry. Child of grace, cease your shivering. All is well. Angels to enfold you in white wings." And as she brushed, "Such lightsome hair. Marigold, flower of love. This will bring him back to your bed. Have no fear. Take heart little bird, sweet marigold. Child of innocence. God's light upon you brings blessings to your marriage bed."

And so continued her litany while she plaited my hair. Such comfort as the Family of Love knows how to give.

I was almost asleep when John returned. He entered with a crashing of the door, his boot steps loud and hasty on the stair. Until he was in the room, panting from the gallop and his drunken tumbling thoughts, the great cattle whip in his hand. And no hesitation in words now, but a fury that untrapped his tongue.

"My grandfather is alive still, but half his motion dead and his speech near smothered! What battlefield and prison could not do to him, you have done."

He flicked the whip nervously. "All say you have bewitched him. You'll not be crossed. You cast the evil eye on those that thwart you – whore, witch that you are."

He lashed at me once, wild in his motion but aimed well enough to just catch my shoulder with a sting that burned and whipped my dull brain alert. I have an animal fear of the whip, and like any dog would cringe and lick the master's hand to escape it.

But it was surely from Isabella that the instinct came to seduce him from his wrath.

I reached the bed, dragging the ribbon off my plait, so my hair would fly, spread on the pillow, poor monogrammed pillow. I pulled at the fastening of my shift, scattering pearls all about, but so that he could contemplate my breast, and guess at the rest of the fair park. I steadied my voice to a syrup of sweetness: "Will you not come to my bed, my lord?"

He hesitated, frowning, and then overtaken by a simpler form of lust he came to me. Cast doublet, dropped breeches, something like groaning. And completed my work by tearing the shift to the hem, violently enough that more pearls spilt everywhere, over the bed, the floor, the room. I mind how long after, the maids still found them, in crannies and corners. He took his look then, discovering what he had craved to know, the colour that the grass grew on the mount of Venus. And thrust himself into me with all the wild energy he might have stuck a spear into a hunted pig. And as he thudded his marital rights my idiot brain kept repeating:

> Jane, Jane, trouble and pain,
> Bitter the bed where you are lain.

And so befuddled by drink and rage you were, my lord, that you were never cognisant that I had, oh so long since, parted with my maidenhead.

Chapter 22

I DID NOT LINGER in your bed seignior. Not choose to lie open-eyed, dully, next the bulk of you who, brute task done, was too deeply mired in sleep to take note of either my presence or my absence. I found a shift and a cloak and left you there, left your bed, left your house, to go sit in the stable yard, oddly comforted by the little sighings and stirrings of the beasts within.

❄ ❄ ❄

The rain was over, the world washed clean, but still enough bruise-black cloud to litter the path of the placidly drifting moon. Ah, the sleepless moon, endlessly promenading the night sky, how She compelled my attention. Pale Ladye, queen of nonchalance, pale as chastity, pale as a waxen corpse.

After the tumble and fumble of a lecherous bed, I longed for the smooth passage of the moon. I longed precisely to be the moon, calmly floating about my business, indifferent to the ruckus and bustle below, silently observing, splendidly ignoring. Is She indeed indifferent or does She feel a puzzled pity, forever gazing down on the follies of mortals? The pity of quietus? She is my Ladye Death and I will attend on Her.

I pay respect to Alice and her waiting on the gentle Ladye Tyme, and her bringing forth of the lovely daughter Truth, but I would be maid in waiting of the pale moon, the silver spirit, exempt from mutability whilst all of great nature below her, goes from change to change. Who would want to attend the meddlesome life-giving sun, as content to breed maggots in a piece of carrion as to bring forth the sweetest flowers? I choose the cool quiet of the moon, putting to peace what has been turbulent, closing heavy eye lids, shushing rasping breath.

I am tranced. I who always had difficulty fastening my mind into prayers to the Lord God and his saints, or even homage to the Blessed Virgin, I fall into a simple and steadfast contemplation, fascinated as a rabbit in lantern light. I see how she is briefly caught and then disentangles herself from webs of black branches or bars of cloud wrack. Without haste or stir, She sails silkily free. And beams down upon me, power to Her handmaid. Cold sweet disinterested power of the moon. I feel it enter my forehead. Almost I hold it in my hands. Such a stillness and command. That I know, I can, I dare—

And suddenly I am terribly afraid. Afraid that I may have already encompassed your death, John, that I have willed your destruction, not knowing how easy I could bring it about. Forget a venal servant, forget a lunatic ancient, how if I should have willed the death of my lord husband, seeing I did so ill wish him in his amorous transports. Where should I stand in the world then? What would I be accounted?

Forgive me Ladye. This white radiance is not the path of light that Irene had prescribed to me. Your misty nimbus is not the halo of sanctity to which Lady Maud bade us aspire.

I closed my eyes tightly and crossed myself. So I abjured the soft magic of the moon. For very fear I put aside enchantment, forwent Her promised power. I resolved to forget the strokes that still burnt my shoulders. To walk ordinary, two feet on the ground. To sleep and wake in a Christian bed. To obey my lord and keep his house diligently.

Chapter 23

LO AND BEHOLD JOHN. I spent the night in recollection of moon magic and on the morrow you are restored to me. However brief – as Ellen warns me – is your remission from pain, your steadied breath, I was glad, truly glad when the Nightingales woke me, to see you partly raised in the bed, able to swallow a little ale and soup. And for me, the ghost of a smile.

She will still dose your nights, our mistress of herbs, and I shall keep watch, and hasten with my story. For though you can neither contradict nor speak for your part, your ever-breathing presence holds me to account, so that the reckoning between us will be as just as maybe.

❋❋❋

It was in a right sober frame of mind that I assembled my little household. They seemed so motley few after the array of servitude I was accustomed to. The slow-spoken herdsman who had witnessed my sorry, sodden arrival, of which he showed no hint of remembrance, was there to ask that his daughter be taken on as cook. At some length he rehearsed her experience and qualities but it was her kindly wide face and cheerful grin that secured Betty the position. Ellen, tiny and trim, standing between the Nightingale sisters, who towered above her, asked for them to be taken on as little maids of all work. How I have learnt to value these two servants, as stalwart-built as dray horses, but doe-eyed and gentle hearted, and much given to languishing dreams of love.

There were lesser people there that morning, like Angelica, a half-gypsy dumb girl who had charge of the wash house, and a tousled lad, Joe Little, who though now well grown the maids still call Little Joe. The yard boy had no place among the domestics, but had crept in under someone's skirts, to catch a view of the new mistress. And others too who might have claimed more of my attention, were I not aware of Mary Sowerbutt's tapping foot, as she played with the cap strings under her chin, and cast sly glances up to the ferryman who stood beside her. He, Thomas Welshman, was to the fore, to present the new lady of the hall with a fine fat salmon. Dark and lively, he was very earnest to describe the great leap of the fish into his boat, into his lap well nigh. With a musical voice and a winning smile, he was clearly a romancer. I thought it best to leave to John to decide how lawfully or not the ferryman took big fish from the Ribble.

To Mary I said, "I am so very grieved to hear that you have lost your babe, Mary. We must all pray God to send you more and stronger children."

"I have already two strapping lads at home, and plenty more to come I daresay." The remark was flung to the kitchen in general, but then very pointedly to me, "Might I ask your ladyship, if the knight, Sir John, has spoken with you for my place?"

So, I thought, it is not yet known that Sir John might never speak again, for any place whatever. I answered her as to how the work would be divided, Mary having charge of buttery and brewhouse and bakery. She was to be on the same wages as Ellen, who would keep order in the house and wait upon me.

Mary flushed angrily at what she plainly regarded as relegation. But she managed a submissive bob, and I expressed a large hope for future harmony in our house.

But harmony is not so easily come by. I do believe, John, that both you and I wished to make a fair start after a bad beginning. The old man did not die, though he was damaged ever after. There still seemed a chance to mend that poor set off.

Of course wedlock is not poetry. It is much housewifery, for which I am but slenderly endowed. It was hard to fasten my life in needles and puddings but I made shift to run a pleasant household, and if your house shone with herbal cleanliness, the bread was good and the ale sweet, and the meats handsome, let it be laid to Ellen's account, who oversaw all. I took such credit as I could and my lord could not fail to be pleased with these things. Though he ever lacked the words to say so, any more than he ever found the words to say what I know, that he repented his brutality. And he strove to be a gentle husband. He did indeed constrain me very little. You made no complaint, dear John, when I removed those many cheap plaster images of sainthood that hung about your house. Which garish colours I replaced with a wealth of flowers. For down here in the seaward valley, wild cherries put on bridal veils of blossom for the end of Lent, blue hyacinth floods the woodland and hedgerows are brightened with patches of pink campion. Campion: that word gives me pause. I stay, quill in hand and endeavour to remember all that name meant to you.

Edmund Campion, scholar, poet, playwright, priest, spearhead of the Jesuit mission in England, pied piper of noble youth, charmer, martyr, traitor. Sheltered and revered to near adulation by the old one. Bitterly thought on by Thomas, whose own name and house had been given when the young missionary broke under torture. Forgiven warmly, sentimentally, by Rosamund, who had a keepsake of his blood upon a kerchief, scraped from among the mortal remnants under the scaffold.

But what to you John? How did your unsubtle mind unfasten the tangle of loyalties and betrayals, of treachery and devotion? I have only thought on this lately. It was never a subject to be lightly broached with you. You answered my single question sharply enough:

"He was danced from manacles. He was pulled out of his length on the rack. What mortal man can promise the strength of his fortitude under such torment?"

Whatever the sentiments among my husband's family, there was no alloy in the affectionate remembrance of simpler folk. For them he was the Captain, Christ's Captain. I remember how in those days Thomas Welshman sang as he brought over the ferry boat and it echoed across the water:

> *Campion is the champion.*
> *Him once to overcome,*
> *The heretics may break their pates*
> *His words will strike them dumb.*

For this was recusancy of a different kind from the one I grew up with. I was well used to Lady Maud's fervent piety, but that was a thing often veiled, ecstatic but secret, even in sacrament and celebration. Here in Samlesbury we were more bold in our subversion, and more strict. Morning and evening prayers were lengthily imposed. We fell to our knees for the Angelus, wherever, in kitchen, hall or field. Stoops of blessed water were in every cottage, and iron-hard Friday fasts were observed in most. The Virgin was everywhere invoked – rough wooden images to be found in wall niches, or hedges, and many floral offerings. Folk crossed themselves for every oath or wish or fear or imprecation, and clacked their beads openly. The very trees stood about, it seemed to me, imbued with stoic and determined faith.

I could not lend myself in heart to such undeviating fervour, any more than I could embrace the pietisms of the Family of Love. I had rather live in the moon, and regard all from a long distance. But I did observe the practices dutifully and endeavoured to obey my husband and accept his prohibitions, both as to study and to society. I did not question the non-acceptance of Alice Nutter in our house. I could very well imagine the discomfort of having that deep-voiced woman speak her mind at John's board.

One guest I was most cheerfully encouraged to welcome was sweet Rosamund, my nervous, prattling mother-in-law. Poor Rosamund. She must have had the fount of speech pent up in the great hall, for she fairly overflowed in my parlour, words coming faster than breaths, as she engaged me with her pauseless stories of this clan I had entered. What had been for me gossip and conjecture took on the colours of a ballad tale, of Rosamund's own particular view.

She told me, almost as one tells a child, the story of children blasted and benighted by a patriarch fast caught in the toils of ancient loyalties, his mind awash with the tales of his own valour and his own favour from the hands of a dead queen. A dead daughter and a murdered lover to pay the price of his certainties. Of two surviving sons, one Christopher, doted upon, sent for a Jesuit, sacrificed upon the stone of hopeless loyalty, and no obliging ram in a providential thicket nearby. The other, Thomas, endlessly weighing allegiance to his queen against obedience to a pope, prepared to change the fashion of his cloak to suit the caprices of princes, if thereby to purchase a little peace and prosperity. But who actually bought himself the withering scorn of his father and the wretched contempt of his own son.

And she most anxious to keep the peace, dear Rosamund, and persuade me to help heal the breach. Which I was indeed eager to do, and played my pretty part in bed – only, I wonder whether you were ever contented John? Or were you always obscurely thwarted?

One source of dissension we did never resolve. Old Mary Snow dwelling in a wattle hut by the brook of Bezza, sought at all times to be a friendly neighbour. She was given out a wisewoman, and if wisdom can be measured by the displacement of hairs upon the head, into warts upon the chin, then Mary would have been a Sibyl indeed. But she was a kind soul, if over liberal with advice. She endlessly brought me little things – a polished acorn, a wild bird's egg, a remarkable stone. John disliked her visiting. Perhaps he knew more stories about her than I did, but I resisted his forbidding. I was too used to beggars at Stonyhurst gates to turn away one poor old beldame.

I gave her bread and milk, and a few kind words, though I chid her when she dabbled in dangerous waters. She showed me once with pride the pence she had gained for offering to make a charm to cure a cow of the shits. I bade her beware of making claims that could be turned against her. But she was too old to be repentant. She gave a smirk and a little skip:

> Here I come, here I go
> Little Mary Snow.
> A penny in my purse
> Is better than a curse.
> If I don't cure your beastie
> I'll never make it worse.

Still, she was not always cheery, and pulled a long face at my growing belly. "Let it not come too soon, Mistress

Jane. Best let your own fruit ripen before you labour to plant an orchard."

For it was true I did labour in my new garden. Ellen had the house, books were denied me and I had enough of my father to desire to plan and build, and make a mark upon the world about me.

I paid little attention to the old woman, and when I measured my pimple against Mary Sowerbutts's already replenished swell, I thought I went slow enough.

Chapter 29

AND SO I LET YOU GO. Opened my hands that kept some tangle of your mortal threads still twined in them. Let the threads untwist, not noticing the fibres unravelling so gently that there was no need of my Ladye to come to clip you off.

You fell away, fell into nothingness so quietly, and I was scribbling too hard. Through my carelessness I did not see, nor hear you go.

But when I paused for thought, there you were, absent. But a shell, a husk, a mask set cold. Sunken cheeks the colour of an old candle, and a sharp and so pointy nose. Only your hands still bore some semblance of living, as if they yet could move, still scratch at the counterpane, or clutch at departing breath.

I kissed your hands that had no warmth left. I kissed the icy smoothness of your forehead, after I closed your hallucinated eyes.

And returned to write my last note.

Even at your deathbed I am writing, determined to capture my last moment with you, before the world arrives and I put on decent mourning garb. So let me keep this minute to tell you John, before the record is washed out with sanctimonious phrases and politic expressions. Tell you that I have a deep sob in my stomach, a clump of misery that I know not how to dissolve. And a longing, unlooked for, to bring you into life again, for you to be a living body, not a thing. A man I tried to love wisely but did not love well.

Farewell my dear, and farewell my little chronicle.

Chapter 25

HOW INFIRM OF PURPOSE AM I. How unable to sacrifice what I had purposed to be done with.

But I have grown used to the dim quiet of this chamber, to the faint crackle and fall of burning wood chips, the slight quiver and dance of a candle flame. And besides those things, to have all to myself, myself alone to please. The household abed, the children quieted, and the key to my memories in my hand again.

I cannot forgo the pleasure of it. Now that my man is in the ground, the clods have tumbled onto the coffin, onto the few frail flowers we cast, my children cast. I have wiped their faces, dried their tears, put on black and draped the house in sombre stuff. I have given sorrowful words to Rosamund and Thomas. I have received sorrowful words from all and sundry, and exchanged them for glasses of Madeira and Ellen's biscuits. I have done all properly.

I am even grateful to discover that your leaving has left a wound in my heart, that I mourn your passing more than I ever fretted against your presence, even against your stubborn excursions into zealotry. And if I mourn you truly, I wish also to bring our account to a fair conclusion.

But I cannot continue to address you in an empty room. I will go on. I tell the rest for myself, as I began. And my judgements must concur with the facts I recollect, as faithfully as I am able.

***

She told no lie, Mary Snow. My first fruit came all unripe. And perhaps she was right. I laboured too hard in my garden, it was my delight. And I had a young squire – great nephew of old William Gaunt – to help with the digging and planting, and to plant a seed of perilous hope in Lily Nightingale's susceptible heart.

Yet I was not unaware of the need for care, even for Mary. I followed her one day into the buttery, where she was clanging among cans and churns.

"Make sure to let Joe Little carry in the milk pail for you Mary. You should not carry the heaviest things in your" – I did not say our – "condition."

"Truth to tell my lady," Mary, with her back against the big stone sink, leaned a negligent hand on her hip, "I spawn so easy that it were no grief to lose a few of the small fry."

I do not know whether it was meant as a taunt, perhaps for barren Ellen, but it was a heedless remark stayed with me through my fruitless days.

It must be that it hurt John more than it hurt me, that first loss. Such a tiny thing, a deformed little homunculus, not much more than a mess of blood and tissue, which Ellen made haste to bear away in a pail, uncovered, so my husband, meeting her in the way, was hit with the horror of it.

He crashed into the chamber where I lay, exhausted. His slow wick lit by anger, vile words came tumbling from him: "Is it hagseed that you fetch me here? Have you wished away, witched away, my child? The very life you carried? What serpent curls about your womb? What envious toad comes to lap your breast milk, after you have destroyed my child?"

I gave no answer to this. What should I say? I lay there wet and empty, too tired almost to fear his fists. But

Ellen, standing wretched with the bucket in her hands, she bravely said, "My mistress has done no harm here. She did most dearly long for this babe. Never could she have ill-wished it."

He was stopped in his fury, standing alongside the bed, struggling with what? His tears, his fears, his longing, his great uncertainty and puzzlement?

I said wearily, "John you cannot believe this nonsense. Even a witch would not deform her own child."

And as he stood silent, I guessed that he was thinking of the Demdike and her misshapen daughter.

It was a struggle for me to speak, but I would have torn away his suspicions if I could. "Do not take heed of fool gossip, of your old grandfather who is—"

"Who is dead," he answered with passion. "I have the news just now." And then the tears flowed.

I whispered, not without malice, certainly with reproach, "You weep for the old man, not for your own child."

He sat on the bed, fists on his knees, gazing into space but not towards me.

"My grandfather was a great hero, tall and brave. Won a queen's favour on the battlefield while yet a boy. His motto, 'Always ready to serve'. He sent the best archers to the Crown. And he in return? Persecuted, imprisoned, examined, disputed with—"

Ellen left the room. He swallowed down his weeping. "But he was staunch. He was unswerving. They could not browbeat him, even though they pauperized him."

I said no word. He pulled his sleeve across his wet face. "Never browbeaten, never afeard – of nothing, no one." Slowly he said, "But he was afeard of you."

He left me then. I knew that a stricken ancient and a deformed foetus stood in his mind against me.

It was left to my women to care for me. I was half asleep, half in a swoon, when I woke to the screams in the yard outside, and the shouting, "No covens here!" and the whistle of the whip.

He had caught her, Mary Snow. She had come bringing parsley for Mary to put into the butter, to soften my hard breasts, to stop the useless milk from curdling, which Ellen was already attending to, but the poor old creature had only thought to help. And got a thrashing for her pains "to within an inch of her life," Joan Nightingale said.

I saw through the window my young husband, as he finished wreaking his terrors on a little old witch. And Bernard Billington, scooping her up to carry her back to her hut, her head lolling, and her face disfigured where the whip had catched it, almost like the pulpy mess Ellen had carried from my room.

I lay back upon the bed, sickly feeling. I could not rise. I was already practised in starvation rites. And I think I knew that, given the setting of the sun and its rising, my lord would be taken by contrition, and certes, contrition being no tongue untier, he would not know how to say it.

Chapter 26

I LAY, RESOLUTELY FAMISHED, I know not how long. And was jolted back into life again by Rosamund. She came, babbling like a little brook, long silted and now freed, freed from the threat of disinheritance, freed also by a gravely silent daughter-in-law who paid her some attention.

She had tales to tell this time, of Christopher and his suffering in the prison of Wisbech Castle, of dissension among the priests, of anointed men falling away from the true conduct of faith.

Perhaps I did not speak but my open eyes and raised eyebrows were encouragement enough for her.

"There is loose living among them and little praying, much loud behaviour and even lewd women, doxies, brought into the prison itself for those who can pay."

A question in my eyes.

"But not Christopher. No. no, never. He joins with a little group, all Jesuits, who strive to a spiritual rule for themselves, even there in the prison. But their very virtue inflames the anger of men who have fallen away from grace."

Did I smile, a very small bitter smile?

"He is they say, a very rage of chastity. And holds the rule most firm. He has been always, to my knowledge, obedient and dutiful, and most faithful. Though I do believe that he went sadly into his vocation, to honour his father, and to put his life onto the scale of this most swinging balance: of England's vacillating loyalties." She took breath to look anxiously at me. "He was writ to, about your marriage and such. Though he wrote often to his father, he never made any mention of it. Perhaps he disapproves of Lady Isabella."

And then more cheerfully, "But we are in great hopes of a pardon, that he may be released and continue his ministry in a wider world than that within the prison walls."

A wider world, where his ministry is proscribed, is counted a felonious crime and sometimes shakes hand with rebellion, is what I thought and did not say.

She patted my folded hands with her plump little own. "But you must take heart my dearest Jane. You must take some nourishment and try to stand and walk about your chamber." She looked as severe as ever she was able. "And then descend to attend upon your husband who is very disconsolate by reason of your indisposition." And on a final joyful note: "And I know there is an invitation come for you to pay a small visit to Dunnow. Your sister-in-law is carrying herself, and full of pity for you. And I am sure, do you ask John properly, that he will agree to your journey. And we can lend a servant to ride with you."

A better respite could not have been found for me – to be with Rick at Dunnow. Even his coarsened manners and profligate carousing were a relief after the strained fervour and loyalties of Samlesbury. And sweet Dorothy, full of care for me.

I felt that Red Rick was back to much of his old affectionate ways with me, until the morning that Dick Assheton arrived unexpectedly and with unusually grim demeanour. He came to ask my brother to bring some servants and some weapons, and ride back with him to Downham. There was big trouble brewing there and a crowd gathering upon the common, he reported:

"Even as I left there were folk coming in from Chatburn,

with ugly face and staves. I thought to stay then, but with my father so elderly, and Richie so weak and nervous, I felt that we needed some reinforcement before the crowd got bigger or uglier. So Red, if you will come straightway?"

The men clattered away with all rapidity. Dorothy sat herself in a rocking chair and I could see that she had no wish to discuss this alarming turn of events. But I could not prevent myself asking why the Assheton tenants, at least, would not defend the lords of their own manor.

Dorothy answered reluctantly: "It is the Downham men that will be found to be foremost in the fray. My father has taken in forty acres of the green. He has dug a deep ditch and erected a tall hedge to prevent the common pasturing and stop the pilfering of fuel. There was much murmuring at the time, but now that we move into winter—"

"And Christmas is soon upon us, and any Christian man would want to fatten a fowl – set a fire in his hearth."

Dorothy sat up straight, pulled the shawl about her shoulders. "You speak in disapproval of my father. The village men have called him covetous, and malicious, but you know very well that he is a kindly gentleman."

"I do not know the rights and wrongs at all Dorothy. Only if they cannot feed their beasts or warm their cottages, how can they live at all?"

We spoke no more about it.

Rick came back fatigued and much shaken. He took the heated ale they had ready for him, and stood before the hearth, frowning and drinking, as he unwound his story.

"It was truly a great crowd – much bigger than when Dickie left – and in foul mood. Many of them carried sticks and pitchforks, not actual weaponry, but to show they could take up a fight if they were minded. We stood our ground, Richie poor fellow just a tremble. The faces in that crowd, many I know, but changed, altered, hateful. A man who beat for us but two weeks ago, and all respectful to be given his dinner, today shaking a great thorn stick and glaring and shouting."

"Shouting? Shouting what, Rick?"

"Why that they wanted the land back, that it was common land, their rights anciently held, that none could close it in, that they should starve and I know not what else."

"And will they starve?"

My brother ignored me. "There were moments when they were fearsome and moments when they were quiet, like wind blowing over long grass. They changed almost in minutes, now listening to Dick, now to some scurvy fellow yelling insults at the lord of the manor. I know not whence this vile rebellious group springs. I hear of a strange ungodly sect at Grindleton, but nobody can find it out. And the witches were there – Chattox shaking and mumbling curses, only the mob drowned her out. But not Demdike. There's none can drown out that one."

His face hardened in remembrance: "It was one of those moments when the crowd is uncertain, moving this way and that. They might have been for turning home, when suddenly they opened ranks for her, to pass through to the front, as if she were a damned queen. It was Silly Jimmie led his grandmother by the hand, with that imbecile smile upon his face. God's Blood they should have been clapped in Bedlam, not suffered in public disputation."

He drank deeply, my furious brother. Dorothy and I neither moved nor spoke.

"She came right to the front to face us, Dickie, poor Richie and me. She seemed growed big, all in black rags, and fearsome with that long chin and hooky nose. Assheton had trouble not stepping back, and Richie shook like an aspen tree. I stood still, my men at the back. And she lifted her arm in the air, all the rags fell down and her arm was skinny, a long white bone. And her eyes were white too, white jellies rolling upwards to the sky, and she started to chant—"

He could not describe it, could not imitate the voice that Demdike used to make carry in a crowded market, or against the winter wind, the voice that put bread and sometimes meat on the table at Malkin Tower, the one power of that now ageing body, but he remembered her words:

> Them as close the land
> And clem the poor,
> Will meet death stalking
> In their own front door,
> Will see their own seed shrivel
> And lament full sore.

Dorothy, my dear pregnant sister, clapped her hand to her mouth, would have done with Rick's story. But I of course pushed him on. "And then?"

"Oh Assheton agreed to make another ditch halfway between, and leave the far side for common use and pasture. And they were dispersed with no blood shed, thank the Virgin's breasts for that."

"All's over then?"

"He's sent for Nowell to witness the agreement."

"Well Roger Nowell must be well used to this sort of thing. The Lords of Read have been fighting for rights over the turf moors at Read and Sabden since, I think, the queen came on the throne."

He was angered then. "Whose part are you taking now, my lady? Would you defend the rabble and the crones?"

But I was of no mind to play the little sister. "Enclosing land is a rapacious thing. We were taught to lament the fever of greed that swept the land when every catchpoll helped themselves to the treasure of the monasteries. But this grab of land from the very poor seems to me a wickeder thing."

"You are an idiot Jane! The poor are increasing like fleas and lice, and the vermin will eat us up if we do not enclose."

"Then you'll not be surprised if they bite sharp while you're doing it."

"Where did you learn such rebel thoughts? It comes from Alice Nutter, I'll be bound."

"I have no need to go to school to Alice Nutter to learn the thieving of great men. Judge Walmsley often said that the highest nobles are descended of the scurviest pirates."

"And included himself in that did he?"

"I am very sure he did!"

"You are a fool Jane." Rick turned away and thumped the fireplace. "I have not the patience to listen to you." And then he turned back. "You are always so . . . contrary. Contrary Mary, Disputing Jane." He sighed then and sat himself down. He gave me a long look that was somewhat melancholy.

> Jane, Jane, if you do not refrain
> Why and Wherefore will prove a fool's game.

I cannot say what of affection and what of irritation went into the rhyme, but we suddenly both realised that Dorothy was silently weeping. And both clumsily produced kerchiefs and kisses. She smiled wanly. "It is just that I am so afeard of that curse," she said, folding her hands, sheltering, over her belly.

Chapter 27

BETWEEN PUTTING DOWN THE QUILL last night and picking it up again, three years have run through my head. Three years of labouring in my garden orchard and producing no fruit of my own. While my serving woman waxed and waned like a plenteous moon. Lost and kept, and some were best lost, advised the kitchen.

Betty was the fount of information there, and I have observed that scraping vegetables is an occupation most likely to release a flow of reflection. I was informed, with apology, that it was no secret that Mary Sowerbutts still fished in the village pond, and was quickest off with her skirt behind a bush, even on the way home from work. That more than Thomas Sowerbutts might lay claim to her bairns, and Sowerbutts himself a brawler and a trouble maker, now lacking the protection of the old knight.

John did not reproach my sterility. I think he blamed himself. Like the old king, he had neglected his wisest counsellors to marry a woman that he craved, and found himself with a wife that he had ever cause to doubt. Rumours of dark magic still clung to the memory of Anne Boleyn. And if John could not very well chop off my head, neither could I dispel his ever recurrent suspicion.

I was not long returned from Dunnow – it was upon the Christmastide – that news was brought that poor Richie Assheton was dead, carried away in a fever of sudden onset.

Elizabeth Southern's cursing, and the near riot at Downham, were well known throughout the county, and

certainly in our house. I had heard Thomas Welshman
singing the tenants' song:

> *Sweet Jesus for thy mercy's sake*
> *And for thy bitter passion*
> *Save us aye the landlord's greed*
> *And that of Dickie Assheton.*

Yet I was not prepared to find among the gifts that
Rosamund brought for John, a small parcel of pressed herb,
which I guessed well enough to be pimpernel. I was truly
vexed. I lifted the little bunch by its dry withered stems.

"Pray what is this?"

Rosamund was all of a flurry, words falling over themselves. "'Tis but a little thing, the scarlet flower you know.
It is a holy herb, the colour of Christ's blood that he
shed upon the rood. I gathered it on holy ground where
Campion stood. It has several properties—"

"As protection against witchcraft?"

"He is a foolish boy, I know, to ask it of me. But it
is Richie Assheton's death has put us all in a shiver of
dread – and besides pimpernel is protection against other
infections."

"Richie Assheton's death can be ascribed to his always
frail constitution. But in any case has naught to do with
John, and naught to do with me."

"I know that Jane. I know that my son is taken with
silly fancies, but he does not really believe any of it.
Besides," she brightened suddenly, "it is a herb when flow-
ering might unlock your womb."

That was a painful jab to me, however harmless
Rosamund meant to be. But mayhap the withered little
bunch brought some benefit. Or could it have been the
words of Mary Snow? I came across her gathering oak
mast. She was always pleased to see me, though she kept

well clear of the Lower Hall. She had a little rag full of acorns that she shook and rattled to show me with childish pleasure. And it was like a child she recited her good wish:

> That acorn has long since fallen from the tree
> That grew the wood
> To make the cradle
> To rock the bairn
> That I'm promising to thee.

But I think it more like that my fortune changed for the words of Judge Walmsley.

I was upon my knees, grubbing in what was to be a knot garden, planting out small box hedging, when a single horseman came splashing across the ford. I was hailed by Judge Walmsley, riding a little mare as gaily caparisoned as himself. I rubbed the clay off my hands onto the sack apron and ran to meet him. He had me up behind him in a second.

We clattered into the forecourt, a rare sight I dare say – the elegant courtier and a most dishevelled woman. John was not amused, coming to welcome a clearly expected visitor. He led the judge with all deference into the parlour, making as if to dismiss me.

The judge flung tasselled gloves to the table. "Oh this is only the preamble John. I thought to run through the outlines of mortgage law for you. I do not touch on private matters."

"It is most kind of you sir. I am very obliged for your visit, but I think there is no need for my wife to be concerned with weighty matters of this nature." And to me he said, "You may leave us mistress. And be pleased to return in the half hour with refreshments for our guest. And change your dress."

That I should require to be given this order! That

I should be so spoke to before a man who cared for me! These moments I hold against you, John, more than I know they are worth. I changed into a decent gown and set a careful tray for Walmsley – the pale wine I knew he liked with sweetmeats, a tiny jug of forget-me-not flower I had sent Lily flying to fetch from the hedgerow.

They had finished business when I entered. The judge, leaning back in the winged chair, gazed appraisingly at the yellow wine, the flecked caraway cakes, and the blue flowers. "It is a pretty tray Jane, if a humble flower."

Lazily he took a glass, while his glance flickered briefly to the silver locket at my throat. "Good then John. I think we have covered the main points of your enquiry. Do not let me keep you if you have other matters upon the estate that require your attendance. Jane and I are old friends and we do have a very bookish womanish conversation I'm afraid."

Even after my own smart I felt for John's dismissal and the judge saw it in my face. He laughed, "Nay do not worry Jane. Your husband owes me large favours and is like to need more. John has not taken the wine. Do you have his glass."

He took out his tobacco box and I saw that I was to have the pleasure of his conversation. He looked at me thoughtfully. "Your husband is a trifle unmannerly. Is he always so curt with you?"

"I do fail to please him a great deal of the time."

"How so? Do you refuse him your bed?"

"Indeed no. I am always dutiful. John takes his tithes with regularity."

He laughed. "You have never recovered from the giant minstrel boy, is that it?"

I said with all dignity: "That springtime fancy is not the obstacle in my marriage, any more than the great love

I still bear my father. I do not think that one love must prevent another. Do you Judge Walmsley?"

"Ah," he smiled, "I think we should need to start defining terms precisely before I could enter into a judgement on that matter."

"Alice Nutter said to me once that there are as many ways of loving as stars in the sky, only half we do not know, and half we do not dare."

"Alice Nutter is a dangerous woman. Dangerous to herself. It is about Alice that I wished to speak with you. You love her do you not?"

"That is another way," I laughed. But he did not.

"We have had her brought up for examination. That is, Roger Nowell had her called before himself as justice, ostensibly on the grounds of some trivial boundary dispute, but he wished me to be there in case that graver matters should arise."

"What – what kind of graver matters? I have not seen Alice this long time. John would not allow a visit."

"Nowell has always tried to seek preferment through tracking down enemies of the Crown. His Catholic neighbours have proved too powerful, but there are other forms of religious disobedience in this kingdom. It was thought we had cleared out the Anabaptists, and some others. But rumour carries news faster than the queen's scouts, and Nowell's large nose was probably designed exclusively for sniffing out heresy."

"But Alice cannot be accused of heresy. She is a good Christian woman, law abiding and honest dealing, known for charity."

"Yes, it is difficult to frame accusation against her. But of course there are many of these little underground sects hereabouts. Some of them – the Family of Love for example – which certainly enjoin their members to fulfil the law in every outward aspect, to attend the reformed church and to pay their tithes, and yet maintain very odd persuasions as to the sharing of property, the equality of persons and even the liberty of the flesh, according to what I have read. Nowell has heard these things undoubtedly."

He continued to savour his smoking, while I tried to collect my thoughts, and then my words. "He has read of, knows of, such groups hereabouts, and searches them out?"

"I doubt he has familiarised himself with their doctrinal convictions in any detail, but he must have a general notion of those factions which represent a threat to our established religion, and hence to the state itself. And as I said, he has a very powerful nose."

"And Alice, was she able to show her innocence?"

"She did very well. It was of this Family of Love that Nowell had heard stories. He pressed her a little on her knowledge of their teachings. She took a very pious tone and expressed her singular devotion to the Holy Family of Jesus, Mary and Joseph. She did profess a humble ignorance on scholarly arguments attending the doctrine of the Immaculate Conception, but affirmed her confidence in venerating the holy household of our Blessed Lord. She even expatiated at some length on the virtuous and law abiding life to be found in the families of many artisans, carpenters and the like." His lips twisted in a smile. "She became quite tedious on the subject."

After a pause he added, "Oh Nowell brought up something about a Manchester cobbler, one of this Family, who it is said, for the sake of his beliefs, cherishes upward of a dozen wives. And then Alice became very lofty, thinking it a sorry mistake to suppose that only libertines would value liberty. The ball went back and forth and Alice held her part very sagely. And it was after all, only a conversation, if rather formally contrived."

"Then he will leave her alone," I lamely said.

Walmsley made an expansive gesture with his pipe: "Nowell like all good tracking dogs will return to the scent. And sedition is a capital crime. I would think – and I am sure you would agree with me, my dear Jane – that if anyone at this time should, by any freakish chance, come into possession of any of the documents, or books of preachments of these whimsical sects, there would be a very powerful necessity to get rid of them." He glanced up towards the smoke curling in the air, and his light voice became steely: "Get rid of them immediately, and altogether."

Before he left, he took me in a bear hug of an embrace. "Do better for your husband, Jane. And make us a manikin. For your adored father, give us a boy, and I'll give him a silver buckler and a sword." He tweaked my nose. "I'll do better than that, I'll give him a share of these," and he patted the fat wallet of documents on the table.

Chapter 28

Dear Alice,

*I write to tell you that I have commenced to make
a garden. I have grubbed up the nettles and intend
to plant many roses. Down here in the valley by the
running water it is much safer for flowers than in your
windy hills. But even here, in Samlesbury, is not the
climate for planting lilies, not at all, I find. You should
take care then what you choose to plant in Pendle.*

May God go with you,

Jane

I wished to keep my note both plain and short, so that she
would easily pick out the warning in the message, but then
I could not forbear to add an extra word:

*I have made an orchard also and the trees are of a size
now, so let us hope the Lower Hall will come to be a
fruitful demesne.*

They had indeed done well, apple, plum and pear. The
harvesting was my great pleasure. One day I was picking
plums, along with the Nightingales. It was a merry occupation, and John, returning from a ride, came to find the
source of so much laughter. I had a wide basket of fruit
cradled against my side. He came to relieve me and took
sudden sight of the bulge of my belly, the shape of my own

little growing thing. The look upon his face was so full of tenderness and hopefulness that my own heart contracted with affection. I nodded and leaned to kiss him over a basket of the sweetest plums in Lancashire.

We entered then upon one of those little periods of harmony and mutual caring that have from time to time imposed upon our married life. It was generous on his part to offer, "If we have made a boy child, Jane, I am sure you would like to name him after your own so much loved father." But I was resolute to help promote the concord in my new family. "Could we not name him Thomas? That surely would give pleasure to your own father." And so it was decided, and so it seemed I was become favourite again.

An answer came from Alice some time later in the autumn. She did not use the complicated message ways of the Family, but sent young Bess, who had to do with relatives in Preston. The girl arrived, jaunty as ever, her cap aquiver with riband, and I discovered that to have one humourist in the kitchen is a diversion, to have two is to invite the very spirit of distraction. I was not sorry that Ellen was absent on a visit to Turner Green, for I thought that Bess and Betty together would have imposed a severe strain on her sober authority.

It was a parcel of young trees – Carlisle Codlings – that Alice had sent for my orchard, along with a basket of the fruit, to show what harvest we might expect. Bess proceeded to discourse on their merits; that they were of good flavour and best of all for the big apple tarts. "Mistress Nutter would have you advised that they require parboiling first, else they will not fall softly."

Betty, not ready to be advised in her own kitchen, remarked with some disparagement on the tapering shape of these apples and Bess maintained that they were as good as any codpieces to be found in Carlisle. Which judgement Betty was prepared to agree with, observing that it would take more than a half stewing to persuade a Samlesbury cod into the falling sickness.

Their exchanges produced much laughter from the Nightingales who loitered near the kitchen jollity. Even Angelica, dawdling about picking up her washing, was grinning, her soundless mirth earning a part in the general merriment.

But Bess was not a girl to be bested. She turned her attention to the maids, suggesting that Lily should take some thought on her attachment to Will Gaunt, seeing as that young man was too fair of face and slender of shank to make a lively lover. Such a one, she opined, as might as well be expected to poke up the fire with a tassel.

"Ye may bate your breath Bess Whittle," the cook defended, "young Will Gaunt is as likely a lad and as well-endowed as any to be found in Pendle Forest."

Bess stood with arms akimbo. "Nay, you can't match Pendle men when it comes to the heave-ho. They're sturdy as oak trees and built with parts like mill posts!"

Betty laughed scornfully, "Piffling brag! From what I've heard, and from them as knows, those great mill posts come whittled down to pudden sticks, when asked to show their mettle."

All these pronouncements as to the relative vigour of local manhood were delivered with very much head tossing and eye flashing. And greeted with increasingly raucous pleasure by my women. But it seemed that Betty had won the bout, for Bess changed her tune to a darker note. Joan was warned to leave off dreaming of Tom Welshman. Bess had just come over the river and formed her own opinion of the ferryman. "That boatman is a singer not a stayer. And from what I hear tell, he's got himself right stickied up in a web could have the strangling of him, did he not take care."

Thinking that she spoke of Mary, I did make some little demur, but Betty was in full flow: "Why Mistress Southworth you did surely know that there's a dark flame lit between that ferryman and Mary Sowerbutts, for all that he drinks many times with her own husband, so hot a flame it could burn your cheek off, here in this kitchen."

Joan protested. "It is not Tom – it is her, it is Mary's fault. She lies in wait—"

Betty warmly supported this view, "'Tis true she is a spider with an ever open web – for any fly."

"And a drunken cunt needs no porter," Bess declared with the loftiness of aphorism.

At which I judged the flavour of the gossip grown too rank. I gave Bess a shilling and sent her on her way.

But in the apple basket I found a small note from Alice:

Dearest Jane,

I understand and heed your advice. There are indeed cold winds blowing here at this time. I rejoice to hear of your fertile garden, and only for fear of reading too much between the lines, have still kept hold of a lamb-swool shawl that I have always meant for you.

Bess certainly carried confirmation of my condition back into Pendle, for the shawl came in good time. It has served all my babies and still as soft as thistledown.

And my son came in good time also, loud and bawling and blessedly strong. And I thought that we Southworths were bound for a halcyon period of good will, which did indeed last until the christening of this so-welcomed Thomas. Perhaps it is not always the dame who turns the wheel. Mayhap a wicked goblin takes pleasure in bouncing up and down the seesaw of peace and dissension. We came down with a thump. Right in the midst of a day of celebration, Thomas puffed with pleasure for his namesake, Rosemary ababble with affection, and John at last able to be proud of me. And my sweet Tom, all curling fingers and snubnosed as his father, teaching me a new thing, a protectiveness near wolfish in intensity.

The sweetmeats and wine were not yet cleared away, and the faithful Catholic gentry friends only just departing, when I heard voices raised in anger. I returned to the dining hall to see Thomas standing like a stag at bay, his face reddened, his voice unaccustomedly loud.

"No, I will not. I will not give way on this. The seminarians I go on sheltering cost us dear. I have already paid a prince's ransom in fines, our house betrayed, ransacked, battered. But these few at least persist in professing loyalty to the sovereign. They are not openly seditious, or known for it. But not Thurston Hunt. Him I will not tolerate under my roof. Priest he may be, but troublemaker he certainly is, and lawbreaker, and stirrer of contention and riot."

John for lack of immediate vocabulary, banged his fist upon the table. "The man is holy – a warrior for Christ. He risks all – does all."

"All," his father gave a bitter laugh, "aye all, all of the old families, all of our own safety."

"Who else will lead us back to Christ?" John was remembering his teachers, "Who else will take us from the grip of an heretic excommunicate queen, and reinstate our true and ancient faith?"

Thomas dropped his voice: "That is treason. You must know that what you speak is capital treason."

My husband laughed, a harsh laugh that I did not know in him. "If it is treason to speculate on the number of her birthdays, or the thickness of her paint, then treason is a crime hardly to be avoided."

Thomas's face was all dismay. "Where did you learn to sneer like that? Where did you learn such cynical humour? You had better wash out your mouth if you cannot cleanse your heart. And rid yourself of these wild notions, and wilder friends. Or you will end with your neck bent."

"I do not fear the scaffold, but I fear the death of mine own soul." John said his heroic piece, his learned bit, and then began to speak earnestly in his own words, the padlock on his speech released at last by the key of anger.

"He is the one man, the only one who can succeed in this venture. He has a name for trouble because he is valiant and eager for any fray in the name of Christ our Lord. And he can bring it to a safe conclusion. He has the knowledge of the castle, he knows what pockets to line, and he has daring. And he can, and only he can, rescue them. Do you care nothing for the holy men who languish there? Are you truly indifferent to the fate of your own brother?"

"John," his father pleaded now, "I have this estate in trust, if not for you, then for your children and theirs. We have done more than our part. Great God, we will be begging for parish relief if this goes on. To have Thurston Hunt in the house is to invite every spy and informer in Lancashire to busy themselves about us. I will not have him and I will not budge."

I saw the look of angry bafflement on John's face and I dreaded his next words. But he spoke quietly enough. "Then he shall come to the Lower Hall. There are still those in Samlesbury who can keep faith." He strode out of his father's hall and was mounted and gone before I had started to collect up my babe and nursemaid.

I rode back slowly with Lily, all the while pondering

on what might come of John's decision. We had poor facilities for shelter compared with Samlesbury Hall. The hiding hole under the main staircase, opening from a loose tread, was an emergency bolt hole only, not a place a man can occupy for any length of time, no genius invention of Nicholas Owen. And the busy ford made the house a dangerous and public place to hide a fugitive. But who in any case was this Thurston Hunt?

I did not wait long to find out.

Chapter 29

THURSTON HUNT was the most restless man I have ever met. When he was not scratching his ear, he was pulling his beard or biting his thumb. If he sat still, he was tap-tapping with his foot. When he looked at me, his uneasy gaze would flit over and past, as if he searched for secrets behind. For secrets were his trade. He and John were in constant close conversation. And I was the more uneasy as I had now my new jewel to protect.

John of course would not make me privy to their discussions, but I could guess well enough that they planned a prison break from Wisbech Castle. And what I did not know, Rosamund was more than willing to tell me. Her view of the priest was, like so many of her feelings, midway between the opinions of husband and son.

"He is a very valiant man, all agree that he is daring and resourceful, and has contrived many wild escapes. But he preaches so strong against the queen as is not to be borne. There is agitation, wherever he walks, and wherever he walks he is in mortal danger."

Rosamund even knew, or guessed, which men were envisaged to be escaped :- Christopher Southworth of course, a priest called little Robert Middleton, and one of already known renown: Robert Nutter.

"Kinsman to Alice Nutter?" I enquired.

"He may well be. He is elder brother to that John Nutter, hung and dismembered at Tyburn past ten years ago. It was John Nutter carried a great chest of catechisms

– washed up by the sea when the ship was wrecked and used in evidence against him."

"And this Robert—"

"Imagine, Jane, before they dragged the sainted John to Tyburn, he was discovered by his brother Robert in the Tower, also imprisoned."

"But—"

"No, only think, to be thrust into the very Pit and there find your own dear brother lying tortured and manacled in that stinking dark. It is beyond belief. But yet so joyous to be reunited, to give love and consolation before John was heaved away to claim his martyr's crown."

"And this Robert, he must have been tortured also?"

"Survived the torture, survived the Pit, survived the Scavenger's Daughter!" Rosamund was triumphant.

"Crushed in an iron corselet, and lived to tell the tale?"

"He is known to be most strong and most courageous, and yearning to continue his ministry – is what is said. He must be of great comfort to our Christopher."

"God preserve them," I sighed.

"God preserve and deliver them," said Rosamund firmly.

❋❋❋

Some of my nights are short because the daily duties which now claim my attention are arduous, or simply eat the hours away. And some of my pieces are short because I have not the will, because I am daunted by the effort of looking into my heart and writing always the truth.

Chapter 30

I SHOULD HAVE BEEN PREPARED, should have been ready, but yet I was taken by surprise that windy night, when the melancholy howling of the chimney was cut by sharp, urgent knocking.

It was John Singleton brought them in, John Singleton my ancient enemy. My husband, at the door in seconds, sharply commanding, "Prepare your sewing room, Jane. It is the nearest to a secret place we have. Have fuel sent up, and meat."

I went to the kitchen to give orders, while four cloaked figures were hustled up the stair. John Singleton embraced my John before he departed in all haste.

My low sewing room under the eaves fairly over-flowed with shapes of men in dark and concealing apparel, badly illumined by the one candle which John, by order of Thurston Hunt, refused to augment. I poured wine for Hunt, noting how his constant stirring was much quieted by the triumph of his enterprise, and, I must suppose, by fatigue. A small and dainty featured man accepted his ration with a gentle, shy smile. Christopher Southworth, his face drawn and eyes shining as with fever, trembled most violently when he took the cup. The fourth priest was as sturdily built as a bear, with bulky shoulders, a heavy neck, and a thick clout of dark hair, marked with a streak of white like a magpie's wing. He accepted his drink with a slow repeating nod.

"Christopher is ill," said John. "Please have a pallet made up straight away." As I went to fetch blankets and quilts he followed me into the closet. "Not a word. Not one word from my talkative wife to these men who have been snatched from the belly of the prison?"

I know I faltered in my speech. "I am sorry John – I was not prepared, I am not prepared. I will go back to beg a blessing. But how much am I supposed to know? How much do I know? What are your intentions? This is very dangerous work."

"You shame me Jane. Our souls were in danger, but not now. Now we have a fountain of holiness, here in our house. We are honoured in our guests above any house in the kingdom."

"You mean to keep them, the priests – how long?"

He gave me no answer. I did indeed feel shamed. I had never before known such a reluctance to share some of the danger of these devoted souls, never known such a slowness to harbour fugitives beneath my roof. I, who from earliest childhood had been privy to the seclusion of holy outlaws. It was the babe asleep in the cradle in the kitchen below which so strongly urged me towards paths of safety and peace. But I was shamed, not for lack of courage only, but for lack of courtesy.

When I returned the fire was well burned up. They had cast their outer cloaks and sat about, eating and conversing quietly. Christopher was already lying on the pallet.

The big man rose to greet me. "Our thanks to you Mistress Southworth. We have travelled hard and what with fatigue and unknowing, we are late in our proper thanks." He indicated fire and feast, but I interrupted quickly: "I would ask a blessing, sir, but I know not of whom I ask that favour."

Thurston leaned forward quickly. "It is sainted Robert Nutter stands before you Mistress Southworth."

The sainted one shook his head, "It is you mistress,

who gives the blessing of refuge and refreshment. But I will bless you in the name of Christ if you will kneel."

I knelt there before the fire. And I knew well what brassy reflections the firelight could make in my hair. I knew how many pairs of eyes were upon me, Christopher's glittering in the corner shadow. But I affected as sober and as humble a demeanour as anyone could wish. This was not a difficult part to play.

The men were weary beyond extreme, except Thurston Hunt, who clung to rehearsing to John the outlines of their undertaking, a geography I could not follow. But when we gained our bedchamber I questioned John. I asked him, asked again, how long these guests should stay.

"Your solicitude, is it for yourself or for these holy men?"

"In truth for both." I spoke carefully. "It is a wonderful, a miraculous escape that they have made."

"It is thanks to Thurston Hunt, who had so delved and thought and planned the execution of it to every last detail."

"And to Almighty God, who has brought his servants out of bondage. But it were a fool trick to deliver them straight into recapture."

That did not please my husband, but I had my word to say.

"Even at Stonyhurst, in that large house and protected by my father's fame and power, we were very careful of the priests. We had them singly for the most part. Whenever two or more are gathered the risks of discovery are so much the greater. And that was before the harbouring of priests had been decreed an act of capital felony, and a hanging offence."

"It is for your own neck that you fear. I am not proud of you Jane, or of your lukewarm welcome. These men are more necessary to our souls than food is to our bodies. You should be down on your knees in gratitude that they grace our house."

I had my fight to win. "I did not know that I was luke-warm. And if so I shall mend it on the morrow. But our safety is not separable from their safety. Where shall the constables first look for Christopher Southworth but in Samlesbury Great Hall, and then with us, in the Lower? He must be most endangered, being nearest his own family."

He could not neglect my sense, my husband, little as he liked my words. "I shall speak with Thurston tomorrow early, and even reflect on what you say. But I had hoped you could rejoice with me in this great exploit."

"I do John," I lied, and climbed with no great grace into his bed.

❋ ❋ ❋

It was already decided by the morning. The men had risen early for prayer and confabulation. Christopher pronounced himself stronger and fit for travel. Safer lodgings awaited him in Yorkshire. The diminutive Father Robert Middleton would accompany him there, and then journey further on alone. Robert Nutter would stay some few days longer in Samlesbury.

They left as swift and secret as they had come, carrying away with them a great portion of the risk I had dreaded. Robert Nutter was a very patient house guest. He mostly kept to my little room, although we had the most faithful of servants. We made an altar of sorts from my sewing chests and tables, and he celebrated mass each day, each pale grey March morning. Just once we were joined by an outsider. Edward Osbaldeston, a quiet scholarly neighbour of ours, contrived to hear the mass with us, himself no stranger to Catholic concealments.

The priest himself was content to stay aloof from the household and yet I knew the whole house heartbeat to his presence. I am always a divided soul. Which Alice so well knew. I had thought that nothing could overshadow the passion I felt for the babe that I nursed at my breast. But an undershadow had entered the house and crept upon me. The knowledge of that broadbuilt man in the attic room, waiting in quiet possession of his soul, steadfast in his mission, grew in my mind. And with it grew a curiosity and a desire that was not possible to assuage – by any virtuous means I knew.

I know of course that impure thoughts may invade the most unwilling innocent mind. And that sins dreamed in sleep do not blacken the helpless virtue. But I am not such a fool as not to know that all occasion of sin is to be avoided, in case a gentle temptation leads to outright trespass.

So at the first I did not wait upon Robert Nutter with overmuch assiduity, but since I could not slight our guest neither, nor fail to honour my husband's wishes, I did perform some general service, without thrusting my presence on him.

We had not many books for him – I think he prayed a great deal. And had some cheerful talk with John, as to itineraries and safe houses. I think he often stood by the tiny window in the roof space, which he kept open despite the cold, looking out upon freedom. That was where he stood, lost in thought, one day when I came to the room with a parcel of clean linen. He was gazing at the river which, leaden-grey and swollen with spring water, was beating a rapid course past the house. I stood behind him, seeing with his eyes – alder and willow just starting to dangle silky catkins, and in the woods beyond the river, there was the tawny haze that is composed of the embryos of many leaves, needing a month or more to break into a spring green riot.

I said, "It is a pity you cannot walk out, Father."

He turned with almost a smile. "I make no complaint Mistress Southworth. The air is sweet and damp, with this expectancy of spring. And I am glad indeed to be in my native county. And preparing for the fray." He comically squared his shoulders.

I said quietly, "You sat very long in prison?"

The smile flitted away as if a cloud had passed over. "We must be tested to serve Our Lord. We would all wish to be about his business, spreading the Holy Word, enfolding our people within the mantle of the true Church of Christ, but if it is His will to have us walled up in confinement, it is perhaps to temper the steel, that we may be fierce and bright swords, to strike the clearer for Him."

I put the linen down, and I said low, as I straightened it, "But they sing of Campion, that he was 'of that noble train, that fight with words and not with swords, for Christ their Capitaine.'"

In his look I had a hint of how he might be angry, but he spoke evenly: "I spoke in metaphor. It was the spiritual battlefield to which I was referring."

"Of course, I know Father." Even though he might think me clumsy and stupid, I did not withdraw. "But there are those who would wrench our country to constancy by violent means. And I would think you must find it very hard to be patient when you have so much endured."

"Our mission is to the faithful, to strengthen and sustain them. We do not consort with violent politicians, nor occupy ourselves with plots and treasons." And then suddenly less lofty, but scrutinizing my face, "Are you testing me Mistress Southworth?"

Then I did retreat. "Ah no, I pray you, forgive me. I wanted to beg a confession of you, and I am already beforehand, turning over in my mind my own anxieties and doubts."

"Your husband has no such confusions."

"I know." I prepared to leave, but I had a last word to say. "My father was a great knight of the shire. He conformed and yet kept faith, and he protected his family. Somehow I fumble in my thoughts towards his solution, now that I have a babe to care for."

"You had better take care of your soul's salvation, Mistress Southworth. The pope has pronounced most severely against such accommodations as your father practised. It were no gift to your babe to have a wavering mother. Come let me hear your confession that Christ's grace may stream into your soul and strengthen your fidelity and courage." He made a gesture that I should kneel, and took a chair beside me.

I made a confession of sorts, worthless by reason of what I did not confess.

He leaned upon the arm of his chair, his hand before his eyes. I wondered where his thoughts flew, while I recited such minor misdemeanours as I could bring to mind.

Chapter 31

IN MY HEYDAY AND HIGH DAYS, and especially when John Spencer was paying his attentions to me, I read a great deal in courtly love poetry. We played a game, competing who could find the prettiest, or most foolish, conceit with which a troubadour would woo his mistress, the cunningest argument to purchase concession of her greatest favour.

So many I remember – how she was exhorted against the wasteful hoarding of her beauties, to be not a ring without a finger, nor a cage without a bird, nor a rose fallen all ungathered and undelighted in. She was warned that her treasure should not be miserly abused in hiding, nor like gold unused, left to tarnish. And the oft reminder that most pleased me, that sweet lute strings harshly jar if left untuned, untouched. All these and other examplars to prove the lover's case against empty and heartless virginity.

Why might not I then turn a table and lament in similar vein the wastage of chill celibacy? Make complaint of such heroic flame and muscle cramped in a hermit's garb, a fine wine yielding no pleasure but slowly souring in dark vaults?

If vestal virgins are besought to broach their sacred vows, could not I then try to make assault upon the harsh abstinence of a Roman priest?

I still kept the copy of *Venus and Adonis* at the bottom of my linen chest alongside a little silver pomander and a scrap of jewelled lace. I could not fetch it out to read it, but

I remembered it well enough. Remembered the pleading entreaty of the goddess. For like a woman, she could only offer to be taken, lacking the force that violators have.

These were fantasies, fanciful thoughts only, that I indulged. My passion for the prisoner within my walls I kept under lock and key, not from virtue only, but from fear of haughty rejection. For we were become good friends. He had forgiven my impertinence, oh before ever I finished my imperfect confession, I do believe, and was not slow to engage me in conversation when I came into his room for some domestic chore.

One time I caught him in contemplation of the river. I told him a tale was told of a fugitive like himself, who had escaped from our house by swimming the river, and that still robed in vestments for the mass.

We both looked at the grey, heaving humps of water moving powerfully past. He laughed and said, "I should have to be very afraid of the searchers to cast myself into that wild water."

"Better the merciful Ribble than the merciless prison," I daintily observed.

"Yes," he agreed, "it would be a preferable death to some I have skirted."

"Pray God you have no such necessity at this time. Pray God we keep you safe Father."

His smile then was gentle, as was his voice. "Safety is not all Mistress Southworth. But I have treasured these days in your safekeeping."

Safekeeping. That was how I thought of our charge and how I reconciled myself to the risks he made us run, and the minor role that I must play. But I was forced to lend him to the great hall, and Thomas forced to open the chapel, when news of his presence had filtered into the community.

It was a sombre chapel at the best, and he himself was robed in Lenten purple and gold, costly vestments that the old knight had managed to secrete. He spoke not long but movingly to confirm the faith of those trusted friends who had come to hear him. So robed and venerated, I felt him to have become both strange to me, and yet familiar, as one of the long line of secret celebrants who graced my childhood home, holding fast our souls, while we oftimes held fast our breath for fear.

As on this occasion the devout assembly was rudely disturbed by a loud knocking on the big door. Thomas was already with his hand on the priest's arm to lead him to safety, when John Singleton returned in haste to pacify the company.

"'Tis nothing, nothing but a tardy tenant come to beg a blessing."

Our collective breath escaped as from a long-stoppered bottle, and all spoke together, laughed and smiled. I doubt I smiled, for a small inward voice was repeating,

> *This game is not worth the candle, the candle,*
> *This game is not worth the candle.*

I could not tell in that moment did I want him most to leave or stay.

I wanted most for him to leave.

The day before his departure the kitchen girls were much occupied helping bake provisions that would last an uncertain journey. And I was busied making over some of John's garments for him. My husband was no puny fellow, but his clothes were like to burst at the seams when stretched upon the frame of our burly missionary. I measured doublet and jerkin over the length and breadth of him. It was a strange and painful pleasure to me, but my most unruly thoughts were quelled by the sight of a webbing of thick cicatrice on his wrists and forearms. "Manacles," I murmured as I inadvertently pushed up his sleeve. "You must have worn them bitterly long, Father, to keep such scars."

"Oh," he said, to lighten my sorrowful gaze, "why long enough to polish off the rust and end with shining fetters. A housewife like yourself might have been proud of me, Mistress Southworth."

And seeing I would not smile, he went on, just partially in jest: "And they had uses too. In the Tower I was not always laid next holy men. So when the prisoners grew noisome, I could always clank my chains, loud enough to drown out the bawdy songs that are not suitable for a priest's conversation. But like to hurt his soul."

I cut and sewed the cloth, glad of the occupation, the while I pondered what a few loose words could do, to make a mark on one suffering so terribly in the flesh.

"Which was the worser of your hurts?" I asked.

"The worst," he said, deliberating, "was the wasteful pouring past of hours, when I was eager to be out and about my Lord's business."

Oh, he was caught in a clasp stricter than the Scavenger's Daughter. What could one red-haired wench plead against the Iron Maiden of vocation? Against the siren of crusade? I could not have him, any more than Venus could win her relief. Adonis, that fair youth, fled her soft arms, to perish on the tusks of a wild boar, in a hunt he had preferred to the goddess' embrace. But Robert Nutter, leaving our sheltering house for a different chase, became not the hunter but the hunted, the quarry of royal hounds.

Chapter 32

AND THE HUNT DID NOT TAKE LONG. It was a very little time before my husband was raging through the house, shouting and weeping that Robert Nutter was taken. Was recaptured. On the open highway, quiet dressed, riding with one other gentleman, seized and thrust into Lancaster Castle.

"He was looked for, I am certain. He sits already in Lancaster. He has been betrayed. By whom?"

Betrayed. He even hurled the word at me, but stayed still when he saw what must have been my dreadful face.

"By no one in this house," I contrived to say, before the knot in my throat gave way into a horrid wail of mourning. Which frighted me as much as my husband.

John, contrite straight way, and reading only faithfulness into my infidelity, was making apology that he had not known how reverent, how deep was my devotion to our tragic guest. And he would go, staunch John, he was resolved to go, to Lancaster, to bear witness to what could be no less than execution.

Rosamund and Thomas were also firm to go. Is this our modern way of making pilgrimage, now that the old saints are denied us?

Rosamund particularly was all exaltation. She would have me go along – she could easily find a good wet nurse in the village, or was I not already drying up in any case? Though she had no great concern, it was of no great moment, for did not prolonged nursing prevent more conceptions, and as we all must hope for—

I was forced to interrupt the flow to say that no, I was not minded to be present at his death, not for any reason whatsoever.

Which reasons she of course could not forbear to give me. "But Jane is it not better that his own people be among the crowd? To stand upon the gallows with only enemies about is very hard. And we could catch any last words he has to say. And we may succeed to get some parts, some keepsake; it is but to do him honour—"

She was persisting as John took her elbow to lead her into the parlour, away from me.

He did plainly have some inkling of the pain I was in, despite the gulf of understanding between us. He spoke to me kindly enough that evening. "You must not grieve so terribly Jane. He will have his martyr's crown which he has so ardently desired."

I had no argument to put to that, but I could not be persuaded to go to witness his winning of it.

I spent that day alone for the most part, the Nightingales delighted to be given full charge of my child. When I walked down to the river I found a bright spring day had broken out about me. A group of wild swans were pursuing their absurd courtship rituals on a suddenly placid water. It seemed that all nature was rejoicing and carelessly indifferent to what was happening a few miles north. Only the lightest of winds was ruffling the new pale greenery, but I thought that it carried across the river echoes from the streets of Lancaster. I have seen the crowd at a bearbait, heard the gluttonous roar that greets the tearing of the flesh, a sound more feral than the dying beast. I am an oddity I know, but I never could endure it. And now I cannot endure at any price the thought of what entertainment the populace might find in the dismemberment of a living human. Of a body I have never been allowed to know.

And still the little wind brought the faint surges of cries to my imagining. I felt helpless in my grief, grief turned to a dull anger that I knew not where to hurl it. Against the throne of a woman who is, according to my husband, 'queen killer and priest killer'? Or against the weathercock of state that decreed that first one and then the other, was the faith we should die for?

But my black reverie was interrupted by the approach of a quiet man. My neighbour Osbaldeston broke off his botanical ramble to come and sit by me. We spoke no word for a while and then with great gentleness he said, "He is fled the rack of this harsh life. He is in the bosom of Christ. He has exchanged the trish-trash of this life for an unfading jewel."

I only said, "Nay, it is not trish-trash to me."

❊❊❊

Perhaps it is because Rosamund talks at such length and such speed, that she has never leisure to observe the effect of her words. She was in a flurry of emotion when she returned from Lancaster, and determined to tell her story to the end.

"Ah Jane, he went so resolutely and cheerfully to his holy death. He mounted into the hanging cart as swiftly and willingly as a bridegroom to the feast. And I am sure the hangman was merciful and hanged him strongly, for he made no sound in the quartering, none that we could hear."

I turned from her, I made to leave, but she most deliberately stayed me.

"I brought it for you, Jane, a precious keepsake, knowing how grieved you were and had so carefully sheltered him. It was not easy neither. They kept the folk well back, even used some men with halberds. Perhaps they feared an escape at the very last. But afterwards some of us surged forward and broke past the soldiers. There was little time, and folk were rough in their hurry, for I swear I near had his hand. They pulled me off but I kept it" – she was so innocent in her triumph – "I kept this little bit of finger."

Then she unwrapped the most precious thing she could think to give me, wrapped in a best lawn kerchief that had got smudged with black ash. A very little bone from such a big man. A little bone that put me sharply in mind of another relic I had been given. And in my head the sing-song voice rang:

> Here is a charm
> To keep you from harm.

And I puzzled to myself as to wherein really lay the difference between these hoardings of remains.

Chapter 33

SO BRIEF A TIME FROM FUNERAL – a little month, one short passage of the moon, and the world is issuing demands for attention. A score and eight of days, long days and short stolen nights. I have snatched but eight pieces of my narrative from the reclaiming hand of daily life. But all is not lost – for I am decreed unwell.

This time I make no pretence. I am unsteady on my pins – I am pasty pale, I am thinner than a bit of string, my eyes are startling and my whole mien disquieting. So saith my mother-in-law, and my sister-in-law. And I am sent out to Dunnow to be loved and cared for. Dorothy even keeps her children from disturbing me. I have long empty days of grace and no one to disapprove my chronicle.

I know that on my return I take up the daily duties of mistress and mother, and I will have an estate to attend to and perhaps remedy some of my husband's negligent stewardship. Knowing this I hasten to reach my story's end, since John's departure should have given me my full stop.

***

I forge ahead, but when I try to recollect periods of mourning it is always the dragging of time that I remember. That was such a summer, of mixed and sultry weather, often expectant for storm. Perhaps because I was myself expectant, time moved very heavily. I often took myself to the water's edge to see the last of the orange sun throwing its gleam across the river, flushing up the sky. And lost myself in a nothingness of thought. My husband in all this time was kindly with me, pleased at the oncoming of another child, and Tom such a brave bonny infant. John brought me delicate fruits, those I had not yet planted in my garden – apricots and greengage. He even agreed to sleep apart from me on very hot nights when I was sickly and uncomfortable. On such nights I would toss about, uneasily awaiting an early dawn.

It was from such a light sleep that I was awakened by the commotion of a summer storm. I lay awake counting the seconds between the tumbling thunder and the jagged arrows of lightning flashing outside my window, until I became aware of other sounds in the intervals, sounds that had nought to do with the growl and flash of storm.

I went down to the kitchen. From the doorway I could make out the shapes of outbuildings and what seemed a crowd of people moving about the yard. For a moment I saw only this dark confusion and then the scene leapt into the sudden fantastic illumination of white lightning, and I snatched glimpses of men carrying crates off a cart, of my husband holding several horses and gesturing, and Thurston Hunt, legs spread wide, in the centre of our yard, directing the operation, as if the thunderstorm and all the heavenly tumult were his, to his command. Even as I watched large drops began to patter, and then the sluices opened and the immoderate rain of this sudden turbulence cascaded down, drowning out the sight and sounds of strange nocturnal activity.

I returned to my bed, quite far from sleep, full of apprehension and curiosity. The hissing downpour ceased as abruptly as it had begun. The storm rumbled away into the distance, as I could hear horses and carts departing. John came back to his chamber and I crept down the stairs.

The cobbles shone in the light of a chastened moon, peering through the tails of storm clouds, to see what human foolishness was now abroad. I saw that the big barn door was padlocked, but I knew where the boards were loose and easy to squeeze through. I was not yet so much grown in the belly. Enough moonlight slid through the gaps of tiles to show me the storage of a quantity of chests, some strong and new, some old and barely lidded, or even just covered with sacking. It took me no time to discover that this was a provision of weaponry, of halberds and pikes and muskets, enough I guessed to equip a serious adventure.

My mind was in a turmoil as I crept back, a turmoil not in any way alleviated by finding my husband waiting in the chair by my bed. His face was hard; all tenderness wiped away.

"I have long feared we had a spy in the house. By Christ you were quick, or else alerted, to sniff our doings in the stable."

I began to shiver despite the night's summer heat. "What in the name of Almighty God are you about John? On what fool trip does Thurston Hunt persuade you?"

"Oh I am sure you would be glad of more information for your masters, but I am not such a fool as to tell you. All I will tell you is this: that I will flog the skin from your back if you breathe a word of what you found in the barn." You were ever thus, my dear departed, ever requiring a flood of rage to loose a flow of words. But if you were inflamed, I was all of ice.

"Your threats are as stupid as your suspicions. I am no informer. Where would I inform? To whom would I inform?"

"You have the means to pass messages, you and your lettered servant. These are dangerous times, treachery is on all sides and double dealing everywhere."

"I cannot believe how that man has addled your brain. I am a virtuous wife and mother. I strive only to keep the peace, which you, I perceive, are bent on troubling."

"The peace, the queen's peace, is but an acquiescence in apostasy, in tyranny, for those content to bend the knee and bow the head before the boot of London. There are still some good men and true, not terrified to spill their blood in defence of that faith for which Robert Nutter gave his life."

"Then go spill your blood, John. Go to Ireland and be a rebel with Essex' men. Go to Douai and learn to be a martyr. But for pity's sake leave me here in peace to guard and love and protect your children. The children God has sent us."

That stayed him somewhat, as it was meant to. I moved behind his chair, placing my hands upon his shoulders, so he should not feel outfaced, but might feel the pressure of entreaty.

"And to protect your good name and fair fame. For you are a good man, John. I am well placed to know it. Not to preserve yourself, but for the sake of this sweet family, I beg you to desist from any hazardous schemes."

I leaned his wet head against me, there where he knew the child was growing, and at length he threw his arms around me, and begged my pardon, and in short space was able to assuage his confusions in my body, and though I was in some fear for the child, I did warmly use him.

It was always the way with us, toing and froing. Once when I was a child, Rick gave me a fledgling hawk that was damaged and useless to the falconers. I took it for a pet, but not being sufficiently skilled I had small success. I gentled it somewhat but never tamed it. At times it might feed from my hand, and at others, unaccountably, would dash from me, perch out of reach, and then from gold-rimmed orbs he would eye me with inextinguishable suspicion. So it seemed with John. Sometimes I would persuade him, by lust or logic, into my arms, but he would, upon a trick of fate, stand suddenly apart and eye me, like the hawk, with an invincible distrust.

Chapter 34

THE VISIT OF SIR RICHARD HOGHTON was as unexpected as it was unwelcome to some of us. He had never visited Lower Hall before, and on the day he chose, we were all taken up with jam-making. I was not really required in this great endeavour, but I had been lured to the kitchen by the hot sweet smell of boiling fruit. And to enjoy seeing my small son happily besmirched with blackberry.

It was Joe Little came running to tell that a noble retinue had crossed the ford, and was approaching the dower house. Despite his breathless forewarning I scarce had time to wipe my face before the noble lord, with a crowd of men at arms, was at our door, being greeted by my evidently perturbed husband. I remember how splendid he was that day, Richard Hoghton, in sable velvet and ermine and a monstrous great medallion studded with ruby. He so far outshone our house that I ceased to care for my smeary apron and escaped hair, but welcomed him with good grace.

John was stammering an invitation to dine, whilst I was passing through my mind the present provision in our house for such entertainment. The knight waved aside John's invitation, instructing his fellows to proceed to the alehouse.

He turned to me, "A cup of wine will do, but send the servant." And returning to John, "I wish to have conference with your wife as well as yourself, John."

And in the parlour he did not sit to commence his tale. "I am come upon a serious matter. I am just back from Garstang, where we have been making investigations into a riot. The vicar there is a godly man who was making efforts to compel his parishioners into a proper obedience for the queen's law. He also has been insisting on church tithes and on attendance. We have been obliged to make arrests of Catholics in that parish who make resistance to this country's laws. And because they are such naughty men in Garstang, and in order to strengthen the cause of good religion, he has lodged with him one of the queen's preachers, sent into Lancashire to combat heresy and superstition in this county."

I observed how his lordly, well-remembered nostrils quivered with impatience, as I attempted furtively to remove my apron.

"Two nights ago the pious man was awakened by musket shots fired against his own house. He went to the window, whereupon another gun was fired, and this time he was very close to being hit. Fearing real danger then, he drew in, and sent his servant into the yard. This man was then shot at, but by good fortune the bullets lodged in the door, where it is plain to see how they continued firing – a veritable pepper pot was made of it."

Joan Nightingale brought in a tray and I relieved her.

"Neither the vicar nor his noble guest managed to see the faces of any of their assailants. We have questioned many of the villagers, but all retain an obstinate silence."

Silence prevailed also in our parlour.

"It is my information and conviction moreover that all this hue and cry is at the instigation of a seminarian, one Thurston Hunt, an evil man for the fomenting of upheaval and conspiracy, and a thorn in my particular side."

I did not look at John and I suppose he gazed at Sir Richard.

"I break my journey here to enquire of you, John, and you also Jane, who must have an ear in the kitchen. Has he been known to be in this neighbourhood? Do you have any scent of him?"

"No – no, we have not. I do not know of such a name." John spoke lamely, looking as awkward as he felt. Lies did not sit easily upon him. Hoghton held his portentous silence. John cast about him, sending me a glance of petition, I thought. And yet I felt almost derision for this husband, who was so hot for conspiracy, yet so miserably unable to dissemble.

I very slowly, thoughtfully began to pour the wine, as if ruminating on his words. And I spoke with care: "There are still any number of priests 'lurking' in Lancashire, as I am sure you know Sir Richard, and when we come upon traces of them, we do turn aside and make a blind eye, for some are good old men and would not make trouble on the estates. The old tenants often have a longing to be buried as their fathers were, to hear a catholic prayer, when they are in need of consolation. But they are not men to lead a mob such as you describe, nor I think is" – and here I hesitated – "Thurston Hunt, a name one would easily forget, though doubtless he will have aliases."

"He has aliases but they serve no purpose. For such a turbulent man as he will not easily be mistaken. I would be glad if you would listen out for rumour of his whereabouts. We are damnably short of evidence. No one will speak, though many admit – cannot avoid admitting – having seen a heavily armed raiding party on its way to Garstang. But no one, not even the vicar himself, is able to identify any member of it. But we will catch him. I have given my promise, a promise in high places. By the year end we will have him."

I presented the goblet with all the grace I could muster. "I wish you all success, Sir Richard. If Thurston Hunt is at the back of such lawless endeavour as you describe, I should be right glad to have you remove him from the neighbourhood."

I had spoken with such strong feeling that Hoghton sure believed me. A half smile flitted to the noble lips, the noble nose became reposeful, and the knight condescended to be seated and even spoke with us on light and family matters. Chiefly he discoursed on the addition of my sister to his family. Her predilection for high fashion had not diminished since her marriage, he was pleased to inform us.

"She affects farthingales as wide and ruffs as high as well nigh any worn at court," he said, with the loud laugh of one accustomed to holding court himself. "She may adorn his house but she is costing William a pretty penny."

I have long known that I am no welcome kin to Gracie. I do not know what credence she may have given to rumours whose shape I cannot guess, but she is as far from me in love as little Carrotnob is distant in time.

When he had left, John and I sat in the parlour opposite each other, and I waited for him to speak. He said at last, reluctantly: "I am obliged to thank you, mistress. I do believe you had the saving of us then, and diverted suspicion from our house."

"I am glad to save you John, but I have no gentle feelings towards that other man. It was a base and dastardly act to organise a raid upon the house of a priest, who did no more than his duty to our sovereign. It is God's mercy that there were none dead that night."

He nodded wretchedly and rose to leave, but I would not let go so easy. "Thereabouts a week ago, you called me a spy. Although you know well, I am none. But if Hunt were to persuade you to such another sorry errand as the riot at Garstang, I would be minded to play informer."

He looked at me from the other side of the divide between us. "There will be no more raids on vicarages."

Chapter 35

NO MORE VICARAGES but he had not said no more Thurston Hunt.

We continued to be plagued – I was plagued – by the visits of this restless man, with his shifting gaze and constant fidgets.

I kept well apart from his presence in our house, and was glad to be excluded from his conference with my husband. And truth to tell, he did not ordinarily thrust himself into my company. Until one late afternoon when he crossed the ford at full thrash. He spake very hurriedly to John, and they both were suddenly solicitous to speak with me.

Thurston Hunt, still breathing heavily, addressed me. "Mistress Southworth, we have need of your assistance again. We need shelter for a flying fugitive for one night at least."

"Yourself Father Hunt?" Even a clown would have heard the unwelcome in my voice.

"No, I will not stay here. But they have taken little Robert Middleton."

I was checked by that, by the thought of that slight figure with the gentle smile. "I am sorry for it. It is a sorrow for us all. Was it in this neighbourhood he was taken?"

"Richard Hoghton seized him west of Preston. He has packed the county lately with spies and informers. No question he knew of our journeying. They fell upon us suddenly. I shouted out to Robert and I am sure he endeavoured to spur away. The agreement for such happenings is that every man must flee for himself as fast as possible."

"But you were faster than Father Robert?"

"I was fast and determined and knew the terrain. Robert was well horsed also but he is a dreamy soul. Learned and dreamy. He is not accustomed to the chase."

John urged the man to sit. "Do you think that Hoghton knows who it was that escaped him?"

"I should think he has a strong surmise, judging from the ferocity with which he yelled his followers to pursue me."

"Robert will not tell," said John firmly.

"No," the man pushed his hand through his hair with a weary gesture. "He is as true as steel. Tiny as he is, he will not break." His unsteady eyes sought mine. "That is a princely man Mistress Southworth. He nursed Christopher with a woman's care, but his courage is that of a warrior."

"A warrior for Christ," earnestly agreed my husband.

"Did he know of Robert Nutter's fate?" I could not help asking. "Did that not put some dread into him?"

"I was with him in Yorkshire that day." He tugged his beard restlessly. "The good soul harbouring us came weeping with the news, lamenting such a tragic death. And Bob answered her with that quiet gravity of his, 'Madam I would I might this day ride a good long way and out of my way, to have so good a chance as he'."

"And you would protect him from that chance?" It was cold anger held me, and yet I knew not what it was most angered me.

"And would not you?" His gaze flickered past me.

John's voice was more simply accusatory. "Would not you Jane, save him while it was in your power?"

213

I answered only, "Yes," and they did not ask for more.

Hunt was already forward with his planning and plotting. "We will most certainly save him from the scaffold if we can. He lies in Preston gaol tonight, but on the morrow he is certain to be transported to Lancaster Castle. If a bold group of men, armed men, could surprise their party, I can collect some stout souls in Garstang tonight, and tomorrow early—"

"I ride with you, Thurston. I would give my right arm for the joy of rescuing Robert Middleton." John put his hand on my shoulder. "And you Jane, you surely would be glad if we could snatch that brave small man from such cruel hands. And give him shelter here before we find him safe convoy into Yorkshire?"

I said only, "I will have a room and all ready for him." Then seeing his face all alight with such youthful ardour I also said, "And I will pray for your success."

John left long before the tardy autumn sun was prepared to lend us any light. He was so hung about with weapons that I thought he might have sunk an armada. And then I pushed him from my mind.

I spent the afternoon at my fireside stitching infant linen with Ellen. She had had high words from Mary Sowerbutts that morning and was very subdued. Since Mary's jibes were usually to do with her cousin's childlessness, I tried to speak cheerfully about this.

"Is it a sadness for you, Ellen, to have borne no children of your own? And sew for others? Or is it that you have the light within you that is the solace of a holy soul?"

I spoke incautiously, but caution was not in the air that day. Ellen kept her eyes upon her work. She said quite low, "I would be a blessed woman indeed were the Lord to light his candle in my soul. But I cannot dare to claim that favour." She stitched assiduously. "And I still do take great solace in caring for your child and this little one who is to come. I love Tom as my own. And that is not all I have," she looked at me quite shyly, "there is a young nephew in Rochdale who I most dote upon – Roger."

"Roger?" I encouraged.

"Roger Brierley – he is a holy boy. He has such a longing to enter the ministry, but I doubt it will be easy for him."

I had no time to discover wherein lay Roger Brierley's difficulties, for at that moment we heard the sound of a returning horse; a single horseman.

I knew the enterprise had failed before ever John hurled his hat and cloak to the floor, with that tearful anger that was ever his way in desperation.

"Taken, all taken. Robert, Thurston, some of the Garstang men."

"They expected you?" I guessed.

"Yes likely they expected us. It was an ambush. As we rode out of the woods, they opened fire. And then more horsemen suddenly on the scene. Thurston was knocked off his horse at the start, and stood battling with his captors like the Lord's own mastiff. We were to snatch Robert and then away at all speed. But he was heavily surrounded. No chance. No choice but to flee. As pre-arranged. Taken – all taken."

He wanted words of vindication I am sure, but I felt nought but dreariness: "So now they have them both. And your friend is like to die."

"Some hope for Thurston." My young husband frowned. "In case of capture he has prepared a document informing on the nobles of this county who support Essex' plans for rebellion."

"Which nobles John?"

"Oh conformers only. Not Catholics. I don't know exactly – probably Molyneux, Sefton, Bishop Vaughan, Richard Houghton."

"He will name names to save his neck? He who has been harboured, he will turn informer? What kind of honour or faith is that?"

"He could argue that since the men harrying papists are themselves disloyal to the Crown, it is no sin to use these facts to free their prisoners."

"And he has explained all this to you. Such Jesuitical equivocation you could never have conceived of by yourself."

And John too wretched to reply.

We did not mention the man's name again. And it seemed that Hunt's proffered information did procure him a stay of execution. He was taken to London with Robert Middleton for prolonged examination. But not to be spoken of in our house.

❋

I was preparing for another Christmas birth. But it seemed that my womb now prospering, was not inclined to throw its tenant on the world too prematurely. The babe, Anne, arrived most decorously at the appointed time, in a white January. The snow stuck fast two weeks or more and drifted in the river valley. I would have been content for it to stay piled to the eaves, so I could stay in that cocoon for ever, warmed and petted by my women, isolated from secret horsemen galloping by night to threaten the safety of my children.

John was polite with me, polite in greeting his new daughter, but some spark of youthful fire had been doused in him. I was neither able nor willing to blow it back into flame. Three unhappy enterprises stood against him in the balance sheet of our marriage. But I was polite also, being more disposed to rock the cradle than the frail barque of our reconciliation. We found a little brief loving in that white world.

But snow, no more than summer sun, will not stay, and soon it was dissolved into the melting mush of thaw. My mother-in-law came to view the new Anne, bringing news of worlds both wide and small.

How Mary Sowerbutts had miscarried again, but too much Yuletide feasting and drinking in that household, she was sure. And tussles between Henry Brierley and Thomas Sowerbutts, again forbidden entry at Turner Green. How there was a great fray between Thomas Sowerbutts and Tom Welshman, and Mary in the midst of it, for all she was carrying, but might she not be the very cause after all? They had grown too wild, Rosamund did verily believe. And other wild men had reaped the storm. Essex was dead. The apple of Elizabeth's eye no longer, he had raised the banner of revolt, and paid with his head. Now that the rebellion lay in ruins, informers might be paid off. In one coin or another.

So with the flailing winds of March, Thurston Hunt and Robert Middleton were returned into Lancashire. They rode in shameful charade facing the tails of their horses, with their hands tied behind them and their feet under the bellies of their mounts. They were taken to Lancaster Castle, with no attempt at rescue.

John spent the blustery March days from the house, furiously riding and hunting, and the evenings he spent deep in drink. He scarcely spoke to me then, not even when news came of the hanging.

Chapter 36

SUMMONED TO LATHOM. That was the message brought by my father-in-law, and it was certainly no invitation to a ball he had come to deliver.

"You are called, we are sent for by the Earl of Derby, for examination, and that immediately." He was standing rigid in the parlour, pale with fear or anger, I did not know.

And it was I who answered him. "What can it mean? Are we to answer charges?"

But Thomas turned deliberately to John: "This Thurston Hunt, Devil take him—"

"Thurston Hunt is dead. He has paid for any misdeeds now."

"Dead he may be but the ill he wrought is still abroad. Did you know he turned informer and of all the crazed things, gave Richard Hoghton's name as an ally of Essex and privy to the rebel plot?"

"I know . . . something of it."

"You don't think that his association with you went unobserved? You cannot think the whole world slept while you played with your masks and muskets."

"Whither does all this lead, Father?" His voice was weary.

"It leads to Lathom. It may lead to prison or worse. It will certainly mean expropriation. God knows what we are accused of, or what sentence we may receive. But we are all to go, you, Jane, Rosamund and myself."

It was I again who asked, "When are we sent for?"

"Tomorrow. The very day tomorrow and no excuse

accepted. We are lucky to go ourselves and not under armed guard."

John was saying slowly, "We will come to the hall then, early, on the morrow."

I made a gesture of refusal, "My babes—"

But Thomas said heavily, "No excuses. I have told you – no excuses whatsoever."

I was undone. The thought of entering Lathom for chastisement, I who had danced and been admired in the great hall, that was intolerable to me. But much worse than the humiliation was the fear of what might happen to our fortunes, or our lives.

John, give him credit, took all in hand, ordered the horses, gave Ellen instructions, and brought me a glass of hot brandy. "Take heart Jane," he said, "you have no fault to confess."

"I will not betray you John. Be sure of that. I will spit lies between my teeth, I will pact with the Devil, before I will betray you, or endanger our children."

He gazed at me sombrely. Somewhere between us love flittered and tried to find a perch.

***

I dressed with great care for Lathom. Gone were the days of my peacock pride, but I still had much dignity to salvage. Ellen and I rummaged in some things I had of Isabella's, for my own gowns were too tight for my nursing figure. I found a dress of rich fabric, steel grey brocade, overlaid with a cobweb of fine black lace. The lace was gathered into a low ruff at the neck and fell into long, hanging sleeves. The trim was very many small jet beads. The same gossamer-light stuff made a veil to the matching French cap, of Mary Stuart style. I did ponder the tact of wearing the fashion of the Queen of Scotland, who now wore neither hat nor head, but in the end I chose to wear it. However I left Lathom, I would enter as a lady of rank. I wore no jewels though, save for a tiny silver locket.

We were received with courtesy, if little warmth. The Earl of Derby sat behind a large desk of some fine wood inlaid with pearl. Two satin-clad pages were beside. Various members of the nobility, many known to me, sat or sprawled about the room. It seemed as though it had been decided to leave the degree of formality in some doubt. But there was no doubting our position, Thomas, John, Rosamund and myself ranged before the desk.

When we took our seats, I could not prevent that old haphazard bit of my brain endlessly repeating:

> *From peacock to spider*
> *And not much the wiser.*

I shook my head to listen to the great man pronouncing against us. He spoke forcefully, as one whose patience is coming to the end.

"This is not the first time we have had cause to rebuke the Southworths – the most unruly family in this so unbridled and bad a handful of England. It is past twenty years since the Privy Council gave instructions to Her Majesty's loyal subjects to root out the bottom of these abuses in Lancashire, being the very sink of popery, where more unlawful acts have been committed and more unlawful persons holden in secret than in any other part of the realm. This county is famed for disobedience and for religious strife. Is it not so sirs?" He solicited the support of the great ones who lounged around the room.

"My lord – the very cockpit of conscience." The drawl came from Judge Walmsley sitting smoking by a long window, and it caused a ripple of mirth around the room.

It being often told that the earl was so besotted a lover of the cockfight that he would have had the birds to sport upon the counterpane where he lay abed, were his wife not violently opposed.

Derby, though, was not diverted. "The queen did her utmost to persuade your father, Thomas, to loyalty, and her great divines contended long and patiently with him."

John spake in heat and haste: "My grandfather was a brave and loyal soldier of the queen. His body was hers to command but he would never yield his soul. He would follow the faith of his fathers – because he was utterly faithful."

I was surprised by John's sudden temerity. It must have been a speech prepared I thought. The great earl was not impressed. He fairly thundered, "Is that what you call faithfulness – an endangered throne, a divided realm, a county bristling with itinerant, warmongering preachers?"

And if John intended to answer this, he was swept aside.

"The seminary priests who haunt the lanes and the shadows and oft times the houses hereabouts, are clergy of a proscribed religion, educated in the territories of a monarch who offers this land an ever present threat of war, under orders of a pope who would be only too glad to tip Elizabeth out of the throne of England."

He paused. The room stayed still. Then much lower but in even more menacing tone he continued, "I do not speak of messages to the Scottish queen, before she was despatched. Nor do I now propose to mention communications with the Earl of Essex and his ill-famed treachery, although there have been slanderous efforts to implicate in this affair, our own most loyal gentlemen."

I glanced at Richard Hoghton's set, bony face, his righteously distended nostrils.

"We have had in this last year disturbances and grave riots, armed bands in assault upon men in orders and constables, and a sullen population which will in no way work with the officers of the law. Those who should lead the way in apprehension of criminals and malefactors connive at concealment. Those with a rightful sword under Her Majesty to redress abuses suffer their power to rust in the scabbard. My Lord Bishop of Chester, what help have you received from our foremost gentry families, in your investigations into the troubled affairs of Garstang?"

The bishop, elbows resting upon the high arms of his backed chair, placed the fingertips of his two hands deliberately together and cleared his throat.

"I have received but small assistance from those families, as from justices and officers generally, which coldness and slackness has been my greatest hindrance."

The earl ruffled the papers upon his desk. "Such audacious insolencies cannot be permitted. We do intend to tolerate this sorry state of affairs in Lancashire no longer, and we will make examples. There is evidence here, and we are persuaded much more could easily be collected, that you have been aware, at the least, of the scheming at the back of many of these disorders. The which, if you wish to dispute, we shall conduct in court of law. But you are neighbour to us Thomas, and old friend. We would rather take a promise from you of future good conduct and co-operation, and an expressed and heart-meant loyalty to our gracious Majesty."

"Indeed your lordship—" Thomas's preparatory words of submission must have come from a very dry throat, but the earl did not suffer him to interrupt.

"In order to express our most profound displeasure, and to convey to you the seriousness of your position, we were minded to deprive you, Thomas, and you John, of all your worldly goods and fortune."

So, I thought, my fear was founded. Beggary is what the man is speaking of.

"But because our gracious sovereign mistress is ever lenient, and loves well her subjects of the north, we have commuted this sentence into a fine to the value of one moitie, one half of the dower house, Samlesbury Lower Hall, and its lands and woodlands, goods and beasts and houses thereon standing."

The room was quietly waiting.

Thomas's voice was as scratchy as an old pen. "Your lordship is right in every particular. We must – we will – mend our ways, and demonstrate how faithfully, how faithfully and scrupulously we are the queen's men, but there is no money, your lordship, no money left in our coffers to meet such a fine."

"We have taken note of the parlous situation you have obstinately driven yourselves into. And we will not on this occasion take monies from you, but take a bond for half the dower house, the other half to fall forfeit if we do not quickly observe a full and loyal allegiance to the laws of this country and its queen."

"What control would such a bond leave to me of my home and hearth?" asked John wretchedly.

"We are in a position to sell you up if we choose," said the earl, "but this moitie has been sold from the Crown to one of our nobles." He glanced towards the judge.

Walmsley put down his pipe. "I have bought the share in your property and will buy the rest if you let it fall to the market again." He did not look at John, nor at me neither, but seemed to direct his attention most through the window. "But you may live in your house and you may enjoy the freedom and income of your lands and flocks for the rest of your lifetime, upon condition" – John did not speak, nor the Earl of Derby, and Walmsley continued coolly – "upon condition that you give your wife complete freedom of worship, since it is known that she would, if let, obey the law and present herself at the church which gives its allegiance to Elizabeth; that you allow her freedom of leisure, so long as she fulfils exactly all proper housewifely duties you may require, so she may tend her garden, or play upon the virginals, or read – whatever – or entertain her friends so they be respectable and bring no stain upon your house. Upon these conditions you may live secure at Lower Hall as long as you please."

He rose and gave that elegant shrug which only a man of fashion could affect. He gave no glance to me or John, but bowed gracefully to Derby and left the room.

Chapter 37

IT WAS A VERY SORRY miry silent ride that took us back to Samlesbury. The rain had made quagmires of the bridle paths. The horses plashed and floundered in the mud. The men on bigger animals rode well ahead. Even Rosamund held her peace a good part of the way.

As we were reaching home, an east wind blew up. A bitter wind to chivvy the horses, to dry up muddy roads, to clear off the clouds. The moon sailed forth. She hung there, round and silvery silent.

"You have been given great favour." Rosamund took advantage of the moonlight to ride up close to me. I answered with reluctance – I had rather silently contemplate the moon – when I said, "I had no foreknowledge of Judge Wamlsley's intentions, believe me Rosamund."

"But how did it come about?" she urged. "The judge did always favour you, we all know. Because of your great father do you think? But even so, this is to make such an example. And to humble John. It is a bitter pill for him to swallow."

"Perhaps he saved John, from penury."

"Perhaps," she agreed. "But how will John endure to have his authority so clipped? Such a grave slight for any man, for any head of a household."

"These are dangerous times for us Rosamund—" I began, and she quickly agreed.

"Of course. We must all seek accommodations now. I think of Anne Line, just last month taken and hung for harbouring. And we have all done the same." A pause.

"And you? Now Jane what will you do?" And before I could reply, she took a quick breath and said, with the affection that paid for all her volubility, "Dearest Jane take heart. Judge Walmsley would not have bought you such expensive privileges had he not believed that you would use them."

Then even Rosamund became thoughtful. As we rode, the moon placidly followed, seeming to come along with us, in her quiet, bright way.

✾✾✾

I did not expect understanding from John and I did not receive any. We supped in silence and the children were kept from the room. At length he sent for a bottle of Stonyhurst wine, the last of Richard's gift, and poured it ceremoniously. With a cold, set face, he handed my glass.

"Congratulations madam. You have won. You have won game and tournament and all. My grandfather said well that you would not be thwarted, but would have your own high will. How you have achieved it, I do not pretend to understand."

I answered feebly I think: "It is not my contrivance, John. I am the most surprised."

Heavy with disbelief he said, "Is it not your contrivance? And do you intend not to take advantage of it?"

I spoke as carefully as I could. "In what Judge Walmsley gave today of freedoms there is nothing unlawful or harmful, nothing that would prevent me being a true and loving wife to you."

"As to that," he said bitterly, "you may be sure I will take my freedom and more. Between your cold thighs, I'll take as many gallops as it pleases me. Go up and wait for me now."

But I knew that he might be long in coming. His cold, heartsick drinking often kept him long by the fire.

I went into my sewing room and took out a quill and paper.

Dearest Alice,

It is a hundred years since I saw you. You have never seen my babes and I have never ceased to miss your talk. Lambing must be nearly over and spring weather to come. Will you make a visit to the Lower Hall? I long to see you.

My defiance did not burn long. I could not make up my mind to attend the little church alongside the ferry. That was too bold an action, and I feared John's rage would know no bounds. In the end, however, it came about quite simply.

On the first Sunday of May our house was quiet, for I had allowed the young servants to go to the maying. I was telling stories to Tom while Ellen lulled my little Anne, when a messenger arrived breathless at the door. The man came begging the master come to the churchyard where a great fighting had broken out. Thomas Southworth had been sent for, to the Great Hall, but it was a furious brawl and the church wardens quite unable to quell the riot.

"What irony," said I, "you are sent for to go to church."

He did go to church in this fashion, and found a noble role for himself, quelling the mayhem there, with the timely help of some of Thomas's retainers.

Late in the afternoon he returned with the church warden, James Winstanley, a pleasant fellow with dark, curly hair and a noble beard, in which he took – still takes – great pride. And with him the constable, who had by contrast a head of very sparse straw-coloured thatch, and a very plentiful lack of teeth. He was a man of infinite good temper and slow breathy utterance, which sometimes taxed the church warden's more sprightly good nature.

With affable dignity John asked me to provide supper for the two men, who had had a turbulent day and been long hours from their homes. The officers of the law did full justice to Ellen's cold meats and jellies, which in no way impeded their enthusiastic accounting of the day's events. It seemed that John, with Thomas's retainers, had indeed put an end to the fighting, but it was a scene of much disarray that they had encountered. John required an explanation of the beginning of the disorders, which James Winstanley proceeded most earnestly to describe.

On this occasion the great garlanded pole had been brought into the churchyard—

"For all it is forbidden," interspersed Solomon Potter.

—and a goodly crowd following and much good cheer as it was set up with flags and kerchiefs and coloured stuffs all streaming. And not rowdily at all they had strewn the straw for dancing and set up tables hard by, and a constant toing and froing between the alehouse and the church green was carrying on—

"Brisk trade at the Boat House" confirmed Solomon Potter.

How it all began, neither James nor Solomon clearly now remembered, but what all had seen was Thomas Welshman light footing it with Joan Nightingale in every dance, till they fell exhausted to the grass—

"Sweethearting for all the world to see," suggested Solomon.

And Mary Sowerbutts had flown from the dance to prevent them in a fury—

"It were a fury of jealousy James," offered Solomon, "it were nowt to do with righteous conduct."

"A fury of jealousy then" James agreed. "However, she was clawing and scratching at them both and had to be pulled off by bystanders, but not before Lily Nightingale had given her a great clout in the face, at which her husband—"

"Mary Sowerbutts's husband, James – Thomas Sowerbutts, that is—"

Thomas Sowerbutts, it seemed, had knocked Lily Nightingale off her feet, whereupon Thomas Welshman thumped Thomas Sowerbutts mightily, and before anyone knew what was about, the whole merry crowd had set about with fist and kicks to make such a great Sabbath breaking commotion—

"—and music from the fiddle quite drownded," said Solomon sadly.

James nodded "And the vicar, poor old George Finch, calling for good order, not heeded by a man jack of them—"

"Might have saved his breath to cool his porridge," thought Solomon.

"But," insisted the church warden, "it is a poor old man and a good old man, and it is not only May Day when the drinkers at the Boat House set up their revels and much unseemly behaviour in God's yard."

Problems with May revellers were not new of course. My own father was induced to sign a bill banning sports and revels. And it was well known, not only in the Lower Hall, that the ferryman and his son were happy to play ducks and drakes with the law, whether it be watering of the ale or the lusty chant of papist songs as they rowed over. There was a little gaming of an evening oft reported, and sometimes dubious persons using the ferry could buy illegal lodging at the alehouse. A little mayhem on the church green would have been well within their capacity to provoke. It was understandable that the old vicar had much ado to keep the peace. All which circumstances and difficulties James Winstanley was patiently and at length explaining.

"And it is the worse, sir," he concluded, "that the chief troublemakers feel sure of the lord's protection. It is known that the folk dancing at the church will not be hauled before the manor court, nor will any offence done to the vicar find redress. And since no member of your lordship's family is ever present at divine service there is no authority to curb their rowdyism."

Solomon merely gave a whistling sigh through his many cavities.

John nodded gravely. "All this will be mended in the future. I will myself officiate at the manorial court, along with my father. And all such grievances will be well attended to."

The men nodded respectfully and waited, as I waited. And John perhaps looked for more words. I heard my own before I well knew I had composed them.

"I do propose to attend Sunday service at St. Leonard the Less. Though I cannot say how much a woman's presence there will help."

And John after another pause said stiffly, but not without some pride, "Any representative of the Southworth family must carry some authority, and cast a sobering influence on those who frequent the place."

James was bowing. "We would be honoured to see your ladyship at church on Sunday mornings."

And Solomon, smiling a very gap-toothed smile: "We'll wipe the dust off the Southworth pew, Mistress Southworth."

Chapter 38

THERE ARE SOME DAYS, remarkable days, which carry more than their weight of memory's gold. That last longer than the hours they counted, that stand proud of all surrounding circumstance. Such was that so merry May morning when I plighted my troth to the Church of England.

We walked, Ellen and I, to the little church by the river. And I wondered as I walked, was it I caused the sun to smile on obedient conduct, clotted the hawthorn with cream flower, misted the woods with bluebell and starred the hedge bottoms with modest celandine? Was it I populated the sunlight with the fragile green of newborn leaves, and caused a thousand birds to flitter and sing among the branches of the lime trees, so that I had a carillon before ever we heard the sweet church bell?

Only the pink campion stilled my heart. But on this blithe day, campion was but a little flower. I bade farewell to the legend of that priest and his fool crusade. More lingeringly I closed down my heart on a scarred and burly figure, who in my memory stands ever watching the flooding river.

A new embrace awaited me. My welcome at St. Leonard the Less was warm enough and respectful enough to rub out many of the slights my dignity has so oft times taken. Solomon and James, widely smiling because it was they had captured the lady of the manor and brought her to church, led me the Southworth pew. When we were seated and Ellen clicked the little wooden door, a rustle of approval whispered round the church. It was not a gawking congregation, but I felt myself to be most cordially accepted. And I could not prevent the wayward bit of my brain singing:

> Jane, Jane, home you are came,
> Virtue and honour attach to your name.

And so I was to become a member of a quite different community of worshippers. No heroic highborn outlaws here, no fervent mystical congregation of the poor. But for the most part a solid prosperous yeomanry, and a benevolent vicar, old enough to have changed his coat four times for the kings and queens of England, and quite prepared to wear it threadbare in order to serve his little parish, and keep his table decently spread.

Indeed I am sure that his loose ministry was a needful canopy to shelter some of the divergent tendencies of his flock. I think of Hugh Cunliffe, the puritany sheriff and his austere wife; of James Anderton and his bonny Scots wife, who would have welcomed King James to descend into our country and nudge us all towards the Presbytery. William Preston's farming family held firmly and simply to the law of the land and loyal service to good Queen Bess, who held the land against civil strife or foreign foe. Hugh Welshman and his unruly son trimmed their papist loyalties to doff the cap to custom and a good trading in ale, and tiny spinsterish Miss Haydock would take in any sewing, be it black broadcloth or gaudy satin. Even Janet Brierley and my Ellen had no difficulty following the spiritual path of the Family of Love within the fold of George Finch's unexacting pastorship.

I see I have not mentioned Gilbert Jackson – I shame to say I did not notice him on that first day – firm friend that he has come to be since. But he was always, he and his antiquarian son, quite reticent as to matters of faith.

When I once made comment on the broad accommodation of the little church, he said, "It must be to do with the saint – Saint Leonard, patron of captives, solace of prison cells. He cannot be a rigorous saint to serve."

So I had chosen my way and my husband could but accept it. He accepted – perhaps endured is truer – the short visit of Judge Walmsley, and the longer and hardly more welcome one of Alice Nutter.

The Judge brought papers for John to sign, and spent no time with me. When he was about to leave I began a deep curtsey but he took me up. He laid a silken finger on my mouth. "No words Jane. No need. I have assured Tom's inheritance. For the rest, what is done is done. I only hope you will be glad of it in the end."

Alice Nutter brought words, however, a torrent of them, and not for my sole benefit neither.

My spirits rose the moment she rode into the yard, slithering from her horse, and stretching out her hands to me. A fond embrace that smelled of tar paste and wet grass and perhaps the must of old books. A singular perfume!

"And where is this unimportant Thomas?" she demanded, "and this inconsiderable Anne?" And professed herself greatly charmed by the wondrous beauty of my offspring. Much blessing then for Thomas and Anne.

And gossip for Ellen, talk of Rochdale cousins and sighing over a beloved nephew and his ardent, difficult vocation.

She poked her nose into the kitchen and treated Betty to a long discourse on cheese, explaining her own admixture of cow milk to ewe's, to produce a cheese of lasting flavour. "It could outlast a sea voyage to my thinking, and might sell well in Liverpool."

She trudged out most cheerfully with Bernard

Billington, and they both leaned upon the five-barred gate and argued the quality of our beasts. I wonder did Bernard make complaint of John's negligent stewardship?

With John she undertook to discuss the Poor Law, a subject he was little disposed to engage at his own dinner table. He answered her shortly: "It is the work of the Church to succour the poor. I want no churchwardens telling me how much to contribute to a pauper's needs."

"Ah there's the rub," agreed Alice. "Who will bear the burden of collection? Your James Winstanley is a diligent man, but he cannot alone summons an entire parish. If begging licences are revoked and great lords like yourself feel that charity is no longer the travail of their conscience, how will they fare, even the deserving poor?"

"I suppose they will have recourse to the justices."

"That's it. Just so. All will depend on the justices. And if your poor are abjectly so, such as they are in Pendle. And if your justice happens to be a Roger Nowell, why great hardship must follow, and from great hardship, I fear, much mischief."

But John returned to slicing his meat, and between his plate and his ale, he threw only nods towards the conversation.

No one was exempt from Alice Nutter's examination or interest. She even put her head round the door of the wash house to give a cheerful salutation to the dumb girl who worked there. And she found time for Mary Sowerbutts. Mary had taken to eating her dinner on a little bench outside my parlour window. She was there nursing her growing bulk in the sunshine when Alice joined her. I am obliged to confess that I tried to play the spy, but I could hear little of Alice's deep voice rumbling along quietly. Only I guessed the substance of their talk from Mary's sometimes sharp replies.

"I give her no physic. She'll grow out of the fits. And no more than Mary Snow can Mother Chattox cure her, who is ever in the shakes and shivers herself. I'll take no physic of a witch's kitchen."

So I knew they were talking of Mary's youngest girl, little Grace of the empty face and late speech. Whose simplicity, they said in the kitchen, was payment for her mother's whoring.

Alice must have offered more unwelcome advice, for Mary burst out, "And who'd wish for strength in a man who lays about him when in drink? And who'd give thanks for half a dozen children clinging at your apron, when your back's near split with weariness from the heavy work?" And I think she was near to tears when she said, "And who wouldn't take a pot of brown beer when you've been shoved out of your place in the house, and made to heed your sour-faced cousin?"

Alice's voice flowed on, not to be dammed or diverted, however Mary might be out of temper. I heard only "and oil of juniper as well, is very efficacious to prevent convulsions, as well as being a great resister of the pestilence."

At length the younger woman quieted, and I could observe how she nodded with docility, and even catched hold of Alice's hand as she rose to leave. For certain Alice had promised to send her some remedy against the child's falling sickness.

Chapter 39

I HAD ALICE FOR MYSELF AT EVENTIDE. We went to watch the sun sliding towards his couch beyond the river. The water was molten gold. We nibbled liquorice comfits she had by rights brought for the children. We sat in rare silence until I said, "So is there mischief brewing in Pendle?"

Alice frowned into the sun. "Plague is reaching scabby fingers into our parts. He does not hold us tight in his fist yet. But there are too many deaths already. More than folk can understand as part of God's daily plan."

"So people are murmuring?"

"If they dare not, or choose not to howl their rage at the throne of God, they may well chuck it at an old hag's door."

"The Demdike?"

"She certainly, but Anne Whittle is sometimes called at, and the enmity between them only increases venomous accusation."

"But Mother Demdike did curse out Richie Assheton. My own brother stood there and heard her."

"She's likely cursed another hundred that never came to harm. You know full well Jane, that young Assheton was a sickly fellow."

"Yes I know that, and also that Demdike can be truly fearful when she is so minded."

"She is called Elizabeth Southern, and that is how she gains her daily bread – a call to Christian charity with the hint of a shadow of diabolic threat."

"Must make for a good rattle in a begging bowl."

"It does, indeed it does. And she is not shy to use it."

"To fright Anne Whittle?"

"That is more a history of old women's quarrels. They are forever falling in and falling out. Elizabeth Southern always blamed Anne Whittle for the hard coming of Lizzie and her poor countenance. And yet Lizzie herself asked Anne Whittle for herbs to help her own labour – such hard travail the Southern women always have to thrust their infants into the world."

"To have helped bring Jimmy forth can hardly be accounted a shining success."

"That poor idiot was born in a ditch. But Anne helped with Alizon, as fair and unblotched a babe as you could hope to see. And Jennet is a pretty child, clever, and sharp as a knife."

"So – good reason for accord."

"And so there was. In thankfulness for Alizon, John Device had promised Anne payment of a bushel of flour once a year. But then come hard times. What a yelling and screaming in Clitheroe market because Device would not – probably could not – pay, on account of a consumption that had eaten the flesh off his face."

"The French pox, that sounds like."

"Aye likely, but even a cobbler needs a nose, and that poor wight had lost his work and his life in a hard winter. But died demented, crying accusation against Anne Whittle having witched him to death, to revenge that unpaid debt."

"You need no witching to pick up the pox."

"No, but rumour, wisps of rumour, they float in the air."

"'Til they snag on branches of fear, held out to catch them."

"Right Jane – and they cluster there."

She sighed and we both contemplated the golden river.

"But it goes on this foolish tale, with a new wrangle. Some rogue broke into Malkin Tower and had away with linen cloth and bags of flour and oatmeal, the quantity which I surely doubt. It sounds a great deal of treasure for that place to house. But Lizzie straightway puts the blame on Anne Whittle. And then the young girls come into the story."

She clamped the lid of the comfit box as if she might within it imprison all of life's stupidity.

"Alizon, for all she is fair of face, is handmaid to her grandma and picks herself a quarrel with Bess Whittle. You know Bess, a flighty girl."

"She has an unguarded tongue."

"And an inordinate love of the flim-flam that a pedlar carries. Both of them, both she and Alizon, have worried John Law to death with their beggings."

"I think it would take more than a loose-tongued girl to unsteady that weighty man."

Alice grinned. "Well now we have Alizon openly lamenting the loss of one cap with pink bows and green ribands. And Bess at church next week flaunting something similar. And the two girls at it in the churchyard like two fish wives over a bucket of spilled fish. And all decent bodies looking on askance at their misbehaviour. While the milk of human kindness dries up like a brook in midsummer."

"But her sister – Anne Redferne stays clear of all this?"

"Our sweet Anne is well occupied in her little cot, with a good man and the new child. You should see her Marie, she is a very pearl. And peace descended on them, now that Robert Nutter is dead. The pox, the plague or the pneumonia hath carried off that scourge of their lives."

"Robert Nutter dead," I repeated. The sun was ready to scald the river with its red rim. "Did you know that other Robert Nutter, priest, lodged with us after his escape from Wisbech?"

"It seems he did not live long to enjoy his freedom."

I threw first one pebble into the river, then two then three.

"So you were enamoured of him, my lady," she said quietly.

"On that day, the day they butchered him, I did bethink much upon your words, upon your anger against religions avid for the blood of martyrs."

She looked across the river, her fingers nervously plaiting into a steeple. By now the water had swallowed the sun, but he had left a trail behind, a crimson and gold staining that lighted up the sky.

"We worship a tortured god man. We sorrow for his tormented death and venerate his message of forgiveness; words to cancel the bond of blood, the law of tribe, to rub out difference – and coercion. And then we proceed to dangle and dismember hundreds of our fellow creatures in the name of this same god man. And only for the fact that they choose a different fashion of showing their reverence, a different way of making prayer or following a different guidance to salvation. I make no sense of this. My mind fairly reels into a faint when I endeavour to unravel the nonsense of it."

"And all and everyone convinced of their own right-ness, and righteousness," I said. Alice nodded, but I, as I used when a child, was bent on having explanation. "And whence comes this swelling of conviction? For mark you Alice, it is but very few have been blinded by a light from Damascus."

"The need to be both in the right, and to impose one's will—" she was beginning thoughtfully.

"But look you Alice," – how quickly I would still become angry with her – "you and your preachments of the inner light. What makes you custodians of the truth?"

"If you ponder on these disputes," she still answered hesitantly, "disputes and arguments that makes us the comedians in religion of Walter Raleigh's description—"

"No, speak not of Walter Raleigh, Alice. How do you, you yourself, prove the rectitude of your belief?"

She disciplined her hands into her lap. She still gazed across the river, where the rosy afterglow in the sky was contending with the creeping grey. "So far as I can understand, from what I hear, and from what I read, it seems to me that we are slaughtering one another in Christendom on the controversy whether salvation is to be obtained through good works, or on authority – authority of the holy words of the Bible, or the teaching of ministers, or the ancient prerogative of the Church of Rome. Or by the inner light of the personal soul."

"I know your belief. Why should you be right?"

"Nay I do not claim; I am a seeker only. But consider: if you think of daft Jamie – I mean Lizzie Device's boy, not the King of Scotland," she grinned at my frowning. "Take silly Jimmy Device, who has not a farthing of sense. Set him before a mountain of scriptures or a flock of doctors of divinity, will you induce a state of sainthood in him?"

"He is not capable."

"Exactly he is not capable, for his own conscience is but a stunted ill-grown thing, could not take advantage of the preaching of Solomon."

"But he can be saved by obedience to the Church."

"How do you know he is saved? Will you stop him riding nanny goats or thieving whatever his sticky fingers can pick up? Will you show him how to tell the truth from lies if he goes to church twice in every day?"

"So?"

"So whatsoever is provided to lead us to the divine light, we can only benefit by using our own inner eye and illumination. And if that guiding light must shine in the soul before we can come to God, then when the soul is quickened by the flame of grace – then no black gowns or hefty commentaries make any matter."

"No churches, no preachers, no disputation."

"If you allow the spirit to fill the quiet seeking heart, the soul will make its own wedding with God."

The afterglow was gone. The light was grey. I laughed. "I would not have called you quiet, Alice!"

"I talk too much for my estate. I know it well. I have never learned to be quiet. But if our Family were allowed—"

"You could have been a preacher. And handy-dandy a new set of precepts and prescriptions. And what would be yours, your precepts Mistress Nutter?"

She ignored always the insolence of my voice. "Oh the substance of my philosophy is simple. I would we were gentle with one another and seek to do no hurt at all, seeing as there is in living and dying much hurt that we cannot anyway escape. And," she narrowed her eyes, peering into the mist that was beginning to creep over the water, "since God is utterly in charge of the next world, we should strive to better manage this one. And make a paradise here on this green earth – for everyone."

"You must be harking on the Poor Law still."

"Oh it would require a greater redistribution than that."

"You would really make upheaval then, the little Family of Love?"

"It is many more than in the Family. It is talked of up and down the land. How to make alteration. Talked of – whispered of."

I gathered my shawl and said: "I would not see you implicated in trouble or turmoil Alice."

"Oh it will not come yet. But it will come. Trust to my Ladye Tyme."

Chapter 40

I ENJOYED MY DEAR FRIEND'S VISIT and I was most
pleased to perform my duty at the little church, but I
did not press my liberties too far. I opened no book and
I did not lift my pen again. But there seemed little hope
of dissolving my husband's gloom. Without forfeiting all
Judge Walmsley's stipulations, I could not see how John
would be brought back to affection, and his displeasure
hung over the house.

We danced these measures so often it seemed to me;
the bow, the handclasp, the pirouette, the separation and
the return. But this time I could not see how to procure
a reconciliation, or create a harmony in the dower household. It was a quite unlooked for solution that old Dame
Fortune offered us.

It is always a surprise to me that not only is the mind
oft-times fastened on irrelevancies, but the sight of the eye
can be captured by small and trifling details, neglecting
or failing to perceive what is of central importance in a
picture. How else explain that my attention was seized by
the sight of Angelica, opening and shutting her mouth in
dumb distress, before I realised that the centre of the yard
was occupied by the escaped stud bull. He was an old heavy
bull of known uncertain temper. Standing there, waiting
with lowered head, he seemed almost to be puzzled by his
freedom, or else mazed by sudden sunlight.

The herdsman was struggling to his feet, after some
clumsy fall, but what most should have concerned me I
was oblivious of, until Joan Nightingale ran like a mad

woman across the animal's path, snatching up my own small fubsy fellow, who was playing all unalarmed by the danger so closely threatening him.

Joan had swept him up and rushed into an adjacent barn before any of us had moved, before the bull himself, perhaps still adjusting his vision to the brightness, had taken proper cognizance of her flight. But doubtless she had diverted his attention, for the herdsman was able to take up the long pole he had dropped, and catch the hook into a heavy ring that hung from the wide blowing nostrils.

I was still stood stock still, as rooted to the ground with terror, with a belated knowledge of what so nearly could have happened. I stayed still even while Joan emerged and Tom was being smothered with kisses of the serving women, and Joan being embraced, and Betty proclaiming that her father was the champion of all time, and would stand alone at the bull bait in Clitheroe and make them all a fortune.

And before I could seize the child into mine own arms, he was in his father's who had tardily arrived and been like me a helpless spectator of the saving of our son. He looked then so very kindly at me, when he gave the boy into my embrace. But it was with thunderous face he called for order in the yard, and demanded to know how the bull had been able to escape.

Bernard Billington came out of the stable, where he had secured the beast, bolted the door, and faced round to John. "The bolt was drawn. Someone had pulled back the bolt. What fool could do like mischief?"

The stablemen, late arrived, shifted uneasily. 'Til one of them jerked his head in the direction of the brewing house, where Mary stood, her young son ill-concealed behind her. It was Joe Little, was the tell-tale. "That lad's been hung about the yard all week. He is forever underfoot and gets right in the way of the work."

John was grim. "Then teach him what he's done and let him taste his welcome in this yard."

They seized the boy from a protesting Mary. His shirt pulled over his head and his hands tied to a tethering ring in the wall. And John sent to fetch the cattle whip.

I should say he was about ten year old, the Sowerbutts's lad at this time. It pained me to see his scrawny back, shivering violently, as I carried my own plump cherub safe back into the house. The girls fed Tom pasties of strawberry jam and made calming camomile for me. But all their chatter and endearments did not drown the screams coming from the yard.

When all was over, John appeared, quite out of breath. "I have chastised the cub," he said. "Do you go now and speak with the vixen."

The brewhouse was dark, even on a sunny day, and perfumed with the sweet-sour of fermenting ale. Little Grace was huddled in a corner next her crouching brother and Mary making shift to clean his stripes with bits of rag. A can of water stood there and a can of ale. She sent both flying as she rose clumsily at my entrance. She stood unsteady in that fragrant gloom and I perceived that she was deeply sodden with drink. She put a hand on hip and tossed her head in her old provocative way.

"Well Jane Southworth," she said insolently, "three nursemaids can't keep your babby from running into harm, but it takes two stablemen and the master to thrash my lad."

Before I spoke, I heard John behind me. "Quit this house now. From now on you have no place here. Do not let you or your brats be found upon my land or I'll have you out the farm as well and set you upon the begging road like your mother before you."

He took me by the elbow and led me back to the house.

I could not interpret the feeling that lay behind his words when he said, "You have been years waiting to be rid of Mary Sowerbutts. Now you have your way."

I would have drawn away from him then, but he held me firmly. "Nay you were right," he said, and to my most surprise slipped his arm about my waist. "Who would have thought that big girl could move so fast? Joan Nightingale must be rewarded."

I said joyfully – is that the right word? I think it is, for I was glad enough to be liked again – "What will you give her, John?"

And he was so cheerful, that elusive husband of mine. "I think she should have enough to buy herself a ferryman."

This was not a truce but a peace treaty, and which we honoured in the main, despite whatever small skirmishes took place by the way. In that resolute peace my womb fruited regularly, and the man has left me with great treasure – my Tom, my Anne, my Christopher, Mary, Gilbert, John, and sweetest Rosamund, who seems like to become as great a chatterbox as her grandmother.

Even to name them so, in script, makes my heart ache with pride, and I am resolved to hasten home. In two days' time, three at most, John Law comes to Dunnow. I will so relieve that pedlar of baubles and knicknacks, that he will walk light as a bird, with an empty pack and a full purse. And the day after, my brother has business in Preston. A wise man after all to go collect his dues after the pedlar's visit. And dearest Dorothy, my sweet physician, has pronounced me properly recovered. Perhaps Rick will have time and patience to talk to me on the ride home. Will he even compose a rhyming couplet at my expense?

Then God willing, I shall recover my brother's friendship, sweeten my husband's grave, embrace my children, and take up the mantle of duty and direction. And snap shut this foolish narrative. Which still I ought to finish. It is I have opened the ledger; it is I should complete the reckoning.

If my harvest was a plentiful one, the same could not be said of poor Joan Nightingale, who was the means of our reconciliation. She did not win a husband quickly even with the dowry John had gifted her. The ferryman was a slippery silver fish in no hurry to flounder in the net of matrimony, and even when caught, reluctant to give up the life of a tippling minstrel. And if she waited long for a husband, she was obliged also to wait for the children she so ardently desired, who when they came at last would not tarry long in this world. Mine is the benefit for I still have that good girl in my service.

I gave my husband plentiful progeny and I curtailed my behaviour to his more or less forbearing. And he, John, set about as best he could to rescue the family fortune by dealing in land and debts. Mortgages and bills of sale replaced the hawks and hounds of his early passion. But the days were past when every Tom or Jack could whistle up a fortune from the ruins of monasteries. And John was no money man. I do believe we were saved from many a calamitous outcome by the advice and acumen of Gilbert Jackson, who associated with him sometime in land speculation. For Gilbert now was become a most regular visitor in our house, liked by all for his good-humoured dignity and careful reticent opinion. And if he much admires me, he makes no nuisance of it.

So I have now the pleasure of masculine conversation in my parlour. We have sober commentaries from Gilbert, antiquarian observations from his son, and botanical information from Edward Osbaldeston. And from time to rare time, politics and gossip from Judge Walmsley.

Chapter 41

WE KNOW FROM PREACHMENTS that all flesh is grass, and all that lives below the marble moon must come to dust. And Alice may have tender thoughts about her gentle Ladye Tyme, but poets know and never weary of telling us, that time is the devourer of youth, beauty's waster, and the mock of majesty.

And yet I could not help feeling disbelief when Great Bess succumbed to mortality. She was queen before I was born. All my life she had ruled the roost in England, seeming as ponderous and immoveable as Pendle Hill. For a moment the world seemed empty, tenantless, disquieting.

But the Scottish James scrambled up into her chair with little delay, and though Rosamund gabbled of pardons and privileges, our lives were little touched. The shower of royal bounty wetted only one of our close acquaintance. Soon after the coronation, Judge Walmsley was knighted in the garden of Whitehall.

I hung ribbons and garlands in our parlour to welcome his return, and was so far contented to see him that I dared a little impudence. "Ah my lord you were post-haste to London to swear your loyalty to the new sovereign. And may we now offer our congratulations on this elevation and ennoblement?"

"You may." The judge allowed my curtsey as long and deep as came little short of mockery, and raised me with the exaggerated gallantry of a courtier. "I have made my vows to our learned fool, and listened to his opinions. I have deserved a knighthood."

If John's congratulatory speech was formal and not fulsome, yet he did attend upon the judge with adequate alacrity. But it was I who brought the taper for him to light his pipe. I was delighted for him, past seriousness, and would not leave his side.

"My lord, I fear your predilection for this weed will earn you no favour with the king, who is known to have pronounced against it."

The judge laughed, "'A custom loathsome to the eye, hateful to the nose, harmful to the brain and dangerous to the lungs.' Oh an unequivocal condemnation. And our privation all the more severe in that the Scottish court is a very infestation of fleas."

"I think the king has pronounced against matters more serious than the smoking of tobacco," observed Gilbert Jackson quietly.

Walmsley nodded. "He has, as promised, caused Scot's book to be burnt by the public hangman."

"And reprinted his own *Daemonologie*?"

"Oh more than that, he intends a new law to the statute book, whereby any act of witchcraft will henceforth be classed as felony, and carry the death sentence."

"So they may swing now," said Gilbert thoughtfully, "not for suspicion of harming to death only, but for a pet frog, a lame horse or even a lucky love potion."

"He has at once defined the crime and placed the miserable objects of conviction beyond all hope of clemency."

"And is it your expectation, Sir Thomas, that he will also now issue commissions to the justices of the peace, to apprehend suspected witches in their areas of jurisdiction?"

Walmsley, blowing his interminable smoke rings, merely nodded.

I was seated on a footstool next him. I said, "That

means the Justice of Read will have an easy quarry to hunt."

He patted my head with his free hand. "The justices of this county have long been badgered for their reluctance to prosecute Catholic gentry. Now Roger Nowell can most laudably legitimately turn from heresy sniffing, to hunt the hag."

I pursued my thought. "You think he will lose interest then, in finding out religious dissent?"

"Ah no, our enthusiastic magistrate is liberally provided with game, and is rousingly hallooed by the royal huntsman."

I looked into his face. He picked up his glass, drained it and handed it to me, saying, "Our new majesty has expressed his particular detestation of 'that vile sect – the Family of Love, who think themselves to be without sin and the rest of the world an abomination'."

And as I continued to look at him, he said with mock severity, "Jane, my dear girl, you do so ever please my soul by wearing that silver locket, that I cannot reprimand you. But you will parch us all into the drought of Egypt if you do not attend to your duties."

Duty – attention to my duties I throw on my side of the balance scales, John, and on the other I must in fairness admit all the wayward sparks in my flesh. For this reason only I will spill some ink to tell of the fleeting adulterous inclination I felt for, most unexpectedly, Ellen's beloved nephew.

It was a result of the pestilential shadow of plague that took across the land again, that caused more shuddering fear in Lancashire than the turmoils and gunpowder plots convulsing London. The spread of it seemed to come suddenly: death tolls mounting, grave diggers labouring, half Manchester perishing, and bills of exclusion set upon every post. At this time Roger Brierley was on a visit to his great aunt and had fallen sick. Some youths of the parish, fearing what infection he might have brought from Rochdale, and sure led on by young Tom Sowerbutts, began a commotion in the alehouse and gave the lad a ferocious beating.

It was Solomon Potter brought us word of it, and of the sorry state the lad was left in – "he is beat up full sore, begging your pardon Mistress Southworth, all swelled and gory."

My poor housekeeper was in such tears and travail, hearing Solomon's wheezingly mournful account, that I had them bring Roger Brierley to the Lower Hall straightway. I helped her nurse him. I read poetry to him and we had some gentle discourse on vocation and conscience. And I wondered how it came about, that I was so often inflamed by ice. By the icicles of chastity and dedication. The chamber of sickness, it is said, is the chapel of devotion, but I think it is rather the cell of concupiscence. Since a nurse doth often conceive too great affection for her charge, as the Queen of Scots had cause to rue. But if the dark wings of Eros seemed to flutter round me while I tended the boy, it was a mere will o' the wisp of lust, nought more than a firefly.

Chapter 42

HOWEVER, ROGER BRIERLEY'S was not the worst hurt to be suffered at the little alehouse on Turner Green. When George Finch's mild life and equable ministry at last drew to its close, there was much speculation as to his successor and some apprehension of a high Puritan preacher. But I think no one was prepared for the startling address of the Reverend James Whitworth.

He stood before the altar, a huge crow wearing neither surplice nor vestment. His skin was paler than milk, with neither eyelashes nor brows to be discerned, but a profusion of gingery curls about his white pate. He gave no greeting to the parishioners but held him still, his large head butting forward as in perpetual reprimand. When we had finished rustling and bustling and clicking pew doors, he let the silence dwell a little before breaking into sudden lamentation.

> *By the waters of Babylon,*
> *we sat down and wept:*
> *when we remembered thee, O Sion.*
> *As for our harps, we hanged them up:*
> *upon the trees that are therein.*
> *But they that led us away captive*
> *required of us a song and a melody.*
> *How shall we sing the Lord's song*
> *in a strange land?*
> *If I forget thee, O Jerusalem.*

That final plangent note had hardly died away before we were startled by a sudden eruption of vociferation.

Mystery! Babylon the Great!
The Mother of Harlots!
And the Abominations of the Earth!

And then more softly the minister intoned the dreadful judgement:

> *And a mighty angel took up a stone like a great*
> *millstone, and cast it into the sea, saying 'Thus with*
> *violence shall the great city of Babylon be thrown*
> *down, and shall be found no more at all.'*

The silence did if possible deepen, and he swept the congregation with an intense gaze. "So spake the Lord for that great city of Babylon. And if this for Babylon, the great and beautiful city, what shall the Lord say to Samlesbury, seeing what pagan and popish practices do there abound?"

There was a gasp from some and a small spirit of alarm flittered like a bat around the church.

"It is the month of May in one week's time my brethren, and I know how you are used to dedicate yourselves to the Lord of Misrule. I do know with what scandalous license you are accustomed in this parish to create festival. Some of you with Romish imaginations will still persist to sing your Mayday songs, the whilst you prance around a monstrous pole, a stinking idol whose veneration does lead straightway to commerce with the Prince of Darkness."

Lest he caught even a whiff of disaccord, the big man moved forward, nodding slowly in emphasis.

"I know it. I have seen it."

And with relish he told what he knew, what he had seen.

"I have seen Misrule's companions decked in every gaudy ribbon and lace, with bells of Hell jingling at their ankles, and on their backs, rich scarves and favours, won of Nellie and Jessie, and Mopsie and Peggy, for lewd behaviour and bussing in the dark. I have seen them, you have seen them, prancing into the churchyard, with pipers piping and drummers crashing and handkerchiefs waving and hobbyhorses dashing into the crowd like a madman's prison broke loose. Or like a devils' pageant out of Hell."

How spellbound we all were by his self-pleasuring oratory. And so enamoured am I by his flights of denunciation that I oblige Dorothy to listen to my rehearsal, before I put the words upon the page.

"But no more will you see evil carnival my friends, my brothers. For I am now your minister and I will reclaim you to the sweet sobriety of the Lord. And I will whip such fleering jackanapes and villainous beer sellers, such drunken dancers and lecher lustyguts as ever I spy, out of this church, out of the garden of this church and so for evermore."

But before he had enumerated more of the n'er-do-wells to be scourged from the parish, Thomas Welshman was upon his feet. Whether the ferryman's son was intent to proclaim his ancient loyalties, or to protect his father's trade, or to contrary a pugnacious Puritan, he took upon him to rise from his seat and break into a favourite hymn.

> At Lancaster Castle three priests took their end
> In glorious victory, true faith to defend.
>
> Of Hunt's dauntless courage let praises be made
> Sweet Middleton's faithfulness ne'er could be stayed.
>
> And Nutter's bold constancy none could defame
> But follow we all in heart now this bold Traine,
> In deathless devotion to Christ Capitaine.

The Reverend James Whitworth was but inspired by this piece of effrontery from the ferryman.

"I know how much the evils of this parish belong to

the rowdy house upon the church boundary. We all know how the hallowing of the Lord's day is defamed and trampled upon by the gamesters and drinkers at the alehouse. For while there are among you those who fail to keep the Sabbath holy for that they must ride and carry on the Sunday, or they must row and ferry on the Sunday, or they must buy and sell on a Sunday, still I cannot think these so steeped in evil as they that do prance in their pride, preening and pricking, decking and painting themselves, to an ungodly gorgeousness. And these vanities are still outfaced by those who wanton at the sign of the ivy bush, this bawdy house that lies at our door."

Even Thomas Welshman's fine tenor could not contend with the clergyman's furious flow, but as he was departing the church door was roughly crashed open, and a drunken Thomas Sowerbutts swaggered to the back of the church, as soused a tosspot as I did ever see. His insolence was more threatening, and unsteady as he stood upon his feet, he yet gave the minister full stop. "How come ye men of Samlesbury, how do you suffer yon red-haired fellow to stand before the altar and preach the word, with no surplice upon him? And you, do you throw snot rags at the face of the law, before you know or man or woman of this parish?"

Majestic in his drink, I know not where Sowerbutts's menaces may have led, had not two churchwardens and the constable hustled him out of the building.

The Reverend Whitworth, having taken breath, seized upon this illustration of his argument.

"Such is the festering disease of drunkenness my brethren, nourished and provided for in this naughty house that stands at hand, where young men are enticed to play at cards and swear, where they may meet with rogues and recusants and lewd women and others of satanic conversation, where they may rest in excess and super-fluity, in gluttony and drunkenness like rats and swine, in brawling and tussling, in quarrelling and fighting, in wantonness, in toyish talking, in filthy fleshiness that does make God more dishonoured and the Devil sweeter served upon the holy day than any other."

But truth to say, our overawed heedfulness was already slipping, loosed by these interruptions, and by the sounds of revelry that came jingling in from the yard. We heard Welshman singing, in different vein:

> *An ugly face, a silly mutt,*
> *Who is this clown of Sowerbutts?*
> *Oh is he not a very knave*
> *To make a privy of a grave?*

And we caught the gist of Sowerbutts's answering growl that he would be pleased to crack Welshman's pate and use his brains for pigswill. Which in no way dissuaded Welshman from a more jovial denunciation of his rival.

> *This bag of guts, how he doth strut.*
> *No maiden chaste but he can smut.*
> *A rogue, a dunce, an ass at rut*
> *Hath kissed the bum of every slut.*

These exchanges and the increasing disorder provided an ironic counterpoint to the sermon, which was growing intolerably long. Invective hath only a short life to command attention, even for such as me who had relished his oratory.

When James Whitworth finally allowed his congregation to escape into the pollution of the drunken Sabbath, the churchyard was indeed a scene of bawdy misbehaviour. The preparations for next week's Maying had in fact already begun, and the ferrymen must have been providing ale at no price at all to rally their supporters and thwart whatever prohibition the new preacher should bring. Benches and trestles were in disorder, maidens of no sort of virtue were displaying their charms, a lone piper was drownded by the village lads in that state of levity that presages fisticuffs, and more than one had already spewed their guts upon the church green.

Solomon Potter made a brave attempt to assert authority. Taking a great breath he delivered his command: "In the name of the king, Thomas Sowerbuts, I charge thee—"

"In the name of the king, Solomon Potter, I charge thee to kiss my tail," Sowerbutts shouted, to the delight of his son who capered and pirouetted to thrust his rump in the direction of the earnest constable.

"I speak for the Church," Solomon did not lose his dignity, "and for the Crown to which you owe allegiance."

"I care not a fart of a flea for such as go to church in there. I had rather hear a hooting owl than that black crow. And I shall have the law on thee – aye on thee, Solomon Potter – that dost tolerate such unreligious practice."

To the relief of this beleaguered officer, James Winstanley was soon returned with a posse of armed retainers from the hall, and they laid about them with staves and truncheons to disperse the crowd. The elder Sowerbutts beat a hasty retreat, Thomas Welshman having already disappeared in good time. It was the youngsters carried the knocks, young Sowerbutts still advising the Reverend Whitworth to drink his own piss and eat his own dung, until a hefty clout shut his mouth, and then his drunkenness turned sour on him.

He went with his companions to look for ale in another house, and found an easy enemy for settling old scores. They beat Henry Brierley senseless and left the hunchback on the floor of the neat little alehouse as near a corpse as made no matter.

Chapter 43

THAT SUMMER WAS A SUMMER OF REMOVALS.

The Reverend James Whitworth was recalled, rebuked for his lack of carefulness in handling the parish, and suspended for refusing to wear a surplice.

Ellen Brierley was obliged to leave my service for a time, to nurse her husband into what is yet but a semblance of life.

My husband also was much removed from the place. The plague left a rare crop of sales, evictions, settlements and the like, and supposedly lucrative transaction. John was hellbent on building a fortune from it and constantly was journeying abroad.

But the most bitter removal was for the Sowerbutts. Both father and son were brought before the manorial court. There was no shortage of witnesses to attest to their constant tussling and brawling and impudence before authority. But the vicious attack on Henry Brierley stood most against them and Thomas was not lenient in his sentencing. They were evicted from the smallholding that they rented from the Southworth estate, and ended in some wretched hovel, the men finding but meagre employment as day labourers.

But that was not the end of Sowerbutts troubling us. This came on one of those mild late summer days when September is promising to blow soft until the fruit be in the loft. Though it was the preserving of meat that was occupying us just then. It is always a merry time, the laying down of plenty before the winter's want, and we were not short of laughter. Jointed carcasses had been washed in the big stone trough until the cobbles ran with bloody water, and when the swilling gave way to the salting, it seemed a snow storm was flying about the yard. Betty herself, a right salted snow queen, was hollering forth instructions and injunctions to the men. Was it always the lot of a virtuous woman, she demanded to know, to be surrounded by such dolts of men who could not wash the flesh without a great watery commotion. And if they could not better work and stack the pieces properly alongside, she would douse them with such a dose of salt as would make their tongues hang out for thirst below their breeches' buttons, to God knew what confusion.

Before she expounded further, Lily Nightingale, now brewhouse mistress, was offering her best ale against Betty's threats. It was in the midst of all this jocularity that I caught sight of John's frowning face.

"Tom?" he asked, and noted as well as I the grins and gestures that his question provoked. It was Joe Little of course who gave the game away, merely by a look in the direction of the far barn. John strode across the yard and I followed him, always nervous of my husband's sudden temper.

He flung the door wide open and the midday sunshine sent a shaft of light across the dirt floor. The thick straw was deadening the quick gasping of the two young creatures in the furthest corner, but I could see the pale orb of my son's bottom, jack rabbiting away between a pair of splayed and slender legs.

John swore furiously and Thomas rolled, blinking and exposed, away from the girl. She sat up and pulled down her skirt and I was dismayed to see the empty vacant face of Grace Sowerbutts.

John flung his son out of the barn and picked up Grace.

He smacked her hard on each side of the face. On the second one I attempted to intervene, but he turned furiously on me. "Get out of this, mistress. The girl has been forbidden to trespass on my ground. She is older than Tom by all the many ways she has learnt in that ill-famed house. He would hardly know how to use his tool if that young wanton had not brought him to it."

I might have said that Tom was of a good age to use his tool, and but a pattern of his grandfather, but why enrage a man with the blood already rushing to his head?

He dealt the girl a last swinging blow that knocked her back into the straw where she lay with fearful shudders and jerking. I pushed him then from the barn and called the Nightingales to help the poor creature. It was some moments before the spasms ceased. Lily took the child against her bosom and Joan brought water for her. At length Grace stood upon her feet. It strangely moved my heart to see her. She was such a scrawny wispy little thing, all frosted with salt rubbed off from Lily in her hair. I offered that one of my women would set her part way home. She had naught but a scowl for me, and all she found to say was, "I'll tell my mam on this beating."

But what I found when I returned to the house was that the thrashing had cost the lord of the manor far dearer than the epileptic girl. Tom was kneeling by his father's chair side, and John was strangely sprawled in the chair, his hand holding a handkerchief filled with blood.

I had noticed that his continual riding forth and trafficking left him often fatigued, and I had warned him of too much commerce in houses where sickness might linger. But such a collapse as this I had not foreseen. The storm that blows up after fair weather oft takes us by surprise. John did not ride out again that day, nor any day thereafter. He declined with the declining of the year, and when winter came he took to his bed, and Ellen nursed him devotedly in the day, and I took up my vigil in the nights.

But in his long sickening, he often looked at me with suppliant eyes, and more than once he begged me, "Jane, use your power for me. I care not what devil you summon to do me good. But cure me of this sickness."

And when I repeatedly confessed my powerlessness to mend what physicians could not cure, he would shake his head wearily. "Do not abandon me wife. I have never asked a charm of you before. Pay me now for my long sufferance."

Is it simply the meaning of that statement that I have sought to elucidate in the writing of this memoir? And to weigh it for truth?

Well you are come to the end, Jane. Where is your conclusion?

Chapter 44

I SWEAR IT. I swear by the Lord God that I had intended to stop, to have done with this foolish scribbling. All that I sought: a correct conclusion, a verdict gracefully expressed and in my favour, but not depriving of full justice my ever uncertain husband. I needed a final flourish with which to fasten the clasp of this slight volume.

Because it was but last night, as I was preparing myself for bed. We have altered John's chamber, Ellen and I, softening his monastic rigour with sundry cushions and hangings, and I had laid on a blue silk bed mantle. A small fire was lit, for the day had been blustery and cold with sudden downpours. I was not inclined to write any more except I did continue to ponder my conclusive, my conciliative, sentence.

The household was abed when I heard the arrival of a horseman. I was perplexed who it might be, and I could only guess it to be my brother, become repentant after our contentious ride home, and come seeking lodging, after some late conclusion to his business. I had no time to put my paper and pens away or myself to rights before swift steps ascended the stair. The door of my bedchamber stood ajar and opened with no sound, as I prepared to confront my tardy visitor.

He was in my doorway like a moulting great eagle, dripping and morose. The hawk face with furrows that time and privation, sure, had clawed deeper than I remembered. He was murmuring something about my candle perceived to be still burning. I was so taken by the surprise of him that for the instant I could think of nothing whatever to say.

He came forward into the room. "I know I am too late to celebrate a requiem for my nephew. But tomorrow I will say mass in memoriam for John – in the hall – if Thomas allows, and he must allow ..."

His voice trailed off, and then he collected himself and said more firmly, "I wished to bring you my condolences."

By this time I also was somewhat collected. I was aware of all my undress and uncapped hair, but I knew that my small fire was the only one left burning in the house, and I bade him leave off his sopping cloak and come near the warmth, while I went to the kitchen to find refreshment.

When I returned he was sitting upon the carpet before the fire which he had fed to a blaze. As I leaned down to pass his drink he caught hold of my swinging plait, so that I spilled a little of the wine, which he was fine and careless of, gazing up at me with dark intent eyes. "I am wondering if you are in need of consolation yet again?"

The effrontery of his gesture and his question caused me to gasp and certainly to lose some self command. And he must have found it an easy thing to tug my hair and pull me down next to him. He removed the goblet out of my hand, and keeping firm hold of my braid, he tore off the ribbon and began, slowly, to untwist the strands.

"I have done this so often," he said in his sombre voice, "plaited and unplaited this rope for you like any serving woman. When you came. And how often you have come through these long years, how often you have invaded my sleep."

I could only stare at him and at his long fingers so carefully untying the tight weave of my hair, as he murmured, "I have tried, God knows, to defend my soul from your wiles, but when you came to me in dreams I could not help but love you."

I tried to pull free. "I did never come to you. You cannot put the blame on me for what you choose to dream."

"You came," he said firmly, "and do not think that I reproach. I never reproached you, for sin is in the will, and in dreaming that will is suspended, even powerless. I never reproached you but took you into my embrace with such a welcome as you cannot have forgot."

He was ever drawing me towards him – the braid grew short. The more he loosed my hair, the more words tumbled from him.

"Sweeter than virtue, fiercer than innocence, are your apparitions to me – my heart's desire become a vision. No succubus of heavenly sweetness ever so troubled a man's dreams, nor holy virgin could so oft and wantonly have haunted my bed."

I could not stay him.

"Where I awaited you, waited on sleep. When I slept my heart waked. And when I woke I craved to sleep, to dream again."

I had not the power to free myself, he had such handfuls of my hair, but I said – feebly I do think – "But you are not sleeping now, sir. You are in my house where I am newly widowed."

"In your bedchamber," he interrupted me and with a sigh that shook him he pulled me in his arms, still murmuring his orison of love. "Let it grow as you were wont, let it grow into a rope to tie us close, a net of fire to catch us both in one sweet flesh together."

I drew back the very little I was able. "Christopher, I am no light woman—"

But he would have none of it. "You are my light, my warmth, my flame. Lying together this night we will burn as a single candle, and banish all the cold of the world."

As he spoke he was pushing the gown off my shoulder in a remembered gesture, encountering oh how little difficulty with this thin muslin, and as he commenced to find out what he would, my memory flared to feel the flower of an old desire unfolding, those long-past tremors that had so surprised me in the wake of funeral.

But I am now no grief struck, love sick child. No green girl I, but a free widow of more than thirty summers, with a mind full of my brother's strictures and injunctions. However Rick would have me put my singleness to profit, I do not need his instruction to advise me what part of a widow's fair estate is unblemished reputation. So I did struggle still, against my own flesh as much as his embrace. "Do not make me your wanton, Christopher. This is the very fruit of fancy. I am a decent woman. You must not take my virtue for naught."

"Your virtue!" he laughed harshly. "You are temptation, you are not virtue. You are enchantment and fascination, you are my beauteous undoing."

And then he stopped my mouth. He kissed me into silence, into breathlessness, into feebleness of will, into the clamour of desire.

How could I have avoided? After the rough rodding of my husband I could no more withstand this ardent gentleness than a moth can escape candlelight. When he left off speaking, it was his hands praised my beauty, played upon me as if he could make music there. Slow fingers counted the nodules of my spine like beads upon a rosary, 'til I was hectic with impatience to know where they would go, to follow their delicate transgression, the trespass that led to my delight.

He called me fascination, as if like the serpent, I could

hold a bird in frozen stillness. But it was not so. This falcon took me for his prey, and flew a pitch so high before the swoop, that it was rapture indeed that my raptor did obtain for me.

As I think on it all, so soon come and gone, I tremble again, my pen writes all awry, and now I do not know whether I was swept away by his towering height of passion, or by my own amazed and wondering flesh.

Some time after fire was spent and candle guttered, I led him into my bed. How little I had thought, when I laid that blue coverlet on, what guest I should be receiving there, or how royal the entertainment. We plied our trade as assiduously, as ardently, as the dark hours let us, until I thought such sport could never end. It is more true to say that I was so steeped in sensation that I could not contemplate ending. But dawn will come – she will not tarry however she be entreated.

The first sullen half light showed – a bed disordered, a heap of flung silk on the floor, and a man who lay beside me, but apart, his back turned, so that I did not perceive straightway that he was weeping. I felt myself an undone lady. I had not expected such an anguished repentance.

All my attempts to rekindle the flame that had burned so fiercely but an hour before were profitless. The glutted hawk disdains the lure. And where lascivious gesture failed, I was fool enough to try argument.

I spoke incoherently I am sure. I could not endure his cold refusal and my own conscience was in confusion. But I tried to represent to him the possibility that he might abandon a life of such great danger and hardship, battle no more against the law of the land, and free himself from the harsh commandment of his mission. I even made suggestion that he serve his maker in the more comfortable ministry of the established Church, where marriage was permitted to the clergy. Where I had found a peaceful haven.

It was then he turned to face me, his dark eyes burning with something that was not lust. "So I heard and tried not to believe it of you. To bewitch my body is forgiveable. Do you not know the difference between venial sin and apostasy? You have betrayed your faith, and you would seduce me into heresy, a heresy I have spent my life's strength to combat."

His last words came upon a sob, but then he caught sight of that slight blemish above my breast, which my mother had accounted my strongest charm. He leapt from the bed as if he had been burned. "Daughter of Satan, your master has left his mark upon you! And I a fool that did not see."

There was naught for me to say. He wasted no more words or time upon his leaving. I will never set eyes upon him again. And I am suddenly weary of this chronicle.

I have told this night's doing, shameful or not, in strict accordance with my promise to tell all, and as you are hardly cold in the ground, good husband, I account this night's revelry into your bill. The reckoning is done and stands not in my favour after all.

I cannot tell another word of my story. I feel my story has told me.

1652.

Chapter 45

I DID NOT CALL IN MY BEST HOUND last night. Because I had forgot her name.

Other things begin to escape me. Some words, some names, cost me pains to dredge up out of the sediment that time has gradually deposited upon my life. When early morning mist gathers and drifts beyond the river, I have at times observed how strange shapes form within it. I can discern momentarily the forms of castles, ships and steeples, in dim and wavering outlines that form, and dissolve, and reform, and disappear, never to be laid hold of. Such nebulous uncertainty now seems to have overtaken many periods of my life. I, who took great pride in my exact memory, now grasp after recollections that sift away like sand between dry fingers.

And if this of long ago, how much more hateful to be unsure of present time, to feel sharp shapes grow mossy and indistinct. Do objects lose their substance with their names? I begin to feel my very life slithering into long tunnels of obscurity.

Beware old woman, that the ruminations of age prove not more tedious than the shallow reflections of youth. For I have good cause to be grateful to my young self, for making a chronicle, however trivial and self regarding, for preserving fragments of my youth. But I cannot allow her to have the last word – to make the only record of what I have been, of what I am. That girl wrote so blithely about herself, such interminable chatter of her lusts and marrying, of her speculations and affections, while unbeknownst a giant shadow was crawling into the sky. I am resolved to take up the story – not the same story, for what could be the same after the summer of 1612? And if I do not tell it now, some other will – and with what veracity?

And besides, and what stirs me most, this man is come into Lancashire, with tales and marvels. But I know of a wonder that befell him, that belike he knows not himself.

So although swollen knuckles protest the pressure of the pen, and a certain dimness hovers in mine eye, I will most certainly begin. To tell the last piece.

To go back – to where that black curtain fell across my life, the rags of it have always dragged like scars across my brain. But to penetrate that black membrane requires that I exert a pressure on this failing faculty, before I am lost in the confusion of old age.

To it, Jane Southworth, go to it. Tell your story carefully and with a proper attention to the truth of the little that you do know.

✱✱✱

There was, as always is, a calm before the storm. Days when I collected my family and household, when I was putting my life in order. My husband recently dead, I was not left short of assistance. Gilbert Jackson and Edward Osbaldeston were on hand, were pressing to render me service and advice. My appetite for male flesh being well and truly sated, I took their help and their solicitude with a very good grace, and total restraint. And believed myself quite free of sinful craving. But like a dying bird, I had one last brief fluttering.

I had received a message that, being gravely ill, my mother wished to see me. I was not dear to Isabella, nor she to me, but the hovering of the shadows creates a need for binding, for the binding of old wounds, for the binding of the bonds of family.

Since Ellen's loved nephew was to ride in that same direction, she offered that he might accompany me to Wigglesworth and there give any help I might require. I look back on that soft April ride as the last memory of an innocent world. We rode through wakening woodlands, as the courteous, serious boy discoursed on the mind of God, with that particular accent that he fetched from Rochdale.

I am familiar with the mobility of hills. Great Pendle has a peculiar capacity for locomotion. Sometimes it lies slumbering in a far off mist, cloud-capped and remote. Sometimes it obtrudes on the gaze with important assertion, heavy and monumental. Sometimes it comes up so close one could almost scratch off the snow with a fingernail. But on this damp, sweet April journey we were surrounded by moving hills. As we rode towards the north, they rose into view, wherever rides and clearings had been carved out of the forest. Slowly they moved, slower than our horses, but ponderously sure, and as our winding paths shifted perspective, we felt their presence, looming and contemplative, enclosing the world.

"I feel as if they ride with us, in protection, like watchful giants," I said to Roger Brierley.

He was eager in agreement. "I think they have the steadfastness of servants of the Lord. I should dearly love to serve in such a place." And shyly he confessed, "I have made enquiries for the possibility of a ministry in Grindleton when I have completed my studies."

"Why this village, Roger? Is it for the sake of Pendle Hill?"

"Yes," he answered quickly, "I should like to climb Pendle every day and pray atop of it. One might have glimpses of angels from there, and hear the songs of Paradise."

"You are as fond and mystical as Alice Nutter," I observed.

He laughed, then added seriously, "But the parish of Grindelton is very holy. Every person in that blessed assembly seems to me like a candlestick, fashioned to hold the white light of the Lord."

His face was rapt as he spoke, and I felt already the scald of the leaping flame, which I was careful to repress, and to conceal with a sceptical question. "Every person?"

"Ah well," he admitted, "there are some who are not ready yet, not grown perfected, but who wish to take part in our devotions. Elizabeth Southern's granddaughter is one making an apprenticeship of the spirit, hoping to grow into grace."

"Alizon Device?" I questioned with, I am sure, even more scepticism.

He nodded. "For all she walks with an old grandmother who frights half the populace and comes of a family known for quarrels and discords, for all that, she asks to be allowed to follow our ways, to be cleansed and renamed in spirit."

I wondered what Alice might have had to do with this surprising conversion, and then I asked him about the preachments he came often to hear in Preston. He was so open, this very young man, so open of heart, and he spake so eagerly and frankly, that I feared he might see the heat in my face. But he was wrapped in his own thought, too determinedly seeking the words that would convey it. Too taken up, thank heaven, to observe the untoward ardour of a widow woman.

"I come most to hear John Winstanley preach," he said. "He is a very fiery rousing speaker, would take the world apart in his hands and refashion it. He does not see Heaven in a blue sky, nor looks for God in a place of glory beyond the sun, but in the soul of every man and woman living."

"I think we do not all inhabit Paradise, nor is every walking human carrying God along with him."

"But Winstanley believes that while men gaze beyond in time, reaching their imagination after a happiness or fearing a hell after they are dead, their eyes are blinded to their own birthright. They see not what is to be done on earth."

"And what is to be done on earth?"

"What is to be done on earth is to live in that primitive freedom for which God had intended his creation, not for the covetous to enclose and parcel up the land, nor bag and barn the treasures of the earth away out of the reach of their fellow men, who must beg or starve in this fruitful land."

"That is but an ancient call, for plentiful charity."

"He is not so peaceable. He accuses the rich very plainly of the double sin of property. First that they enjoy land got in the first place by the sword, and by the sword sheathed in the law, they hold it."

"So who is this Winstanley, that will so ferociously castigate every landlord in the country? Is he a learned divine, or a dreamy itinerant tradesman?"

"He is a joiner, a carpenter of sorts. Not too poor a profession for one who comes to preach the word of God."

I heard how he rebuked my irony, but irony was my protection. "To wrench the world to his notion of a just order. It is not the first time I have heard such sentiments, but they were better not spoke aloud. Here in green woods you may say your piece, but this Winstanley is a fool to shout out in the market place."

"He is not alone," the young man answered firmly,

"and they are not my sentiments neither, but up and down the land you will hear such things being said."

"I am glad they are not your sentiments."

"It is not the way of the Family of Love, to proceed by violence. But there will come a day of reckoning, even for such as wear a crown."

"You are very impudent in your certainties, young man."

"And you, Mistress Southworth, have you not your own certainties also?"

I looked through the pallor of almost green leaf, through the mist of something softer than rain, and answered very slowly. "I am not certain. I have a divided soul. I with myself do not always agree."

By that I touched him, or rather he was bold enough to touch my hand. "I will pray for you, Mistress Southworth. That you be enfolded in the love of Christ, and in the love of your fellow men."

And then we left the love of Christ and the love of fellow men. We left the cool April day. And I entered Wigglesworth Hall.

Chapter 96

MY MOTHER'S HOUSE was suffocating hot, and dark with many curtains drawn, not on account of death, but to preserve Isabella from headache. She was herself ensconced before a roaring fire, in a large wing chair, mountainously padded with embroidered bolsters. She bore a long-suffering look, but not a dying one.

"Our mother is much recovered," said Grace severely, with a look on her face that seemed to say, 'else you were come too late'.

"I am not inclined to die just now," said Isabella. "You need not have come. I sent for you before time."

"But now I have come and am very pleased to see you recovered. Perhaps I can help Grace take care of you for a little time."

"You have never helped before," said my sister with no good grace.

"But I have great suffering," lamented Isabella, "and Gracie is a tender nurse. I have dolours in the limbs from the gout, and even worse in the gut – it has riven my belly like a knife, like a scald of boiling milk, 'til I have wept to God to take me from this life."

I contemplated the ruins of her beauty with little compassion. Her catalogue of complaints irritated me, and as I noted the various dishes of sweetmeats that lay around the supposed sick room, and the pitcher of sugared wine in the hearth, I could not forbear the suggestion that if she forced less work on her gut, it might repay her with less pain.

My sister tutted, and my mother threw me a baleful look. "Always you have more to say than you have right to speak. Always you are opinionated and troublesome, Jane. I wonder how long you mean to stay at Wigglesworth. Your brother is promised to come tomorrow eve, and it were certainly best you were not here."

"But you sent for me to come. And why ever should I be deprived of seeing Rick?"

"That was before—" said Grace, but Isabella had not finished with my offences. "You surely must know in what way you have offended him. Apart that you have abandoned and betrayed the faith of your ancestors, I have learned how you misbehaved at your first marriage, and how you treat with disdain your brother's advice and arrangements towards a second. You always speak out of turn, and you behave so as to provoke scandal."

She had put herself out of breath, but before I had well opened my mouth to protest, Grace had took up the charge.

"You have to do with witches. In Rick's house you defended the Demdike, even when she made great affray, and brought the Devil Himself to kill Richie Assheton."

I do not think I disguised the contempt I felt. "I spoke only against enclosure and I hold that view to this day. Nor do I believe that Elizabeth Southern has Satan at her beck and call. And Richie Assheton was sickly a good while, and not believed to live so long."

"Well now is all paid for," said Grace in a loud and contented voice. "They are all cleared out at last. The Demdike is hauled off to Lancaster with old Mother Chattox. Just yesterday they were took."

Those two old women were of no consequence to me, but still I felt a shudder in my heart. "Old Anne Whittle too," I said sadly. "She has done nothing but dispense remedies and bring children into the world."

"And Anne Redferne, she also. Off to Lancaster Castle, the lot of them, along with Alizon Device, it being that girl that started the whole investigation."

"Not Anne Redferne, dear God, there is no sweeter person."

"Ask Robert Nutter if she is a sweet woman," said Isabella, "if you could get him out of the grave to answer."

"And poor little Alizon Device, she is not capable—"

"You still go to it—" began my mother, but Grace sat stiffly erect in her chair, and spoke less loudly, but with more intent.

"Alizon Device has bewitched a man to nigh death. She has been examined and has confessed herself to witchcraft."

"Ah no," I still confusedly protested. "Why would she confess herself into the hangman's noose?"

"Because there is no doubt. She was pestering John Law, the pedlar man, bothering him for pins or such, and when he denied her she stood off and stamped her foot, and gave him a bad look. She has told all of it. Prompt he dropped down upon the floor and was incapable of motion, and after he was found and carted off to the alehouse at Colne. She came to beg his pardon, but he was still dire afflicted, his speech all smothered and half his motion gone. He is a good man and he did forgive her, seeing her so very contrite. But then his son came over from Halifax. Abraham Law, he is a cloth dyer and no fool. Seeing his father so afflicted he desired to call the witch to account and reported all to Roger Nowell."

"And from that?"

"And from that all the other derived. Alizon confessed herself and named the others, who have all now had examination and, as I say, they are on their way to Lancaster's dungeons."

"And no one to help the poor creatures?"

"You still go to it," said my mother, who was out of all patience with me. "You will leave nothing alone. You will contaminate us all with your interest. Your brother will not tolerate your contrary taking of sides, and I will not have him thwarted and annoyed by your nonsense!"

After this outburst, she required some medicinal drops to calm her ill humour and the chest cramps I had undoubtedly caused.

But after supper when Isabella was abed, Grace said to me, "It were better for you to leave, Jane. Our mother is right, you cause much bother and nuisance. And Rick is like to be as annoyed as any if you embark on your 'Oh the pitiful', when we do well to be rid of them."

"What can it matter to you," I said wearily, "whether they come or go, these poor folk?"

She said, "Aside from their claims and demands on our charity, on us and all our neighbours, and their filth and displeasing aspect, they stain our reputation with their garbled prayers and their tit-tat of holy ceremonies. They tag on to the tail of true believers, and what with all the fury attendant on Jesuit exorcisms, we need to cut cleanly off from all suspicion of dealing with magical charms."

"I cannot believe you perceive them a danger."

"You may have your own opinion, Jane, but it were best you send a messenger to your servant to return on the morrow and escort you home."

"He is not my servant, and I will go alone at first light," I said.

I resolved rather to go to Roughlee and talk with Alice, before returning to Samlesbury.

Chapter 47

IT WAS THE FIRST TIME I had ever ridden such a distance alone, servantless. Perhaps this in part accounts for the cloud of despondency which was heavy upon me, far over-topping any fear of louts or vagabonds. Nor did I fear to lose my way, for while part of my mind was remembering directions, my inwardest thoughts were wandering other paths, of surmise and disquiet.

As I rode southerly I could not rub out of my mind that other, northbound road. I could not prevent myself imagining the progress of those poor women, roped and dragged through the long winding trough between the Bowland Fells. No friendly guardian hills those, but wild barren heathland rising bleakly from the narrow road, swelling and folding away in desolate beauty, comfortless to the limits of vision.

And after the felons' road, the castle, high and mighty, awaiting them.

Although such imaginings made me wish to hasten, it was late when I came to Roughlee. At Crow Trees it was Hugh Redferne came to take my horse. He clasped my hand briefly, with no word, and followed me into the farmhouse.

Alice was seated by a big fire, gazing into the flames as if she would find an answer there to a hard mystery. But she rose quickly to come to me, to embrace me against her, fiercely, as I were the only sure thing in a world of thistledown. And kept tight hold of my hand when we sat down.

Joan Gentle, with eyes reddened and swollen, brought us drink and set about laying the table. Hugh took his place there – I had not thought to see him look so elderly. And still no one had spoke. I was at a loss in that grieving farm kitchen, and I spoke some of my bewilderment.

"What is to be done? How could they be so suddenly pounced upon?"

The shadow of a smile crossed Alice's face. "I cannot forever answer all your questions, Jane. The first I do not know, the second is easy to guess."

But it was, oddly, Joan Gentle who took up the burden of explanation. "It is Alizon Device who was always half crazed with waiting on her grandma. But I cannot clear in my mind why she would name Annie, when all her quarrels were with Bess."

"It makes little difference," Hugh at last found words, "why a simple creature casts her malice at the wrong person. Once declared witch, confessed witch, Alizon may name any names, and bring whomsoever into accusation."

"It was by hap or chance," Joan halted her laying of platters on the table, to follow her thought, "a trick of fate that the pedlar fell down just as Alizon was probably ill-wishing him. The man has long since been buying calamity with his great paunch and his plum-purple face. Who could be surprised?"

No one answered and she went on with her work and her commentary. "With John Law down on the ground, Alizon must have believed she had found the knack, learned of her grandmother. Believed she had a power."

I could not help reflecting. "It is a puzzle to know when happenchance comes by accident or by intention."

"Happenchance means without intention," said Alice severely.

"But it is a confusion," I insisted. "I only just yesterday heard that Alizon has asked to be accepted into the Family of Love."

Joan nodded. "They even talked of a naming day, but she is a feather light, like to be blown in any wind, blown any which way. I deem her a lost soul."

Alice sighed. "Alizon is not a girl who has lost her way, she has never known her way. She is a child, not a simple idiot like Jimmy, but with such childishness. She asks for the Lord's grace, and she runs after trinkets. She would be a member of the Family of Love, and she helps her grandmother with spiteful spells. She is not good nor bad, but puzzled. Very puzzled I should say."

I felt the necessity then to abandon my own puzzlement and to think harder on ways to help. "How can we save Anne? Is there a way?"

Alice sighed again. "I must go to Malkin. They will be in such a wilderness of fear. Lizzie is not taken, nor Jimmie neither – yet. Already the rumour flies that the folk at Malkin Tower would hatch a second gunpowder plot to blow up Lancaster Castle, in order to free those women. They are like to break into much stupidity."

"The fools," said Hugh bitterly.

"Aye, foolishness is all their undoing," said Alice.

I could not endure to see Alice so cast down. "I shall go to Nowell," I offered. "I can perhaps endeavour to explain. It was plainly the apoplexy, this of John Law, and has confused the girl into confession. I have known a similar thing – an old and heavy man, in temper. This is not beyond understanding. And Nowell is a learned man, not compassionate, but not stupid neither. And to drag in Anne is such nonsense. I will go and talk to him."

Alice spoke quickly. "Jane you shall do no such thing. To speak with Nowell now would serve no more than to spit in the wind, and the Lord God knows what will blow back in your face."

"Then I shall go to Judge Walmsley. Tomorrow I will ask his help. Give me a bed for the night and I will ride to Dunkenhalgh first thing. He will advise how we may save Anne at the least."

Alice I think feigned to be reassured, but none of us found much to say at that supper table. Alice asked Hugh Redferne for a hymn to give us courage and hope, but it was long before he could be prevailed on. How sorrow does translate people. The thoughtful and judicious steward broke into an angry anthem:

> Why fum'th in fight the Gentiles spite,
> In fury raging stout?
> Why tak'th in hand the people fond,
>   vain things to bring about?
> The Kings arise, the Lords devise,
> In counsels met thereto.
> Against the Lord with false accord
> Against His Christ they go.

And Alice in a voice unexpectedly rough and harsh, prayed, "Oh my sweet Annie, Heaven save you. Dear God preserve that woman in the castle of cruelty."

❉ ❉ ❉

It seemed that all the folk I visited that time were unwell, all seated by a fireside. The judge lay reading in a long, extended chair, wearing a quantity of silken shawl. He put down his book when I entered, but he did not rise to greet me. The welcome was all in his face. "My dearest Jane what do you here? The servant says you come alone and I perceive you are in some disarray." He waved me towards a chair. "Be seated, take your breath, and let my man bring you some wine."

As I endeavoured to compose myself, he tapped the book he had been reading. "This friend of mine, Montaigne, is of the view that no man should be executed, without there is a luminous clarity of evidence." He nodded to me with great seriousness. "'A luminous clarity of evidence,' how I honour that phrase. I doubt there will be overmuch luminosity in the summer Assizes at Lancaster."

"So you know why I am come – to seek your help for Anne Redferne. If someone with authority could speak to Roger Nowell. I myself even thought to go to Read Hall, but Alice Nutter forbade me."

"Alice is right, Alice is always right. Nowell has made his snatch. Like any good game dog he will not let go 'til he has laid the bird at his master's feet."

"Is there nought to do?"

"Words dropped into the right ears, or coins dropped into the right pockets will not help here. The trial must go forward."

"So they are lost, lost!"

He took up his pipe and waited for the servant to bring a taper before he answered me, and I thought he drew more solace from the tobacco than the wine.

"Nowell will lean on King James, that's sure. He is very familiar with the 'Daemonologie'. So he will be certain to use the confessions of the accused to incriminate their fellows. And between promises of fear and hope, he may elicit, may help to invent, ignorant statements, that he can twist to any pattern of evidence."

He continued to speak slowly, evidently contending with pain. "Bromley will be in judgement and probably James Altham also. Bromley is an honest man, not exceedingly clever, but fair. And he is very mild with juries, which means they will be much affected by the feeling in the court. So – demeanour is everything. I have seen many poor fools blather themselves into a noose. Silence is golden, and sober dignity a powerful advocate." He added in a low voice, "And some consolation in case of failure."

He smoked on and I waited on his words. "Torture is forbidden, but searching for devil's marks is examination, not torture. If the prisoners could hold unbroken to their innocence, if they can retain some shreds of decent bearing—"

"Despite incarceration?" I interrupted.

"Despite incarceration," he agreed. "They might yet escape."

"And no confessions?"

"Certainly no confessions."

"Shall I try to send word with these warnings?"

"No by God you should not!" He raised himself with difficulty in his chair, and it might have been my father instructing me. "You should keep clear of all this Jane. You may pray for them. But you should stay out of all commerce with these people. And Alice too, it were better that she should not meddle."

I began to say that it were impossible for Alice not to meddle, but he waved me away with his much be-ringed hand: "Pray for them Jane, and pray for me, but keep well clear."

Chapter 48

HOW LENGTHILY I DO PURSUE the prologue to my own theme. I shrink back from tearing away the last rag of forgetfulness, from revisiting my darkest days

❊❊❊

I simply do not remember how or when we knew that James and Elizabeth Device were taken, along with folk I did not know. But I do remember the silence in our kitchen, and the wretched hangdog look of Thomas Welshman, who brought the news of Alice's arrest. And Ellen, so very quietly asking, "Did she go alone?" and the boatman shrugged and said, "They say a man went after, a tall stooping man, a shepherd it is thought, followed all the way behind the cart, but did not speak to the soldiers, nor to the prisoner neither."

I went to the river alone, to weep for Alice, to cudgel my poor brain to think of someone I could ask to intercede for her. Standing there by the water, I remembered the shouts from Lancaster's streets that I had imagined blowing down, on the day of Robert Nutter's hanging. And despite the exceeding fine summer that came, I never could shake off the melancholy that hung like mourning clouts about our house.

❊❊❊

One bright morning Solomon Potter was brought into the parlour, wheezing mightily, sneezing apologetically through his sparse whiskers and sparser teeth, come to inform me that he was ordered to accompany me, to bring me before the local magistrate.

I cannot describe my disbelief. He was obliged to repeat his instructions again and again, and each time with more splutter.

I was in full mourning still for my husband, but I immediately bade Ellen fetch my crimson silk cape. Was it to emphasise my rank, or my contempt, or simply to bolster up my courage?

I swept into Robert Holden's house with as much arrogance as I could muster. I knew the young man as kin to an ageing magistrate who sometimes assisted Roger Nowell. He sat before a table piled with books and documents, and was about to embark on some unctuous sentence.

"So," I said on entry, throwing Judge Walmsley's advice to the winds, "you have heard of arrests in Pendle and think what slander you may throw upon the virtuous womanhood of Samlesbury?"

The justice shifted his papers about – I swear his mother's milk not dried upon his chin – "Mistress Southworth, I am bid to ask you certain questions is all. If you would kindly make answer to me I shall not keep you many moments. Please be seated."

I stayed standing, letting him see my furious face.

"It is reported – I have here a deposition from John Singleton – that your husband's kin, Sir John Southworth, did believe you to be an enchantress and did go in fear and avoided you on that account. Is this true to your knowledge?"

"You use the reported words of an old man half out of his wits and dead these many years, with no power to retract them, and you would on such slender reason call me before you?"

"It saith that the late Sir John Southworth feared for your husband's life, that you might kill him, and that your husband himself was ever in fear of you."

"My husband as you too well know is dead also, five months past, and cannot stand here to defend me from your infamy. I have only the evidence of seventeen years of faithful married life, of an orderly house, of seven children of promise, of my place in this parish and my good name."

The young man pursed his lips, fiddled with his papers. "Did you know a woman by the name of Mary Snow?"

"Mary Snow! I knew an old pauper woman of that name and gave her often a cup of milk or a piece of bread. Is that a crime?"

"And did you never suspect her of witchcraft?"

"Of course I did not. She was a poor wisewoman who used herbs and simples. That is not witchcraft. She never did ill to anyone."

"But did you not beg a charm of her to break your barrenness – before these children came?"

"I marvel into what filthy drains your spies go raking to procure such nonsense evil stories. I cannot imagine who told you such a thing, but I am sure that such a pathetic evil-minded tale would be laughed at in the very court, Mr Holden, and you yourself the laughing stock of the county. A charm for barrenness! When you have more to accuse me of than an old man's babble and a little kindness to a beggar woman, then call for me to answer a serious charge and I will make you a sensible answer." I did not stay 'til he had risen to bow me out before I was through the door.

But so they did, they called for me, but not to go to Robert Holden's house. This time both constable and churchwarden awaited me. Solomon Potter stood twisting his hat around in his hands, weeping unashamedly. James

Winstanley said, "Mistress Southworth, God forgive us, we are charged to take you to Lancaster castle."

I wanted to laugh, loudly, unbelievingly, laugh as my father might have laughed to put these feeble retainers out of countenance, to dissolve the menacing moment, but my voice came out curiously meek. "Why James this cannot be. I am loved and respected in this parish. I have not harmed a soul."

He stood silent, in terrible unease.

I spoke stronger: "Do you know James? Who stands to speak against me? I pray you answer for the love of God."

His eyes cast down, James reluctantly answered, "Grace Sowerbutts has a story to tell against you."

"Of witchcraft?"

"Aye."

And then there was that taste in my mouth, of iron and ashes, the taste of real fear. And I felt as if my whole life, of seeking and evasion, of compacting and accommodating, all my efforts to find a solid rock to stand on, all were come to a headlong stop at this moment. I was frozen in time and could not imagine the morrow. My future had simply been taken away.

I knew my eldest son had entered the room and I could hear Lily and Joan drawing the other children away from the parlour. From a great way off I heard James's voice: "Gilbert Jackson is waiting in the yard. He is urgent to speak with you."

I think I frowned in incredulity, and Solomon put in, "It would have been more than my life's worth, Mistress Southworth, not to have told Gilbert Jackson what has befallen you."

I turned to Ellen to bid her I know not what, and James said, "And Ellen Brierley must go too, along with Janet her mother."

It was hard to stay standing on my feet. And James in that mournful voice continuing, "We go now to fetch Janet. It will give you a little time, Mistress Southworth, and you too, Ellen Brierley, to collect such things as may be needful to you."

And then Gilbert was in the room, and a leathern bag was on the table. "I will ride with you, Mistress Southworth – Jane – I will ride with you. We may purchase you some clean accommodation. And I have brought my grey mare to be your mount."

Thomas stepped forward, "I will ride with my mother. I thank you, sir. It is my part."

I saw his face as white as whey milk, and I could guess what spectres of guilt had come to haunt him, and I over-mastered my paralysis. "Thank you Gilbert. But it is Thomas must go with me."

The man, in kindness, tried to insist, but I was able to repeat, "Thank you, but there is no question."

"Then for God's sake take the money. It is the language of the prison keeper." He turned to Thomas. "Take it and demand good housing for her." And to me: "And I do beseech you ride my big mare. She is very steady, like a rock, and she is tall," and to my probably uncom-prehending stare, he murmured, "she will carry you well above the crowd."

I went like one dazed in a dream, on that journey. And like a dream, the most of it has evaded my recollection. Snatches remain, pictures in my mind: Angelica's dumb distress at the yard gate as we rode away, Tom's too drawn, too young face, the long swaying stride of the big grey mare.

Not so far on the way we were met by a posse of soldiers, who relieved James and Solomon of their escort. We halted atop a small hill, affording a view of John of Gaunt's huge fortress. The men not roughly but jestingly advised that I avail myself of the view, this being where most prisoners commenced to weep.

To me, at that moment, it was almost insubstantial; a castle floating on clouds, standing proud of the sunlit bay of the sea. It did not take on reality, until we clattered through the city streets and the towered facade rose above us, as we mounted the short, sharp incline to the gate. The long grey neck with its hanging mane swung high before me, as the horse quickened her pace to mount the slope, almost trotting under the louring massive gateway. 'Abandon all hope,' saith the poet of Hell's entrance. It should have been writ over the portal of Lancaster Castle. The gates closed behind us with a clangour that waked me sharply out of my dream. I could not bear to leave the horse, had difficulty to clamber down from the warm, living breathing creature. I clutched at the coarse mane for one childish moment before we were led off, led off to be seen by the Keeper of the Prison.

Thomas Covell, a fat man with hooded sleepy eyes, was slow to speak.

My son pushed forward, desperate to play his part.

"I wish to provide for my mother and her attendants as seemly accommodation as may be possible, and for her to be treated with the consideration that her rank demands."

He was brusque, much too brusque, as he brought down on the table the heavy leather bag.

Covell blinked at the word 'demands,' but did not look at the bag. "We have foreseen your request," he answered in a tired monotonous voice, "and Mistress Southworth is allowed a room of considerable comfort but it will cost – a great deal." Barely did he let his eyes flit towards the money bag. "We have reserved a small room over the gate, with an adjoining chamber. She is allowed one waiting woman only. Strictly only one may be allowed."

Before Thomas could begin to argue, I approached the table.

"Master Covell, this old woman is sick and requires the attendance of my waiting woman. I ask you the great favour that you lodge them together, with the other prisoners if need be. And that you allow Alice Nutter to be brought out to serve as my waiting maid."

I knew this request was beyond the scope of my privilege, and neither I nor Covell looked at the bag, being both so much more worldly than Tom.

He said tiredly, "I will permit it then." He scrawled numbers upon a sheet before him, and glanced up at me. "It is August, you will not require hearty fare I think. But we will see you properly served, Madam. Your son and I will draw up the reckoning, Mistress Southworth." And briefly nodded his dismissal of me.

The dream gains in clarity. I see the narrow stone spiral leading to the gatehouse room. I remember being thankful for its decency, for the stone bed covered in straw, for the adjoining chamber just big enough to keep the slops pail in, but most of all for the tiny barred window, that spied down into the courtyard below, and up into a slice of sky that let in the light of day.

I stood at the window, and I saw my son enter the courtyard, untether the horses and, leading the grey, he waited for the men to open the gate. He cast never a look behind as he urged the horses outward.

Chapter 49

I STILL TURN THE PAGES of my youthful manuscript, and I marvel how blithely I reported on the wheel of Fortune, not knowing how frantic fast it could spin, into what depths it might tumble the unwary soul.

Since those days of long ago, the world itself has toppled upside down. We have been shook with civil strife. The folk have risen. We have severed the very head and new powerfuls arise. It is all indifferent to me. Full forty years have lost me a son, and him I counted more than kings and crowns.

But Alice was right as to the buzzing of the bees. I am not so sure of her belief in the beauteous daughter, Truth, emerging from the womb of Time. Except this man has come into the north, and he now dares say aloud so much of what the Family of Love whispered secretly. Oh I hear tell of how he preaches the secret spirit, the divine light in every soul. How he looks for freedoms, disdains authority, despises deference. And there are crowds going to meet him – Seekers from Yorkshire and Lancashire. What would you make of George Fox, Alice?

What did I make of her when they brought her to my cell? They brought her that night. No one expects a wholesome appearance out of a dungeon, but I could never have let myself imagine such a falling away. Who was thin, was become skeletal skinny, her once weather-tanned face now a ghastly tallow drawn over protruding bone, her dark hair white as a shroud and wildly unkempt like a furze bush, her gait all faltering and falling, and her stench like she brought the midden with her.

I used Gilbert's money to marvellous effect. We had water brought that was warm, and clouts, so I could wash her. It was a long washing. In all the works of mercy I ever undertook, this was the most pure hearted, the nearest I ever came to holiness.

I fed her a very little and gave her drink. She was blinded by the evening light, but kept reaching to touch me, and then murmuring, "I cannot believe it – such joy, such joy." It made my heart weep to see so derelict a creature from such a hell hole, professing joy. But everything I did to ease her increased her thankfulness. And when we were done, and her tears had stopped helplessly trickling, she lay upon clean straw – the pinnacle of comforts – and slept, as peaceful as babe in cradle.

I lay next her. The troubled sleep that fatigue and fear had driven me into did not last long. When I woke, the sounds of guards and soldiers in the courtyard had ceased. A silvery silence had entered our prison cell; bands of bright light striped the stone floor.

I crossed to the tiny barred window, and there she was, queening it in the night sky, with an attendance of many stars. I gripped the bars that fractured her light, remembering the night she had seemed to offer me a gift which I had refused. How if all had been different? If I had then devoted myself to lunar worship, entered the service of Diana, gained secrets of her chaste power? Power that I had willingly renounced, to tread a path of domestic duty and marital complaisance. A path of ordinariness that had fetched up in these stone walls. Now had come the time to regret the magic that I had abjured. So might I have preserved myself, better than an ordinary virtuous life had done.

I wanted no truck with peasant sorcery, with clay dollies and talking cats and upside down prayers. I could not distance myself too far from the village feuds and ignorant foolery that were the stuff of gossip, and had dragged us all into this prison. What I longed for was the grace and silence and poise of the moon. Longed for a more ancient magic that could have me away, above all the tether and terror down below.

I concentrated my gaze upon her, seeking a state of contemplation, striving to recover the sensation of my wedding night, willing myself to transform this helplessness, into some semblance of power, hoping for a sign that would show me how to release the jaws of the trap I was caught in.

But this night I perceived a puzzle upon the face of the moon – a faint uneven shadowing that gave her an expression slightly interrogative, perhaps faintly amused, an expression of uncertainty, almost an O of surprise. I could not decipher it. Did she feel the distress of her handmaiden? Was her influence deflected by the iron bars? Were the walls of John of Gaunt a fiercer barrier than the drifting clouds?

I could find no connection, make no communion. The scrap of secret knowledge that I had buried deep in a crack in my soul, now that I had prised it out, was turned out feeble, useless. Howsoever my body was constrained in the cell, my mind could move into no refuge neither. Until the idiot part of it began repeating inside my head:

> *Jane, Jane, whereto are you came?*
> *Dishonour, disgrace, sorrow and shame.*

I heard the changing of the watch before I lay down again on the pallet next to Alice, and something of her peacefulness persuaded me to oblivion.

Those days in the gatehouse cell: time out of time, out of the world, when life was stopped, the whole whirligig halted in mid revolution. Four days out of fourscore years is not too much to lose, but that space has marked me. I lost more than time, lost part of myself, or else I found an emptiness that appalled me. What is certain is that I lost some fair image of myself. I found I was not courageous – I had nor faith nor hope nor acquiescence. But my cell mate had them all.

And how she strove, my friend Alice, with her little strength returning – and it was truly a wonder how much of the old Alice did come back. How she strove to fortify me, to imbue some part of her spirit into mine so poorly failing. She made wry jests, solemn exhortations, told stories, even devised contests. She tried every device to cajole a child into patience. And I am astonished to think of it, how in those stark hours I could still play the petulant child to one who loved me so generously. But so I did, let her take the brunt of my distress.

When she quietly enquired why I was fallen into a sullen silence, I said bitterly, "I have been wrenching my mind to confront the fact that we are likely entering upon our death."

"Death is not the worst."

"No perhaps it is not the worst of it. But I am not ready to die. I am very fearful. I have children, a babe – my little Rosamund at home. And I do not know my way to Heaven. I am not of your Family of Love and I have found no church to which I can make true profession."

She looked gravely towards me. "But you are on your way to Heaven." And in the old dreamy voice she intoned, "I believe that the spirit of God is like the honey bee. He plies in the flowers of the hedgerows as eagerly as in my lady's bower. He has no need to put names to the flowers of his love. And he will not thrust his sting into the nettle flower because she has not the fragrance nor the legend of the rose. But gathering sweetness from all who open the petals of their soul, he will transmute that love into the very food of Paradise."

"All you are lacking is a pulpit," I said, with a sourness I could ill disguise.

"Pulpit or market square," she said, "there is nought I should have so dearly loved to do, as teach folk the ways of the Lord."

"I mind me what my father once said to you, that preachment is not fitting in a woman."

"There are as many ways of serving God and loving Man as there are stars in the sky—"

"And half we do not know, and half we do not dare," I interrupted, in imitation of her slow preachy voice.

"But you remember everything." She took nothing but affection from my mockery. "Because you listen hard, which is what has always rendered you so dear to me. But since you are now my entire congregation and since our best friends must be upon their knees just now to petition for us, let us also kneel, Jane, and endeavour to pray well. To pray even against your disbelief will do us both good."

As well as frequently praying, she was also constantly expressing her immeasurable content to be with me "Though I would give my every last lamb to have you out of this dire strait, yet for me it is a pleasure I never looked to receive before my death."

She also professed herself well pleased with the "princely entertainment" I had purchased from the master gaoler. He kept his bargain, old Covell. We were fed; not daintily, not copiously, but fed. And the wine he allowed was harsh and comforting.

"He is a fair trader," said Alice judiciously, "a cruel examiner but a tolerable innkeeper."

"You are a market woman to the last, Alice Nutter."

I am sure she marked my every smile for a triumph. She spoke but briefly of the rat hole she had left, for she knew it smote my heart to think I had sent poor Janet and Ellen there, into the lightless cellar, where terrified wretches lay in their own befoulment, with barely enough water and bread to keep souls in their bodies. And indeed Demdike's soul had already escaped that ancient body.

No wonder that such an aged woman should succumb to like privation, I thought.

"Dead of fear more like," said Alice, "dread of examination. Hunger and dirt were no strangers to Elizabeth Southern and the light of her eyes is long since gone. But the probing and fastening on of stories by clever men pitched her into such a state of mental confusion and bodily pain as made death a welcome guest. But not before the terror she had endured was spread among us all, like one scabbed sheep will so fast infect the fold."

"It does not bear thinking of."

"You are right. And no good will come of thinking on it. What is past our help let it be past our grief. It cannot be mended, but it can be prayed for."

As well as these frequent calls to prayer, she thought to pass the weary hours in sharing recollections of past joys and loves. She took a deep interest in the pieces that I chose to tell. When I questioned her in return, her ravaged face lit up with a memory of the itinerant mystic boy who had brought the message of the Family of Love, along with holy books smuggled in bales of cloth and wool.

"Using the packhorse trails," I said sententiously. "That was a criminal offence Alice."

She nodded agreeably. "It was for the Perfects, teaching how we should be transfigured, godded with God."

There were other diversions in this incarceration than Alice's dreaming up stories to entertain me. There was an oft tramping of steps and rattling of bolts as Covell allowed messages from the outside world to be delivered to us. I had enough coins to keep the prison guards content to mount our narrow stair, and when I rued the bribery, Alice spread her hands, "Even gaolers have a livelihood to earn."

One time a thick roll of blanket was thrown in to us. "Gilbert," I said without hesitation, "he is always of a practical turn of mind," and we were both awed by the luxury.

Not awed but moved to tears by a little wooden box containing one red rose, and a scrap of parchment with a misspelled scrawl: "the shurburn rentil."

"I have my red rose," I said to her sadly, "of redemption or of passion. Where can I find you a lily for your days of light?"

"We will have our lilies soon enough."

Alice was returned the leather bag that had been confiscated on her arrival at the prison. We pored over the contents as wonders: a book of prayer, some lavender sachets, a kerchief, a phial of limeflower water, a tiny pair of iron-rimmed spectacles. Only in the evening did she rummage out a little clay pipe, package of tobacco, a tinder box.

I was for some reason incensed by this. I said severely – oh God forgive me – "This is a prison not an alehouse, Alice." And she replied imperturbably, "To every churl his cheer my dear Jane."

❊❊❊

No diversion but a call to bitter recollection was the entry of the king's judges into the city. From our eyrie we could hear the fanfare of trumpets, the jingle of bridles, the tramping of pikemen and the applause of crowds. I could not forget my father proudly riding off to the Assizes, and I reflected helplessly on my so much changed fortune. I shook at the immoveable iron bars in baffled, bewildered anger. Alice sat behind me said, "So the great men are come. Mayhap they are the ones to send us to Heaven."

It was late, after we had supped, that I received the last missive of that day. It was a brief note from Judge Walmsley:

> *My dearest girl,*
>
> *I cannot help you. I am beyond help myself. I do but weakly wanton with Death and he will soon have ravished me. Be brave. I do believe you may fly free. Listen to Alice, if that is possible. She is the wise old bird. And come to my funeral – it will be splendid.*

Chapter 50

I AM COME TO THE VERY BOTTOM of my well, and if I were to look up I would see no stars.

Not a well, but a cesspit more like, surrounded as I am by a mass of shaking, slithering, stinking humanity. Penned in with demented, gibbering, trembling, tumbling idiots, who can hardly stand in the daylight, and whose stench would worsen a pig pen. And across the courtroom I observe half the gentry of Lancashire and Yorkshire, ridden out to see the great witch trial. Seated in commodious benches, curious, aloof, elegant – Heskeths, Talbots, Gerards, Hoghtons – my father's friends in whose houses I have danced, conversed, folk I have frequented, been welcomed by, and sometimes even gratified with my graceful wit.

"Death is not the worst of it," saith Alice, and how right she is. This, this is the worst of it. I care not for the many-headed monster of the gawking populace and their jeering, fleering faces. It is to stand like this in abjection before my father's confreres that wrings my pride. I could die for shame, would rather die, would rather mount the block, would rather sit in a death cart so it would rattle me away from this degradation. I would be dead and gone, a slab upon a marble monument like my father, but out of reach of a humiliation which is so far beyond anything my simple bastardy could have fastened on me.

The longing is intense, to be away, out of it, and I wish strongly I had no connection with the poor woman standing in the dock. Who am I after all? Jane Southworth, who is she that can be brought so low? Surely she has nought to do with me. With me? And if I am not myself who am I? What am I? I have great fear that I am a nothing. But I put this fear away. I embrace my nothingness. I am not obliged to share Jane Southworth's ignominy. I have been many things in my time, played several parts. Now I will play spectator, recorder, as if my soul has flown up into the great arched beams of the hall to observe this playacting beneath.

To observe. The judges in solemn elevation, the magistrates ruffling documents, the dapper little clerk, Thomas Potts, skipping about the court, perusing instructions, distributing documents, whispering consultations, with ever and anon an obsequious bow towards the platform of the judges. I find the man detestable. Perhaps even more than Nowell. Roger Nowell: the years have been kind to him, his beard as black as ever. He has gained somewhat in flesh, but also, it is evident, in confidence. The peasantry grows quieted as expectation gathers. There is silence in the court awaiting the first to be named. I needs must swallow down the hate that is collecting like bile in my throat. I must abandon Jane Southworth. I am become nought but a memorising brain.

Roger Nowell rose heavily from his desk, requesting the indulgence of the court and leave to give a summary of confessions already taken at Fence, which evidence was collected for the arraignment of Elizabeth Southern, known hereabouts as Old Mother Demdike, which subject had died in Lancaster Castle and now was called to a greater reckoning. But yet these same confessions might be shown to throw light upon many facts that would arise from questioning others of the accused persons throughout the trial. He was of opinion that while copies were available for their Lordships Judges Bromley and Altham, and for any gentlemen who might wish to peruse them

– Potts leaps up with alacrity, eager to provide such noble gentlemen as are literate – yet they were confusing and repetitious documents, and for the clarification of the jury he would be glad to read the substance of them aloud to the court. On being granted this permission he proceeded to read statements from all the members of Elizabeth Southern's family.

It was a matter of some indifference to the body of the court to hear the self-incriminating evidence of the old woman who was now beyond castigation, but her stories set the tone for all that was to follow.

Nowell aroused the interest of the crowd first by describing the particular devil to whom Demdike admitted giving her soul, and who had carried out her revenges. This was 'Tibb', who sometimes appeared as a boy in parti-coloured coat, and sometimes as a brown dog. The magistrate went on to describe an argument between Demdike, together with her granddaughter Alizon, and one Richard Baldwin, a miller at Wheathead. This was a story plainly known to many in the court. I could see some moving their lips in memory of the exchange, but it was Nowell who gave life to the words. He quoted with great energy the miller's threat, "Get off my ground you whores and witches, or I'll burn the one of you and hang the other!" and Demdike's retort, "Go hang yourself Richard Baldwin." But he lowered his voice to repeat her curse:

> "I'll pray for you Baldwin, still and loud.
> I'll pray every day, in every way.
> I'll pray in the light and I'll pray in the dark."

How satisfactory it was for our justice of the peace to be aware of the slight thrill that slipped like a sigh around the court. Indeed the mastery of thrills proved his great talent. He played with the attention of the court, carefully varying his performance to produce fearful whispers, or excited murmurs, or howls of indignation. He would have disgraced no actor's troupe out of London. Indeed I have to think that even Judge Walmsley would not have bested him now, set as he was upon a stage of his own choosing, with a text of his own most purposed devising. As I watched Nowell manipulate the mood in the hall, I also noted how the faces of the jurymen reflected the exuberance of the low fellows, and the more reticent and subdued nods and twitches on the gentry benches.

Before he sat down, Nowell told of the witch marks he had discovered upon the bodies of old Demdike, old Mother Chattox, and Alizon Device; how the Devil had sucked under Demdike's left arm, but the place he would have to suck of Mother Chattox was on her right side near the ribs. And on Demdike's granddaughter, Alizon, the Devil had chosen to suck at her breast under the nipple. The Devil's places being clearly verified as insensitive to pain, which he, Nowell had carefully assured himself of, this being one infallible test of a witch, as specified by the King's Royal Majesty himself.

A shudder passed through me to think of that heavy hairy man so painstakingly assuring himself of the places where no pain could be found. I had to banish the images very quickly if I was to keep to my place of observation up in the rafters.

The court waits again for the naming of the first to be arraigned. I am glad I do not exist. I think those about me hold their breath. I have no recollection how long the particular silence lasted, but it was a relief when Anne Whittle was brought forward onto the little dais of accusation. Her palsy was now so bad, her head near bobbing off its stem, and her teeth in spasmic chatter, that I feared she could only worsen throughout the course of the day and she might fall all to pieces, and lose her senses and end in fits. She made a great effort to hold herself together as she passed through the gate. She gripped the rail in front, gathering all her strength to plead not guilty as charged.

Roger Nowell rose ponderously from his table, suave, respectful, but a little excited nonetheless. He was entering into his fame. Would their lordships permit him to recapitulate that part of her confession made at Fence, and pertinent to the present proceeding? He read slowly and carefully, in a way which allowed me to guess at his own questions.

No, Anne Whittle had said, no she had no part in harming Richard Baldwin, miller of Wheatfield.

Nor would she have done so if the Devil bade her.

Not if the Devil threatened to catch her and bite her, she would not have helped him to injure the man or his family.

But on being asked for an account of the trouble with Robert Nutter of Greenhead, she did willingly testify that she had found the landlord's son Robert Nutter at her daughter's house and he was trying to force the girl, to take his pleasure of her, which her daughter, Anne, refused with all her strength.

Which made that man very angry and he mounted his horse in a fury. And before he rode away he shouted that when he came to inherit, he would evict them from that place, and set them houseless upon the begging road.

Yes she was afraid of him.

She was afraid of what he might do – ravish her daughter until his lust was full.

Yes she cursed him in her heart.

And would have killed him if she could.

But Anne Redferne's husband was a peaceable man and would not let her curse out loud, but she did curse in her heart, long and deep.

And if the Devil came to her and offered, she would ask him to be rid of Robert Nutter.

She did ask him to kill Robert Nutter.

The Devil came in no strange shape.

He was not like any animal.

Not a cat or a dog – but like a man. He came like a man.

She forgot what he was called.

He was called Fancy.

He came to do her bidding.

He said he would kill Robert Nutter.

He did kill Robert Nutter, for in one quarter of a year that man was dead.

The room was quiet by now. But Nowell had more confessions to produce. Before she died, Demdike had told the same story of the attempted rape of Anne Redferne, but she had added how she herself, along with a particular spirit, little black cat Tibb, had watched Annie Chattox making clay images of Robert Nutter. But she herself, Mother Demdike, refusing to help them shape the spell, had angered Tibb, who shoved her into a ditch and made her spill a whole can of milk.

Then a statement was read from a farmer called James Robinson. This witness had told how Mother Chattox had spoiled the beer in his house one time he had hired her to card wool for him. And how she was well known to be a witch, she and her daughter. And he did also affirm that he, James Robinson, had been in service with Robert Nutter, and he had heard him very angry with Thomas Redferne, and threatening that when he came back out of Wales, he would get his father to evict the Redfernes or he would pull their damned house down himself. And Redferne was a very peaceable man who said, "You will think the better of all this when you come back." But Robert Nutter never did come back, but died, as they say, bewitched.

After that Nowell read Alizon's statement from Fence, a story of the old feud between Demdike and Chattox. She told of the theft from Malkin Tower of linen and oatmeal, and of Anne Whittle's daughter, Bessie, wearing stolen clothes, and especially of a cap of green ribbons that she had worn at church. She also told of how her father, John Device, was so much afeard of Anne Whittle he did covenant with her to pay one bag of meal each year, so that she should not harm him, and when he could not pay she, Anne Whittle, did bewitch him to death. And on the matter of bewitching Robert Nutter and others, she agreed that Annie Chattox did used to make images out of clay, which she herself had seen them making, though Anne Chattox tried to hide them under her apron.

Then there was further testimony from James Device. That idiot boy had elaborated the same story of the making of clay pictures, with gruesome details of skulls stolen from a graveyard at midnight, and teeth pulled out and used for spells. I could so easily imagine how that great moon calf must have rolled his eyes and squinted as the magistrate encouraged his necrotic fantasy.

But in all of this was so much malice mixed with nonsense, as I could not believe it would be enough to drag Anne Whittle down.

But Nowell had not finished with Anne. He proceeded to offer further testimony from Fence. I do not know how long he had held the women for examination, but it seemed clear to me that this was a later stage, and a more demented stage, of Anne Whittle's ordeal. I pictured the old woman, cajoled with who knows what promises, spiked in how many places, confused by her own confessions, producing yet more self-damning babble.

There was a long account of Anne's being sent for to amend the soured ale of a farmer's wife called Moore. And

Nowell quoted in full the spell she confessed to using.

> *Three Biters hast thou bitten,*
> *The Hart, ill Eye, ill Tonge.*
> *Three bitter shall be thy Boote,*
> *Father, Sonne, and Holy Ghost*
> *A God's name.*
> *Five Pater-nosters, five Avies*
> *And a Creede,*
> *In worship of five wounds*
> *Of our Lord.*

Now some discomfort on the gentry benches – how many seated there had been given just such a penance by a rambling priest hearing their confession? I have myself had any number of avies and pater-nosters assigned for even childish misbehaviours.

However the traditional recitation might lighten a burdened soul, it did little to cure Mistress Moore's spoiled drink, and an altercation ensued, with the result that the attendant devil, Fancy, then bit a brown cow of the said Moore, which cow went immediately mad and died six weeks later. And so it ran on: what Fancy could not do, in biting cows to death, and spoiling milk of folks who had contraried the old woman, taking in his stride of course the killing of Robert Nutter.

A sad incoherent tale of nonsense, but it answered the crowd well enough. Anne was in a paroxysm of shaking, out of her mind with terror. I knew that Nowell could make her say whatsoever he pleased.

When Elizabeth Device stood next upon the prisoner's dais, I wondered what deliberation had taken place to assign the order of appearance of the accused. The old one, Demdike, with her sightless face and pronouncing voice, feared far and wide for her curses and menace, she would have convinced the court at first sight that here was business with a witch. Dead in the dungeon, she was lost to the prosecution. But Anne Whittle, with wobbling head and aged shaking body, with trembling spittled lips and gobber teeth, why she would do near as well for the picture of an evil crone. And now here was come Lizzie, not so aged, but with fearful disfigurement and a vile temper, might be counted on to rouse the rabble. And Lizzie gave her pennyworth.

At first she stubbornly denied the charges of witching to death one Squires of Burnley and one Milton of Roughlee. Even when Nowell read out her confession taken in April, she shook her great shaggy head, refusing to confirm her own sworn statement. She resentfully denied her son's description of the procuring of Squire's death by making clay images, as she denied the killing of Mitton for that he had refused her mother a penny piece. More passionately she denied witching to death John Robinson, for calling after her for adultery and the making of a bastard child. And equally vehemently denied taking any part in plans to blow up Lancaster Castle.

Nowell was not impatient. He quietly asked that Jennet be brought in. Great stir now in the court. People at the back craning up and trying to stand on boxes and bundles to see the child brought in to cry out her own mother. Jennet was a picture of transformation. Cleanly and tidily dressed – a neat little nine year old if ever there was one – how different from the ragged scowling mother she had come to indict. And though a little timid at first, she seemed not greatly displeased with her role, seeming to bloom under the amiable favour of the great men who spake to her. Nowell led her gently through the evidence and she answered in a small shrill treble, which was clearly audible throughout the courtroom.

Oh yes her mother was a witch. She had told her so

herself. For three years that she knew of. And she had seen her devil many times. He was in the shape of a little brown dog called Ball. And she had heard her mother tell Ball to kill John Squires, who died near enough straight away. Yes she heard her mother call up Ball to kill Henry Mitton. And three weeks after, Henry Mitton was also dead.

Then Lizzie's fury broke out. I know not in what proportion fear or rage possessed her, but she tried to come down to get at Jennet, and was forcibly pushed back by the constable as she gave voice to a stream of oaths and curses on the stinking shit she had brought into the world for children, on the Devil's whelps and turds that stood against her, on all the fucking cunting judges and the festering black bubo magistrates, and the lawyers who would grind in Hell for a fee and all the villainous world that tricked her children into lies would hang her. A lifetime's bitterness as the ugliest beggar's drab in Lancashire spilled and spewed from her mouth as they dragged her away, condemned herself utterly.

Jennet is crying now and Nowell bends to console her. He wipes her face with his own kerchief, telling her sure that she is a good girl and need not be afraid. But she has some trouble to summon back that reedy little voice. A tall table is carried in and Jennet lifted onto it. The judge condescends to praise her for the help she is giving this loyal justice, and bids her speak up well and tell her story. Now Lizzie is well away, the girl takes up her courage, and starts afresh, pleased with her part, set high up in the courtroom.

It was on good Friday last there was a great assembly of witches at Malkin Tower. There were about twenty people there. They had a feast. They had oh so much to eat – there was beef and bacon and a great roast. The roast was a sheep stolen by Jimmy the night before. He stole it in Barley. He killed it and spitted it. Her mother was there as well as her brother. Some of the people she did not know the names. But some she knew. Her uncle Christopher Howgate and his wife Elizabeth. And Dick Miles, his wife of Roughlee, and others she did not know.

I stay up among the rafters. I do not look at Alice. Nowell asks the favour of the court to read the statement made by Jennet's brother earlier at Fence.

Now we have it, more nonsense.

Jimmy had willingly elaborated the story of the Good Friday feast, with more details of the projected delivery of his grandmother and sister out of goal by blowing up Lancaster castle and killing the keeper, Thomas Covell. And having thus devised, the witches all departed upon ghostly small horses, some of one colour, some of another, and when they were so mounted, they straightway vanished into thin air. And he named some present at that assembly, including the mother of Miles Nutter.

It is well for Nowell to read out this testimony, for James himself can neither speak nor stand. His legs flail about as if he is a man of straw. The constables are obliged to uphold him on the dais. The creature is in a gibbering fear, and when his name is called, his bowels must have given way, to release their steaming terror, to the discomfort of the constables, and the applause of the simples. The stink of his squitter has provoked a deal of merriment among the groundlings, and caused a fluttering of disdainful kerchiefs in the elevations.

Nowell neither smiled nor frowned, but quietly, inexorable, read the confession taken at Fence – of one little dog, Dandy, who was the Devil, and the many folk Dandy had bewitched to death at Jimmy's command. How Dandy helped him kill Mistress Towneley who had once given him a thump for pinching kindling. And John Duckworth who never gave him his old shirt after promising it.

It is enough, enough, but the good magistrate has still a little trick in his sleeve, to throw some discomfiture among the Catholic members of the gentry benches. Dear Lord, the man has his sweet revenges now.

Jennet is lifted up again to recite a charm or two. A charm to get drink into the house that her mother taught her:

"*Crucifixus hoc signum vitam Eternam. Amen.*"

A small gesture of encouragement from Nowell and Jennet embarks bravely, clearly, on a long and confused ballad. The infant voice, commanding silence even of the louts and gawkers below her, chants of the Holy Cross, of Mary Mother Mild, of the Keys of Heaven, of Sweet Jesus' Redemption.

So Jennet gives us Jimmy's favourite spell, and whether of benediction or malediction it still causes unease among the Romist members of the nobility. But for the poor simpleton himself it is already superfluous. There is nothing can save the demented wretch from the rope.

Anne Redferne came last that afternoon. Silent she stood. One long plait behind her back, she somehow contrived a decency of appearance, her stillness a contrast to all the cursing and blubbering that had gone before.

She did not strive or protest beyond swearing her innocence. Robert Nutter's ferocity was well known. He had wreaked his will on many other women than Anne Redferne, mayhap even on some who stood within the court.

And perhaps Roger Nowell was tired by late afternoon, or sated with success. Or Judge Bromley was in need of a stoop of wine. However it was, Anne's ordeal was short, and the verdict, like a ray of dawn breaking into a black night, brought her in for innocent.

Chapter 51

WE ATE OUR MESS OF POTTAGE in silence that night, each occupied with thoughts. We were both searching in the entrails of the day for a magic rune to foretell our fates.

I said at last, "He has gotten three. Will it suffice him?"

Alice shook her head. "It is a puzzle how to impose on their belief. Maybe Anne Redferne's demeanour helped to save her. I am rejoiced for that dear girl, with a sweet babe and a good man waiting for her. But I did not think that Nowell would let go so easy. I do not know what it augurs for us."

"Jennet—"

"Jennet has tried to name me, but misremembered. Jimmy was nearer, near enough, but he is now beyond speech, incapable of more harm. As for Jennet, Nowell has schooled her well and she is a clever little minx. But I cannot think there is much more for her to tell. Whereas Grace—"

"—is a dolt, a straw head, a peabrain. Whatever Mary Sowerbutts and Thomas have laid on me of malice—"

"It may amount to very little. There must be some good hope there."

"Hope is itself a torment. I think hope lies too close to sorrow.

She said with some briskness, "Sorrow pays no debts. Pluck up your heart girl. You may be set at large tomorrow."

"And if not—"

"If not we shall be together, and we will give courage to one another, courage and grace."

"And if we are separated—"

"We shall stand together as long as we are able, and thrust our thoughts together when we are not. We will pray hard for each other. And if one of us escapes" – a faint smile creased the thin lips – "she must send all her courage on an angel's wing."

"I am not conversant with angels."

She looked at me then with such tenderness. "An angel's wing is but another word for love."

It was then I commenced to weep. Slowly, surely, without volition or sound, my tears fell down like the soft small rain of April, with neither glub nor sob nor heaving of the breast. Quite as they had their own life that was apart from me.

Alice grasped my hand. "My sweet girl, the worst the morrow can bring is a good death. Let us rehearse our courage, let us practice noble words upon the scaffold."

I was obliged to smile. Only Alice would think of such a singular whimsical device to bolster the courage of a self-sorry subject.

I made an effort: "I could imitate Mary Stuart, and lament a state of undress, who never was immodest before."

She was immeasurably pleased with me. "I have a fondness for that Protestant divine, who went to the burning, with the vow to light thereby a candle for England as would never after be put out."

"I think the Catholics have the most wit. What of Thomas More, that begged a hand in mounting the scaffold, on the promise that he would shift for himself on the way down."

She nodded thoughtfully. "I think we of the peaceful persuasions are not the best humorists. All the best jests have a whiff of contention."

All that I had to give Alice was my approbation of her tobacco smoking, but it was not a nothing to give her. She bade me lie upon the bed whilst she sat upon the floor setting out the pipe, the tinder box, the small tobacco pouch, the last treasures of her prosperous life. I have this vision of her, before the very last, as she leaned her back against the stone wall, an ancient shepherdess, with a bush of wild white hair and few teeth left, with little flesh upon her frame, and eyes sunken into dark hollows, puffing upon a little clay pipe, as if lost in a dream of contentment. She puffed and talked and while she talked her voice took on the old deep timbre.

"When I consider terrible doings to death that have been transfigured by great grace, I do bethink me of a sect of people, called something like the Giovanni, came from an island away to the south of France. It was a Frenchman I met at Blackwell market told me the story, and it stuck in my mind for they were a group much like the Grindletonians. They believed that man and woman were equal before the face of God, and that the land and its creatures were created for the sustaining of all, and in free marriage and free parting, and such like wicked doctrines. So no surprise my lord bishop could not suffer them to live unmolested but sent a hue and cry to root them out. In this island are high mountains, very jaggy peaks, he said, against an ever-blue sky. This group retreated into a high mountain village, where people willingly sheltered them, they being folk of such peaceable loving ways. But the bishop had many soldiers, and to be sure there are always informers. He found them out and had them roped together and tied to the stack built for heresy burning. And he most strictly forbade all Christian ritual. The villagers could not save them, but still they disobeyed the bishop and stood around in sorrow and in defiance, singing the Mass for the Dead, for their blessed souls, as their living bodies burned. When the flames shot upwards fiercely, suddenly, as they do, a large white dove seemed to fly out of the very heart of the fire. As the villagers sang, so high as they were, the mountain tops called back their chanting, and the white dove circled above the fire, and the mountains were calling 'Kyrie eleison, Christe eleison, Kyrie eleison,' until the burning was over, and the bird flew off and away into the highest peaks."

I thought but did not say to her that there would be no white doves flying up from Lancaster's grimy streets. We could hear how the clamourous confusion outside the prison walls had increased even from the previous day. No 'Lord have mercy' there.

And yet I fell into a light sleep, when I dreamed of standing in a church porch dressed for marriage. And it was my father, my great red-bearded father stood at the rail waiting for me. And I was troubled, not troubled to go to my father, but troubled by the wedding gown that was soiled and stained by my disgrace. I heard him say, "You know I look to you Jaynie, to protect my name and guard my honour." And I woke pondering how I should not soil or stain his name.

My father sure was no saint, he very harshly pressed men into soldiering to pay his Crown dues. He played at ducks and drakes with a Catholic conscience, and I did not care to know how many village wenches he had deflowered. But I would not for my life dishonour him. I would defend his name ever until my dying moments, which promised to be not far off.

Not far off in time, but far from my acquiescence. It is for old age to declare that the best of life is over, in effort to achieve content before the growing shadow. But I am young and lusty. My blood runs thick. I cannot easily

317

submit to this harsh shortening, this iron frost on my blooms not yet fallen. I know that no design of mine can wrench the pattern of my life into a safe familiar channel, but my mind still scutters about like a frightened rodent, tracking and back tracking a terrain with no exit. Finding no way out, I close my eyes, close my mind, for I know not how many moments, and then sharply wake again, cold and fearful.

Mostly Alice was praying, but she was too tired to stay upon her knees. One time I woke, she was standing by the barred window. She saw me awaken and said, "This is a pagan queen sails the sky out there, Jane. Think you she would help us resolute Christians?" Another time I woke she made some light remark, and I said, "Save one jest for the last word, Alice, for the end." And she said, "Not the end Jane, not so. It is but the commencement. It is but the serving man come to take the hood off the lantern of our souls."

Chapter 52

My name is Richard Southworth. I am son of Thomas, now deceased, and grandson of John Southworth, also deceased, himself grandson of Sir John Southworth, knight, long deceased. I am grandson of Jane Southworth of the Samlesbury Lower Hall, dower house to the great hall. I am devoted grandson, and I would dare say favourite, for it is of me she begs this favour. And I do so willingly agree for I understand that this is an important task that I undertake, to set her mind at rest, to complete her narrative, to free her soul to find its bourne.

She shakes her head, she protests my interjections. She fears I may become as prolix as herself. But I have steadied her in the pillows. One has set her drink beside. And I am her obedient servant. I have taken up the quill, there at the table where she did herself begin, and now we are agreed. She will dictate and I will transcribe her words exactly. Exactly, we are agreed.

✾✾✾

No besmirched wedding gown, but decent mourning black. No flailing sobbing incompetent, but a gentlewoman fit to govern a manor house. No dribbling, drooling lump of prison rot, but the daughter of a noble house, with still-bright hair, and a presence to command respect, even in this courtroom.

This is what the curious dream had brought me, a capacity to assemble fragments of my courage and the rags of my pride, and to face up to my judges as queens have done before.

They called us first that morning, Covell paying some attention, the three of us together, myself with Ellen – oh so reduced – and Janet barely clinging on to life. My poor servitors, aligned on either side, not Shireburn retinue at all. But in my new-found pride I had some space for compassion, and bid them pluck up their spirits, while I stood tall, tall as any tree, let them fell me who would.

And it was, after all, not Nowell who affronted us but the scarcely-bearded Robert Holden. I felt a kind of heartened scoff take hold of me. What a feeble adversary. It is after all a duel, only one side is forbidden all movement and all speech, save "Not guilty," clearly and proudly pronounced.

I had never staggered, that I can promise, nor would I have wavered at all, had I not seen a ghost arise from the gentry benches. My full red-bearded father stood up as my name was read, stood stern and tall, during the indictment of Janet Brierley, of Ellen Brierley, of Jane Southworth, all of Samlesbury, for devilish and felonious practices, and recourse to wicked arts and witchcrafts, upon Grace Sowerbutts, whose body was near wasted and consumed away by their ill usage.

I had the bar to clutch at, and I was only for one moment near to swooning, at sight of this supernatural visitation. But in the second moment I perceived it was Red Rick, it was my brother stood there, stood in silent statement, in silent witness to my innocence, stood and did not move whatever foul evidences were presented against me.

Then Master Holden, in emulation of his powerful colleague proceeded to read statements of examination conducted at his own home in Samlesbury. It was in the main but the busybody trash of gossip, must throng any full and public life. An honest yeoman William Alker who had heard such and such, others who knew the old knight to fear Jane Southworth's bewitchment powers. More pertinently, my old adversary, John Singleton, had told how Sir John would take the long way into Preston, for fear of crossing the ford by John Southworth's house, although it was the nearest and easiest way. And the old knight had also feared for his grandson's life, believing that Jane Southworth had exercised her hellish powers, on the day – and maybe on the night – when she was wed.

So: a very little knot of truth in all that tissue of confusion. Oh Moon Ladye, that was an ill turn that you played on me, to give me pause, when I would fain have been cast iron in mine innocence. But then I toss it off, the doubt. I do perceive how much of nonsense and fabrication and ignorant foolery is being ladled onto the scales against us. I will but hold my head the higher.

And so to Grace Sowerbutts. In truth she was a somewhat weakly version of the other child accuser. Paler and frailer, though older, she was tidied and cleaned like Jennet. Only unlike Jennet she did not so much relish her role. Instead of that sharp shrill voice, Grace could only produce a timid mumble, so that the court was obliged to strain, to crane, to hear.

But Holden encouraged her, called her by name, bade her speak up like a good girl. She held her hands before her apron, she took breath as he told her, and commenced a recital like a dame school child.

It was a story how she was haunted and vexed by some women. Chiefly she was troubled by her grandma Janet Brierley, her aunt Ellen Brierley, Jane Southworth also, wife of late John Southworth of the dower house and one Doewife, or Snowife – she trailed into uncertainty.

But at the lawyer's bidding she picked up her tune – how these four women had violently pulled her by the hair and laid her on top of a haymow. And then soon after how she was met by Janet, who had taken the shape of a black dog, who pushed her over a stile and made her fall. But she was not hurt, only fearful, and went to her aunt's house at Osbaldeston, until she was fetched home by her father. And on the way home she told him of all the doings of her aunt and grandmother, which she had never told anyone before.

As the flow was becoming a gabble, and not easy to hear, the judge leaned forward and asked why she had not spoken of these things before. She pulled up short, answering that she could not, she did not know why, but she could not.

"And this was the only time that you were met by the black dog?" Holden encouraged.

"No," she found her thread again. She was met by her grandmother again, in shape of a black dog but with only two legs, who kept close to her, until they came to a deep pit of water, and the black dog pushed her towards it, persuading that it was a fair and easy death to drown herself.

"And how did you escape this watery death?" Holden asked.

"By one who came to frighten the dog away."

"Which one?"

"By a thing in a white sheet. That then departed also."

But the black dog had continued to persecute her. It had carried her into Thomas Welshman's barn, that is the ferryman's barn, and covered her with straw and hay and lay atop of her – she did not know how long, for her speech and senses were taken away, and when she came to herself she was in a bed, in the said Welshman's house, where they had carried her, and she was fetched home by her father and mother.

The court began to stir as, I can guess, the spectators at

a play might groan at the tedious parts. And there was a good deal of this coming and going home, and Holden not adept at pushing forth the narrative. Until at last he was obliged to remind her of the time she went to Welshman's house, with her aunt and grandmother, at dead of night.

She nodded, "When all the household was abed and the door shut fast."

The judge leaned down again. "How did you enter then?"

She did not know. "'Twas Janet must have opened it."

And it was Janet went into the chamber where this Welshman lay with his wife Joan, and from that room she brought a little child, that Grace did think was abed with its father and mother. And set it down before the fire.

Now here was some substance. The court quieted and Grace gaining at last some assurance, spoke stronger.

Thereafter Janet Brierley did thrust a nail into the child's navel, and then took a reed quill into the hole she had made, and sucked at it for a good space of time, then after put the child back into bed. And she was sure that not Thomas Welshman, nor his wife knew the child was taken from them.

"It did not cry this child?" asked the judge.

"No it never cried."

"Is that not strange?"

The girl bit her lip, twisted her apron, then offered hesitantly, "But it did thereafter languish, and not long after died."

They had not finished with Welshman's child however, these Brierley women. For later they stole the child from the Samlesbury graveyard, Janet carrying it to her own house, where it was boiled in a pot, except for parts they roasted on the coals, and at this midnight feast, they did earnestly persuade Grace to eat some, but she would not.

And afterwards they seethed the bones, and kept the fat from the stew to anoint themselves, for as is well known, such grease can make a witch change shape or fly in the sky.

The story pleased the groundlings mightily, the judges not so much.

"What became of the bones, after all this cooking?" James Bromley wanted to know.

The girl was ill at ease with question. The bones she thought were put back in the grave.

"When, the next night following?"

She did not know. She did not see. She did not know for sure they were returned. And she could not say by what means they were got out of the grave in the first place.

The girl's manner of telling the tale, her hesitation and uncertainty, her plain discomfort with questions, none of this was likely to compel belief in persons of judgement. And indeed she was asked to repeat her oath that what she spoke was truth. Timidly she repeated it. Holden gave her water to drink, and she was settled down.

I do not believe that Janet Brierley understood a word of what had been said, and I know that for Ellen all passed in a fog of horror. But my cold brain lost none of the words. And I waited for myself to enter her story.

Chapter 53

I do love my grandam, but I do not love the story she obliges me to tell. And even despite her strong resolve she drifts into somnolence at moments. And leaves me free to rest my arm. Rest and wonder, wonder how she embarked on it at all.

❋❋❋

Robert Holden lacked altogether Nowell's insidious leadings on. He had to say baldly, "And what of Mistress Southworth? You have not mentioned her in this account."

Grace pondered for a moment and then found her story. About a half year ago she, Grace, was used to meet with Mistress Southworth, along with Janet and Ellen Brierley, at a place called Red Bank. They met at night, every Thursday and Friday, for the space of a fortnight.

Quiet in the court while she takes a breath, a deep breath.

And when they came to the riverside they were met by black things.

"What sort of black things?" the judge enquired.

"Four black things – of giant size, that walked upright like men, but had no faces of men, had no faces at all. And they carried us over the water."

A sigh like a light breeze ruffling water slid round the court.

"Like men you say?" the magistrate encouraged.

Perhaps Grace knew she had missed a piece, because she repeated determinedly, "Aye, black things with no faces but with horns, big stags horns and," she frowned in the effort of recall, "and they walked on hooves, but with little hooves so they pranced along." Another pause. "And with tails also," she said, but a little doubtfully, "tails with barbed ends, and their endowments," here she spoke with a rush of confidence, "they were most huge and fearsome to behold."

That brought her to a full stop, as if appalled at the recollection, or else defeated by her task.

"And they carried you over the water," Holden urged on her recitation. "Over the Ribble river?"

Grace even looked contraried now, puzzled or tired, and contraried. I thought she might sink into stubborn silence. The judge leaned forward: "Leave her Master Holden. Let the child give her her story with no more interruption, or I foresee she will let all go."

Grace heaved a sigh and found her place again. "Yes over the Ribble to the far side. And on the Red Bank side there was a feast prepared which all set down to eat. But not I. It was such food as I never saw before – my stomach heaved to see it. The others ate and my grandmother sauced me that I did not eat, and the others all bade me, but I did not."

Here she stood firm that she did not eat. And after the feasting, the black things danced with the other three women, disrobing them in the dance, as made them shrike, and pulled them down upon the ground, whereupon they did abuse their bodies.

"And you yourself?" Holden could not forbear to question. And she with reluctance admitted, "My body was abused also by the black thing that was with me." She sighed, "I was abused and I was greatly afeard."

The girl was certainly tired now and she had come to another blank. The devils' saturnalia must have taken some effort of imagination, or memorisation. After a pause Holden was permitted to prompt his witness. "Do you have any more to tell of Jane Southworth?"

"Yes." With an effort she started on her last piece. How Jane Southworth, that widow, did meet with her at her father's very door, and carried her into the loft and put her down upon the floor, where her father found her and took her downstair and laid her in bed, because from very first meeting with Jane Southworth her speech and senses were taken away from her. And upon the next day Widow Southworth came again and took her out of bed, promising that what she did last time was no harm compared to what she would do now. And left her up atop of a haystack, for which all the neighbours searched, 'til she was found by one's wife, and was laid in bed again, where she was, as she said, speechless and senseless for two or three days. But when she was recovered, this same Jane Southworth came again and laid her in a ditch face down, 'til she was found again bereft of all her senses for the space of a whole day and night.

Holden could not stop the babble now. Some ancient vengeance had took hold of her, and she was loud enough.

That upon a Tuesday after, the said widow woman finding her near Tom Welshman's barn, carried her therein and upon Grace's struggling to be free, the widow woman thrust her head into a gap in the boards, and lay upon her, and there spelled her, which sent her back into a fit that lasted until Thursday night.

All this was rich meat for the groundlings. What Tibbs or Fancy could compare with a cannibal coven, with an insatiable predatory widow, with giant devils carrying women across water to feast and fornication? Yet even the rudest rascal must have felt the shadow of a doubt as to the veracity of Grace's tale.

It was a hubbub in the body of the court greeted the conclusion of her evidence. And a buzz of surely speculative talk amongst the elevated folk. I dared not look at my brave standing brother. The judges now in serious frowning conference. Master Potts upon tiptoe.

And in all this hiatus and confusion, Alice's bony fingers, prodding in my back, and she herself, who had gotten near the dais, hissing in my ear, "Ask who set her on. Demand to know who schooled her so."

Bromley looked gravely across at us: "This is a tale of abomination given by this witness, fouler by far than all the doings in Pendle. Prisoners at the bar, do you have aught to say?"

"Ask, Jane, ask!" her so insistent whisper, as I knelt myself down, and the poor Brierleys alongside. "My Lords, I do beg of you to ask who set this girl on. To ask Grace Sowerbutts by whose means she is come to create this sorry tale. I beseech you, my lords, to question her who set her on."

Then for some moments we had truly provoked disarray. Grace seeming dumbfounded that I was given a voice, commenced a trembling and a weeping, and all she answered to the Judge Bromley's repetition of my question was "I know not, I know not." And upon his pursuing how it could be that she knew not who taught her so to speak, her father, Thomas Sowerbutts, red faced, arising in the body of the court, demanding that Thomas Welshman be examined, to establish the veracity of his daughter's account. And indeed Welshman was called, and a sorry witness for the prosecution he made, wretchedly admitting only his child's sickness and early death, and knowing nought of any other thing.

But they were disturbed, nobles and commons alike, some shouting out the name of Master Thompson, the master all knew to have schooled Grace Sowerbutts. And Potts afoot from one bench to another, conferring as to whom he should officiously summon next. Until old John Singleton arose, stiffly, from his place, asking permission to give his piece.

It was at his own house Grace Sowerbutts came to learn her catechism with Master Thompson. "But I knew not that what he taught her was a catechism of Hell." The old man did not look towards me, but the apology in his look – if apology it was – he directed to my still-standing Rick.

The judges demanded quiet. Bromley returned to questioning Grace, severely now, but she was fallen all to pieces, protesting her great ignorance, how she had learned her part, had tried her best, and delivered a most hard lesson, but to these last questions she never had been taught an answer

"And this Master Thompson?" suggested the judge.

Grace had lost all her props. Twas true, she was took by her mother to Master Thompson to learn her prayers. And certes it was he had taught her all these things to say. That she herself knew not.

It was now Judge Altham pursued her.

No, she confessed trembling, her grandmother never was in no black dog.

And she knew naught of boiling babies, nor ever did she traipse in Samlesbury graveyard.

The Widow Southworth never did pester her for all she had prevented her mother employment at the dower house

And the black things – it was the master had explained to her about devils and their misbehavings.

"And who," asked Bromley, "who is this master of yours – Thompson? Is he schoolmaster or divine?"

"No it isn't Thompson," sobbed Grace, "that's the false name for hiding. It was Master Christopher Southworth who is our priest sometime in Samlesbury."

Chapter 54

My own uncle, backward of three generation is found out the villain of the play. I do not care to write down these defamations of my family. So I have said to the aged lady, and we are agreed that I am allowed to insert my objection, so long as I am strict with her reply.

✳✳✳

Richard, Richie, light of my soul, you are not engaged in this to protect your ancestors, nor to take upon yourself the burden of their defence. You scribe only for an old woman, who is grown too feeble now to wield a pen, but worse, whose eyes are losing light enough to perceive the letters she would write. Remains that I am deeply grateful for your good assistance. But you also write what comes nearest truth. I am no sot nor dolt – I know that what I am set on remembering now must perforce be partial, or heavy coloured, but it is an honest history. Or else we should let all scurrilous playwrights, all lurid pamphleteers, all obsequious clerks, and whatever else of fantasists, have all the telling of the tale. Let us for mercy sake, let us assist this old Ladye Tyme, in her dolorous travail, to bring forth a lovely daughter – for Alice's sake.

Come Richie, it is no time to squirm and cavil. Let us not be squeamish, let us return to Alice.

To Alice, blameless Alice whose thin fingers had prodded me into my own safety, while her ordeal lay still in front.

What could I say to such a one over prison dinner? My own throat was stuffed up with a complexity of feelings. I was of course full of amaze. Who lay behind the accusations against me, I had never dreamed of. Amaze, relief, the slow letting go of terror, even a wild feel of triumph that could have laughed out loud, all were in the mix, as well as great pity and great fear for my friend.

We sat some while in silence. And he had sent up such a dainty collation, old Covell, on our day of trial. For pity or in hope of some advancement? Who knows for what? There was cold tongue and sweet apple preserve with clotted cream cheese and figs, and white bread and white wine.

"Eat Jane," at last said Alice. "We should not disappoint the master torturer in his efforts to lighten this day of judgement."

"Do you hate no one Alice?"

She disdained the question by asking another. "Christopher Southworth. And you never thought it?"

I shook my head and she looked hard at me. "But you have lain with him?"

"The once only." I swallowed down some wine along with an impulse towards prevarication. "When he came near me it was like a spark in dry corn stooks. A flame that danced where it would, and I incapable to douse it."

"You made merry?" What was in those unfathomable sunken eyes – malice, pity, envy? Or something I could not lay hold on, like complicity? "But only once?"

"Once. But I would have lain with him forever, in proper wedlock. Would he have renounced that fool mission and accepted the lawful religion of this land."

"You told him so? And he having pitched his entire life to fight that establishment. Worse than any prick tease you must have been to him."

"He was torment enough to me."

"Aye a flame so fierce is apt to leave burned scars. Or to provoke a delirium of the imagination, such as he rehearsed to that young girl."

I said quietly enough, "Violent delights bring sinister ends, and it were near enough sinister for me."

She grasped my wrist: "Jane, it is nigh certain that you will fly free."

"I owe you my life Alice. I know that. I do believe I am safe now, and it is you have saved me."

"Showed you the way to save yourself."

"But can you do the same? If Jennet is produced against you?"

"Nay they will not let the same trick work twice. And Jennet is no weakling ninny, swift to be discomfited. I do not know what will be brought against me. But I am resolved to hold my peace."

"That was Judge Walmsley's counsel."

"It is the counsel of the Family of Love, which I have most of my life neglected. But I would be glad now if you would finish this magnificent repast, and leave me room to pray."

Chapter 55

My grandmother has laid abed these two days, without bidding me continue my task. I come frequently to her chamber, to take up the quill, await the request that I have promised to fulfil. It is not the light of her eyes only that is fading, but I see how her bodily strength is slowly ebbing like a tide, and I know, I know as I love her, that she still has to do, to say, before the sand is dry.

✾✾✾

I wager that this dear amanuensis of mine has taken the occasion of my absence to insert lines of his own, has written of his grandmother's declining powers. Is it not so Richard? Ever a truthful child, you nod, and copy down all my words. But my words Richard! You have no part in this story. Return to my account if you please.

If Robert Holden had failed to keep hold of Samlesbury's slippery fishes, Nowell was determined that none should escape his net. It was with dull surprise and grief that I saw Anne Redferne called again. Despite that she had been acquitted of murdering Robert Nutter, she was now called up to judgement for murder of his father, old Christopher Nutter. It was grievous to me and I know to Alice, that having escaped one indictment, she had now the old one's death thrown in the scales against her.

The magistrate was implacable – this we knew, but the folk also were impatient. Noontide food and drink had only fuelled their worser appetites. There is this feeling in the court that the prey are escaping. Sure there will be aged bodies to hoist upon the gallows. But where is the prospect of a young wench, to provoke a sharper spasm in the onlookers, as she dangles there, slowly throttling in the turning air?

Well Anne Redferne would do. Comely yet, despite the prison filth, standing still despite her fears, she was just such a one to make a sweet morsel for the ravishment of execution.

And it was, in truth, feeble evidence he brought against her, reading his endless examinations from Fence, this time from Robert Nutter's sister and brother. Sister Margaret had agreed that her father feared bewitchment, but for all Nowell's pursuing, she could not be got to agree that the old man had ever named Anne Redferne.

And the brother John's evidence seemed to me only to favour Anne. Though Robert Nutter had weepingly begged his father to have Mother Chattox and her daughter lodged in Lancaster's gaol, the old one would have none of it. John had quoted his father's rebuke: "Thou art a foolish lad, is it not so. It is thy misbehaviour."

Surely on this they could not have her. But Nowell still had a little playacting to do. He repeated Robert Nutter's assertion as it were a given truth, and most rousingly expressed that one's furious threat, that he would indeed on his return procure them to be laid where they would be glad to bite lice in two with their teeth.

Almost a hurrah was felt in the courtroom. It was astonishing to me that the lecher's vindictiveness could turn the court against her.

Anne Whittle knew it; she pushed through, pushed onto the prisoner's dais. She fell upon her knees and pleaded desperately for the innocence of her daughter. It was she, Anne Whittle, Mother Chattox if you will, who had done all, all the clay pictures, all the curses, all the killings. She, not her daughter, not Anne, who was innocent as morning light. She sobbed and pleaded, and strangely she did never shake nor tremble. They had to drag her away.

And after Anne, Alice. Old and stiff and stern. How many in that gathering may have benefited from her charity through the years? They were quiet to hear her, the old sonority of her voice come back, clanging like a bell in the attendant hush, as she claimed "Not guilty." And then she shut her lips and would not be dragged into any sort of refutation.

Indeed what was the use, against such nonsense as was brought forth? Nowell forever reciting examinations from Fence – a stupid story from Jimmy, how Mistress Nutter had bewitched Henry Mitton for that Mitton had denied his grandam, old Demdike, a penny piece.

A penny! Alice! It was past belief even of the groundlings.

Now the court was subdued. My brother had disappeared. I even had difficulty to believe he had ever stood there. I think Anne Redferne had satisfied the blood lust. I curiously felt that no one looked to see, nor so much wished to see, Alice indicted.

Apart Roger Nowell. Mayhap he had come now to his hardest test. In a compassionate company Alice may well have excited the least compassion. Neither fallen into utter piteous decrepitude, nor preserving vestiges of youthful beauty, she stood hard as a board, plain as a pikestaff. But of such honour and charity as none could imagine fastening heinous crime upon her. Even their lordships judges were beginning to frown.

But Nowell had much at stake – a hungry ambition to feed, a career to build high, a road into the king's favour. He had caught no religious defectors, was ever wary of his powerful papist neighbours, and had proved unable to discover the underground networks of dissent. But witches he could deliver up to James, and this was one to cause a stir in the county, with wealth enough to make sequestration a tempting prospect. And sure there was that about this woman he would not be sorry to trample down.

He swiftly abandoned Henry Mitton and his penny piece, and picked up another parchment. Back to Jimmy's account of the great witch meeting at Malkin Tower. Now reading carefully, with studied emphasis, Nowell reminded the court of the plot there hatched to blow up Lancaster Castle and kill the keeper, in order to release those prisoners accused of witchcraft. He touched lightly upon that greater plot, that had filled half London's cellars with gunpowder, a plot some seven years past, but still awesome enough, and of such moment, to linger in all our minds. And if Jimmy did not know the names of all the witches present there, there was one who did.

Jennet was brought back and lifted onto the table. He patted her hand and spoke something encouraging to her. But she was becoming a seasoned witness. She quickly, clearly informed the court of the Good Friday meeting, all witches which she knew because her mother had so informed her. There were upwards of twenty present, whereof two were men. They met upon twelve of the clock, and she recited a string of names, only slightly stumbling as she misnamed Alice again, as Dick Miles wife of Roughlee. She had given her statement with great alacrity, perhaps too much so, for their lordships were not overly pleased with her evidence, and I doubt Nowell was pleased at her slipping over Alice's name.

Then came a pause in the proceedings. But a pause full of business. I am flown up into the rafters, to observe the hurly burly below – the judges deliberating with the lawyers, the magistrates commanding the constables,

Thomas Covell brought up, Jennet dispatched into another place, and little Tom Potts back and forth about the court, as in an ecstasy to perform his clerkly duties.

It was commanded to arrange a line of suspects, some of the accused, some of the innocent spectators. And to set them all among. Oh what a dithering was there, what mirth and shoving, what scuffling and protestation, what clowns they made, these peasants summoned out, to the joyous malice of their fellows. And what a shuffling and tottering of prisoners, what fearful, hopeful, faces stood in that line.

Jennet was called back. She was to pick out if she could, what woman had been at the witches' feast. The judges were most serious with her. Which women were at Malkin Tower upon Good Friday? How did she know them? By name only, or by face? Could she therefore tell if one stood there before them?

Yes, said Jennet, she could do that. On being bid, she stepped forward. With barely a pause for deliberation, with scarcely a frown for scrutiny, she approached Alice, took her by the hand, and clearly recited to her, for the court, where she had sat at the feast, who had sat next her, and what conference they had had.

Nowell had not finished. He spoke with the judges, as to further test the veracity of his witness.

Jennet was asked, "Did you see at the gathering one called Joan a Stile?"

"No." Jennet smiled as she shook her head. The child was well schooled, she understood the test.

"Or Margery Makepeace, was she at the meet?"

Another smile, shake of the head.

"Or Daisy Daw?"

She had seen only certainly Mistress Nutter, and they stood before the court, holding hands, the clever child and the tall woman with a face like stone. A dumb show more telling than speech. I wrenched my heart away from her, that dear friend. She was captured and I was still free.

But we had not finished with masques and suchlike. Let the London theatricals come down, let Hoghton's players strut and play, we had as good a piece as they.

A weeping maiden upon her knees, begging forgiveness of a poor cripple that staggered onto the scene. Alizon Device, claiming no innocence of magic, but repenting, with rivers of tears, the wickedness she had brought about. She confirmed all the story of the pedlar's refusal to give her pins, and her own, powerful, ill wishing. But it was a touching spectacle, and we listened to her confession with rapt attention. All had to do with one black dog, that had sucked at her breast below the paps, and this one had at her command, lamed the reluctant pedlar, and after which she had no truck with no black dog, not ever after.

And John Law, stricken as he clearly was, confirmed her words. Upon Alizon's pleas, upon her knees weeping, humbly begging his forgiveness, he, the sufferer, he did vouchsafe the same, and would have gone to take the wench's outstretched hands, but that his son who was supporting him, did look more grim.

So we were told that Abraham Law, cloth dyer in Halifax, being sent for at the time his father was laid low in Colne, finding that parent speechless and lamed, had set out to find Alizon, and bring her before the magistrates. He had thus set all in motion. And the son confirmed now that John Law, the pedlar, was heretofore a goodly man, of stout and sufficient frame. But behold, his head is drawn awry, his eyes and face deformed, of thick and stumbling speech and twisted limbs, his strength departed. A goodly man laid low by Hecate.

Whereupon the judges demanded of Alizon would she

reverse the spell she had cast upon this man. And Alizon confessed she could not. That it were like her grandmother would have done so, were she alive – no one doubted Demdike had all such in her power – but she, Alizon, possessed no such spell.

Such a lamentable, such a piteous spectacle was there presented to the court. My Lord Gerard, Sir Robert Hoghton, and other Catholic barons who had some stake in this, rose up to express their great pity for the pedlar man, and their own willingness to assist in provision for his relief and maintenance. And the sprightly court clerk was on his feet, babbling of the mercy and clemency of judges, the charity and condescension of great men.

I do perceive a great fatigue in my grandmother. She is cast back into the pillows, and yet it seems to me she laughed at her conclusion. A strange laugh and a whisper that it cost me some effort to capture.

Mercy and charity – God save us. God save us all from the pity of pitiless men.

Chapter 56

HOWEVER HARD I TRY, pressing my fingers into my forehead, it will not come back to me, the moment that I parted from Alice. Nor can I recover much of my own feeling upon the pronouncement of our verdict: "Janet Brierley, Ellen Brierley, Jane Southworth, found not guilty of the offence of witchcraft, contained in the indictment against them."

A greater degree of solemnity was demanded for the reading of the death sentences. A threefold call for silence before Thomas Potts presented to their lordships the names of those prisoners we already knew to be marked for the hangman. I must have turned to her then, surely would have tried to embrace her, at the least to speak in farewell. But the memory is gone, not darkly obscure, but a clean empty hole.

What I remember well is standing alone in the court-room, the prisoners having been dragged away, the officials with their documents dispersed. I stood near tranced. I had no inkling of what I should do, where I could go. I could scarcely move, let alone think. Until my sweet boy came flying into the hall.

"Forgive me mother that I have caused you this long wait! Master Covell is most scrupulous in his reckoning."

And out into the light of a declining day, into the smell of air that was not fetid, though yet we stood within the prison walls.

A little group awaited me: the good church warden and our stableman with mounts for the Brierleys

– featherweight now, the both of them. And holding the other horses, a tall likeness of my father, let all go to take me in his arms, and wept, and whispered "Jaynie, Jaynie," into my hair. And I remember, as I clambered onto Gilbert's big mare, clearer than Rick's embrace, I remember the feel of the coarse grey mane, the rough comfort I had never thought to feel in my hands again.

She pauses such a long moment, I make bold to interject a question. "They took you home, grandmother?"

Not yet young Richard. Do not lay your pen aside. It is not the end. Alice would say it is but the commencement.

We clattered out from under that frowning gate into a right Hell's kitchen. They say that fiddlers, dogs and flies come to feasts uncalled and here they all were a plenty. In four days every Tom and Dick with a roasting spit, a barrel of ale, or a tray of puddings, had taken up a stall in Lancaster's streets, and the crowds were thronging eagerly.

"They are foddering in the kennels now." It seemed my brother could not restrain his bitterness. "Tomorrow they will be baying for blood."

But I rode high on the big grey mare, so closely attended by my two red-haired squires, in resemblance not unlike this young scribe, who I perceive is impatient to finish.

I have protested her injustice, I have reaffirmed fidelity to my task, but I wish to have her took home in this story.

So was your father, anxious to have me home. But my brother had purchased accommodation for us in a little farm nearby. No more than I, could he endure to stay within the city walls. The family were one-time tenants of my father and full of willingness to please the Shireburn family. They laid a groaning table which I am sure they could ill afford, and which I could not touch.

I was upon my knees much of that night, but I did not pray, or I think it was not prayer, for I had no desire for commerce with the God that had the ordering of our days. I sought a way to send my love to she who must be preparing for her morrow to end all. But to little avail. Sleep perpetually overcame me.

Shortly after dawn, I walked into the fields. I heard the early morning rumble of a city. I marked how it swelled like a distant river rising, as all the mortals there awoke and set about their business. I stayed away from the farmstead, an indulgence begged of my now so compliant brother.

When I heard the sudden yelp of sound before a mounting roar, I knew as if I was there that the death carts had just emerged from the looming prison gateway. I knelt in wet and gentle grass, praying the God I did not know to spare her suffering. Prayed from my own incapacity, my own sorry showing as a friend, and more intently than I had ever asked a favour in my life. So hard I strained that I summoned into my mind a clear picture that I knew to be true: how she stood in the last cart, wild white hair blowing, gazing at the world she was leaving, while foul and filthy yokels ran alongside, striving to keep up. In my praying – or in my concentration – I sought another image: of a tall woman on a hill, snow flakes on dark hair whipping in the free wind, a smile of delight as she cradled a newborn lamb. I imposed this image upon the other. I sent it to her with my best will.

And that is how I touched the angel's wing. For now I was not only seeing Alice, I was seeing what Alice saw. For she had long since ceased to observe the frantic crowds around her. She was drawn into her own inner vision.

She was living in memories, swift pictures that startled and vanished like lightning flashes, but came from her into my mind. Some I did not know but guessed – a wide-browed young man with a huge bale of books slung over his shoulder, surely that early lover. Others were familiar to me – a pious little wedding group, an old man singing anthems to rebuke the powers of the world, a tall, stooping, silent shepherd.

I strove to stay with her as the tip carts mounted the steeper slope to the gallows field, and the Cumbrian mountains came into view, and the sunlit edge of the sea. A sea that may be glimpsed, some days, from Pendle Hill, for she was back in that loved place.

But the spirit that had released her from the present moment could fly as well through future as through past. And the image that was brought to me was another shepherd, taller, straighter, stronger, with many, many words.

I have been contraried somewhat, even vexed, and finally struck by wonder at the recent coming into our county of this George Fox, drawing such great crowds out of Lancashire and Yorkshire to hear his preachments. His followers, who call themselves Friends or Seekers, Shakers or Quakers – I know not rightly – it is said they claim to pursue inward holiness and outward equalness, in many the same words as once whispered the Family of Love, words which sure would have lit the hearts, confirmed the hopes of that ardent congregation. Seeming to me now, as I think on, that he is come express to fulfil the aspirations of that folk, to take them on into history. He, George Fox, also was cried out for witch, knew bitter prison walls, and herded sheep in his youth. What is it that sheep have to do with visions? They say the Witch of Rouen minded her father's flocks before she heard the angel voices.

So this man strode into her mind, into Alice's vision,

walking the hill where she had passed the most of her days. As the cart completed the ascent, there were always crowds about her, but in her inner eye – and in mine, that was reflecting her's – they were crowds of kindly intent, eager folk who came to hear that man recount the tale of how he climbed atop Pendle Hill, where it was the Lord vouchsafed him a great vision of peace and content. There was a rejoicing in Alice's heart.

They took her out of the cart, and but one short step to mount, but she was going forward to meet these people he had envisioned, clad in white raiment, bearing wands of arum lily. They were waiting for her, the white-robed saints, and that image grew bright, dazzled like a star, and in the instant vanished. I knew the particular moment that Alice's sensible perception was extinguished. She was gone where I could not follow.

But I should tell this fellow – or perhaps my grandson will do it for me – that Alice had dreamed his dream before ever he was born.

I wonder does she wait for me now, among her shimmering saints? Would I be allowed, her concupiscent, sceptical friend, in that blessed company? For she was ever indulgent towards me, Alice, and forgiving.